SPARKS FLY UP

The Lost Story of Margaret Fuller

CAROL STRICKLAND

Paperback ISBN 978-1-63226-168-7
eBook ISBN 978-1-63226-169-4

Published by
All Night Books
PO Box 3131
Westport, CT 06880
allnightbooks.com

Book and cover design by Barbara Aronica

For Sid, my bedrock and my pinnacle

CONTENTS

PART TWO

INTRODUCTION

This novel is fiction, but its characters were real. They were alive in the 1850s, which was a turning point for America—years when, for the first time, a distinctly American literature appeared. It was also a time of social upheaval, when women and abolitionists were struggling for "a more perfect union" with equal rights for all. Margaret Fuller's voice was among the most articulate, demanding revolution in all spheres—individual, cultural, and collective reform.

During that time, Concord, Massachusetts, was a cradle of creativity. Since the 1830s, Ralph Waldo Emerson had fomented a philosophy called Transcendentalism. This idealistic view preached self-reliance, intuition, the inherent divinity of humanity, and learning from nature. Emerson wished to assemble a covey of gifted intellectuals in Concord, among whom Fuller, Nathaniel Hawthorne, and Henry David Thoreau were prominent.

Margaret Fuller was arguably more brilliant—certainly more loquacious—than other geniuses in the Concord cohort. An early advocate of women's rights, her challenging ideas both incensed and inspired her friends. Like an extinct star, whose rays reach Earth long after its demise, Fuller still sparks controversy. Although her voice has been lost for more than 175 years, her story should no longer be.

PART ONE

CHAPTER ONE

Fall in New England

NOVEMBER 1849, STOCKBRIDGE, MASSACHUSETTS

"Utopia, here we come!" Cary flapped a blanket in the air. As its pouf deflated, she settled the cover on a flat rock. She avoided a crumbling pile of brown debris she suspected of being dried droppings and kicked dead leaves over the unseemly impediment to high spirits. *Joie de vivre* restored, she crowed, "Revolution—that's the flag Margaret marches under: for women's rights here at home or a beautiful, unified republic in Italy." She drummed a few martial thumps on her pencil box and hummed "Yankee Doodle" with a relish uncommon for a woman of twenty-nine years.

"Even if the old world's not ready for her dream world?" mumbled Sophia, opening her pencil case with a precise click.

"That's it," Cary said. She narrowed her eyes and sketched the lake called the Stockbridge Bowl with slashing strokes. In constant motion, she scrawled on a drawing pad, hiked her voluminous skirts around her knees, and stuck a pencil behind an ear amid the disheveled scrolls of red-gold curls tumbling down her shoulders. The landscape took form under quick scratches.

The drawings the two ladies produced were as unlike as they.

Caroline Sturgis Tappan (known as Cary) looked more like a spangled gypsy than a serious *artiste*. As she swirled a maelstrom of graphite curves on the sheet, gold bangles jangled on her wrist.

Sophia Peabody Hawthorne, forty, hugged a homespun shawl

around her shoulders. A stiff bonnet enshrouded her slicked-back hair, every wayward curl tamed into genteel submission. She tipped the straw rim to block a ray of sun that jabbed her eye like a luminous dagger. "If you ask me, revolution isn't beautiful. It's messy." She squinted and held up a pencil to gauge the height of a pine and expertly drew its outline on the paper. She added curved lines on the trunk to suggest rounded volume and scattered staccato dashes for pine needles. As Cary watched, Sophia penciled in a light grid of lines to scaffold the scene.

"Ever the professional artist," Cary sniffed. Her own version of a tree resembled a palm more than a pine. The half-hidden profile of a sprite peeked out through scalloped fronds. She sketched a jubilant child raising a fishing pole above the lake. Two tiny fairies dangled from the line. "I prefer invention," she muttered, "insight, not outsight."

"You're like Margaret." Begrudging admiration tinged Sophia's voice. "What do you hear from our crusading heroine, La Signora Margaret Fuller Ossoli?"

"Her last letter from Italy was truly tragic." Cary smeared pencil lines into a smoky blur with an index finger. "She had to flee Rome for Florence."

Sophia waved away a buzzing horsefly. "Revolt tore everything apart in Rome. It's like those broken statues of old Emperor Constantine. In one piazza you see his giant stone foot. Sculpted fingers lie on the ground in another square, huge as tree trunks. What a sad, benighted country. Italy isn't even one nation. It's separate city-states, each ruled by a foreign despot." She sighed. "Two years of desperate fighting! What did they gain? No independence; just massacre! They need some Minutemen, like in *our* revolution, not wine-swilling papists." She looked pleased at her summation.

"Everyone said Margaret was daft to go to Rome, instead of writing for the *Tribune* in New York," Cary said. "She gave up everything to be a foreign correspondent."

"The *first* ever foreign correspondent—and a lady! Imagine . . ." She sighed. "Nat and I told her not to go." Sophia, absolved of complicity in Margaret's misguided decision, wiped her fingers on a lace-fringed handkerchief. "War is no place for a lady, no matter if she's intrepid like our Margaret Fuller."

Sophia shook her head, flattened a crease in her paper, and penciled in a heap of fallen leaves in the foreground. Margaret could traipse around the globe till the heavens fell, but Sophia had better things to do right at home. Unspoken was her thought: more *lady-like* things. Her ringlets jiggled in the breeze. The scent of honeysuckle floated in the air, and she sketched an aster in the grass, even though none was evident.

Cary added a dark cloud in her sketch to shadow the little fishing child. She revised his demeanor from jubilant to watchful. She sighed, "Margaret says it's not safe for them to stay in Italy. She's coming home."

Sophia gasped, "Returning with a husband and child!" She placed a pencil in its case, snapped it shut, and leaned forward. "Who would have predicted! She always preached that marriage was slavery for women! Her ghastly book likens wives to chattel. Margaret as good as vowed to remain celibate all her life—a life of the mind, not the body, I might add." Sophia loosened her shawl, warmed by her devotion to domesticity.

"You haven't told anyone except Nat, have you? The few who know she succumbed to matrimony are astonished, not to mention disbelieving."

"I'll believe it myself when I see her," Sophia said. "Margaret as a paragon of wedded bliss?" She rolled her eyes, smoothing her skirt. "I pray she's found a true soul mate in that Italian fellow. She always envied my partnership with Nat."

"*You* can talk of the joys of marriage," Cary said. "You and Nathaniel are deliriously happy. We don't *all* have an entertaining husband and esteemed author in the boudoir."

Cary cast her eyes down. "Before marriage I called my own Will 'the Great Unknown.' I thought him redolent of mysterious promise." She drew thick Xs across her sketch, slashing the paper with her pencil point. "Hah!" she laughed, a rusty sound more like a gate rasping closed than a response to humor. "Now I know him! He never speaks, the most unsociable of men! It's like living with a hole in the wall. . . . Or a mortician," she added under her breath.

"I admit Will is arresting, a *poète maudit* type." Sophia couldn't suppress a shiver. "Those dark eyes—that brooding intensity—it almost frightens me! He *is* rather withdrawn, not exactly jolly as a hoe-down."

"More like silent as a gravestone. Why oh why . . . ?" She didn't finish. In the ensuing silence, Sophia studied waves ruffling the lake while Cary stabbed a finger with ferocity at a ruffled mound of clover. She plucked spikey blossoms and twined them into a circlet. She placed the clover wreath on her hair. "Queen of the fairies!"

"Watch out!" Sophia swatted down the chain of flowers. "A spider!"

Cary's eyes filled with tears. Sophia patted her friend's hand. "You must be strong for the children. There's solace in routine."

Cary's voice cracked. "Routine! I want to be wild, extravagant, not a man's property! Women are more than brood mares. That's what Margaret taught me. What a new life she found in Italy!"

"I'd say it unleashed her inner savage," Sophia said. She hesitated, then plunged ahead. "Tell me, Cary. Do you regret not marrying Ellery Channing? I know you two courted when you were younger."

"*Courted*! That's one way of putting it." Cary looked off into the indecipherable distance of her youth. "Ellery and I were . . . let's call it 'inseparable.'" She reddened. "He wrote me passionate sonnets! And, oh, when he recited them . . . !"

"I can almost see him in his rolled-up sleeves, tossing that mane of long hair over his shoulders." Sophia seemed hardly immune to Ellery's charms.

"He's the complete opposite of my stuporous husband." Cary admitted. "With Ellery, you never, *ever* know what comes next. He's like a pirate, stealing one's heart, then off to another adventure."

"Poor Ellen, married for eight years to that rascal." Sophia smoothed an errant wrinkle from her apron.

"What does Ellen have to show for it—three little children whom Ellery ignores and a shanty of a house, where she's sole breadwinner!" Cary said. "Margaret was horrified when her little sister married him. I may have been taken aback when I heard they were engaged, but I'm well rid of him."

"Why do Waldo Emerson and Henry Thoreau adore Ellery?" Sophia wrinkled her forehead. "Nat calls his poems execrable."

"Ellery's like a racehorse with no tether. Some admire the flashing hooves and dust he kicks up."

Cary stood, brushing pine needles from her skirt. She tugged Sophia to her feet and pulled her to a dory tied up on shore. "Come on, Sophia, my hearty! Enough parlor talk! Let's take a spin on the lake. I'll steer and strike sail to no one!"

She loosened the stays and unfurled the sail, hoisting it up the mast squeaking. A breeze billowed out the canvas with a *whump*! Cary pulled the line taut and manned the tiller. The sheet swelled with a pregnant puff of wind. They zipped forward, slicing a V in the water at the stern. Mallards scattered, quacking with indignation as the boat routed them from mossy reeds. "Tell me, Sophia, how do you and Nat like the Little Red House?" she shouted.

Sophia gripped the gunwales of the hull as the boat heeled over, nearly spilling her into the water. She righted herself from the diagonal and answered, "Well, it's certainly *little*, like a tiny coop for baby chicks, but we're happy. I thank you for offering us an escape from Salem."

"You must like the fact that it's red, especially now that Nat's novel is selling so well."

Sophia turned her face up to the sun and laughed. "Yes, red is perfect for the author of *The Scarlet Letter*. Nat says he even wishes he had scarlet slippers." She giggled as they scudded across the lake.

"Whoopee!" Cary yelled, her face freckled with splattered droplets blown by the wind. Her bonnet zigzagged up and down like a kite behind her, its ribbons knotted around her throat.

CHAPTER TWO

In Italy After the Failed Revolution

NOVEMBER 1849, FLORENCE, ITALY

Margaret Fuller was determined to evince steely stoicism. *I must write a column to show I still exist*, she told herself as she paced beside her husband on the banks of the Arno. They stepped over coils of guano deposited by vociferous geese and avoided the squashed, bullet-sized olives splattering the ground.

Austrian hussars marched nearby in spotless white, gold-braided uniforms. Their shiny patent leather boots clanged on the flagstone path. Margaret darted deeply derogatory glances at them. The soldiers were so proud of their curved swords and ridiculous helmets curling forward like an onrushing wave. Delighted with the spoils of war, they shoved aside errant Italian children who had the temerity to cross their path.

Margaret could barely contain her disgust. She clutched Angelo's hand tightly. It was all she could do to keep him by her side. She knew his fingers itched to strangle the strutting invaders.

The Palazzo Vecchio clock tower tolled twelve times. Funereal bongs dissolved one by one in the autumn air. Margaret frowned at the buff-colored sparrows that hopped on the path before her, ignorant of the disgrace to their homeland. "At least Florence isn't in ruins like

Rome," she told Angelo. The tall, dark-haired man, a target of coy gazes from ladies they passed, looked young enough to be Margaret's son rather than her husband.

Margaret regarded a gurgling fountain where stone cherubs poured sculpted urns of splashing water into a pool. Angelo cupped his hands as frothy bubbles calmed. He scooped up a drink and rubbed cool liquid over his forehead.

Margaret's face contorted in memory. "Near my chamber on the Via Barberini, cannon balls blasted a beautiful villa to rubble. In the garden's dry fountain was a marble nymph. Its head was blown off. I saw human bones splayed out on a crumbling wall! And a dog—licking a dead soldier's face!" She shuddered. "These things I *must* tell my readers!"

Angelo removed his hat, bowed his head, and thumped a strident sign of the cross on his chest. "I remember vultures circling everywhere," he said. "Rooks followed them to pick the bones clean." He wiped streaks of tears from Margaret's cheeks with his thumbs.

Would Horace Greeley give back her treasured slot on the front page of his *New-York Tribune*? Margaret had been his star reporter. Fifty thousand readers had been devouring every story she wrote by the time she left for Europe, just three years before. New Yorkers used to flap the broadsheet in each others' faces and quarrel over her columns. Stir 'em up! Make 'em think! That was her goal.

She recalled her more daring articles. At coffee shops on the Bowery, outraged readers erupted in howls: How dare a female columnist befriend prostitutes released from prison? How could she berate gentlemen who patronized, then condemned, these Women of the Night? How could a purportedly proper lady—no matter how lauded for her intellect—broach such a disgusting subject in print?

The women she conversed with in Sing Sing Prison, those "from the lowest haunts of human vice who had been tempted to pollution," she wrote, "show a sensibility and sense of propriety that would disgrace no one." What? Gasps, as much as rabid attention, greeted her articles. Far from chastising her for immodesty, Greeley rejoiced in her boldness. "More, Margaret," he urged. "Keep going strong! We got 'em by the balls!"

Why, Margaret asked herself in near desperation, *doesn't Horace write me? Ever since I wrote him that I am married and have a child, nothing but silence. Is he shocked? Scandalized?* A committed reformer as he was, her ally in challenging the public, did Horace think she'd betrayed her principles?

Margaret had never actually *vowed* not to marry. Well, maybe she did, insisting that her only love was Love of Liberty. She told her friends being a Vestal Virgin was preferable to being a man's property. All her disciples—upper-crust young ladies in Boston and New York—knew that their idol considered marriage a form of slavery. Chastity was much preferable. But that was before she met Angelo Ossoli in Rome. Before he pumped her heart rate into a tizzy. *He is the first man to love me not for my wit or my Latin and Greek, but for me, myself*, she reminded herself. At the thought, she felt flip-flops in unmentionable regions.

When Margaret finally divulged the truth of her liaison to her family and closest friends, she had some fancy explaining to do. In her much-delinquent missives home—after two years of guarding the secret of their affair—*no, call it a union,* she thought—Margaret defended her lover as an enlightened partner.

"My Angelo Ossoli is different from American men," she assured her mother and Cary. "He's different from Italian men, too—a war hero and devoted to me!" *If anyone in their household is a servitor*, she told herself, *it is he. Far from a domestic slave to Angelo, I'm more his queen.*

To many acquaintances in New England, Margaret knew, her choice of husband would be inconceivable. "Others esteem me for my talent at embellishing subjects," she wrote Cary. "The man with whom I have united my destiny simply loves to be with me, even when I am silent. He is an obscure young man of no intellectual culture, whom you may see no reason for my choosing. Yet I will never regret acquiring this sweet, sincere companion. We are of mutual solace."

Margaret confided her matrimony—and the existence of her little son—first to Cary. "Ossoli is unswerving in his love for me. He tends me when I'm sick and cares for little Nino with tenderness. I don't give a fig for the world's opinion of him," she wrote. "People call it *wedlock*, but, in truth, my wedding has *unlocked* a trove of sweetness and joy."

Cary, perhaps unwisely but in the interest of preparing Margaret for the criticism that awaited her, wrote back, "The holy mob is saying injurious things of you, which I lack details to refute. Meddling curiosity rages. Some nasty gossips claim Angelo is an ignorant gigolo, unacquainted with books or ideas, and even more absurd, they say you 'bought' him!"

With what funds would I buy anything? Margaret huffed to herself, lamenting her impecunious state. From the height of celebrity (or perhaps notoriety), her starry status as the most learned woman in America had fizzled into obscurity. Three years abroad—even while sending impassioned dispatches back to *Tribune* readers—hastened her slippage into anonymity and poverty. Her urgent pleas, begging Americans to care about Italy's fight for independence, sank without a ripple of public notice. So far from American shores, Italy's concerns seemed irrelevant to her countrymen, especially when a gold rush was raging! The unfortunate fact of Italians' proclivity to Catholicism and their widely accepted status as feckless sinners, lacking get-up-and-go gumption, cemented Yankee indifference. A taunt circulated in proper Boston: "Italians boast, shout, and fling garlands, but they cannot *act*."

Americans were oblivious to what Margaret discovered in Rome. As she wrote Cary, "Italians possess an exalting capacity for intense passion, a trait absent in New Yorkers obsessed by Moloch. My readers have not witnessed, as I did, heroic young men fighting like wounded lions. They didn't hear their cries of agony as they lay maimed or dying. Their glorious Republic, overthrowing foreign rule, lasted only a hundred and forty-three days. Our own republic born in Revolution endures. Yet it has lost its way. In my last dispatch, I importuned Americans, 'Rest not supine in your easier, more prosperous lives. Do not hug yourself in selfish content with your profuse fortune.' I pray a lust for gold has not cankered America's noble heart. My foremost task is to wake up my countrymen, not to lull them into porcine complacency but to *think*!"

With no money and those smug Austrian warlords dogging the couple as suspected traitors, a return to the States was urgent. *How will America greet me?* She tortured herself with incessant worry: *Will they think me a fallen woman, an emblem of immorality? An irritating scold? Or*, as Margaret pondered with scant hope, *a pioneer New Woman forging a path to freedom?*

Can the woman I've become, she wondered, *live in provincial America? Will I be ostracized?* She was especially nervous how Concord friends like Ralph Waldo Emerson and Sophia and Nathaniel Hawthorne would receive her. "I expect Ossoli will be nothing to Mr. Emerson," she wrote Cary. "Waldo will never understand what we have in common. I go home knowing my reception will be painful and difficult. Yet, if my life be not wholly *right,* it is not wholly *wrong*."

She kicked up a spray of dirt, recalling Emerson's most recent letter, a masterful mélange of affection and reserve: "Although I had hoped to lure you to our little Concord," the revered philosopher wrote, "it is undesirable for you to return only for the prospect of publishing your proposed book. Stay in Italy for now, but we will want you and must have you here *in time*."

In time, thought Margaret. *The time is now, Mr. Stick-in-the-Mud! My book will show my countrymen they must link hands and hearts with the cause of freedom, even across an ocean . . . if I can get the book published!*

Angelo saw creases of sorrow furrowing her face. He kissed her hand and she felt a zing of pleasure. "*Principessa,*" he said. "*Avanti, mia cara.*" He steered her around a puddle that threatened to muddy her long skirts. She lifted them above the muck.

She was hardly oblivious to the admiring glances cast on Angelo by young Italian women. She noted their puzzlement when they perceived his devotion to her. Margaret raised her head in pride. *If only those who called me a moldy old maid could see me now!*

They entered the Piazza della Signoria and saw on the loggia Cellini's statue of Perseus. The demigod held Medusa's severed head aloft in triumph, her eyes blank in death. Perseus's winged sandals trampled his victim's corpse.

"Perseus with his cursed sword!" Angelo spat on the ground. "I think of the brave women who defended Rome. Fighters all! You were there beside me on the last night of the siege, *amore. Insieme,* together, we manned the Pincian Hill."

"Yes, after cowering under a cushion on my sofa the night before, certain with each blast that you'd be killed. I had to join you on the wall," she said. "If I could've sold my blood or hair to help, I would've done it. All over the city, I heard booms, then shrieking whistles and cannonballs exploding. Roofs caved in, walls crumbled, blood pooled in the streets, groans of the dying in every piazza." She pulled her shawl tightly about her shoulders and nodded towards the sculpture. "Medusa is a fearful Gorgon, but to me, she's heroic, an emblem of courage."

Angelo all but clicked his heels. He nodded and pounded a fist on his heart. "*Assolutamente!*"

Margaret raised her chin and stood straight as an unbroken column. *Courage, don't fail me now*, she thought. *My fire may be banked, but I will not be extinguished!*

CHAPTER THREE

Two Writers in Florence

FEBRUARY 1850, CASA GUIDI, FLORENCE, ITALY

"After Rome of the Emperors, after Rome of the Pope, will come Rome of the People!" Elizabeth Barrett Browning recited the popular creed to her guest Margaret Fuller. She raised her teacup in a semi-martial salute. "Isn't that what the Revolution was all about?"

The two women—both esteemed for literary endeavors—were a study in contrasts. The English poet Barrett Browning was frail, delicate, her long brown hair draping both sides of her face like tent flaps. So long an invalid, first confined to a sickroom by her father, then cocooned by her husband the poet Robert Browning, she seemed ethereal as a moonbeam.

Fuller, with her substantial bosom like a warship's prow and American air of invincibility, leaned forward in her armchair. She clinked her cup against Browning's, signaling solidarity. The strike of porcelain vessels was so unforeseen a collision, it propelled the poetess backward in her chair. "Exactly!" Fuller agreed in full-throated approval. "I'm so glad to find you in sympathy with the Revolution."

Elizabeth amplified her usual whisper to a more audible volume, mirroring her guest's vehemence. "As, indeed, how could I be otherwise?"

"Fight we *must*, and fight we *shall*!" Margaret said. "The Republic will rise again!"

Nearby they heard skittering as their little sons, Pen and Nino, evaded the attentions of the nursemaid Lily Wilson to play hide-and-seek. Both toddlers searched for places of concealment. Pen crawled under a long, red velvet curtain. Nino upended a wastebasket full of crumpled paper, placing it over his head. His shriek mixed fright and pleasure as Wilson hoisted the basket and said, "*Bravissimo, bambino!*"

The two authors smiled at their sons' antics. "It seems we have much in common, with our little tots," Margaret said. "We've both been blessed after marrying late."

"Yes," Elizabeth nodded. "Who would've predicted it, both bearing a child at our advanced age?"

She offered a plate of grapes and roasted chestnuts. "I must tell you, Mrs. Ossoli, I admire your book, *Woman in the Nineteenth Century* —a capital masterpiece! You make the case for women's emancipation so forcefully."

Margaret knew that the poet's father had isolated his sickly daughter from normal life. It was no wonder she resented male dominance. For years, Elizabeth's father had confined his adult daughter to bed, considering her too feeble to stand on her own feet. Or even to meet others. Elizabeth confirmed the widely known story: "For years I was virtually imprisoned in my room. My father meant well, but I was his hostage. I had no freedom."

"Thank goodness you escaped," Margaret said. "How brave you were to elope with Robert! How cunning to come to Italy." She clapped her hands in tribute. "*Brava*!"

"Your book," Elizabeth asked, "what led you to the subject of women's rights?"

"My own father treated me like a possession to brag about, not a child to love." Margaret looked down. She frowned. "My father demanded that I master Latin before I was six, then French, Italian, and Spanish by twelve. Every night, I had to perform for him like a trick pony." The words of Caesar, Virgil, Horace, Cicero—she recited them all in her piping, childish voice. "I stood straight in my pinafore—I was all a-tremble, terrified I'd forget a word."

Words spewed out of her. "Papa was determined I be exceptional. Only a prodigy would do for a daughter. If I once failed to translate a word properly, he rapped my knuckles and said, 'To excel in all things should be your constant aim.' Do you know," she asked, "what Papa demanded on my fourth birthday?"

"That you eat your spinach?" Elizabeth attempted a joke before noticing tears in her visitor's eyes.

"He said, 'I will love her if she learns to read!' I had no natural childhood. I had to put on the fetters."

"But it made you brilliant," Elizabeth said. "I suppose our family history inspires us both to cheer for Italian independence."

"And," Margaret added, "women's equality."

"Precisely. Do you know," Elizabeth said, "until I was near forty, my only companions were books? I was kept so inert in my sickroom my father used to place a feather on my lips to see if I still breathed. My bed was my chariot; poems were my steeds."

Margaret looked around the poet's drawing room, taking in the patriotic décor: green walls, red upholstered sofa and armchairs, white millwork. "You're very brave to display the banned colors of the *Risorgimento*."

"What a tragedy poor Italy is brought to heel! What an exhilarating day it was two years ago! Tens of thousands from all walks of life—high to low—paraded for the Republic. The mob waved kerchiefs and banners, blew horns, bellowed songs. What a joyful racket! The streets were packed with patriots. All the church bells pealed in unison. Through that window I heard the heart of Italy beating strong, laughing and crying with rapture. A child's pure voice was singing '*o bella libertà*.'"

"In Rome," Margaret said, "they lit a bonfire in the Piazza del Popolo. Gusts of sparks flew up to the deep, blue-black sky. Trumpets blared, bells rang, drums throbbed like my heartbeat." She shook her head. "I thought it was a new era beginning, no longer an embryo but stumbling to walk before leaping in giant strides."

The two women sighed and hung their heads, their sorrow intensified by the Republic's swift demise. "The future is not lost," Margaret said. "I'm writing a history of the rise and fall of the Revolution. I'm anxious to do it historical justice—my contribution to the Cause. Something memorable must come out of my troubled existence."

"*Bravissima*, Margaret dear! It will be your best book! What are your plans? Where will you live with your Marchese and little Nino?" Elizabeth refilled her guest's cup with strong tea.

Margaret's face clouded. "I'm deeply homesick, yet where is my home?" She paused to consider. "Ossoli speaks little English. Living in America will be a trial for him, a lonely exile. We adore Italy; nonetheless, we must leave. He was almost arrested days ago, suspected of being a radical revolutionary. Which, of course, he is! In our rooms he insists on wearing his Civic Guard uniform—a soldier to his core. The Austrian police follow us everywhere. When we stroll with Nino in the Boboli gardens, spies hide behind every statue and pop out to frighten us." She lowered her teacup to the table with a clatter. Her voice dripped hatred. "You know how they treat rebels: imprison, torture, execute—the three prongs of tyranny. It's imperative to leave!"

"Plus," she straightened her shoulders, "I must resume my career to support the family." With a finger, she scribbled a flourish of words in the air to illustrate her calling. "And bring my book to the public."

"Your husband is a Marchese, an aristocrat. Surely he has means."

"Hah!" Margaret barked. "He's the youngest son of a minor noble family. They cut him off without a *sou*. He fought for the Revolution, while his family was in the Pope's retinue. They'll never forgive him."

A door opened with a flourish. Ossoli himself blazed into the room, saying "*Perdon*" and bowing as he removed his hat. He beamed at Nino and Margaret as if they'd been separated for one year instead of one hour. Margaret's face kindled into a broad smile. Nino barreled into Ossoli's legs at full speed. The young man hoisted him to his shoulders, laughing and tickling the boy.

Margaret rose and clasped her husband's arm like an anchor in a storm. "You know, Elizabeth, when I came to Italy as Margaret *Fuller*, little did I know I would find the *fullest* life imaginable. I have acquired a bejeweled and sturdy scabbard in which to sheath my spirit." She touched her husband's cheek.

Elizabeth winked at Margaret with a trace of envy. "Always the wordsmith."

Margaret waved good-bye. "Farewell for the nonce."

The tall soldier bowed. "*Arrivederci, Signora*."

What does she see in him? Elizabeth wondered. *What can they talk about? Maybe they don't talk. She certainly glows when he appears.*

After Lily Wilson escorted them to the door, the lady's maid returned to the drawing room holding little Pen, a squirming, ample armful.

"That boy is so fat and rosy and strong that I'm almost skeptical he's my child," Elizabeth told Wilson.

"His grip is most prodigious," Wilson confirmed, extracting a curl from the boy's grasp. "He wants to march around, but he's too encumbered with frills." She touched the little boy's embroidered blouse, lace collar, and velvet pantalettes. "These clothes you insist he wear! He's a babe, not a fancy Renaissance courtier."

"Did you see how he scampered about with Nino? Freedom of movement—the most salubrious thing for children. They should never be shut in a nursery! Margaret agrees with me. She takes her son with her all over Florence. On foot—for the poor couple has no carriage."

Wilson shuddered. "Perhaps there's such a thing as too much freedom."

"Nonsense! To what do you refer?"

"I encountered them in the Uffizi galleries . . . with the little boy.

You know I refuse to look at paintings of nude flesh. Such shameful displays! Well, little Nino was scrutinizing, even—I would say—*ogling*, the Venus de Milo's unclothed torso! At such a tender, susceptible age!" She plopped Pen down on the floor, and he scuttled off in pursuit of the Browning spaniel.

Elizabeth laughed. "Your modesty knows no bounds, my dear Wilson!"

The maid looked affronted and insisted, "I term it piety, not modesty!" She went on: "That so-called Marquese Ossoli! He looks like a babe himself! He must be barely twenty-five and she, Madame Marquesa Fuller Ossoli—forty at the least!"

"It does not behoove us to speculate." Elizabeth looked uncomfortable and brushed crumbs from the table. "I admit they're an unlikely couple. What a strange species of marriage! She talks so fluently; he hardly speaks."

"Are they even married?" Wilson could not abstain from voicing doubt. "Everyone questions whether the little boy was—pardon my frankness—conceived within the bonds of wedlock." Her face reddened. "Please excuse my indelicacy."

"*Basta,* Wilson! The Ossolis have enough opprobrium from American Puritans. I've heard—when Madam Fuller appeared in Florence with unexpected accessories like an ambiguous spouse and incontrovertible child, her friends were astonished. I actually feared meeting her. The acquaintance was apt to be socially awkward."

"And theologically dangerous! I've heard Mrs. Fuller Ossoli venerates the Holy Bible *only* as literature, not the Word of God!" The proper Wilson could barely voice such sacrilege.

Her mistress popped a grape in her mouth. "She told me—quite jovially—she never 'pretended to be a Christian, except in dabs and sparkles here and there.' True religion, she told me, can be found anywhere *except* in church." Elizabeth removed a grape pit and made a sour face. "Yet I wager she's been baptized in blood."

"Heathen," Wilson muttered.

"Margaret agrees with her teacher Mr. Emerson," Elizabeth added, "that whoever would preach Christ's teachings must say nothing about Him."

She picked up from the table a toy wooden top, painted in the red, white, and green hues of the forbidden flag of freedom. She pulled a string that wound around it. Balanced on a tiny point, the top spun in frantic circles. Her little son crawled to her side, attracted by the chop-chop whirring sound. Before he could grab the toy, it toppled over, wobbled, and rocked to a halt.

"Ah, to keep one's balance, to stay upright in this topsy-turvy world," Elizabeth said to herself. "There's the rub." Her curls fell forward, veiling her face. She reached for paper, dipped her quill in an inkpot, and scratched a few words:

"This sinner was a loving one—
And now her spinning is all done."

CHAPTER FOUR

What Came Before— A Friendship

DECEMBER 1836 THROUGH 1839, BOSTON, MASSACHUSETTS

Margaret Fuller was twenty-six—nearly a confirmed spinster—when she accepted Bronson Alcott's offer to teach in his much-touted Temple School in Boston.

To Alcott, its idealistic founder, the institution was a Temple of Learning, inhabited by inherently divine, although still inchoate, angels. Margaret doubted both her pupils' godliness and their brilliance, but her idol Waldo Emerson almost worshipped Alcott. Plus, she ascribed to the school's progressive pedagogy, emphasizing not rote memory and recitation but independent thought. Then too, after her father's untimely death, Margaret had to earn money to support her mother, brothers, and sister. From a bookworm dreaming of a European Grand Tour, overnight Margaret became the family's only means to stave off poverty.

Three positions were open to gentlewomen: teaching, needlework, or marriage. Sewing she could do—but too reluctantly to turn into a vocation. Marriage, she could not. "Why be a housewife," she asked her students, "if you could be a genius?"

That left teaching. Proud of her linguistic prowess, she gave lessons in Latin, French, German, and Italian literature to upper crust teenage girls. Although she had considerable book learning to impart, Margaret preferred not to stand aloof as an omniscient lecturer but to inspire and befriend her pupils. More than occasionally, however, she grew impatient with what she termed her students' "barbarous ignorance." Often, she was impelled to belittle their effusions with harsh sarcasm. Superficiality had no place in Margaret's pantheon, even if these girls of elite breeding stock were adept at trivial prattle.

One girl in particular drew her: Caroline Sturgis, a seventeen-year-old redheaded beauty incapable of uttering a mundane cliché. Offering her protégé bountiful attention in extracurricular chats, Margaret soon began to call the young girl Cary.

Cary was a rebel after Margaret's own heart. Unable to curb her temper or her tongue, she'd been expelled from Dorothea Dix's Boston school for young ladies. Cary refused to subscribe to conventions for ladies' deportment. When her teacher required passivity, Cary was prone to mock her and complain of a lesson's absurdity. When others calculated sums on their slates, Cary sketched a cartoonish Miss Dix wielding a turnip rather than a piece of chalk. Her docile classmates practiced sentence structure; Cary penned a poem declaiming the torpid state of their brains.

Cary's defiance stemmed from her father's sternness. A self-made millionaire who grew up without benefit of formal education, William Sturgis worked as a seaman from the age of sixteen. Through dint of tireless effort at self-improvement, he rose to be captain of a ship at nineteen and, not long after, was admiral of a fleet. His source of wealth: he bartered with Northwest Indians for plush sea otter pelts and sold them in China for a lucrative profit.

Though immensely rich, Sturgis lived in Spartan simplicity. He had no patience for his daughter's shenanigans. After Schoolmistress Dix pronounced Cary intolerable and ungovernable, Sturgis enrolled her in the Temple School, thinking it would tame her. He little suspected she'd come under the influence of the most idiosyncratic woman of the time, Margaret Fuller.

Margaret and Cary had in common no-holds-barred candor.

Regardless of etiquette or the blandishments of discretion, they both spoke the truth. Direct, frank, they avoided the niceties of tact.

In their scorn for mere politeness, they shot a fusillade of saucy retorts at unwary miscreants. During a performance of Beethoven symphonies at the Boston Academy of Music they were annoyed by the constant buzz of a pinkly pretty young flirt, simpering and giggling with her escort throughout the concert. After disapproving stares failed to quell the girl's loquacity, Margaret turned to her during intermission and unleashed her ire: "I hope that, in the entire course of your life, young lady, you will not suffer so great an annoyance as you have inflicted this evening on a large number of music lovers."

"*Touché*!" cried Cary. She'd found her perfect model. After that, they were intimate friends, despite the near decade's difference in age. Cary responded to Margaret's charge to "be all that you can be" by pursuing her talent for art. "Total freedom!" she declared, showing Margaret a penciled sketch of an imaginary scene.

Margaret's brow furrowed as she perused the drawing of waif-like fairies levitating above ruins of a castle. Nothing could be further from her view of women's roles. "Hmm," she said. "Among Boston ladies, wings are scarce as crocodile teeth. Freedom," she instructed, "requires awareness of reality."

"Precisely!" Cary agreed, sketching in a king's crown plopped in a mud puddle. "And knowing when to oppose tawdry reality with one's own superior vision."

Their friendship was not without rifts, as might be expected when two such outsized egos collide. When Margaret decamped from Boston to Providence, Rhode Island, to teach at a new school, she hoped to enlist Cary as her roommate. She wished to save money by sharing the rent, but Cary's responses to the invitation were at first enthusiastic, then evasive, and finally negative. Margaret, who prided herself on magnetic power to attract prized students, was hurt. Was her planet losing its most resplendent satellite?

Only later did she discover it was Cary's father who had put the kibosh on their growing intimacy. The beetle-browed Captain Sturgis refused to advance money for rent, lecturing his daughter on the ills of family philanthropy. "A promiscuous giving of alms is injurious to character," he wrote Cary from a far-flung port where he was engaged in accumulating said alms. "Dependence on charity leads to imbecility of purpose. If I yield to your importunity in begging these funds, it would produce more evil than good."

In actuality, Sturgis feared the taint of Margaret's influence. He knew Miss Fuller was allied with infamous savants like Ralph Waldo Emerson, godless intellectuals who were known as Transcendentalists. "I'd as soon swallow a porcupine," he declared, "as let my daughter live with Miss Fuller!"

By 1838, the Transcendental crew was the scandal of the Old Guard. Had not Mr. Emerson blasphemed in his Divinity School Address at Harvard? "He disparages Christianity, which he calls 'the cult of a partially-divine Jesus,'" gasped cigar-smoking gossips in top hats. "Heresy!"

Sturgis was appalled at the latest trend known as The Newness. Its adherents, among whom Cary was a conspicuous member, formed a coterie known as Young America. At barely eighteen his wayward daughter embraced indecorous fads like wearing ankle-baring bloomers, listening to lively music, and spouting new-fangled slang. Unburdened by the necessity of work to buy food or frocks, she indulged her every whim, even if her reckless behavior gave her elders the vapors. Cary had been seen in public not wearing a bonnet—like a peasant!—her long hair tumbling down her back. And corsets? No sign of any whalebone strictures on her comely person. Even worse, she was heard whistling as she ambled down a country lane. (*Be still, my heart!* Captain Sturgis thought, recalling the adage "Whistling girls and crowing hens—they don't come to no good end.")

By 1839, the twenty-year-old Cary was practiced at—and proud of—defying her father. Which was why Margaret questioned her reluctance to become her roommate. "Is there another reason you won't come?" she asked her protégé. "Does it have to do with that barbarous young man who's courting you?"

"You mean Ellery Channing?" Cary blushed and looked away, suddenly absorbed in flapping a leather glove to fan her face. "Ellery's been my friend since childhood."

"You're not a child any more. You've outgrown old friends just as you've outgrown hair ribbons. Besides," Margaret pronounced, "he's a wretched poet!" In her view, mediocre poems were a capital offense.

"But what an adventurer! Ellery says he's heading West, a pioneer! He'll build a cabin and write paeons about the prairie." Cary sighed, a faraway look in her eyes.

"His paeons will be as flat and featureless as the prairie." Margaret slapped her knee.

"I admit Ellery and I differ in our opinion of you. He says you're overladen with book learning, dogmatic, arrogant—that you'd make a semi-clever, third-rate man."

Margaret seized her parasol to stalk out. Cary quickly amended, "Wait! I told him you're large-brained and even larger-souled."

"We'll see who comes out on top, won't we? I or that pompous vagabond!" Margaret rearranged her crinolines, smoothing out untoward flounces. She looked directly in Cary's eyes. "I'm planning a subscription series of Conversations in Boston. Will you sign on?"

"It goes without saying." Cary pulled on her gloves. "A salon for ladies! A thousand times yes!"

Cary was keen to enroll in Margaret's latest venture, where a subscription became—for Boston's female intelligentsia—a sign of aspiration to Higher Thought. Women were forbidden to speak in public from a podium, as Waldo Emerson did so successfully to fatten his purse. But to listen to the most cultured woman in America in a private setting, what a thrill! New England's foremost maids and matrons gladly paid out of their household stipend to converse with their idol. Little did these subscribers know her message would undermine their complacency.

CHAPTER FIVE

Stirring Conversations

NOVEMBER 1839, BOSTON, MASSACHUSETTS

Cary had heard so much about Sophia Peabody, the talented painter and sister of Lizzie Peabody, who owned the bookshop that hosted one of Margaret's first Conversations. The room, lined with bookshelves, was packed with the best and brightest of female Bostonians. It was Sophia whose acquaintance Cary most wished to cultivate. Sophia had exhibited her paintings in galleries, a rarity for a woman! She had won commissions to do oil portraits and sculptures! Indeed, her copies of famous paintings hung on the bookstore walls, offered for sale. Most tantalizing, Miss Peabody was said to be secretly engaged to the reclusive writer Nathaniel Hawthorne!

Cary knew that Mr. Hawthorne was living in the agrarian enclave of Brook Farm, an idealistic new community set up on Transcendental principles. "I didn't realize Mr. Hawthorne subscribed to the romantic ideals of Brook Farm," Cary said to Sophia as they settled in their chairs. "I wouldn't have thought a utopian experiment was his sort of thing."

Sophia, recognizing a kindred spirit, was eager to speak of her beloved. "Alas, he has absolutely no illusion that the commune will prove a model," she answered. "He lives there only to save money on lodgings, in the hope that he can pursue his literary vocation at night. He had the naïve misconception," Sophia explained, "that after an afternoon's work on the farm, he could pen his romances at night.

Unfortunately, fatigue overwhelms his muse. After shoveling manure for hours, he can't pour out his soul on paper. His soul, he wrote me, is perishing under a dung-heap. Please excuse my indelicacy."

"I appreciate your candor," Cary said. "Tell me, why did you enroll in Miss Fuller's Conversations? Do you agree that women are denied proper education?"

"Most certainly." Sophia was adamant. "What an irony, that Boston boasts of its pretensions to intellectual refinement, but it applies only to men. They go to Harvard, while their sisters stay home to crochet. I confess to feeling hero-worship for Miss Fuller," she went on. "Margaret is not only a genius of talk; she has a great gift for friendship. I'm blessed to consider her a friend."

Standing in front of the bevy of belles, Sophia's sister Elizabeth Peabody tapped a ceramic bust of Plato with a penknife. "Attention, ladies," she said, calling to order those who packed her parlor. Giddy gossip hushed, silence fell, as thirty adjusted frilly skirts and leaned forward to hear the wisdom of Margaret Fuller. Cary's stomach churned with nervousness as her mentor, known as the deepest thinker and most stirring speaker in the country, cleared her throat. Margaret sat like a sybil on a tripod wearing a green velvet gown. She was rather plain, in truth, but with such colloquial adroitness that as soon as she began to speak, only her wit was evident. Her eyes shot sparks as her words electrified her auditors.

"Consider *The Odyssey*," Margaret began, "the first recorded instance of a man telling a woman her voice 'should never be heard in public.' Telemachus is privileged by being Odysseus's son; he has the effrontery to tell his mother, brave Penelope, to leave and tend to her weaving. Then there is poor Philomela in Ovid's *Metamorphoses*. She is raped by Tereus, who cuts out her tongue to prevent her testimony against him. History and myth are replete with men forcing women to be quiet. It is time for us to speak out!"

The women stirred, rustling their petticoats. They snapped their fans shut and waved them in the air. Some jumped to their feet, stamped, and clapped, shouting, "Yes!"

One conspicuous nay-sayer who remained fixed in her seat, unswayed by Fuller's rhetoric, was Lidian Emerson, wife of the revered Ralph Waldo Emerson. "A woman's place is in the home," she whispered, "not ranting from a podium."

Cary felt impelled to demonstrate her status as Fuller's star acolyte. "Even earlier than *The Odyssey* is Hector's putdown of his wife Andromache in *The Iliad*." She preened at the group's attention, raising her voice. "When Hector says he'll fight Achilles and his wife weeps, begging him not to risk certain death, he tells her, 'Go home. Leave the cares of war to men. Tend to your housework.'"

Margaret nodded. "Yet another instance of denying a woman the right to speak her mind. Hector says, 'Get back to your loom and spindle.' She noticed Lidian's unease and asked, "Mrs. Emerson, do you have a thought to add?"

"What's so wrong with sticking to our knitting?" She held up a sock she intended to mend on the stagecoach ride back home to Concord. She poked her index finger through a gaping hole. "Who else will mend the tatters? Certainly not my husband, Mr. Emerson."

Margaret rejoined with more gentleness than asperity, "Perhaps Mr. Emerson would benefit from knitting a sock, not just knitting his brow in philosophic thought."

Her listeners tittered. Margaret continued, "I merely wish to note: by venturing into traditionally male-dominated areas, women are subject to verbal abuse, as if being smart or witty or discerning is a crime against nature. Regrettably, men fear intelligent women like you, Lidian, women who speak the truth."

Lidian retorted, "I am neither thawed nor convinced by your examples, Miss Fuller. Are we expected to learn from heathen Greeks? Already, people say the doctrine of Transcendentalism is atheism in disguise. Are you saying pagan Greece is superior to our Christian nation?"

Margaret, delighted to debate, answered, "Our civilization is more advanced in many ways, especially in mechanical devices, but we should show respect, not contempt, for Greek myths. They express aspiration and potential."

Sophia nodded her approval, and Margaret smiled. Sophia whispered to Cary, "When she looks at me, or—more accurately—into me, I am so under her spell, I feel life without her would be empty—no, more than that. It would be wrong."

"Woman is at present too straitly bound to give us scope," Margaret declaimed. She made fierce eye contact with each and asked, "Who are you? Are you all you can be, more than a decorative appendage to a man, destined to bear his progeny? Can you see yourself as a surgeon or a senator, a college professor or a barrister, or why not a sea captain?"

Gasps and general hubbub ensued among the audience. Women let out bursts of air, as if they'd been stifled for years. Margaret had said aloud the unthinkable: women could be anything, do anything! The ladies poured out secret dreams.

"My hope when we married: to be my husband's true partner in metaphysics," Lidian mumbled. "But now I knit socks."

"I will be an artist of brilliant, original paintings!" Sophia shouted, nearly breathless.

"Life is an art," Margaret answered. "You are not merely an artist but a work of art yourself."

"I want to throw aside my gloves, whip out a sketch pad, and start drawing straight away," Sophia crowed. "My fingers itch!"

Cary caught the contagion, her heart pounding with exhilaration—*the idea of equality*! She sat up straighter, almost levitating. *A sea captain!*

Margaret peppered the crowd with questions and listened to their responses, pushing each one further into the realm of imagining.

"I dream of going to medical school, becoming a physician!" one said.

Another: "I want to study archeology, to dig up mastodon bones!'

"A botanist!"

"An engineer!"

"A journalist!"

Although such professions were closed to women, Margaret challenged them: "This is *le grand peut-etre*, in French, 'the big perhaps.' You must make it real! Roots and fruits! My goal is to plant a seed, one that takes root and grows into your own fruitful, original thoughts. And actions! Our identity as women does not condemn us to be merely passive listeners. We must tune our harps to play a grand symphony!"

"What a concert that will be—treble and bass in harmony!" Sophia trembled with excitement.

The crowd gathered up bonnets and cloaks and steered towards the exit, jabbering in a high-pitched, most unladylike manner. So wrought up at the thought of her unlimited potential was one young lady, that she knocked the ceramic bust of stoic-faced Plato off its pedestal. Margaret caught it before it shattered. "No harm, my dear," she reassured the flustered woman as she restored the bust to its plinth.

Sophia approached Margaret and curtsied, saying, "I can't stop myself from gushing. I feel all kindled! You're my Priestess! My Queen!"

Margaret emitted a most unqueenly bark of mirth. "Please," she said, laying a hand on Sophia's arm, "you are as much a Queen as I. Now sally forth and do royal deeds."

Lidian alone tsk-tsked to Cary, "Ever since Mr. Emerson delivered his lecture attacking the veracity of Biblical miracles, ministers are saying Transcendentalism is evil, that it will lead believers astray. Mr. Emerson says the best part of church is the silent sanctuary before the preaching starts. Imagine!"

"Well, you know what your husband thinks of Evil—that it's just temporary, before developing into Good," Cary countered.

Margaret approached Lidian. "Conservatives think all change is audacious. Please, Lidian, join our new generation. The time has come to reform and transform the old ways."

"Hmmph!" Lidian snorted. "Ask yourself, Margaret Fuller: aren't you motivated by vanity? Isn't it egotistic to trumpet the virtue of self-trust?"

The two veered into a corner to continue the argument.

"I vouchsafe Margaret will win her over," Cary whispered to Sophia as they donned their shawls, bonnets, and gloves. "Transcendentalism is all the rage among my crowd, but it's hardly understood by the mob. I heard one man seize on the 'dentalism' part of the word and surmise that it means an operation on the teeth."

Sophia laughed and invited Cary to a tea shop next door. "I hope my enthusiasm is not so excessive as to appear ridiculous," she said, settling in her seat inside. "When it comes to Margaret's prophecies, I seem to suffer from a surfeit of ebullience."

They ordered plum pudding and attacked it with gusto, their mouths smeared with purple juice, eyes shining with exuberance. Cary admitted she shared Sophia's elation, which inspired Sophia to speak. "Finding your sympathetic ear emboldens me to divulge what I've so long kept secret." She blushed with pleasure, bouncing with hardly suppressed glee.

"You allude to your engagement to Mr. Hawthorne? A secret only to his mother and sisters."

"So you know! What a relief to eschew concealment! May I speak freely? My heart is so full. I yearn to tell all to a sisterly soul."

Cary nodded. "I am your servant."

"Mr. Hawthorne's letters from Brook Farm are full of his labors, which chiefly involve spreading manure and disseminating hay. Poor dear—his smooth hands are only acclimated to holding a quill! I gather my Love has traded his frock coat for a farmer's overalls and his pen for a pitchfork."

Cary pictured the immaculately attired author in ploughman's garb, his chest sweat-soaked and straw in his wavy brown hair. Not an unpleasing image—Hawthorne was as handsome as a Greek god.

When Cary had seen him on a street in Salem, she froze in admiration, staring so boldly that the writer reddened in embarrassment and strode off.

Sophia chattered on, unstoppable once the dam of silence was breached: "Nat seems jealous of my fascination with Queen Margaret. When I write him panegyrics on her eloquence, he writes back, 'Would that Miss Fuller might lose her tongue! Her Conversation sounds like a Babel of insane talkers.' Yet I know he's not immune to her charms. Even though he's sequestered at Brook Farm, I keep him abreast of my pursuits—most notably my interest in women's advancement. As encouraged by sessions with Margaret."

"How does he respond?" Cary asked. Hawthorne was associated more with The Oldness than The Newness.

"Not well," Sophia admitted, "but I'm sure he agrees with me that our marriage will defy tradition. Our union will surely allow equal artistic endeavor." She looked at her hands and sighed. "If only we could be together! Instead, I have to read in his letter—intended to be facetious, but I found it unsettling—of a visit to Brook Farm by Margaret and a cow. He had the cheek to compare Margaret to a 'fractious cow, apt to kick over the milking pail.' A cow!"

"That analogy is hardly enlightened—or flattering," Cary interrupted. "I hope you scolded him. Remember *The Odyssey*. When Telemachus is rude to his mother, she corrects his error."

Sophia rallied. "Let me explain. Margaret, it appears, gave Brook Farm a milk cow from her family's stock. Since this cow refuses to mingle with the herd, Nat refers to it as a 'Transcendental heifer.'"

"Outrageous!" Cary said.

"Humor, alas, is not his strongest epistolary talent," Sophia sighed. "Said bovine, he confides, evinces a firm attachment to Nat, following him around the barn and mooing for ear scratches. I infer Margaret, during her visit, also stuck to his side like lichen on a tree." Her brow wrinkled at the thought.

"I'd say your Mr. Hawthorne has spent too much time on the manure pile if he can't perceive Margaret's merit," Cary said. "She's more a powerful bull than a smitten milk cow."

Abashed, Sophia confessed, "I felt a pang of envy when Nat wrote that he's 'content to be Miss Fuller's milkmaid' when she visits. He's always so reserved, taciturn as the tomb with everyone except me, but he wrote that he and Margaret gabbed for hours when she was there. Yet—despite their rapport—he's downright critical of her! He implies Margaret is conceited. Miss Fuller has, he writes me, 'a very good opinion of herself.'"

"She's entitled to it!" Cary blurted. "As if any woman has to apologize for her intellect!"

Sophia set her fork down with an unladylike clatter and wiped plum juice from her lips. "I long to shout our secret engagement to the world—even to inform cornstalks and cows that Mr. Hawthorne and I are betrothed."

She smiled broadly, a look that turned to surprise as she glanced out the window. "Land sakes alive, there's Ellery Channing!"

Cary, suddenly rattled, tucked wayward curls behind her ears and pinched her cheeks to redden them. "He's coming in!"

The tall young man, radiant as a spear of sunshine, approached and swept off his hat in a showy fashion. Ladies at nearby tables perked up and stared at him appreciatively. "Greetings, fair maids!" Ellery said to Sophia and Cary, bowing. "How fortuitous to see you, just as a poem popped into my head. Tell me what you think." He straightened and recited:

"Few friendly voices cheer me on,
Few dear caresses comfort me,
I seek thee at the glow of dawn,
Come pick wildflowers, glazed with dew!"

His eyes bored into Cary's, then he pivoted and bowed to his rapt audience of female tea drinkers. The young ladies giggled and squirmed in their chairs.

Watchful mamas proffered stern admonishments. One matron hissed to her daughter, "A seedy rascal. His shoes are orange!" She flapped her fan energetically, as if to banish toxic vapors.

"I bid you farewell," he told the two. With a wink and a wave, Ellery sashayed from the tearoom. He smirked and threw a kiss, confident his auditors had relished his poetic offering.

"Well, Mr. Ellery Channing is certainly different from my Mr. Hawthorne, who is taciturn to a fault." Sophia shook her head in amazement.

"His poetics are weak, although the sentiments seem strong," Cary allowed, flushed to the roots of her red-gold hair.

"Do you know him well?"

"Ellery and I used to spend summers together . . ." Cary trailed off in revery.

"Nat compares Ellery Channing to a flat rock skipping merrily over the surface of a lake. One marvels at the impetuous leaps, but that scamp will never make a big splash."

Cary's dreamy expression was leavened by vexation. "Big splashes are highly over-rated."

CHAPTER SIX

Discord in Concord

1839–1842, CONCORD, MASSACHUSETTS

The group attending meetings of Boston's Transcendental Club lamented that they were misunderstood, even maligned as dangerous radicals by the ignorant public. To rectify that error, publicize their enlightened beliefs, and advance the backward state of American culture, they proposed to publish a literary magazine called *The Dial*. When Emerson declined the honor of editing it, as did other leaders of the movement, they anointed Margaret Fuller as editor, shunting the burden to one unlikely to refuse. It was a thankless and payless task, which she performed through 1842, badgering Club members for essays and poems to fill each issue's promised 136 pages.

Working on the magazine required Margaret to stay at Emerson's house in Concord for weeks at a time, a sojourn she welcomed: to share a house with her idol! "I long to know him to his roots!" she told Cary. "He's our country's most daring intellect!"

Margaret hoped her proximity to the Sage of Concord, as Emerson was now known, would ripen into intimate friendship. Yet Waldo remained aloof on his solitary Olympian peak. "I apologize for wearing a churl's mask and for maintaining the prickly armor of a porcupine when I consult with you," he told her. "Draw not too near to a porcupine, lest its quills wound you." He withdrew to his study to work. "Life paralyzes art," he said as he shut the door.

Margaret was not one to give up. She had dealt with a man's icy reserve before. She had suffered grievously from her father's severity and was determined to win over Waldo. She would ingratiate herself with an arsenal of wit, erudition, and—most effectively—compliments. Not a pretty sight for those allergic to sycophancy, she courted him with conversational brio. "I look through your telescope, Master," she told him, "and I see the universe."

At first, Emerson found her unrelenting torrent of talk tiring. *We shall never get far*, he thought. Gradually, his granite façade cracked into a smile and—at Margaret's scathing humor—melted into outright chuckles, a sound that left Lidian slack-jawed in surprise: *Mr. Emerson—not just smiling ironically but audibly laughing!*

As the months rolled on, the Great Man came to value Margaret's candor. "Before we trouble ourselves with the supernatural, let us be completely natural," Margaret admonished him. "You reverence the stars, but if they be too distant, let us examine the pebble lying at our feet."

"You are all poetry," he told her. "I am all prose."

"Philosophy alone is dry," she added. "It must awaken echoes in the heart."

Emerson nodded. "It's impossible to hold out against your assault. Your mind intoxicates me."

Hardly affection, Margaret thought, *but perhaps esteem will blossom into true partnership.*

They developed the habit of reading to each other after noonday dinner. After evening supper, they went for long woodsy rambles or moonlight rows on the river. On one such excursion *à deux*, Emerson and Margaret fled the house, practically skipping, giddy after drinking glasses of hard cider. As they disappeared down the lane, trailing laughter behind them, Lidian stamped her foot and shook a broom at them.

Cary, who'd accompanied Margaret to Concord, also felt excluded when the two luminaries absconded. She saw Lidian scowl, with one foot poised on the stairs, ready to mount to her chamber and slam the door.

"Are you ailing, Lidian?" Cary asked. "May I help you?"

"What ails me is the state of my marriage," Lidian exploded. Her voice shook as she unleashed a string of complaints she could no longer suppress. "I know you're great friends with her, but I must speak or I'll surely combust. Mr. Emerson invites Queen Margaret to stay here for weeks. They talk and talk. He says more in one hour with her than in a whole month with me. And you know Margaret—she's irrepressibly chatty with everyone, but with me she avoids supper. Too busy with her editing, but not too busy later for a stroll with Mr. Emerson."

She continued, ignoring Cary's silence, "Yesterday I asked her to take a turn with me outside, knowing how I need fresh air." Lidian gasped with umbrage: "She said she was already engaged to walk with Mr. Emerson! I couldn't help it—I burst into tears and retired to my chamber."

Lidian paused, straightened her spine and leveled her voice: "Now, 'tis I who chooses to absent myself from the supper table. But I will admit, Margaret is not so inert to feelings as Mr. Emerson. When she heard me crying, she knocked on my door and asked me to walk with her. I confessed to her that I envied her bond with my husband. When I agreed to marriage, I had hoped for a similar intellectual union."

Cary patted Lidian's arm. "Margaret admires Waldo so, but I see your point: you are equally worth spending time with. They ignore me too, you know. I'm considered too unlettered to partake of their high-toned dialogues."

Lidian raised her head. Her eyes sparkled with mischief. "Would you like to hear my Rules for Perfect Conduct here?"

Cary nodded, relieved to see Lidian's spunk return.

Lidian picked up a folio of papers inscribed in formal calligraphy "Transcendental Bible." With a tinge of rue, she said, "I wrote these commandments in jest, but you be the judge of their veracity."

Lidian recited: "First, a commandment Mr. Emerson firmly adheres to: 'Never confess a fault. You could not have committed it and who cares whether you are sorry?' Second, here's one addressed to lower folk like me: 'Are you not ashamed to wish to be happy? It is egotistical.'"

She giggled and wiped her eyes. "This one is mean, directed against my ill health: 'Loathe and shun the sick. They are in bad taste, and may untune us for writing the poem floating through our mind.'"

Her mouth formed a downward U of hurt. Her voice grew stronger. "Perchance this one applies to you as well as me," she told Cary: "'Despise the unintellectual, and make them feel it by not noticing their remarks, lest they intrude into your conversation with those of greater intellect.'"

"I had no idea you have such a gift for satire," Cary laughed. "Can you enlighten me further? This is my chance to solve some mysteries, while our betters—our perfectly divine, infallible friends—are enjoying their tête à tête."

"You wish to hear *me* speak? How vastly original!" Lidian murmured. She raised her voice. "You truly wish to interrogate my opinion? How novel! I am usually overseeing arrangements for our visitors. Never am I solicited to speak my mind. Would there were any hole to creep out of this most servile post as hostess! Oh, the insupportable ennui!"

"I'm sorry we seem to be exploiting your hospitality," Cary said.

"No, I apologize for my outburst. I welcome your company, Caroline. Someone from the wider world, from a bustling city, is exactly what I need. I do so miss my home in Plymouth. Lamentably, I am trapped in this provincial village—Mr. Emerson's choice of residence, decidedly not mine. Concord—the Athens of America, as Mr. Emerson calls it—hah! Concord slumbers and stifles, devoid of the decencies of civilization."

She went on, "Why, do you know, besides relegating our family life to this rural outpost, Mr. Emerson even insisted on changing my name?"

"You are not Lidian?"

"I am Lydia, called Liddie during all thirty-three years of my independent life before marriage. Apparently, that name was too pedestrian for our transcendent Mr. Emerson. He decided I should be called Lidian, after a Greek musical scale. And so I am. Ironic that my name should be so high-falutin' when my daily existence is so dull, without a scintilla of lyricism."

"I have another question: could you tell me why the house is called Bush?"

An ironic grin flickered across Lidian's face. "You've heard of the Burning Bush in the Bible? Where our Heavenly Father spoke to Moses?"

Cary nodded, although she had little truck with Old Testament legends. Or even the New Testament—all balderdash in her opinion.

"Mr. Emerson fondly hopes and fervently wishes The Divine will speak to us here at Bush. He is a prophet leading everyone to freedom."

"Will God communicate without setting this Bush afire?" Cary asked, her voice not devoid of sarcasm.

"If our Lord obeys his infallible creation, Mr. Emerson," she answered, "indubitably." And then the solemnly-inclined older woman's eye flickered in an unmistakable wink.

The two years of Margaret's editorship of *The Dial* were not an unalloyed success. Albeit infinitely more ambitious than the sentimental, sensationalistic magazines then extant, the publication's trumpeting of unorthodoxy was deeply suspect.

Leaders of establishment thinking called the magazine's issues less intelligible than "duck tracks in the mud." Reviewers deplored Dialers' scorn for popular American literature. "How dare they label home-grown writers 'mincing flunkeys' because our esteemed authors imitate hallowed European authors?" one editor wrote. "Longfellow, James Fenimore Cooper and their ilk are just fine, thank you very much," reviewers wrote. "American writers' refined work is polished, not rambunctious; it is urbane, not wild with rustic originality!"

To Margaret, the magazine was too tame. "How far it is from the snarling eaglet I wanted," she told Emerson. "It has not fire and flame enough."

"We are still fermenting," he placated her. "So far, we have much surf and foam from hitting the breakwater of American complacency, but we have no treasure left behind. We're not yet bad enough!"

One effect of Margaret's labor was that she was celebrated as the only woman at the helm of a serious cultural journal. She reaped both plaudits and censure—"hail to her" and "to hell with her." Just as she was renowned in Boston for her Conversations, she now gained respect nationally, even internationally. *I'm recognized as a person of substance—at last!* she thought. *All those books were not for naught. If Papa could only see me now.*

Her vocabulary became even more erudite. When introduced to a new acquaintance, she was apt to say, "How fortuitous to meet you" instead of "How d'ya do?"

Her essay in *The Dial* calling for wider opportunity for women caused an uproar but made Margaret a heroine, a warrior for women's rights in a world where there were none. At every social occasion, she brazenly denounced laws that limited women's autonomy. "The New Woman's day is dawning. We have waited here long in the dust; we are tired and hungry, but the triumphal procession must appear at last," she proclaimed. Her interlocutors either swooned with admiration or sniffed into their handkerchiefs with dismay.

Her assault on Emerson's affections did not turn out so well. For her, mutually respectful friendship was not enough. Margaret pressed her Master for a closer relationship—partaking of a romantic tinge on her part. Emerson froze her out. When she walked too closely by his side, clinging to his arm too tightly, he pulled away. She found herself left working at her inkwell alone more and more. Emerson increasingly turned to twenty-one-year-old Cary as his companion on woodland jaunts.

Cary was proud when the Great Man chose her. Margaret's demand for total loyalty had taken a toll on her. As a student grows, the teacher-student hold constricts until the pupil breaks free. It was time for Cary to leave the nest and try her wings. Cary walked out with Waldo, head held high, as Margaret watched from a window and dabbed her blurred eyes.

Lidian knocked on Margaret's study door and entered bearing tea on a tray. She nodded towards her husband's domain across the hall and said, as she fed sticks into a crackling fire, "He always chooses youth and beauty over ripeness."

Margaret spilled a slosh of tea on her skirt.

"One must tend one's own garden," Lidian said. She muttered, "A plant will not grow to maturity in a mighty oak's shade," and slipped from the room.

Cary stayed a spell in Concord without Margaret after her mentor's *Dial* editorship ended. She was often the sounding board as Emerson tried to free himself from Margaret's charisma. On one evening ramble to Walden pond, they saw a streak of moonlight in the pond, broken into a hundred incandescent facets by a breeze ruffling the surface.

"That dissolution of lunar radiance reminds me of Margaret," Emerson sighed.

Cary poked him in the ribs, a jab that made him start. She grabbed his walking stick and held it out of reach. "Such maundering dialogue may work in a lecture hall, Waldo, but say plainly what you mean! I'll withhold your cane until you're direct with me."

He plopped down on a mossy boulder and threw pebbles in the water. Their widening circles overlapped and dissolved. In a contemplative mood, Emerson spoke, "I remember when Margaret first visited. I resisted her charm. Her nasal voice repelled me and her habit of always squeezing her eyes shut—distracting. Then when I listened to her talk—so droll, so learned, so challenging—I never gave another thought to her appearance."

A silence followed. Emerson seemed to be digging into memories. He changed the subject to recollections of his first wife, Ellen Tucker. Cary was surprised, so closely had he guarded details about his adored child bride.

"I remember when I met my Ellen. It was the end of 1827 when she was sixteen to my mid-twenties. Never had I met someone so lively, so pretty!"

An all-encompassing smile split his face. "Ellen introduced me forthwith to her pets—how she loved animals! Her beloved spaniel Byron barked most snippily at me, vexed no doubt by my obvious attraction to his mistress. My darling girl held out a delicate finger for her canary to perch upon, she fondled her white mice among their wood shavings, and called in the field outside to her lamb, which came bounding up for a treat. I was smitten, besotted as I could never be again."

Cary was astonished. Was this chatterbox the iceberg she had come to know? She nodded to keep him talking.

"My 'kindling smile and dulcet speaking tones'—as Ellen called them—prejudiced her in my favor, even though I was only an itinerant preacher at the time. She found both my voice and words golden, she said, and I'm sure I glowed like all the crown jewels in the Tower of London. My angel was consummately bright, witty, and well-read for her age. I begged her to show me her poetry, impressive for one so young."

Cary sat up straight. *Ellen's poetry?* Was not Cary herself author of remarkably profound poems? True, she signed her poems in *The Dial* with only the letter "Z," but Waldo knew they were hers. Hadn't he praised them and asked to see Cary's drawings?

Emerson, oblivious to Cary's hauteur, went on. "During the next year, we deepened our acquaintance in letters. Ellen was bold; she overcame my reticence when she wrote, 'I love you very much, dear Waldo, and would like to be wholly yours if consistent with your future plans.'"

He laughed, looking like a schoolboy who'd stolen a tart, and continued, "How could I withstand such an avalanche of affection? Of course, I knew she was consumptive, which increased our urgency to get engaged—hard to believe more than twenty years ago. We married in Boston. We shared nearly two glorious years. My poor girl was often ill. When I found blood on her collar or the sheets, I was distraught. We tried every possible treatment, sleeping in a tent outdoors, drinking gallons of milk, exercising with dumbbells each morning. Once we even bumped along in a buggy for two hundred miles as part of outdoor therapy."

He fixed Cary with a delighted look and bragged, "We used to laugh and sing and dance together, if you can believe that of me."

"Hardly," Cary said. "I think of you as a mountain of reserve."

"Margaret and Lidian tax me with an incapacity to express emotion or show affection," he admitted. "If only they could have seen Ellen and me together! I lost no opportunity to demonstrate my love. When reading or writing, I'd call out to her, 'Ellen, my lovely love, I do dearly love you!'" He looked proud rather than abashed.

"So you have a heart as well as a brain!" Cary said, patting his hand. "No one suspects this side of you."

He hung his head and picked up a pinecone, which he flung into the pond. As the sound of its splash died away, he said, "In early 1831 Ellen Louisa Tucker Emerson died. Frail as a snowdrop, barely twenty. My angel's last words were 'I have not forgot the peace and joy.' With her died my vocation as a Unitarian minister—and all my hopes for earthly happiness."

He swallowed a lump in his throat. "For one year I walked to her tomb every morning. I spoke to her spirit; I left flowers and poems on her grave. Some thought my grief had driven me mad. I left the ministry and went to Europe to find myself again. After Ellen died, I thought I could never love again. My marriage to Lidian, as you have no doubt perceived, is a most solemn union."

He seemed to come out of a trance. "Where was I? Oh yes, Margaret!" His demeanor changed from melancholy to factual. "Margaret couldn't be more unlike my Ellen. Our friendship was strictly platonic—until Margaret tried to make it more." He straightened his cravat and cleared his throat. "But what a mind she has! Her every utterance is either outrageous or brilliant. I fear her wit if she ever turns it on me."

He took Cary's hand. "You remind me of Ellen—so young and lovely and daring. You'll say anything, try anything!"

An awkward silence fell between them. To break it, Emerson pointed to a shockingly pornographic fungus, the aptly named *Phallus impudicous.* It sprouted at the base of a nearby spruce. "Pray, what could Nature be thinking of when it created such a plant?" He averted his eyes and frowned. "It looks like a scurvy drawing in a privy."

A flock of gnats buzzed in front of their faces. Cary handed Waldo his walking stick. "I thought you a lover of Nature in all its forms."

"If I had lived back when the world was made, I would've volunteered some very valuable suggestions." Emerson took her arm and tugged her upright. Her skirts billowed in the breeze.

Just then, ripples reached their boulder, slapping waves on its granite back. A boat separated the water, trailing an enlarging wake, as a young man who bristled with energy rowed towards them. "Halloo, Waldo and Miss Sturgis! Ahoy!" Henry David Thoreau called.

"Please, call me Cary. And may I use your first name?" Cary asked as Thoreau beached his rowboat's bow on the flat boulder that projected into the pond.

The short young man blushed—as was his wont when confronted with any members of the female persuasion other than his particular friend Lidian Emerson. "As you like," he mumbled, then screwed up his courage to ask, "May I offer you two an excursion on the pond?"

Emerson brushed dust from his trousers, waved away a cloud of gnats and turned around. "Not today, my brave Henry. I've already overstayed my allotted hour for recreation. My study beckons." He strode off.

"I accept with pleasure," Cary announced to Thoreau's chagrin. She stepped into the rowboat, grabbing gunwales on both sides to steady it as it rocked. She installed herself in the stern and addressed the rower. "Now, Henry, it's my chance to plumb your depths. You usually disappear whenever I've approached you in the past."

"I have a pronounced antipathy to idle chitchat," he said, "but plumbing depths is a wholesome activity. Do you wish to know how deep the pond is? Local people say it's bottomless, but using a fishing line and a stone, I measured it at just over one hundred feet."

"Absorbing, I'm sure, but tell me—what I wish to know is how Margaret gained your confidence. I see you more at ease with chipmunks than with most women. And Margaret is hardly the feral sort."

Thoreau, at first shy, gradually warmed to his tale. Words poured out while he rowed. The fact that Cary sat behind him and he kept his eyes on the pond made his thoughts flow.

"A while ago Margaret stayed at Bush all summer. She and Waldo were "Dialing" on the first volume. I was twenty-three, a raw, beardless schoolmaster just out of Harvard College. Margaret was thirty or thereabouts, mightily impressive for her learning. Waldo encouraged me to submit poems and essays to *The Dial*, but Margaret wouldn't accept them, no matter how Waldo cajoled or how often I revised and resubmitted."

"Were you angry?" Cary asked, dangling her fingers in the water.

"Pshaw, no!" he said. "Margaret isn't like other ladies. Most are silly, delicate, sentimental, fanning themselves and dropping a hanky for me to retrieve. Excuse me for speaking the truth. No nonsense for Margaret! No coy games, just blurting out her meaning straight."

"Truth is her goal," Cary agreed, already feeling she was betraying her friend by usurping Emerson's affections. She scooped up a water lily and inhaled its citrusy aroma.

"If she comes into a room where I'm sitting, she has no wish for me to rise and offer her a seat," he said. "We don't shake hands every time we meet. Such a waste of time! She once said she'd as soon take the branch of an elm tree as take my arm walking. People in town think her brusque, farcical even. To me, she's honest!"

"You speak the truth too," Cary said, relinquishing the flower back to the pond. "Oh look at that trout zoom through the water! I wish I could swim like that."

"A fin is better than a foot for swimming," he said, twisting around to view the fish. "I noticed Margaret accepted many of *your* poems for *The Dial.* What's your secret?"

"Margaret wanted rude poems that make a virtue of non-conformity, poems more at home in a tavern than a parlor." Cary squared her shoulders, straightening from her languid posture. She doffed her bonnet and shook out her hair, hairpins pinging into the pond. "She calls me a genius, but who knows?"

Thoreau frowned at the sinking hairpins without comment, then said, "One spring evening I took Margaret for a row like this. We stayed so late the moon sank down and the whip-poor-wills sang to us. An eastern breeze rustled the water into scalloped waves, carrying the scent of apple blossoms. When fireflies started blinking, she clapped her hands like a child seeing birthday candles."

"You make me feel inadequate," Cary said.

Speaking almost to himself, Thoreau continued, "One time I threw pebbles at her window just as dawn cracked open the day. 'Miss Fuller,' I called, until she raised the sash. I invited her to sail with me on the Concord River. 'Come see Heaven with me!' I said. She called me a gallant guide." He blushed with pleasure. "What a curious, provoking, restless mind she has!—'What's this? What's that?' she kept asking.

'Why are andromeda leaves glossy-green on one side and glowing-red on the other? Why does the warbling vireo's song end on a high note? How do ravens fly upside down and do somersaults in the air?' She even likes my flute."

"What naturalist lore did you teach her?"

"I told her how jewelweed oil cures poison ivy itch. She liked the water walkers gliding over the pond and asked me why frogs' eggs look like billowy foam floating on the water."

"Look at those dewy cobwebs on the grass!" Cary pointed. "They look like fairy hats."

Thoreau snagged a green frog from a log and handed it to her. She didn't flinch but held it in the cup of her hand before releasing it to a lily pad. "All very well and good, Henry—your mutual admiration society with Margaret. Were you being so pleasant to entice her to accept your verses in *The Dial*?"

"No! I want to improve my writing, to hear her frank opinion. She's right to push me. I don't mind that she's ruthless. My essays *were* rough and self-righteous. She said one essay didn't flow naturally, that she 'could hear the grating of a tool on the mosaic.'"

"Oh dear, she is always one to ignore tact."

Thoreau warmed to his recollection. "The best teachers are tough, not tender. My analogies lacked fluency. 'More concrete experience, less abstract thought!' she told me. 'Your encumbrance of rhetoric clouds your meaning, smothering the facts. Too much upholstery and not enough framing!' I've taken her words to heart."

"I'm glad you bore it well. She can be hurtful and blunt."

Henry aimed the boat at a sandy patch of shore and ran it aground. The bottom scraped on pebbles as the boat came to a halt. "What I remember most of all is her faith that I would one day be greater than Waldo," Thoreau said, with an air of disbelief. "Astounding! He's my paragon of excellence! 'One day, you'll go a step beyond that icicle

Waldo,' she prophesied. 'One day, you'll cut the puppet strings.'" He stepped from the boat and scratched his head.

"Margaret has a gift of drawing out your inmost hopes—dreams you're embarrassed to tell anyone," Cary said as she alighted on dry land. "My dream is to be a great artist. What's yours?"

He looked towards the woods. "The villagers laugh at me and call me a lazy, good-for-nothing wastrel, but I've long wanted to build a shack here at Walden Pond and live in it alone. It's probably a foolish fantasy. Everyone thinks it's a joke, but it's no joke to me. Margaret told me, 'Do it! Where Waldo grapples with his thoughts, you must leap, climb, and swing with all your force! You put flesh on Waldo's ethics. He thinks, ruminates, lectures. You live!'"

He tied the rope to a tree stump. The wind stirred up his tousled hair. "Would that it were true!"

"One more thing," Cary tucked her hair back under her bonnet. "Where can I find Algonquin arrowheads?"

"Everywhere!" Thoreau stooped and plucked a rough-hewn stone arrowhead from a jumble of wild cranberries. "Seek and you will find."

CHAPTER SEVEN

Sophia and Nathaniel Hawthorne, Marital Concord

SPRING 1842, CONCORD, MASSACHUSETTS

The newly wed Sophia and Nathaniel Hawthorne made their first home in the Old Manse in Concord. Emerson arranged the rental beginning on their wedding day. He hoped to lure literati and progressive thinkers to the village to form a colony of like-minded souls. Sophia was a devotee of Transcendentalist ideas—chiefly the faith that her intuition emanated from divine purpose. Her husband had no such sunny optimism. In the short stories he was beginning to get published, he dwelt on humanity's dark impulses.

The Old Manse was indeed old. A former parsonage for Emerson's step-grandfather, it was built in 1770. Visible from a window was the North Bridge, the site of the battle that kicked off the Revolutionary War. Soot stains from thousands of fires in the massive chimney blackened the interior walls. Its back faced west—past the apple orchard—towards the placid Concord River, which glowed at fiery sunset. The apple trees were spindly, past their prime, yet on fall evenings when the wind blew, Hawthorne heard apples tumbling down. Their plop-plop-plop signaled, he said, "perfect ripeness."

Emerson's boarder and handyman, Henry Thoreau, planted a vegetable garden to welcome the Hawthornes. They made much use of it, having almost no income. Beans, corn, and squash grew abundantly, as did currant bushes, cherries, and more pears than they could eat or preserve.

"I love pear trees in bloom—like a bouquet of white clouds on each trunk," Sophia said, "yet I dread the duty their fruit imposes." In autumn, the whole house smelled sweet, fruity. Rooms, drawers, even the cellar stored surplus pears. Whether Bartlett, Bosc, or Anjou, Sophia constantly sliced, baked, and made cobblers, trying to stay ahead of fruit flies before the yellow pears turned mushy and soft.

The lane to the Old Manse was weedy, since the house had been empty for years, aloof from village hubbub. A major charm for Hawthorne, handsome as Apollo and antisocial as Hades, was the manse's distance from the road. "Not every passerby," he told Sophia, "can thrust in his head to derange my solitude and disturb our domestic tranquility."

For Hawthorne and his bride, life in the Old Manse was paradise. Together after a secret engagement of many years, they were blissful. "We are as happy as could be without being ridiculous," Sophia reported to her sister Lizzie.

Their union began as an equal partnership of artists, just as the lovers had pledged while courting. Nathaniel worked upstairs on his tales, while Sophia rambled woods and fields, sketching landscapes for oil paintings. She replaced faded ancestral portraits of dour clerics, which stared at them with beady-eyed disapproval, with her own more cheerful subjects. In her brightly lit scenes, mythological figures romped with winged cherubs, scenarios designed to amuse rather than instruct.

When they arrived by buggy directly after their wedding, they found the old house embowered. Lidian Emerson had installed bouquets of lilies, daffodils, and hyacinths in every room to dispel the house's musty odor. Lidian brought presents of freshly made bread, as well as butter and salt.

"My Lord Nat and I are finally together!" Sophia crowed to Lidian. She stated the obvious but—to her—it was still a miracle. "I feel I've died and gone to heaven without the necessity to die first!"

"May the Cloud-Land that is Concord ever dispel discord for you," Lidian said tersely, an edict that did nothing to shadow Sophia's joy.

Hawthorne reveled in his role of lord of the manse. He rose early, bathed in the Concord River—though he complained of its muddy sluggishness—and caught trout, which he brought home for breakfast. While reading a book, he fried the fish, roasted potatoes, and ground coffee beans for his pretty wife. In the afternoons, he sawed and split wood like a demon and undertook repairs, fixing the bellows and repairing the arm of a rocking chair, which had a disconcerting tendency to fall off.

When fall came, purple asters dotted the grass and buzzed with bees. The corn had long since tasseled and goldenrods waved their tops in the breeze. Flocks of geese took their leave as sweet fern changed from olive-green to crinkly gold. For the Hawthornes' first Thanksgiving—just the two of them—they dined on quince, dates, baked apples, bread, cheese, and milk. Sophia even contrived a pumpkin pie, although she had not much prior experience with cookery.

Troubling intimations—such as poverty and neglect of Hawthorne's literary merit—cast the only pall on their sun-blest lives. Every morning Sophia set out with her sketch pad. One day, she was drawing a somnolent turtle, half-immersed in mud at the pond's border. Suddenly a pout-fish swam by, flicking its tail casually. In a flash, the turtle seized the fish in its jaws and tore it to shreds. Sated, the turtle lapsed back into slumber in the mud bank, disguised as an innocent stick.

At the sudden display of nature's menace, Sophia shivered. *Such aggression is surely an anomaly*, she assured herself. Nature, Concord, and the Old Manse held nothing but happiness for her. There might be the occasional splinter when she ran her hand over the rickety stair rail, but on the whole, life was splendid. Sophia and Nat formed an indissoluble unit, keeping to themselves, since, as she told curious villagers, “my beloved has an abomination of visiting.”

The couple’s mutual harmony was so complete only one minor quarrel intervened. A month after they moved in, they went for a walk, holding hands all the way. Sophia nearly skipped like a carefree child. Even Hawthorne, usually so silent and withdrawn, was effervescent. He’d escaped at last from his labors at the doomed Brook Farm, and Sophia was released from her mother’s care! Sophia turned to take a shortcut, aiming to tramp through a field of tall grass, on her way home.

Hawthorne stopped her, tugging her back. “It’s unmowed,” he urged. “Stay on the road. Don’t trample the hay before the scythes come to cut it.”

Sophia shook him off and took her own path. She clomped through the tall grass, running her hands over the blond spikes and breaking the stalks with her boots. She enjoyed the swishing sound of her passage, only regretting that Nat wasn’t with her to share her progress.

They met on the other side of the field. Sophia looked back at the yellow hay she’d trampled. She saw where her feet had flattened a corridor. “I see my error!” she told Nat. “Sorry to disobey, my Love! I should’ve yielded to your superior knowledge of husbandry! I’ll never be so naughty again!”

They embraced, and she kissed him with mounting passion. “My naughty girl,” he whispered in her ear. The newlyweds dropped to a bed of pine needles in the woods. Her petticoats and the buttons on his trousers proved no obstacle to what became a torrid bout of passion. Doubtless their overly long engagement heightened such honeymoon fervor.

One neighbor on a visit to the Emersons, Margaret Fuller, was almost witness to their enthusiasm for physical contact, which Sophia termed “blissful dainties” in her journal. Margaret had long declared her disapproval of marriage as a form of subjugation for wives. She’d vowed to remain a virgin, independent of romantic ties, yet she couldn't help but notice—and be intrigued by—Sophia and Nathaniel's ardor. Anyone who lived on a farm, as Margaret had, knew the basics of sexual congress, but to see persons she admired in the throes of passion—now that was fascinating. *In a purely anthropological sense,* she told herself.

It happened one summer day when Hawthorne presented his young bride with a bouquet of crimson cardinal flowers. "I had to compete with hungry butterflies to pick these for you," he said. Sophia was so grateful, she tossed the flowers on a table and wrapped her body around his. She hugged him so close, she virtually plastered her form to his body. She nuzzled his ear, uncaring that his wing collar scraped her neck. She could almost hear his gold watch in a waistcoat pocket ticking. Its beat mirrored her pounding heart.

At that moment Margaret barreled in without knocking. The lovers sprang apart, gulping down their quick breaths and straightening their clothing. Margaret regarded them with intense curiosity, not at all discomfited to surprise them in a moment of passion. Sophia hid her embarrassment well. She took her guest's bonnet and shawl, bade her sit, and served her tea. Red as a raspberry, hair disheveled and garments in disarray, Sophia made small talk and spooned an extra ration of sugar in her cup.

Margaret, not a bit unnerved, said with a frank sparkle in her eye but no sign of perturbation, "It seems I have a genius for interrupting."

In fact, Margaret and the habitually laconic Nathaniel had grown close, moving past impersonal cordiality to intimate talks. That evening after tea, as shadows lengthened and hoot owls began to holler, he walked her back to the Emersons in the moonlight. When he returned—after a rather too-lengthy time, Sophia felt, for she'd been drumming her fingers impatiently on the sideboard awaiting him—his countenance glowed like the shiny moon itself. He was actually humming!

Hawthorne excused the deviance from his habitual reserve: "Such is Margaret's influence. Her mirth unsettles my foundations," he chuckled. Noting Sophia's set shoulders, he soothed her: "You should know that Margaret considers our marriage a happy duet, a union of equals."

Sophia agreed, almost as if to convince herself. "We are penetrated by joy in our first home, like Adam and Eve in Paradise." Then she frowned, replacing her aura of beatitude with a trace of doubt. "I'll never understand how Margaret can hold marriage in such low regard. Home is the great arena for women, as our blessed partnership—wide and deep and equal—amply illustrates."

"Ah, but perhaps our marriage is an exception." Hawthorne straightened his collar and smoothed his immaculate mustaches.

"I always feel excessively tame compared to Margaret," Sophia admitted. "She is so . . . *modern*."

"In a way, she's like Waldo, everlastingly rejecting all that is, in search of . . ." Hawthorne looked thoughtful before concluding, "she knows not what."

"In search of autonomy!" Sophia burst out. Her forceful exclamation was a departure from her usual docility. "A boon routinely denied to my sex!"

"Please, my dearest Dove, spare me the Transcendental fervor! You'll recall Margaret reproves us for our devotion to each other. She calls it 'mutual seclusion.'" He blew her a kiss.

"Just so," she said. Sophia adjusted pearls in her auburn hair. Her mood clouded as she recalled a lapse in their vaunted mutuality. "I remember once when I was imprisoned inside all day with a toothache. You were walking back from the Emersons when you came upon Margaret, lying on a bed of clover in the woods reading a book. For hours, you didn't come home—not until Waldo appeared searching for Margaret, annoyed to have lost her company."

"Ah, yes, Margaret and I talked and talked—of our childhoods, of the virtues of being lost and found, of climbing mountains." Hawthorne straightened his cuffs, no trace of remorse for his long absence evident. "I prefer to view a distant mountain with its hint of an unattainable peak from afar. Margaret claims the panoramic vista from a summit crowns the effort of the ascent. I still remember her exact words—my God, that woman can speak like a seraphim! When she ascends a mountain, panting with effort, she describes it as, 'Some part of me seems to escape through the loose grating of my ribs.'" He touched his chest.

"I have no doubt of her eloquence," Sophia said, her mouth a straight line.

"Just as you should have no doubt of my undying devotion to you."

"My peerless Love!" she flung her arms around him. "I know that others wish to hear your thoughts. I shouldn't be selfish. Waldo can hardly get enough of your company, even though you try to withhold it."

"The man entraps me whenever we walk with him and Lidian. I pity her; he so readily abandons her. She's not the jolliest companion, but she is a woman of common sense and intellect." He smiled at his buxom wife and licked his lips. "She's a bit bony for my taste."

"I think the reason Waldo has such an attachment to you," Sophia said, "is that everyone else parrots his sayings. It's refreshing for him to encounter a different viewpoint. You are only and all yourself, nobody else."

"Little does His Serene Highness suspect how bacchanalian I am when not fending off his attention," Hawthorne said with a seductive smile. "If he could've seen you last night dancing and swaying to the music box and enticing me to join you, I doubt he'd be solicitous of my so-called Wisdom. Your lively performance would earn you the head of John the Baptist." He drew his bride to his lap.

"It was the dance of the seven veils, but I'd gladly throw them aside for my lord." Sophia unbuttoned her bodice with one hand and flounced up her petticoat with the other.

CHAPTER EIGHT

An Outsider Infiltrates the American Athens

WINTER 1842, CONCORD, MASSACHUSETTS

By the Hawthornes' first winter in Concord, the bloom was not exactly off the rose but frost was decidedly on it. It was so cold, a mist of frost like a white snood covered Sophia's hair—even inside the drafty house.

"Why are you singing so loudly?" Hawthorne tugged a woolen scarf to his mouth.

"To distract me from the cold. I am becoming a pillar of ice. My thoughts begin to hang in icicles."

A further source of chill was Hawthorne's increasing isolation. When he and Sophia took tea at the Emersons', he was stonily silent, answering questions in monosyllables and rising to stare out the window at the snow. He insisted on taking his leave before Sophia could finish a morsel of brown bread. As she rose she apologized to her hosts. "I'm sorry. My lord has an anathema of visiting."

Emerson helped her don a cape. "No explanation necessary. Nathaniel always rides his horse of the night."

They tramped home, dodging snowdrifts and icy patches on the path. "What," she asked, upsets you so?"

"That rogue Ellery Channing barged into my study today with his usual goblin-gleam. He asked for my help. Apparently, a rumor is circulating that I'm to become editor of the *Miscellany*. That vile young man wishes me to publish his fatuous poetic reflections. And pay him five dollars a page for his dismal verses! An advance would prove my good faith, he had the gall to say!"

"Is it true? Has anyone offered you a post?" Her heart pounded, tom-tom-tom. A salaried position would do much to alleviate their pinched household.

He spat. "If so, they've neglected to inform me. I can hardly afford a cigar. No one pays *me* five dollars a page for my stories." His boots squeaked on the glassy ice. "Waldo thinks Ellery a genius, but all the talent I see is his extraordinary ability to be idle. No vulgar usefulness for him. Do you know what he said when I disabused him of the notion that I could pay him?"

Sophia breathed a cloud of frosty breath and shook her head.

"'No matter,' he said, as indifferent to silver as a grasshopper." Hawthorne imitated the younger man, speaking with an air of self-congratulation. "'I shall never desert the muse. Rich or poor, I will stick to her,' he declaimed. What a ridiculous gump! That prince of inanity should have been whipped often and soundly in his boyhood!"

Sophia grabbed her husband's arm to steady herself, and Hawthorne slowed his pace on the slippery path. "Now, now, dearest," she said. "I knew Ellery as a boy. He was never whipped and likewise never loved," she said. "His father was my doctor. As a boy, Ellery always seemed full of fun, leaping like a cricket, cracking walnuts and throwing snowballs in chapel. When he was but five, the poor little boy's mother died and Ellery was shipped off to distant relatives." She shook her head at the memory, then said in amazement, "Now he is Waldo's protégé. He must have some merit."

"If only he would give up poem-mongering!" Hawthorne was firm. "Anything sets him off versifying. I do believe he'd write an elegy for a worm if he stepped on one." He gripped his waistcoat and struck a pose, mimicking Ellery's lordly mien when impelled to compose.

"Oh wanton worm, thou art both dirty and dead.
The earth—now thy grave—was once thy silken bed.
Et cetera."

He couldn't stifle a sly smile as Sophia burst out laughing.

"Ellery means well," she said. "When I pulled up turnips from the garden once, Ellery offered to clean the grit off them and dry the leaves. He plunged the turnip greens in a bucket of water, grabbed a pillowcase, stuffed the greens inside, and twirled it around, his arm whirling like a windmill. Water drops went flying. But when he dumped the greens out, they were covered with feathers!"

"Was he inspired to invent an ode to a turnip?" Hawthorne asked.

She shook her head. "He seemed uncharacteristically chagrined. All he could do was shrug and say that I could cook *navet à plumes*." She chuckled, then turned serious. "I don't know what Ellen Fuller sees in him besides a pretty face, yet it's clear she loves him to distraction."

"He only loves two things: Nature and Poetry." Hawthorne reconsidered. "No, make that three things: Nature, Poetry, and his imperial Self."

"I remember how Margaret rued her sister's hasty marriage to Ellery. She couldn't hide her disapproval."

"Ellen was smitten by Ellery's superficial charm. So is Waldo." Hawthorne stamped his boots to dislodge clumps of snow. "Waldo has the unfortunate habit of accumulating so-called geniuses to make Concord a private utopia. This poor country village is infested by his collection of oddly behaved halfwits, most of whom consider themselves solons of the universe. They are simply bores of a very intense water."

"Speaking of water, I'm sure our pump is frozen," Sophia said. "Let's bring some chunks of ice to melt on the fire. At least we can wash our teeth and fill a hot-water bottle."

Hawthorne began to slide on the slick ice. "Come, my love! We can skate without skates!" He hooked arms with her, and they glided down the icy lane, whooping. Her cape filled and billowed like a sail. Scooting down the path, nearly out of control whizzing downhill, they barely avoided a heap of teetering stones. "Wheee!" Sophia shouted.

"Whoa," Hawthorne pulled her close. "Let's get inside, not that it's much warmer there."

• • •

The next day Sophia appeared at the Emersons' white farmhouse. She basked by the woodstove with Lidian, grateful for its warmth. They both set sewing baskets on their laps. "I apologize for our abrupt departure last night. Nat had a bad case of the glums." She unrolled a length of yarn and attacked an embryonic wool muffler with clacking knitting needles. "It seems an unwanted invasion by Ellery left my lord with a lingering foul taste."

Lidian dropped the nightcap she was mending to her knees, so eager was she to discuss the character of this recruit to Emerson's stable of young poets. "Mr. Emerson attracts hobgoblins of flesh and blood to his orbit. Odd ducks like Ellery Channing are drawn to his alpine atmosphere of lofty thought."

"That's just what Nat thinks. Why does Waldo continually pick up clever young men and dub them brilliant?"

Lidian grew heated, despite the howling wind battering her windows. "Who knows? Ellery Channing is an appalling poet," she sniffed. "He has his head in the clouds and feet in the mud. His only trade is loafing." She warmed to her metaphors as if they had been long mulled over in private, awaiting a receptive ear. "He's like a hot-air balloon with no rudder, floating and drifting."

"He must have some redeeming grace. He's Margaret Fuller's

brother-in-law. Her sister Ellen loves him, or she wouldn't have married him."

"Poor Ellen," Lidian sighed. The subject of Ellery's wife's trials was much on her mind. "Ellery is unalterably incapable of providing for his family. A lazier fellow never existed."

"He comes from good stock," Sophia noted, as if genealogy compensated for character flaws. "His great-grandfather signed the Declaration of Independence, his father is Dean of Harvard's Medical School, his uncle is a revered Unitarian minister."

"To be fair," Lidian allowed, "Ellery's lot has not been easy. His mother died when he was little. Since his father couldn't rear the children, the poor boy was sent first to a distant aunt, then banished to boarding school before his ignominious departure from Harvard College. Now his father bestows a stipend rather than love. Dear Ellen has to support the family by keeping school, while Ellery does nothing but ramble the woods with our Henry and compose his vapid poems."

Sophia's ball of yarn rolled off her lap and she retrieved it before the cat could pounce. "Ellen could've had her pick of husbands. With those blond ringlets and dark-blue eyes, she looks like an angel." She picked out a ragged row of knitting and resumed. "Of course, Ellery is an excessively attractive young fellow too. With his shoulder-length hair, he looks like a pioneer. I'd like to paint him."

"Good luck on getting him to sit still long enough for a portrait," Lidian said. "He's like a perpetual motion machine. Excluding motion allied to industry, of course."

"I'm most curious to know what you think of his poems," Sophia said. "Based on the ones I've read and, of course, Mr. Poe's infamous dissection of them in that review, he seems a poet of exceeding ineptitude. Yet in person he's charming, a true *bon-vivant*. Why is his verse so tedious?"

"He refuses to let anyone touch his poems," Lidian explained, her needle darting in and out at increasing velocity. "Every word is sacred, a gusher from his divine spirit. He's ingested the Transcendental adage 'Trust thyself' from root to stem. The more you try to pin him down, the more responsibility you give, the farther and faster he flees. He does not even care if his poems are published or paid for." She paused, piercing the flannel with ferocity. "More's the pity for poor Ellen."

"I remember when we first saw him here in Concord," Sophia recalled. "The first utterance out of his mouth when he met Mr. Hawthorne was, 'I feel a poem coming on!' Nat said, 'Pray, do not let us prevent your withdrawal to commit it to paper. Hie thee to a garret post-haste, young man, ere the fickle muse abscond.'"

Lidian guffawed. "As if anything could stop him!"

Sophia went on, "He burbled some lines like:

'Beauty is unleashed upon the hills,
Fields and forests, frothy rills.'"

The women giggled as Sophia continued in her best Ellery imitation,

"'Joy abounds in blossoms springing,
To the syrupy melody of small birds singing,
New life and new thoughts pop up zinging'!"

"Zinging?" Lidian held her stomach, which ached from laughing. "No!"

Sophia wiped her eyes, then more seriously asked, "What about his character?"

"Ellery is a God-despising pagan," Lidian proclaimed, her eyes fiery. She produced a much-thumbed Bible from her apron pocket and gripped it like a lifeline. "His god is Dionysus. Do you know—when Henry plays an Irish jig on his flute—Ellery and Ellen dance on the grass, even on the Sabbath!" She shuddered.

"That sounds rather delightful," Sophia had to admit, recalling her dance as Salome for an appreciative Hawthorne.

"I enjoy Henry's flute tunes as much as anyone, but I cannot countenance dancing on the Sabbath." Lidian glanced upwards for heavenly approbation and continued, "My little son must learn a hymn every Sunday." Between pursed lips, she added what to her was the coup de grâce: "Ellery Channing is a satyr."

Sophia looked puzzled. "You do not mean, in regard to marital relations . . . ?"

"Do I not?" Her voice rose in outrage. "Ellen Fuller, just twenty-one years old, was so infatuated that she agreed to marry when she barely knew him. A whirlwind romance, which she felt was divinely inspired. Ellen would save the wastrel! She'd give him love and encouragement! Those lovesick children got engaged after just two weeks' acquaintance! And Ellery—in a fit of Emersonian intuition—persuaded himself she's the one true mate for his soul, even though loyalty was heretofore absent from his character. The man is like a pitcher with no handle."

"A youthful marriage," Sophia said, "does not produce a satyr."

"Pray let me continue! Have you heard how Cary Sturgis and Ellery Channing were once in love?"

Sophia shook her head—all the encouragement Lidian needed to accelerate. "Caroline Sturgis, Margaret's best friend and Mr. Emerson's frequent walking companion, is admittedly a beautiful, wealthy, talented young woman. A redhead, and you know how those gingers are . . . Cary is every bit as irreverent as Ellery. I do believe she also detests Our Savior Jesus Christ."

Sophia gasped and missed another stitch. She gave up all pretense of knitting and leaned forward.

"A few years ago, Margaret introduced Cary to Mr. Emerson. And now that vixen visits us here at will, staying even when I am gone!" Lidian exhaled in disgust. "She and Mr. Emerson exchange long, verbose—I would even say intimate—letters, as Cary does with Ellery. My noble husband shares her letters with me, as if that excuses their dalliance!"

"I do not believe there's a dalliance, dear Lidian." Sophia reached out a hand in comfort.

"Listen!" Lidian raised her head. "After Ellen and Ellery wed, he came to Concord alone to find a house for them—at Mr. Emerson's invitation. But even though his bride was presently expected, Ellery chose to abscond and visit Cary on her private island—for who knows how many days? And who knows what mischief they were up to? He told us it was the last time to see her before becoming a boring married man! As if that excused his desertion! When Ellen arrived, full of anticipation to be reunited with her new husband, no bridegroom!"

Lidian wiped her hands on her apron, as if to remove a stain. "Poor Ellen asked me plaintively, 'Where is he? Do you think Cary has seen him? We should write her. He sets such store by her letters.' The poor girl was despondent. She set out a daguerreotype of him and mooned over it. Mr. Emerson and I were frantic with worry."

Sophia shook her head. "What happened next?"

"After a few days, Ellery waltzed in, unrepentant as a bluebird, kissed his bride, and explained that he has a 'wandering' temperament. 'Wandering'—what an understatement! A euphemism for selfishness. I don't understand what dear Henry sees in him—or why Henry and that rascal are inseparable."

"For that matter," Sophia said, "what does Waldo see in Cary? He's such a deep thinker, and she's so young and frivolous."

Lidian's voice was broken by tears. "All the things I am not." She threw the torn nightcap back in her sewing basket.

"I do like Cary," Sophia said. "She may be a shameless flirt, but one can't hold youth and beauty against her. As a wedding present, she gave us that bust of Apollo in our parlor."

“The one with a red ribbon around its neck?”

“Yes,” Sophia said. “The ribbon hides a crack. Nat and I bumped it while dancing, and the head broke off. I glued it back together and hide the seam with a ribbon.”

“If only,” Lidian whispered, “we could mend all cracks so prettily . . .”

CHAPTER NINE

A Visitor Appears as Margaret Works, Cary Sulks

OCTOBER 1844, FISHKILL LANDING, NEW YORK

Cary pounded out a rafter-shaking tune on the piano at the bungalow she shared with Margaret. Her fingers thumped the keys angrily, belying the jollity of the tune. She ignored Margaret's disapproving look and bellowed the popular lyrics:

"When young, my heart was bent, sir
Upon a nice young beau
There's time enough for lovers
So don't impatient grow
Just take your time, Miss Lucy—"

Margaret threw down her pen. She flapped a page in the air to dry the ink.

Cary finished singing, "Miss Lucy, Lucy, oh!" and played a discordant clash of notes. She rose from the piano bench to pace in a circle around the parlor. "Don't look so disagreeable, Margaret! One can only rusticate for so long without succumbing to ennui."

"It won't be *so* much longer," Margaret sighed. "I only have a few weeks left to revise my *Dial* essay into a book before I go to New York City." She reddened with pleasure, rolling up her sleeves as if ready to fling herself into the maelstrom of newspaper reporting.

"That's all very well for you," Cary said, "but what am I to do then . . . nursemaid my mother, spend my days in idle gossip at tea parties?" She stomped her foot.

Margaret looked at her young friend swishing her petticoats around as if swatting flies. "Do what you were born to do!" she said with vehemence. "Write poetry, pursue your art! Have I taught you nothing?"

"I only write letters now," Cary retorted, as if that pursuit absolved her of further responsibility. "We can't all have a contract for a book on The Woman Question. Or a promised position as *Tribune* columnist." She pulled from a desk drawer a ribbon-bound sheaf of letters festooned in spidery black ink. She shot a smug look at Margaret. "Of course, Waldo asks me to include drawings in my letters."

"I've been meaning to speak about your growing intimacy with Waldo." Margaret eyed the fat bundle of envelopes. "I was once his preferred correspondent. Now he has frozen me out. I'd hate to see you suffer the same fate. Let's walk by the river." She drew Cary to the door.

They donned bonnets, shawls, and leather gloves and picked their way on the rocky, moss-strewn path by the Hudson. Ragged vines on denuded branches whipped over their heads. The sky was lowering, leaden with dark clouds. "No more bright autumn days; soon winter arrives." A quickening wind snatched Margaret's words and stirred the river into white foam. Her head down to navigate a rough patch, she murmured, "I was once a leaf, grew a stem, and became a flower. Now I'm a dry husk, thrown aside, a bird without wings."

"I don't mean to replace you in Waldo's affections." Cary grabbed Margaret's arm. "I was once your disciple. Now Ralph Waldo Emerson is my teacher." She smiled and raised her head to proclaim, "I am his muse."

"I gave him pearls of great value. He gives me chuckstones of granite," Margaret muttered. "His love does not survive the wear and tear of years. He's captivated by you, but you'll be succeeded by a new sport replacing the old. You're in the summer of Waldo's affections. But an autumn die-off and wintry ice are inevitable." She stumbled, steadying herself with Cary's arm.

"Come now, Margaret. . . . Just because I'm no longer bewitched by you! Jealousy does not become you."

"Not jealousy; it's concern. Waldo's affection soars like an eagle now, but it skims like a swallow. There's no depth to his love—except for his own thoughts," she insisted.

A train whistle screeched its lonely howl nearby, and the chug-chug-chug of wheels grinding on tracks grew faster and faster. A poof of smoke billowed overhead.

A tall man in his late twenties appeared trotting on the path, holding his slouch cap on his head and running to catch up with them. "Ladies! My queen and my princess!" He swept off his hat in a flourish and bowed. "Greetings from Concord!"

"Speaking of shallow . . ." Margaret said under her breath.

"Ellery! What are you doing here?" Cary gripped his hand with joy. He kissed her fingers.

"Don't you have a newborn babe at home?" Margaret asked. "How can you leave my little sister at such a time?"

"How could I not?" Ellery replied. "That little goblin does nothing but squall. The strain has surely wrecked my ears. We named the bobbet after you, you know—Margaret Fuller Channing, although I shall call her Greta. Your namesake has your talent for robust expression, dear sister-in-law." He addressed Margaret but only had eyes for Cary, who linked arms with him and turned him back on the path to their cottage.

Once seated in the parlor, Cary beamed at him. "I'm starved for sparkling conversation. Margaret does nothing but scribble away at her book! All I hear is scratching of pen on paper. Tell me, Ellery, what brings you to us in Fishkill?"

Ellery stretched out his legs, as at ease as a lizard on a leaf. He planted his boots on a pine stool, the picture of contented indolence. "Margaret, you're not the only one to secure a position on Horace Greeley's *Tribune*. I too am a *Tribune* journalist."

"What? Gainful employ?" Margaret reacted with shock. "A first for you."

Ellery ignored her sarcasm. "I've already started—months in advance of you, Margaret. I am wearing the harness of a regular, salaried job, just as you've always wanted." He continued, "Of course, writing poetry about rocks and rills is more to my taste than penning prose on the vices of speakeasies. So tedious: assignments, deadlines, interviews with idiots. I've come to this bucolic Eden to rest and recover my energy."

"No!" Margaret protested. "You'll be fired! Remember your last disastrous attempt at a profession: a so-called farmer in Illinois! You did nothing but sleep!" She racked her brain to think how he might retain his job. "I know! Come with me and Cary. I aim to visit the Mount Pleasant Female Prison in Sing Sing. I want to interview the inmates for insights for my book on women."

"I hardly think my *Tribune* readers will want to read about lowlife criminals, but I'll gladly accompany you as chaperon." He picked up a book titled *Guidebook for Tourists and Travelers* and leafed through its contents. He stabbed his finger on a page. "I see prisons are among the attractions recommended for visitors. Poorhouses, insane asylums, hospitals, too. Apparently, one can 'witness every form of insanity and depravity' at the New York Lunatic Asylum," he read. "Now that does sound entertaining."

"A welcome change from the insanity of sitting here all day watching Margaret work." Cary giggled.

"I go not to gawk at imprisoned women," Margaret assured him. "I want to talk to them as friends, to make people aware of their plight, to expose injustice."

"Their plight!" Ellery scoffed. "Surely you jest. Those jailbirds are criminals, hardened lawbreakers guilty of prostitution, public drunkenness, shoplifting."

"And worse," Cary added. "What about that Henrietta what's-her-name, who slipped arsenic in her husband's ale?"

"She was beaten by that drunken beast," Margaret was quick to note. "He threatened to turn her out and take her children away—as was his right by law. If a law is wrong, one must not obey it." She tucked a stray lock of hair behind her ear.

"It's all for her book," Cary explained to Ellery, who yawned with indifference. "She wants to investigate the unfortunate class of women from the lowest haunts of vice."

"These women have been trampled in the mud to gratify the brute appetites of men," Margaret said. "What do they have in common with women of the upper class who submit to man's lust in exchange for a life of ease? Those women are locked in a bare cell. Married women are trapped in a gilded cage."

Ellery shook his head. "If you say such things, your book will certainly stir a breeze. Or perhaps a gale."

"I seek the truth," Margaret said, "not to *titillate* but *illuminate* and *mitigate*."

"And here I thought to *rusticate* was the apogee of boredom." Cary dragged Ellery to the piano. They sat side by side on the bench as she hammered the keys and sang a rousing chorus of "Take your time, Miss Lucy." Ellery sang harmony, flipping his long hair out of his eyes and pounding bass notes. He produced a harmonica from his trousers and improvised a cascade of melody concluding in a crashing crescendo.

"I see loud music doesn't upset your sensitive ears," Margaret said to him, "only a babe's cry."

CHAPTER TEN

An Unlikely Excursion on the Hudson

OCTOBER 1844, FISHKILL LANDING
AND MOUNT PLEASANT, NEW YORK

The next day, Margaret twisted her thick hair into a tight bun buttressed by tortoise-shell combs. She shrugged on a plain black shirtwaist dress over her shift and turned her back to Cary for buttoning. "Promise me," she said, "you won't flirt with Ellery. I don't care that you knew him first. He's married to my sister. He's a father—no matter how neglectful."

Cary secured Margaret's row of buttons, then lifted a colorful, sprigged muslin dress over her head. She settled its ruffles on her shoulders and smoothed the hem. She arranged her russet ringlets with care and dimpled at her image in a silver hand mirror. "You insult me to suggest such a thing. No matter how misguided I consider Ellery and Ellen's hasty marriage, it's done!" She added under her breath, "Even if it seems he has adopted a toddler rather than found an equal partner!"

• • •

A steamboat arrived at the dock with flags flying. Its paddlewheel churned murky water into foam, and a loud whistle split the air. Margaret covered her ears with her hands and walked up to the top deck, followed by Cary and Ellery racing up the stairs laughing.

"Roll on, majestic Hudson!" Ellery declaimed, as Cary spun in a circle, arms outstretched. When more decorous passengers bumped into her and glowered, she joined Margaret and Ellery at the railing, watching the countryside stream by on the river banks. The calliope piped jolly, high-pitched notes. A breeze fanned their faces, and field workers on shore paused their hoeing to wipe their brows and wave.

Cary gasped when her first glimpse of the prison came into view. It was high on a bluff, a limestone structure fronted by Doric columns and a blank pediment. "It looks like a temple!"

"A temple of tragedy for jail hens," Ellery said. "It's the first prison only for female convicts," he read from the guidebook.

"The classical façade lends dignity," Margaret jotted in a notebook. "The idea is not a place of punishment but rehabilitation, a reformatory. I'll call it 'transformatory,'" she penciled.

"What sublime bosh!" Ellery nudged Cary.

They entered the warden's office, ornate with its carved wooden mantel over the fireplace and a heavy desk that bespoke serious business. Eliza Farnham was a reformer who had spearheaded construction of the facility to protect women both from male guards and other prisoners. "I'm pleased you could come, Miss Fuller," Farnham said, shaking hands with her guests. "I've admired your writing in *The Dial*, especially your essay on the need for women's rights. We'll give you a tour of our building."

The trio saw the library, stocked with secular books like Charles Dickens's novels as well as religious tracts. "We emphasize education here," Farnham explained. "Most prison libraries contain only Bibles. Our residents write daily in journals, reflecting on their lives. They sing in our choir and stage theatrical productions. We have the only nursery in a jail."

"I applaud your use of the arts to elevate their minds," Ellery interrupted. "But if you ascribe to humane treatment, how can you lock them up in such tiny cells?" He pointed to a row of bathtub-sized cubicles, with bars across the front, barely seven feet long and a yard wide. Inside was no window, only a chair, shelf, and cot that unfolded from a wall.

"The women spend only their sleeping hours inside," Farnham said. "Prisons before ours required solitude and silence. We allow social engagement. Women work together in the gardens; they make buttons and trim hats."

"Trimming their lust for vice makes more sense," Ellery whispered to Cary.

A child-sized dwarf with a large head and bright eyes ran up to the matron and pulled her long skirt. She aimed an imploring look at Farnham, who shook her head and detached herself. "No one has come for you today," she said, not unkindly.

In response to Margaret's questioning look, Farnham explained, "Some showman brought her from Holland and abandoned her. She was convicted of larceny for stealing an apple from a fruit vendor. Whenever we have guests, the poor woman rushes to see if someone has come to collect her."

"I would like to talk to some of the women, please," Margaret said, raising her hand to stop the tour. She summoned a woman nearby who was sweeping and guided her to a chair by the long dinner table. They sat, knees touching, and chatted while the others resumed the tour.

"I'm Margaret Fuller. I'm most interested in knowing who you are, what brought you here, what your hopes and dreams are, how you and your sisters feel."

"My name is Polly," the woman answered, straightening the straps of her apron. She met Margaret's eyes and said, "I stole a bolt of wool to make coats for my children before last winter. That's why I'm here." She spoke softly: "I dream of returning to my children—their father is dead, gored by an unruly ox. I wish to become a dressmaker."

After twenty minutes' conversation, Margaret released Polly to her labors and snagged another woman to sit with her, a full-figured woman named Lettie whose hair was dark at the roots and yellow at the ends. "I am what men call a fallen woman," she said with no trace of shame. "As to why I sold my body, I'll tell you. For money. Girls born like me have few choices: work in the mills, as domestics in a house or tavern, or marry and be a man's slave. Miz Farnham has us keeping a journal, writing about our lives. I ain't much for writing, but I call the chapter about my so-called Life of Crime 'Thrills and Frills.'"

Margaret scribbled notes. "What about school? You could learn enough to be a governess or keep school."

Lettie barked out a bitter laugh. "Hah! Not the likes of me! I want an easy life, pretty clothes, good food, a decent place to live. Is that asking too much? The quickest way is the way of the streets. So I became a prostitute, not in a brothel but on my own. I was whatcha call an 'independent purveyor.'"

Margaret wrote faster, afraid to miss a word. "What do you wish for?"

"I want to sing at the top of my voice and be heard—even hailed. I want a full embrace from a sufficient love, someone who respects me. I want to meet even gentlefolks' eyes—not as a fallen woman but someone who picked herself up and stands tall in my own right." She gestured to her hair, then stood and seized a mop like a jousting lance. "And I want to stop dyeing my hair and let people see its chestnut-colored glory!" Margaret saluted her as Lettie strode off.

In the carriage back to Fishkill, Margaret, Cary, and Ellery debated what they'd seen. After she described Lettie, Margaret sighed. "She can't do it alone. We must change the social institutions to give her a chance. We can't rely on male legislators to make changes. Collective action! Women must stand up and demand our rights!"

"Just like your motto," Cary mused. "Let them think; let them act!"

"You dream, dear, deluded Margaret," Ellery chided. "Self-culture, self-reliance—the only cure! These women's afflictions are the first step towards their growth into noble individuals."

"Pish-posh," Cary said. "How can affliction effect a cure?"

He put his hand on her knee. "Recall our master Waldo's prescription," he answered. "Solitary reflection and immersion in nature will lead us to recognize our errors, to pungently feel remorse—sharper than a scorpion's sting—and to realize our inner divinity." He raised his voice like an orator winding up. "Suffering is redemptive. Heed intuition, then seek *internal* reform!" He looked at Cary for approval.

"Suffering leads to divinity?" Cary tested the words in her mouth as the carriage juddered over ruts in the road. Her body bounced first against Margaret's ribs, then collided with Ellery's legs.

"What do you know of suffering?" Margaret challenged. "Both you and Ellery are coddled by your rich fathers' handouts. Your keels will never grate on a rocky bottom. You always glide over the shoals."

The carriage jerked and jolted, lumbering into a crater in the road, then shuddered to a halt. Leaning like a toppled deck of cards, the three passengers tumbled out of the halted coach. The door, which hung open, tilted to the ground. A rear carriage wheel spun off into a meadow, flattening tall stalks of cardinal flowers and alarming bees that buzzed in their red hearts.

"Well, this is a fine kettle of cod!" Margaret said, brushing dust off her skirt.

"Did you just say my keel never grates on the rocks?" Cary surveyed the immobilized carriage, its axle embedded in mud.

"Allow me, ladies!" Ellery bounded off in pursuit of the errant wheel, trampling high grass and purple coneflowers. Blue chicory blossoms dotted the sere field as he loped.

"He's in his element," Cary said, shading her eyes with a hand after removing her bonnet, askew on her head. "It's remarkable how happy Ellery is under an open sky rather than confined under a roof." She felt a flutter in her gut, similar to the tumult she used to feel years before when she and Ellery were teens playing at courtship.

The driver tugged at the stuck axle and said, "Would that a blacksmith might happen along to help. Settle yourselves, ladies. This may take a while."

Margaret sat on a boulder shaded by a tree and began to write in her notebook.

"Working—already?" Cary asked. "What are you writing?"

"Recording my impressions while they're fresh. We must finish our American Revolution! Founded on the principle that 'all men are created equal,' entitled to 'life, liberty, and the pursuit of happiness.' There can be no justice, no honor, no true republic until equal rights are extended to women and our enslaved brothers and sisters!" She wrote with such force, she broke the lead tip of her pencil with a *craaack*. She took out a penknife and sharpened it.

"Ooh la, la, Margaret," Cary said. "You're putting your hand in a hornet's nest if you say things like that." She fanned her face with the guidebook.

"I care not whether sympathy or opposition greets my words. My essay on women in *The Dial* was not *bad* enough. It was too pious, too timid. In this book I'll rouse the laggards and scold the lukewarm. Married women must wake up and admit their life is a raggedy tragedy until all barriers to our dreams vanish."

The driver overheard her passionate words and let out a loud huff, which he disguised as a struggle with the axle.

"Yes!" Margaret persevered. "I mean equal access to education and universities, to all professions, to ownership of property, decision-making in marriage . . ." Her words trailed off as she scrawled.

"Cary!" Ellery called from the field. "I've found the runaway wheel! Come see!"

Cary followed his mashed track through the grass, stopping short as he held up his hand. "Look!' he said. "A snake is coiled around the wheel. I have an idea how to lure it away." He scooped up handfuls of honeysuckle flowers growing in profusion on the remains of a split-rail fence and placed them in a small, bowl-shaped pool. "Snakes love sweet water. They also love music." He took out his harmonica and began to play a slow, sensual tune. The snake lifted its head in his direction, darted its tongue in and out, and slithered off the wheel towards the pool and Ellery's music.

"You're a snake charmer!" Cary said, her eyes wide with astonishment.

The snake oozed into the pool and plopped on a rock with an air of content, while Ellery tugged the heavy wheel upright and rolled it back to the carriage. "*Voilà*, my good man," he said, presenting it to the driver. "The prodigal wheel has returned to its brothers!" He used a sturdy branch to liberate the axle and lever it into a horizontal position. The carriage stood, truncated like a three-legged bull.

A milk cart approached from the north and halted on the track, blocked by the listing carriage. "Come, my good man!" Ellery called to the solidly built dairyman. "Help us attach the wheel, then you can continue your journey."

When they had wrestled the wheel back on its axle, Ellery conferred with the milk cart driver. He leapt to sit beside the dairyman and waved farewell to Margaret and Cary. "Toodle-ooh, lovely ladies! I leave you to travel up river, while I must hie myself with this fine gentleman back to Gotham! My work awaits!"

After he left, Cary asked with a sullen air, "What—or who—else awaits him in the city?"

"Whatever it is," Margaret said, distracted, "that cheeky jackanape will never succeed." She licked the tip of her pencil.

All the way back to Fishkill, Margaret scribbled in a notebook perched on her knees. Cary studied the passing landscape. She fidgeted and tried to arrange her face along lines of indifference. She sniffed a bunch of honeysuckle she had tucked in her bonnet, sucked the nectar out of a flower's pistil, then threw the wilted blooms out the window.

CHAPTER ELEVEN

Margaret Courts Controversy

FEBRUARY 1845, NEW YORK CITY

The first edition of *Woman in the Nineteenth Century* by S. Margaret Fuller sold out all 1,500 copies in one week, was reprinted, and sold some more. Margaret instantly became a celebrity, lauded as the most outspoken—and learned—woman in America.

Even her rival literary critic, Mr. Edgar Allan Poe, noted the book's "independence" and "unmitigated radicalism." "It's a book few women in the country could have written," he wrote, "and no one in the country would have dared publish, with the exception of Miss Fuller." The book, he added, was both "warmly abused and chivalrously defended." Discussed in every parlor, its call for women's equality occasioned widespread ridicule, scorn, and derision. The critic Rufus Griswold found the author's message offensive, "an eloquent expression of her discontent at having been created female."

Only a few brave hurrahs seconded Margaret's observations. The writer Lydia Maria Child praised Margaret's courage and "contralto voice . . . deep, rich, and strong."

Ellery was no longer at the *Tribune* to witness Margaret's new notoriety, having been dismissed after a short tenure, due to his disdain for actual labor. *Tribune* readers evinced a pronounced aversion to his pallid poems, much preferring to read about crime and civic corruption.

After her book's launch, Margaret's friends worried for her reputation. Sophia Hawthorne and Lidian Emerson—aware of the cloud of scandal descending on their friend daily in the conservative press—determined to caution her.

Lidian pulled a gauzy veil over her face, only raising it to peek at a street sign in Gotham city. "Commerce Street. Isn't that where Margaret said to meet her? I see no establishment here that looks remotely decent." She sniffed and avoided a steaming pile of horse manure on the street. Two squealing piglets chased by scruffy urchins dodged around her long skirt.

Sophia tugged her cloak tightly closed. "Miss Jessie's Tearoom, she said. It's at the back of that rowhouse."

"At least she didn't choose a coffee house, where rowdy men congregate. But what if Undesirables are present? Floozies or worse? Lord protect us! I wish Mr. Emerson were here to chaperon."

"Courage!" Sophia took her arm and guided Lidian inside a wood-framed house to a table where Margaret and Cary awaited. After cordial but decidedly tepid greetings, Cary lifted the teapot off an alcohol lamp and poured, offering thin slices of buttered toast to the Concord duo.

Margaret noted their disapproving looks. "I don't suppose you came to congratulate me on my book's success?"

Sophia removed her bonnet but not her gloves. She set down her teacup with an unladylike thump. "Margaret, dear, I confess my horror at what you have written is unfading. Most indelicate," she whispered, "to suggest that women have the same desires as men in the bedroom!"

Cary came to Margaret's defense. "Sophia—can you doubt it? You and Nat are always entwined! You can hardly keep your hands off each other!"

Sophia blushed to the roots of her hair and stared steadily at her plate.

Lidian produced her Bible, waving it about to exorcise the demon of sensuality. "Praise God, Mr. Emerson and I have no such base proclivities!" She raised her chin, setting down a crust as if it were

Eden's poisoned apple. "The Bible says a wife must obey her husband. What you propose—discussing physical congress with one's spouse—unthinkable! It would upset our whole social system, lead to unbridled, heathen licentiousness!" She gasped, catching her breath, and gripped the Bible to her chest. "Sodom and Gomorrah come to earth!" She shuddered. "Procreation—not lechery—is the sole inducement to sexual congress."

"Women should be more than a husband's broodmare! More than a decorative or battered utensil! Why should the alternative be to resign oneself to being a forlorn old maid?" Margaret blurted. "I call on lionesses to rouse from their stupor! We must have freedom of choice!"

A lady at a nearby table overheard, sneered, and stood up, ensuring that her voluminous skirts did not make contact with Margaret's, in mortal fear of contagion. "Well, I never . . . !" she muttered as she swept from the room.

Margaret leaned forward to explain. "I have no children of human birth, but I have brave disciples. My book encourages future generations to grow up unfettered! I am not preaching to Transcendentalist converts as in *The Dial*. My *Dial* essays were like words written on water, washed away with the tide of prejudice. In the book, it's like my words are incised in stone! With my newspaper stories and this book, I speak to all women! My voice is heard; I have influence!"

"Heard perhaps," a skeptical Cary interjected. "But heeded?"

"I pray not." Sophia squared her shoulders. "Your view of men is ignoble."

"Irreligious!" Lidian seconded.

"In our society women are degraded, treated like overgrown children," Margaret countered, "excessively dependent and devoted to serving their husbands' selfish needs."

Cary distributed slices of cake to each plate. "Margaret says things plainly, which no one before has dared broach. She wishes women to explore their feelings and discover their needs."

Margaret straightened and said, “I will be my own husband, wife, parent, and priest. The women I interviewed in prison taught me. They are the defying sort. So am I!”

Lidian recoiled. “You revel in the odium projected on your head!”

“New knowledge, new thoughts, new hope!” Margaret speared a layer of sugared icing from the cake and ate it.

“I find the book rather too dense with examples from mythology, like an overfurnished room,” Cary said, “yet I agree that most men are like little boys, hoarding all the toys and marbles. What we women need is not a home but a ship on the infinite ocean of possibility.”

“And courage!” Margaret licked her lips.

Sophia and Lidian blotted their mouths with linen napkins and stood. They nodded good-bye. “And perhaps,” Sophia said as her last word, “women need a good heaping of humility.”

“Not to mention piety!” Lidian thundered. She swiveled to turn away and marched off, her posture ramrod straight.

Cary watched their receding backs and frowned. “Are you going too far, Margaret? You’ll alienate all those who care for you. You must be careful in your audacity.”

Margaret sat up, regal as Athena on her gold throne. “I care not for jeers of the horrified. I am smoldering. I will burn to ashes unless I burst out in heroism!”

“Burn if you must,” Cary warned, “but take care not to be consumed.”

CHAPTER TWELVE

Diverse Paths for Would-be Journalists

APRIL 1845, NEW YORK CITY

After Boston's prim Puritanism and Concord's high-minded moralism, New York City agreed very well with Margaret. She adored her work at the *Tribune*, no matter how Waldo dismissed it as "running on a treadmill of newspaper foolishness." Half a hundred thousand readers hung on her every written utterance. Her articles adorned the front page of the *Tribune*, next to a column by a firebrand named Karl Marx. Her emblem concluding every article was a star shaped like an asterisk. With its pulsing ribs radiating out to electrify the reader, it looked like a cross between a daisy and a spiderweb. Readers knew her asterisked articles would provide spicy food for thought.

Before, I tootled a tinny tune, nearly inaudible, on a penny whistle. Now I blast my thoughts with a loud trumpet, she thought with pleasure.

No matter how much crime and drunkenness—not to mention odorous horse droppings, cackling hens, and mud-spattered pigs—littered the city, Margaret felt liberated, sprung from the trap of Bostonian propriety. She exulted in cosmopolitan life, telling herself, *New Yorkers are vehement, adventurous, rowdy*—all qualities she chose to emulate. Walking and riding horse-drawn cars all over the city, she was fearless in investigating every corner. Even if she stepped in the occasional lump of manure.

"Why do you even bother to write, when you talk so well? Conversation is your natural element. You are greatest when you drop the pen," Emerson told her. She ignored him and kept writing, reviewing books, theater, music and—more and more—defending the underclass.

"Having such a various population," she wrote Cary, "impedes the too-rapid spread of mental epidemics. In New-York, there's no Puritan contagion. I've discovered my true self."

"My goodness gracious," Cary exclaimed on one visit, "You're four inches taller! Are you on stilts? For the first time since I've known you, you're standing straight! What happened?"

"You know my spine has been curled since childhood," Margaret answered. "Hunching over books or a desk made me even more bent." She thrust back her shoulders. "I see a mesmerist here every week," Margaret said. "Have you heard of Dr. Théodore Léger? A brilliant practitioner—he puts me in a trance and improves my spine and my spirits." She bounced on tiptoes. "You see the new Margaret! I'm no longer a crooked stick."

With her salary, Margaret bought beautiful, fashionable clothes. In the Big City, she was no longer a high-and-mighty Transcendental Queen but an avant-garde sophisticate. No pious provincial, she interviewed prostitutes in prison and helped them find jobs when released. "Tear down the doors from their jambs!" she crowed to friends in sleepy Concord.

Invited to all the city literati's most exclusive parties, Margaret relaxed her distrust of men. One in particular, a smooth, blue-eyed German named James Nathan, whom she met at a New Year's Eve soirée, was especially attentive. "Have another oyster," he urged, with his gloved hand on her elbow. "Then wash it down with champagne." He quoted a poem by Goethe, Margaret's foremost love.

Their acquaintance flourished. Soon enough, Nathan was strumming his guitar and singing *lieder* to her. "Your German is perfect," he flattered her when she attempted to speak a language she knew only from books. They walked his Newfoundland dog Josey by the East

River, throwing a ball for the dog to chase. For months, Nathan and Margaret met at art galleries and concerts. They corresponded every day in long, flowery letters. Margaret's rhetoric became increasingly fervid.

"*Mein Liebster*," she wrote after Nathan serenaded her one evening, "you rouse in me so many thoughts and feelings. Every hour you grow upon me and the root strikes to my inmost life! Your look fills my eye and your voice my ear."

Do I finally have an admirer, she asked herself, *a man attracted by my whole person, not just dazzled by my brain?* When she strolled in parks with him, their hands often brushed together. She began to rest a gloved hand on his arm. When Nathan whispered in her ear at concerts, Margaret felt a thrill.

She dismissed as spoil-sport malice repeated warnings from her brother-in-law Ellery, who witnessed assignations between Margaret and her beau. "He's using you, Margaret. Nathan is smitten only by your fame. He wants a job at the *Tribune*. Don't fall for his honeyed talk."

Margaret was angry and even angrier when Ellery's predictions proved accurate. Just when Margaret's romantic fantasy was at a white-hot peak, Nathan absconded to Germany, no offer of *Tribune* employment having been forthcoming.

After four months without a letter, she wrote Nathan, "Hast thou ceased to cherish me? Alas! I say, and once again, Alas! Our days and nights gone too soon, too long! Where are you?"

Margaret was more than despondent when she discovered her fancied lover had sailed off with a mistress in tow! During the whole time he'd wooed her, Nathan had been living in sin with a "loose" woman, Nathan's landlord said. Margaret ripped a crushed flower the cad had given her from her bosom and handed it to a blind beggar.

So much for men! she thought. *Very well then, a virgin I'll remain.* She looked forward, raising her chin. *I must shroud my heart to escape deadly wounds.*

She'd been foolish, blind to Nathan's true character. *Was it just my position that attracted him?* she wondered. *He said he saw the dame in me. Does that mean he saw at least a vestige of physical charm?* She looked at her reflection in a shop window, then at Callery pear trees lining Bowling Green in full, flossy bloom. *Why am I so plain when springtime is so beautiful?* she asked herself. As couples on the street snuggled together and whispered in each others' ears, she squared her shoulders and sighed, "Alone again."

Her only solace was that Ellery, who had witnessed her infatuation and betrayal, was not rehired by the *Tribune*. Daily journalism, as Ellery had discovered, required an inordinate amount of disciplined labor, an activity he found unendurable. Back to Concord he went—to his feeble poetry, his wife Ellen (pregnant with another child), and their overly noisy progeny.

Fortunately Ellery was able to elude responsibilities at home. Thanks to Emerson's largesse and a generous contribution from Cary, the lucky young man could realize Margaret's dream of European travel. Ellery convinced the Sage that the only obstacle to his achieving universal adulation was a lamentable unfamiliarity with Old World culture. He would surely succumb to despair, he informed Emerson, without such exposure. The Sage raised funds for his protégé's voyage to Rome. Once arrived, Ellery began his Grand Tour with hyperbolic expectations.

Unfortunately for his hopes of enlarged acclaim, he discovered familiarity with Old World culture was no ticket to fame. The inhabitants of the Eternal City went about their affairs without notice of the distinguished visitor among them. They twirled their pasta on forks, indifferent to Ellery's presence. When he presented letters of introduction, they babbled in rapid Italian and too soon showed him the door. He had not even the chance to regale them with a poem of his composition.

After only sixteen days in Rome, Ellery abandoned his aesthetic explorations. *White marble statues—even if ancient—are,* he concluded, *highly overrated as conduits to Higher Thought.* For once, his poetic muse faltered. No poem to rival Tennyson's leaped from his pen. He could only rhyme Fountain and Mountain, then Culture with Vulture. Even his *pensione* in Rome was disappointing. Butts of cigars littered the halls; spittoons were nigh to overflowing.

Disheartened by his European exposure, Ellery took a fast boat back to Boston. He claimed—often and loudly—to fellow passengers on the Cunard steamer, "Concord's brooks and orchards are vastly superior to Roman piazzas." He neglected to mention his frustration at Romans' inexplicable ignorance of his personal excellence.

His promised literary opus on Rome, which was to be his masterpiece, would languish for years in the form of yellowing notes in a battered trunk. "Just wait!" he routinely told Emerson. "The images in my mind are evolving. When fully fleshed, I will astound the world with my insights!"

CHAPTER THIRTEEN

Two Operatic Writers: Fuller and Whitman

FEBRUARY 1846, NEW YORK CITY

In the metropolis, Margaret's social and cultural life was at an apex. At the Astor Place Opera House, quite by accident, she encountered a fellow journalist named Walter Whitman, a reporter for *The Brooklyn Eagle*. They had both gone to review Rossini's *Semiramide* and found themselves sitting side by side.

Margaret was moved by the majesty of the music. She clenched her hands and nearly swooned when the soprano sang her arias. She was oblivious to her seatmate, whose light-blue eyes brimmed with tears as he listened. Whitman's whole body responded to the music, the notes rousing whirlwinds of feeling as he twisted and bounced in his seat.

Whitman's face was glowing as he hummed a few bars, tapping his toes and conducting the air with his arms. Only later, when he found his arm entangled in Margaret's shawl, did he realize he'd been squirming in his seat. She was just as hypnotized by the drama as he and noticed nothing. *Oh, the agony—the Queen discovers she cannot marry her beloved*—Margaret thought to herself, nearly overcome with emotion.

When the last notes died, signaling intermission, Whitman and Margaret discovered they were entwined. His cane protruded under her wrap. He made awkward efforts to dislodge it, only resulting in drawing her closer, as if ensnared. "Please forgive me, madam," he began before stuttering, "Wash the gum from my eyes—if you're not Miss Margaret Fuller!"

Emerging from the spell of the music, she acknowledged her identity and they stood, at which point Whitman said, "Blimey, but I fancied you much loftier. When I read your book, *Woman in the Nineteenth Century*, I imagined you a giant!"

"Not even," Margaret demurred, "a literary giant."

He bowed. "Walter Whitman, at your service, reporter for *The Brooklyn Eagle*." He couldn't stop himself from babbling as if he'd unearthed a diamond in a dungheap. "Miss Fuller! Well, bless my bones! You're not at all starchy or stuck up! I was picturing you like a marble statue of Plato high on a plinth. I read every article of yours! I even cut them out to keep them."

"Since our persons—and possibly our fates—are now entangled," Margaret said, putting him at ease, "let us get to know one another, Mr. Whitman."

They chatted throughout intermission and, since Whitman insisted on escorting her home, continued in the Fourth Avenue horse car afterward. Margaret did what she did best, seeking his inmost thoughts, pushing him to disgorge secret hopes.

"Music wrenches ardors from me, which I didn't know I possess," he confided. "It fills me up, pouring from the tenor's mouth straight to my soul. It's almost Rabelaisian," he said, seeming embarrassed by his fiercely erotic response.

Margaret didn't flinch from the earthy allusion. She encouraged him to go deeper.

"It's like when I walk on the beach and hear the endless waves barreling in," he said. "The sound is delicious. It whispers and roars to me, telling me to write what the sea says."

Margaret had spent countless hours by the East River watching schooners and dangling her ankles in the shallows. "What does the sea tell you?"

Whitman's response was unexpected: "At flood tide and ebb tide, the sea says the word 'death,' which starts one thousand echoes warbling in my ears."

She looked startled. "Death? How can that be?" *Death by sea?* Margaret's worst fear!

"Death is different than you think," he assured her. "And luckier. The sea is not the end of life; it is full of life. The waves sing to me; they slap the shore, tumbling pebbles in a circle as they whoosh in and out. It's the sound of applause, like a thousand hands clapping for a beautiful aria."

She looked shaken rather than comforted. On the omnibus ride, the streetcar jolted up and down, jouncing over ruts. Margaret held a strap, swinging back and forth like the clanger on a bell. "I feel like one tossed on the high seas," she said. "I'm happy when joy knocks on my stateroom door and unhappy when it retreats." Her mood darkened as she remembered Nathan's abandonment. She sighed. "I'm now riding high on the crest of the waves, but when I plunge into the dark troughs, I fight alone."

Whitman looked concerned, and she patted his hand. "This is the state of all women, unless we withdraw from life. That I will never do."

They descended from the car amid a tangle of vines and overgrown fields. Did she live in this distant farmland of upper Manhattan, so far from civilization? As they proceeded down a rocky path towards the East River, Margaret took his arm. She caught his eye and challenged him: "You must find, Mr. Whitman, then fulfill the unknown want of your soul. If poetry is your true calling, you must write the song of the sea. We need brash, brave poems to smash the old, petrified forms and breathe big gasps of life and love. We need poems as vast as America's prairies, as wide and wild as our cascades."

Her voice rose to an ecstatic pitch as she charged him with creating "a truly American literature, with original ideas that animate fresh currents of thought! I want an American bard as wonderful as our rivers, as luxuriant and flowery as our fields, as strong as the rocks beneath our feet!"

"I'm just a disreputable Grub Street reporter," Whitman allowed. Then he raised his chin high and announced, "But I can be more! My hopes and ideas have been simmering, simmering all the while. You bring them to a boil!"

A whip-poor-will sounded its lonely notes and Margaret shivered. Whitman felt he had gone too far. He reverted to the subject of music, admitting he used to prefer minstrel-show tunes to European orchestral pieces. Opera, he'd assumed, was too high-brow, only for the elite. But seeing how people of every stripe bellow its tunes in the street and dance halls, he was converted. "Opera," he declared, "is not one barleycorn less powerful than 'Buffalo Gals.'"

Margaret—ever the critic—seized her moment to regale him with her flawlessly expressed opinions. "I deplore the chattering of backbenchers at the opera house, which distracts my concentration," she said. "I also hate the recitatives' flimsy melodies. And most opera singers' stilted performances, their near-burlesque gesticulating and lack of dramatic talent? Odious! When they try to express passion, their acting hardens to wood, without fire. Their pretense at grief or joy is tepid—mere stage-strut and vulgar bombast."

Whitman nodded in agreement, as if he were reading her review in the *Tribune. Gad! Would he ever write as brilliantly as she talked?* He felt a throb of envy.

"The baritone's pretense at despair was that of a person with a toothache or a person who has drawn a blank in the lottery." She smoothed her leather gloves.

Whitman was desperate to match her oratory. "Opera and poetry," he ventured, "awaken the senses to the majesty of the body. To the glory of life." He spoke faster, in a rhapsody. "I find letters from God dropped on the ground. Where others see a ragtag street urchin or a fallen woman or a cab driver, I see the divine."

His face glowed. He was talking with a writer he revered! When she spoke, he felt her eyes shoot sparks; she became incandescent. It was like hearing all the instruments of an orchestra and all the soloists sing and soar together—a symphony in full! And her laugh! Like a child's, full-throated, unabashed, rolling and rollicking.

He saluted her farewell as she tugged open her door.

The next day Whitman bragged to his colleagues, "When Miss Fuller and I talked on the omnibus, her whole body was in motion. Her wit flashed like heat lightning—a burst, a boom, then on to the next explosion. Ideas spouted out of her faster than a horse's clopping hooves. I felt dizzy. Margaret Fuller is like a top spinning so fast it's a blur. I think her pulse must beat ten times faster than a hummingbird's wings."

Whitman paused. A bird's twitter wafted on the wind, and two mockingbirds hopped on an oak branch above his head singing in full concord. A sudden breeze swayed the tree to and fro, like a cradle violently rocking. Leaves rustled, and a spray of acorns rained down, pelting his head.

He looked up and whispered to himself, "She told me to write a song of myself. Maybe it will be a song of herself."

CHAPTER FOURTEEN

A New Margaret Blossoms in the Old World

MARCH 1847, TO ROME, ITALY

One advantage of living in New York and becoming known as a progressive reformer was that Margaret met many like-minded citizens, including wealthy couples whose sympathy for the poor didn't impede an accumulation of their own riches. One such couple, Quakers named Marcus and Rebecca Spring, were so taken with Margaret they offered to finance a Grand Tour of Europe for her, if she would accompany them and tutor their young son, Eddie.

Margaret was ecstatic. It had been her lifelong wish to experience the glories of European art and history not just relayed through books but firsthand. She arranged with Horace Greeley to become the *Tribune*'s first foreign correspondent, sending "Things and Thoughts from Europe" to an audience in the States.

As she wrote in her final column on American soil, "Farewell, New-York City! I go to behold the wonders of Old World art and hope to bring home some packages of seed corn for Life in our New World, especially the part assigned to women in the next phase of human progress."

Margaret's letters from abroad appeared regularly in the newspaper. She recounted meeting *literati* in England including poets William Wordsworth, Matthew Arnold, and Samuel Taylor Coleridge, as well as the contrarian Thomas Carlyle. Everywhere, she was feted as a superior savant, an oddity from what Europeans considered the wilds of America. "My book and *The Dial* are read here with earnest interest and warm appreciation," she wrote Emerson. Those with intellectual pretensions vied to make her acquaintance, surprised to see she wore lovely frocks rather than a coonskin cap.

In Paris Margaret sought out the notorious libertine novelist George Sand. Sand's reputation for multiple extramarital affairs (including with the composer Chopin), for wearing men's trousers, smoking cigars, and being an outspoken supporter of women's rights increased Margaret's desire to know her. Even her masculine pen name caused outrage in Americans' timid hearts, but Margaret—maligned herself—felt a kinship. "I vibrate perfectly with her," she confided in a letter to Cary.

In a tête-à-tête over tea and macarons, she found the French woman most congenial—and audacious in not kowtowing to conformity. "What a pioneer you are!" Margaret said in French, "a powerful voice for change."

"We both see the festering wounds of our society," the French author told her.

Margaret reported her favorable opinion of the novelist to her *Tribune* audience, terming her "genuine, pure, and free from even the suspicion of error." *What's next*, her shocked readers wondered, *condoning adultery? Celebrating debauchery?*"

"If one's conduct be false," the author urged Margaret, "give it up. But if it be true, keep to it."

Margaret was not one to affect ladylike diffidence or pander to men's conviction of their superiority. In European society parties, her wit made an impression—positive and negative. Her relentless colloquial flow was apt to render some auditors tongue-tied.

At one garden party hosted by minor royals, she was at great pains to make an impression. Guests first surrounded her, then scattered, exhausted by her incessant raillery. One cornered gentleman repeated

"Just so" after her every utterance, then backed away, overwhelmed. Undaunted, she bombarded the morning-coat-clad gentleman with bon mots. The hapless man wiped his forehead with a silk handkerchief and lapsed into silence. He grabbed a glass of claret like a lifeline and slunk away. "Too much, too strong," he muttered, as he fanned himself with his top hat. "These Americans!"

To most new acquaintances, she was considered a traveling celebrity, a virtuoso of loquacity. Her brilliant repartee inspired not a few admirers. Margaret was pleased that Europeans—at least those in the literary circles she frequented—prized wit more than a pretty face.

One fan was the notorious Polish poet in exile Adam Mickiewicz. A handsome rake and sensualist by reputation, he bowed and embraced Margaret at their first meeting. "At last I meet this vaunted American author!" he said. Rather than pecking at her cheeks, he planted a kiss on her lips. When he squeezed her in a tight hug that lasted long enough to raise eyebrows, Margaret's heart pounded. "Mademoiselle Fuller," he said, "Enchanted! I am your servant."

The poet knew of her hostility to men. "I have read of your low opinion of matrimony," he said. "As I understand it, you are resolved never to succumb to marriage." Mickiewicz stood close and looked Margaret directly in the eye. "I urge you. Give up your foolish vow of celibacy."

Margaret's mouth dropped open in shock: *no one talks like that in polite company!*

He continued, "You must abandon Puritan morality and accept the pleasures of European life, my dear. You have pleaded the equal freedom of women in a masculine and frank manner." He kissed her hand and retained possession of it longer than manners dictated. His mouth twitched in a seductive smile. "Give up your virginity—that will be your deliverance. Live and act as you write."

A story circulated that Margaret fainted dead away and collapsed on a sofa, so electrifying was his charge.

In any case, the two writers found much to discuss in subsequent, frequent meetings. They strolled the boulevards of Paris, talking and laughing until late in the night. Her chaperons, the Springs, were glad to pry her from his clutches and explore other cities.

Margaret's newsletters to the States were more than glossy travelogues. She found poverty and working conditions appalling in industrialized English cities—and said so without euphemism. She bragged of hobnobbing with political revolutionaries. Her friendship with the Italian socialist Giuseppe Mazzini was pivotal. The charismatic Mazzini persuaded her to care deeply about Italy's divided state, split into eight foreign-ruled principalities. In her columns, she trumpeted the need for a unified, republican government encompassing all the peninsula's city-states.

As the ferment of revolutionary movements, riots, and barricades spread across the whole of Europe in the 1840s, Margaret became impatient with guidebook-toting tourism. She wished to embed herself in Rome to see history in the making. Breaking with propriety, she extracted herself from the Springs' well-meaning chaperonage to establish her own domicile in Rome.

"I wish to be free," she told Rebecca Spring, who fanned herself in dismay and sniffed cologne from a handkerchief. "From infancy," Margaret went on, "I always knew my path would be difficult. I have been shunned and persecuted as an oddity."

Rebecca ransacked her mental trove of platitudes for a means of persuasion. "My dearest Margaret, what will your mother say if we leave you here alone?"

"If I cannot live absolutely true to my nature, I do not wish to live. Trials will ripen my character."

Much debate among Margaret's fellow expatriates centered on the wisdom of a single woman living alone. Gossipers insinuated possible romantic entanglements. *That famous Polish poet—reputedly quite a rogue—with whom she was friends in Paris? Were they perhaps more than friends?*

And in Rome, her effusive praise of young Tom Hicks, the painter . . . *unseemly? Didn't she rave about his talent a bit excessively?*

Hicks insisted on painting her portrait, which of course entailed many intimate sittings *à deux* in his studio. Margaret's modest chamber on the Corso was continually overflowing with wildflowers he bestowed. Oil and water are known not to mix, but, in Hicks's studio, oil paint and champagne seemed to meld harmoniously.

One young man, a recent graduate of Harvard named Samuel Higgins, had known Margaret in Boston. During Margaret's Conversations era, he'd deemed her a scornful, arrogant man-hater. On renewing their acquaintance in Rome, Higgins claimed the warm Italian sun had melted her. One night, he danced two cotillions with her and admired her low-cut Parisian gown. He found her not sarcastic and haughty but convivial and jolly. "Miss Fuller even drank whisky punch with me!" Higgins bragged to his comrades. For the young men who'd embarked on the Grand Tour for cultural polishing, Margaret's at-home Monday evenings became a mandatory stop. "St. Peter's today or St. Margaret's?" one wag asked his fellows.

For Margaret, the Old World became a New World. Rome was a revolution for both her *and* the country. "One cannot change the world," she told visitors, "without changing oneself." So confident was she, she even relaxed her constant stream of witticisms with new acquaintances. "I'm no longer a freak of nature here," she wrote Cary. "No longer seen as a man's ambition in a woman's body." When she went to Hicks's studio to pose for her portrait, he was astonished she could remain silent for fully half an hour.

One bit of brass in that Golden Age was Italy's fitful struggle towards independence. The liberation of Italy was blocked by foreign despots, but Margaret still hoped a glorious future would dawn. She resolved to rouse sympathy for the rebellion and inform the world of the fight for freedom.

Scribbling away in her chamber one day, she had an unexpected visitor. "Captain Sturgis!" she exclaimed. "What brings you to Rome? Is Cary all right?"

Cary's father, the gruff Boston baron of the fur trade, bowed and reassured her he didn't bring bad news. "I confess my motive is paternal intervention in my daughter's affairs of the heart."

Margaret looked confused. "I'm relieved but also intrigued," she said. She took his hat and ushered him to a chair. "Do continue, sir."

The sturdy man of seventy years, impeccably dressed in the finest waistcoat his fortune could buy, crossed and uncrossed his legs. He seemed unsure what position would best serve his end and finally settled on a ramrod-straight posture, feet planted on the floor. He plunged forward with his mission. "Let me say at the outset that I believe your influence on my daughter, at a very impressionable age, was deleterious to her womanhood. Yet I appeal to your love for her. Help me and help her."

Margaret recalled how he had tried to steer his daughter away from her. She shut her notebook with an audible clap. "How, sir, may I help?"

He spoke deliberately, as if explaining the basics of an exotic foreign language. "A young man of good stock named Mr. William Tappan is courting Caroline. You must have heard of him in her letters?"

Margaret shook her head. "I am ignorant of any courtship."

"I suppose she's been reluctant to mention it, for her favor of the young man is far from certain. Yet I deem him an acceptable match, regardless of their incompatible personalities. He comes from a wealthy family. I'm confident his intentions are honorable, and Mr. Emerson has a high regard for him—although Tappan is far from loquacious, rather withdrawn, in fact."

"You understate his shallowness," she interjected. "I know the man. Call him what he is, not taciturn but downright torpid—Will Tappan is a tortoise compared to Cary's jack-rabbit!"

Another comparison occurred to him, and he floated it to kindle Margaret's consent. "Perhaps a union between an exuberant, voluble filly and a colorless plough horse might be to the advantage of both—taming one and enlivening the other?"

Margaret's expression was skeptical in the extreme. Sturgis gritted his teeth and persevered. "I'm aware of how Cary changed as she grew close to you, Miss Fuller, how she became resistant to ordinary domestic duties. Under your thrall, she vows to remain a 'heroic' virgin, forsaking a man's protection, and never accede to marriage. This concerns me. I worry for her happiness. She's fast approaching the age of spinsterhood—nearly twenty-eight! This may be her last chance."

"I am even more advanced towards obsolescence," Margaret said, "past my mid-thirties. Do you pity me? Have you ever considered that a more fitting appellation than *Old* Maid may be *Bold* Maid?"

The thought had clearly never crossed his mind. Startled into alien mental territory, he let down his mantle of invincibility and rubbed his forehead as if to wipe away a stain. "Forgive me if I seem severe. I partially blame myself. Her refusal of matrimony is consistent with your teachings, but it may also be due to my own pitiable marriage."

Margaret looked him in the eye. "How well do you know your daughter? If you think her pliable, you're mistaken. You accuse me of unduly molding your daughter, but Cary's too headstrong to obey any counsel she opposes."

"Which is why I approach you, Miss Fuller, as her cherished friend. Please, persuade her to accept Tappan's proposal."

Margaret stifled a chuckle, then abandoned all pretense at gentility and laughed out loud, slapping her knee. "I have some acquaintance with both the man and his deplorable poems. A union between your daughter and Mr. Tappan—the epitome of dullness—would be like perfume wasted on the desert wind."

Margaret held up fingers to elucidate for him, one by one, the major tenets of her ethos. She made a case for women's emancipation, naming goals such as equality in family decision-making, ownership of property, custody of children, access to education and all professions. Not to mention women's suffrage! "It's Cary's duty to develop her talent as an artist and furnish an example for future generations. I fear, sir, you aim to force a miserable mistake on her."

He hung his head. "My negligence constrains her to either marry or be condemned to a half-life of family servitude. You're aware of my wife Elizabeth's mental breakdown and the strain of suicidal mania in our family, I assume. If Cary remains single, she'll be a prisoner to duty. Do you know her sister Elly has died?" His voice broke, and he cleared his throat.

Margaret nodded. "I loved Elly. What a gifted poet!"

"Now Cary is obliged to be her mother's custodian. My wife and I live apart, you know. I've only recently learned how dire Elizabeth's condition is. Night and day, she roams the halls of the nursing home in a trance, pacing and pacing, eyes unseeing, never speaking except to moan unintelligibly. Cary alone cares for her. What a toll this takes! Cary must escape. A kind husband will save her."

Margaret did not hesitate to disabuse him of the idea. "She must save herself! Marriage to a dolt like Tappan will increase her suffering."

Sturgis reached for his hat and rose to leave. He was not accustomed to being thwarted. On a ship or in business, a captain's word is law.

"You know about your other daughter Susan's marriage, don't you?" Margaret could not forbear speaking the truth, no matter how unwelcome. "She's miserable, desperate, yoked to a man far beneath her. She rails at the gods in her letters for making her a woman. She wrote me, 'Why do men go to Harvard and I can only go to tea parties?'"

"*Damme!* I can manage pirates on the high seas better than my daughters in drawing rooms!" he growled.

Margaret feared she'd been too harsh; he reminded her of her own father, who'd died years before. Her Papa had never displayed the slightest paternal affection—so steely was his mien as she performed pirouettes of learning to elicit his praise. Captain Sturgis too was stern, but he did not hesitate to show love for his daughter. A pang of compassion impelled her to clasp his hand. She presented him a glass of claret and plied him with her trademark lively chat. Gradually he softened. With humor and biscuits, she disarmed him. He even found himself agreeing with her comments on the submission required of wives.

Having been disposed to disapprove of Margaret's influence on his daughter, Sturgis was surprised to find her so congenial. Could they be friends? She glowed rather than frowned when she talked! *Perhaps*, he thought, *I misjudged her*. For a Captain of Industry not overly given to jocularity, he laughed out loud at Margaret's satiric jibes. Her accounts of young *Baedeker*-toting Harvard graduates checking off an itinerary of European treasures to "finish" their claim to aesthetic omniscience were diverting. She described hordes of dandies trampling the Pantheon marble floor in sentimental rapture, perusing their guidebooks more than the architecture.

"*Baedeker* says to note the overhead oculus," she mimicked one young tourist. "Noted! Now let's move on to a trattoria for chianti. Touring is thirsty work!" Captain Sturgis burst out laughing.

Between his business dealings securing lucrative contracts for delivery of Chinese tea and opium, Sturgis returned several more times to visit and enjoy lively banter with his daughter's friend. On one visit, he and Margaret were sharing a meal of cold turkey, mayonnaise, and champagne when a tumult erupted on the floor below. They heard loud, stormy curses and shouted threats of violence. Heavy objects shattered, crashing into walls, and sounds of breaking glass invaded the room. A frantic *madre* pounded on Margaret's door. She begged for help: "*Signorina Fuller, aiuto, per favore!*" They dashed downstairs to find two curly-haired brothers in fevered combat. One waved a knife blade near his brother's throat, fended off by the other brandishing a cudgel of firewood.

Sturgis, who had proved his courage against marauders more than once in the China Sea, raised his cane to intervene. Margaret waved him off and inserted herself between the two men. She spoke to them in Italian, persuading each to drop his weapon. The brothers magically forgot their dispute. As their mother wept with relief, they hugged and kissed each other's cheeks and sat down to bowls of pasta. In thanks, *La Mama* presented Margaret with a pot of polenta and a basket of boletus mushrooms.

To round out his impressions of Rome before he left, Margaret took Sturgis on a tour of the Vatican by torchlight. As shadows played over incomparable art, she described the Raphael frescoes with intense passion. On his final day, the two rode horses at full gallop to the top of the Pincio Hill, reining up just before the precipitous drop-off.

Margaret looked down on distant ruins of the ancient Roman forum. Her mood turned melancholy. She hailed the broken temples and arches in Latin: "*Ave atque vale.* If only I can leave something to inspire future generations." The wind whipped her light hair into a froth. "I am not the same person I was in Boston. How thankful I am to have entered this larger life! But always I want more!"

They strolled on the parapet in full sun, and Sturgis opened a parasol to shelter her. She waved it aside. "No need! I fear no natural elements and no tyrants." Her eyes lit up with inner fire. "Tell Cary to act out her character, to follow her instinct or she'll always regret it. Imperfect as love is, we'd suffocate without someone to love."

She spoke of the revolution brewing and her hope that Italy would be a democratic state with universal suffrage and human rights for all. "A wave has been set in motion, which will not stop rolling and rising until it casts its freight of liberty on the shore. I want to see this drama play out. I want to be part of it, whether as actor or historian."

She stumbled over a root but caught herself, slowing her pace. "I have presentiments of doom," she admitted, clutching Sturgis's arm. "I doubt that Destiny will leave me long in this world of struggle. I am tired of keeping myself up in the water without corks or strength to swim. Yet try I must; try I will!"

CHAPTER FIFTEEN

Lost and Found

APRIL 1, 1847, ROME, ITALY

Margaret's companions the Springs, along with their high-spirited little son Eddie, were preparing to leave Rome for points north. Margaret was resolved to stay. First, one last visit to St. Peter's with her benefactors. It was Maundy Thursday, the day of the Biblical Last Supper. It would be Margaret's last supper with her hosts as well. She hoped for her own transfiguration after their departure. *Alone at last*, she thought, with minor trepidation but major anticipation.

The three Americans peered on tiptoe over tourists' shoulders at Michelangelo's marble *Pietà*. "How does he make stone look so soft and supple?" Margaret mused. "And how does the Virgin Mother look so young? Grief-stricken, yet no wrinkle furrows her brow!"

"The miracle of art," Rebecca speculated. She and her husband wandered off, arranging for the three of them to meet later. Margaret headed for a chapel to hear vespers. The singing filled her soul with ambiguous longing.

Afterward, when Margaret arrived at their rendezvous in the vast basilica, no friends appeared. People began to filter out as bells rang to signal closing and the sun slipped down outside. "Alone" began to lose its appeal, and Margaret, nearsighted, squinted and whipped her head around with an increasing air of fright.

The marble walls around her lost their luster, turned cold and hard like a clamped-shut oyster shell. Soon she and one young man were the only ones remaining. The stranger came closer. In the dim light she could see his features mistily. Her innards did flip-flops. Her pulse quickened. Her heart pounded a drumbeat against her ribs.

The young man was tall and slender, with moist dark eyes lighting up his handsome face. "*Signorina*, may I help you? You seem disturbed," he said in Italian.

"I am lost," she answered haltingly in his language.

Politely correcting her, he replied "You must mean you have lost your way or lost your friends—not that you are *persa*, which would suggest you are dead, fallen to perdition." He smiled and took her arm to guide her out.

Chagrined at her linguistic error, she forgot how inappropriate it was to speak to a stranger, especially one who set her heart aflutter. "Yes, I have lost my friends. How shall I get back to my lodging?"

"Allow me," he bowed, clicking his heels with a military air. "I am Giovanni Angelo Ossoli. It will be my honor to escort you."

Adventure! Isn't that what her book-bound life had been missing? In the dying light, Margaret beamed as Ossoli searched for a carriage. Giving up the quest as fruitless, he insisted on walking Margaret back to her room through narrow, zigzagging streets. She was delighted to cling to him as he conversed with her and steered around beggars and piles of excrement. She excused this extreme proximity by rationalizing that here was a real native—she could practice her Italian! The fact that he looked so striking made the excursion all the more exciting. Margaret tried to steady her pulse as she practiced her grammar.

When they arrived at her address, Ossoli relinquished her arm, touched his walking stick to his hat, and bowed. "*Ecco, Signorina!* You are not lost but found!" He saluted and withdrew as she pulled open the heavy wooden door.

In the stairwell waiting for her were Margaret's friends the Springs. "Thank goodness you're safe!" Rebecca exclaimed.

"Indeed," Marcus said with relief, "you look none the worse for wear. In fact, you look positively luminous. I hope it's not moonburn or malaria."

"Actually," she said dreamily, "I feel that my hard, marble armor has melted into soft silk. You were right, Rebecca. Miracles abound in Rome!"

CHAPTER SIXTEEN

Not Alone Anymore

APRIL 2, 1847, ROME, ITALY

The next morning, Margaret looked outside her window to the street below. She saw a young man pacing back and forth in front of her building, twirling an ebony cane. He leaned against a wall and glanced up, then continued strolling. Her rescuer from the night before—what was he doing here? Ridiculous! He must be ten years—or even more—younger. *Yet what does age have to do with anything in the Eternal City?* she thought. She quickly exchanged her wrapper for a day dress, tugged on boots, and carefully arranged curls under her favorite bonnet.

As she emerged into the light from the doorway, Margaret thought of her Italian lessons. To say a babe is born, she'd learned to say, it is "given into the light." That was how she felt—newly born in the light of this old city and new world.

Ossoli brightened when he saw her and closed the distance between them, bowing and removing his hat. He came to return a handkerchief, which she must have dropped, he explained, holding out an embroidered hanky that was totally unfamiliar to Margaret. He blushed that his pretext was so transparent. She invited him to accompany her to see her rambunctious pupil Eddie. Ossoli gladly accepted and seized her arm, tucking it inside his elbow with wicked closeness. *It seems Italians' concept of propriety between unmarried gentlemen and ladies is less structured than Americans'*, Margaret noted mentally, thinking of using the idea in a future column on Cultural Differences. She had a pleasurable awareness of ropy muscles in his forearm. *What must it feel like without gloves*? she wondered. Her cheeks pinked.

Her young pupil Eddie was playing outside when they approached, happily jumping on a chalked hopscotch grid on the ground. Margaret noted another Cultural Difference. Instead of numbering progressive squares from one to ten, as money-mad Americans did, Italian children leaped from a square labeled "hell" at the bottom to one at the top called "heaven." *Philistine numbers versus theology—that says it all, doesn't it?* Margaret thought.

"Come, Eddie," Margaret urged her charge. "Let's go to the Villa Borghese gardens."

The boy gamboled along beside them, raking a long stick with a satisfying *clack-clack-clack* over the spindles of each metal fence he encountered. He stopped to pick flowers as the two adults, absorbed in talk, mostly ignored him.

Ossoli explained that he was the youngest of five children and that his father and brothers were all in service to the pope. He agreed with Margaret that the new pope, once thought to be reform-minded, was turning out to be more conservative, crushing people's hopes for self-rule. A shame, they agreed. Despite his family's papal ties, Ossoli was open to Margaret's ideas for revolution.

Seated on a bench, their heads nearly touching, Margaret and Ossoli didn't see little Eddie stand on the edge of a fountain, balanced like a tightrope walker. He stretched an arm to float a bouquet of flowers in the pool, then was startled by loud quacks of a mallard swimming in the basin. Eddie windmilled his arms to no effect, then fell with a great splash into the water. Margaret and Ossoli looked up to see him thrashing, flailing, sinking.

"My God!" she cried as they rushed to the fountain. She stepped on the rim, prepared to leap in and pull Eddie to safety. Before she could so much as wet a pinkie, Eddie exploded to the surface for a third time, raising his stick in one hand. Ossoli leaned his long form over the water, grabbed the end of the stick, and pulled the little boy out. Flopped over the edge of the basin, he coughed up spurts of water as Margaret hugged his soaked body.

"Grazie mille!" she cried to Ossoli. "Saved again!"

The miscreant mallard flapped its wings in a flurry, indignant at the turmoil in his normally quiet pool. As Ossoli carried the dripping boy away, the duck preened his iridescent tail feathers with a yellow bill, restoring his smooth equanimity.

"Let's buy you a *grande gelato*," Ossoli said, and Eddie, none the worse for his dunking, nodded joyfully at the word "gelato."

CHAPTER SEVENTEEN

The Italian Resurgence

SUMMER 1847, ROME, ITALY

Margaret's acquaintance with Ossoli ripened apace. He haunted her residence, bringing flowery bouquets and chocolates. When she received English-speaking guests, he stood aside. Silent, he fixed his gaze on her with worshipful adoration.

"What does she see in him—beyond his good looks? So young, so virile!" American ladies wondered.

"What does he see in her?" gentlemen questioned. "He can't even understand her discourses on art and literature. He simply stares at her like a contented cow!"

It was Ossoli's non-intellectual simplicity that won Margaret's affection. For the first time since she had to recite lessons for her father, here was a man who appreciated her not for what she said, but for herself. She did not have to dazzle him with word play and arcane knowledge. If she mentioned Goethe, Aristotle, Beethoven—even Shakespeare—he looked blank, unacquainted with their *oeuvre*.

Margaret and her unlikely beau strolled the avenues, installing themselves on benches in many a piazza to discuss political affairs. The painter Tom Hicks had to work on her portrait from memory, since she no longer frequented his studio.

Goaded by Margaret's republican fervor, Angelo—for so he insisted she call him—became allied with the rebel forces, hiding this apostasy from his conservative brothers and father. While his family wore the uniform of the Pope's guards, Angelo joined the opposing Civic Guard, donning proudly its brown uniform with red piping and brass buttons. A younger son inclined to break with his elders' demands, he readily accepted the *Risorgimento* slogan of "for the people, by the people." Monarchy, autocracy, theocracy had ruled Italy for too long. It was time for democracy. Margaret thrilled at the echoes of her country's revolution. *Born too late for the upheaval of 1776, now is my time to shine! And to think my ally is this young man!*

Margaret wrote her Polish friend Mickiewicz of Angelo's ardor, saying frankly, although vaguely, that the young man had "taken liberties" with her person. Kissing, she learned under Angelo's tutelage, was more exciting than reading about Abelard and Eloise. The poet approved the connection and urged further liberties. "Your organism greatly needs the physicality of Italy," Mickiewicz wrote. "Enjoy your life and body—breathe it in through all your pores."

She trembled; her hand holding the letter shook. *What was he saying? Free love?* She was a long way from Puritan Boston. "You say you are struck by the beautiful build—*la bella figura!*—of men and women in Italy," Mickiewicz went on. "Know that you are also beautiful. Do not live in bondage to books and ideas. If you are to be a truly free woman, give all for love. Accept and respond to the legitimate needs of your organism."

Margaret gasped. *My organism? Am I the sole judge of my needs?* The thought set her heart beating fast. *Legitimate needs? . . . Assalutamente!* No one and nothing would constrain her. *Angelo?* Certainly he was rather young, but she basked in his adoring regard, jubilant that he preferred her company to the nubile signorinas who fluttered around him. *Why not? If I am ever to be a woman in full, I must not cower.*

Ossoli affected her like music. *My heart beats with joy that he sees beauty in me*, she thought. *When I'm with him, I'm happy—not a state I'm overly familiar with. Perhaps I'll do things that may invoke censure. Yet I'll act as I ought, act as I must.*

Everything in Rome was changing. Peasants, middle-class workers, and artisans as well as liberal patricians—all were demanding resurgence, *Risorgimento,* of the people's power. Young men flocked to the Resistance. They paraded, marched, and drilled with guns and swords. The times called for heroism.

New world. New Margaret, she thought. When Angelo next caught her in an embrace, she did not turn her head or push him away with a chaste hand against his chest. Now that she had her own chamber and the Springs had disappeared, she was free to absorb Angelo's lessons beyond Italian. When he touched her, she felt fully alive.

Yet no matter how ardently she indulged the "legitimate needs" of her organism, her independence was too precious to relinquish. When Angelo begged her to marry him—in secret, since he could not let his family know he married a Protestant—she refused. *He is so much younger . . . and almost completely uneducated. An unseemly match, to be sure.* She couldn't risk ridicule. Romance heated her body, but her mind was far away . . . far above.

Margaret heard that Emerson was in France and hoped to see her. In a quandary, she wrote Cary and hinted of her new freedom. She wondered if "dear Waldo" would appreciate her liberated self. "Candor and ardor are my new watchwords," she wrote Cary. "I intend to show Mr. Iceberg my whole self. Will he melt?"

CHAPTER EIGHTEEN

Worries About the New Margaret

JANUARY 1848, CONCORD, MASSACHUSETTS

Cary hugged Sophia tightly. "Thank you for meeting me. I'm so befuddled by Margaret's last letter from Rome! She wants to meet Waldo in France. I don't know what to tell her!"

Sophia Hawthorne placed a lump of sugar in her tea, the picture of complacency. "Why shouldn't she meet him? It'll do her good to inhale the bracing atmosphere of New England. She is becoming too continental. Did you read her column praising that shameless hussy George Sand? Unthinkable!"

"I fear French loose morals are infecting her. She seems to imagine a 'liaison' or some such may occur with Waldo," Cary whispered. She swiveled her head to be sure they were not overheard.

"Good Lord in heaven!" Sophia leaned forward. "You can't mean intimate relations with Waldo? Impossible!"

"It does seem unimaginable," Cary admitted. "I've known him for ten years. He's a most frosty soul. We exchange weekly letters, but always on a high plane of thought."

Sophia broached a subject that had long aroused curiosity. "What about all those walks you and Waldo take together in the woods, those moonlight paddles in a canoe? You two are inseparable when you're in Concord."

"I assure you, he's never done more than sigh and dart longing looks at me. Our friendship has more light than heat."

"And Margaret's feelings for Waldo?" Sophia asked. "During the years they edited *The Dial* together, Nat and I saw she was in love with him. *I* knew it. *Lidian* knew it. Probably everyone knew it."

"She told me," Cary was quick to say, "that when she wanted more than talk from him, he pushed her away. His reputation is spotless."

"Would that we could say the same for hers." Sophia radiated the piety of a happily married matron. "Warm climes make people hot-blooded. I remember when I lived in Puerto Rico as a young girl; even *my* head was turned." She sighed in nostalgia.

They drank their tea down to the dregs. Cary examined her cup as if she could read the tea leaves. "It's true that Europe has transformed our New England Margaret." She lowered her voice. "I wager that dashing young Ossoli is not the only man who hankers after her. People say he never talks, but he must do *something* well!"

Sophia's hand fluttered to her chest. "Caroline! What do you imply?"

"Only that we think we're such free thinkers here in Concord—in the vanguard, plotting a radical route, nourishing thirsty souls in the wilderness. Everything seems possible. The country's in a ferment; utopia lurks just around the bend." Cary seemed to be thinking aloud. "Perchance Europe is really where change happens."

"The times are certainly in an uproar," Sophia agreed. "Nat tells me that seventy model communities have been founded. *Not* that one like Brook Farm is a true ideal or even practical." She frowned.

"When did our zeal for The Newness become cold gruel?" Cary asked. "Waldo still preaches the same, stale dogma of Self-Trust. We see how that insistence on ego has infected someone like Ellery. That man-child makes poor Ellen's life a misery."

"As much as I've diverged from Waldo's Transcendental notions, I do not applaud Margaret for stepping away—and stepping out on her own," Sophia said, fierce in her upright decorum. "I fear her radical ideas. If you have any influence over her, encourage her not to tempt Waldo. It would be sacrilege to his marriage vows, a violation of morality."

"Do we even know Margaret anymore? She wrote a very un-Margaret letter telling me I should 'give all for love' and fulfill the 'legitimate needs of my organism.' Then she asked if I am keeping company with Will Tappan." Cary raised the lid on the teapot and saw it was empty. She slammed the cover down with a resounding *chunk*. "Will Tappan! Let my father marry him if he's so keen on the blighter!"

Sophia mumbled under her breath, "You're not getting any younger, Caroline Sturgis."

CHAPTER NINETEEN

A Proposition for Emerson

JANUARY 1848, MARSEILLE, FRANCE

Emerson had just arrived and unpacked his trunk. He lined up his socks in a rigid phalanx as if preparing for battle. A porter knocked on his hotel room door to say a visitor awaited him in the conservatory. Emerson's heart skipped a beat. He realized how much he'd missed Margaret since she'd been abroad. She had been his best audience, invigorating their sparring matches, giving as good as she got in argument. Both friend and foe, she sharpened his thoughts no end. Never could he get away with a sloppy, half-baked idea. Her acuteness contributed to his success as a lecturer and essayist.

Yet a major drawback perturbed their collaboration. He remembered how in Concord she had tried to kindle their friendship to more warmth. "My heart is a blazing hearth," she'd said, "yet you never warm yourself by it. You love my words more than me." Probably true. At this meeting on foreign turf he resolved to assume a paternal demeanor.

He blushed to recall one particularly galling occasion years ago, when they were editing *The Dial* together. Margaret had actually plopped down on his lap—on his very person! She had suggested they could correct a manuscript in that unseemly position. Emerson lost no time in shuffling her off his limbs. Unrelenting originality was tiresome; Margaret could take things too far. Casting off all conformity to decency takes a toll, one he was unwilling to pay.

As they reunited in France soon after New Year's, the Sage's reserve came near to melting. When he entered the glass-enclosed dining room, he inhaled the heady scent of orange trees forced to blossom prematurely. Margaret, he saw at once, had changed. She was more . . . womanly.

Margaret's last letter to Waldo, announcing her intention to meet in France, had overflowed with warmth. "Love me all you can," she wrote. "Let me feel there are pure hands stretched out towards me, if I can claim their grasp."

She referred, he was certain, to platonic love, but it was still a bit *de trop, n'est-ce pas?* Such a passionate effusion unnerved him—and not a little tantalized him to see its consequence. Always with Margaret, the seesaw of repulsion and attraction levered up and down.

Everyone knew—Margaret more than anyone—his nature was not demonstrative.

Now, seeing her for the first time in two years, he stretched out his hands and she hugged him in a tight embrace. "Two kisses, Waldo, *de rigueur* here." She smacked both his cheeks with gusto.

"I bow to your superior continental knowledge," he reddened and pulled back. "How well you look!" He extracted his hands from her grip, and they sat down at the white-linen-covered table.

"You must have the oysters!" She signaled a waiter and in flawless French rattled off an order for mollusks and champagne. Emerson, a bit taken aback by her forthright takeover of the ordering process, nevertheless smiled gamely.

Their ebullient conversation and a surfeit of bubbly loosened him up more than was his wont. After they dined, they strolled in the hotel garden, stopping under a secluded pergola at a safe remove from a prickly cactus. Margaret nodded towards the succulent and encircling palm trees. "The microclimate here fosters semi-tropical species. In Italy, warmth produces luxuriant growth year-round."

Emerson was forced to acknowledge the wholesome effect on

Margaret personally. Blood surged to her face and bosom; she seemed to glow. Or was that perspiration? Her words to him, so free and frank, were, he felt, a trifle *unbecoming* to a lady.

"I stand in the sunny noon of life," she announced, "What concerns me now is that my life be a beautiful, powerful, in a word, a *complete* life." He had the uncomfortable impression that by "complete" she meant both intellectual expression and physical passion. Yet, he wondered, how complete could her intellectual life be with a lover whom Emerson had heard described as an all-but-illiterate Italian? He affected an air of jocularity. "Tell me, Margaret dear, is it true you have a young Italian admirer?"

She nodded with a trace of pride. "You say, 'follow your intuition.' I have done so and have no regrets." She paused, then went on. "I have done things that may invoke censure." She looked her mentor directly in the eye.

A most surprising thing—unique in Emerson's experience—happened next. She pulled him up from the bench and attempted to embrace him. Alarmed and losing the air of detachment he always cultivated, Emerson untangled himself from her grasp and offered a chaste handshake.

He straightened his cravat and backed away, saying only, "Um, er, just so, I'm sure." He extracted a silk handkerchief from a pocket and swabbed his perspiring forehead.

Ignoring the rebuff, she intensified her assault. "I no longer feel suffocated." She stepped closer as he retreated, nearly colliding with an urn of purple bougainvillea.

"I have begun to drink deep of this cup of life!" Margaret pressed on. "I had been living a life of bondage. Now a new era has begun. I've become a New Woman of a New Epoch."

Emerson recoiled, and for every step he took backward, she took one forward. He began to feel panic, like helpless prey pursued by an undaunted lioness. Words had never failed him, and he summoned his mighty baritone to quell her advance. “I say, Margaret—remember yourself!”

“I don’t remember the timid woman I was. I’ve learned things which you cannot learn from books. I challenge you to recognize my legitimate needs as a woman!” She took his hand and pressed it to her bosom.

Emerson snatched his hand back, as if burned by a hot iron. “I beseech you. Control yourself, Miss Fuller!”

Margaret crumpled and sniffled into a handkerchief. Through her tears, she choked out, “You’re destined to remain an undeveloped man, Mr. Ralph Waldo Emerson, philosopher of solitude. I’ve discovered, and I wished to share with you, a new, vast, tumultuous class of human emotions. Accepting a need for pleasure is perhaps my most radical act. I surprise and delight myself!”

Moved by her outcry and hoping to restore her dignity, he placed a hand on her shoulder to comfort her. “My dearest friend, I have always lagged behind you. Give me time to catch up.”

He returned to his room, leaving her slumped on the stone bench. She straightened as she watched him recede, his back straight as a poker. *If a union of mind and body is blocked*, she thought, *other paths beckon.*

CHAPTER TWENTY

Emerson Explains

MAY 1848, CONCORD, MASSACHUSETTS

Restored to the serenity of his pastoral estate after his European trip, Emerson walked with Cary in his pear orchard. He regarded the small nuggets of fruit dotting the branches, still undeveloped. "Those tiny pears remind me of my time in France. When I saw Margaret in Marseille she called *me* 'undeveloped.'"

"You never speak of your meeting with her. Why?"

"Our interview was astounding—I try to erase it from my memory."

"How so?"

"I was glad to see Margaret after so long apart," he began, stabbing his walking stick in mounds of green moss. "You know there's no one to whom I can talk with as much animation as she. As we sat at lunch, my first remarks were as an old friend. I asked, 'Shall we not again talk as we used to and serve and love one another? We can build in Concord, when you return, a covenant of hearts and minds, even though you may find it a naked and unatmospheric land, devoid of the ruins of antiquity, of which you have become so fond."

"What a beguiling invitation," Cary said with dry sarcasm. "You speak like a fusty book."

"I fear I was too gushing, perhaps signaling an excess of enthusiasm or too liberal imbibing of champagne. I was sincere when I told her, 'You've been important to my imagination and still retain importance for me. You're one of the few who love what I love.'"

"Her reply?"

"You know Margaret—never at a loss for words," he said. "She came right back with, 'You've given me your conversation, your wise counsel, your partnership with your mind. Now I want you to give me no less than your whole heart.'"

Cary gulped. This was exactly what she dreaded. Waldo was galloping into the lion's den. "How did you respond?"

"I was confused. Margaret went on in overly heated terms: 'Open your doors to my sunshine and morning air. If not, you're not the friend I seek. I want your passion as well as your intellect,' she said." He blushed crimson. They sat on a wooden bench, a body's length apart.

Cary had to know. "Your reply?"

Emerson shifted, shaking his legs like a dog flinging off water. "I didn't know what to say or do. I tried to elevate the discourse to a higher plane. I referred to an individual's need for intellectual and personal freedom, saying, 'I don't wish to exchange my present prison for a larger one without bars. I wish to break free of all prisons.'"

"I find that a circuitous response, as I'm sure Margaret did."

"Yes, she had an air of reproof. 'You agitate others, but you yourself are never agitated,' she said. 'You experience no ecstasy with any other, only lonely eloquence. My relationship with you involves no axes, no arrows, no nectar, no growling, enchantment, or loving.'"

"I marvel that you remember her precise words so clearly."

"How could I forget? They're seared into my brain." He looked Cary in the eye. "Margaret said many complimentary things. 'You inspired me to rebellion, and now I've gone further. The essence of Transcendentalism is freedom,' she said. 'You set me free, and in Italy I've become a free woman!'"

"*Bravissima*!" Cary exclaimed.

Emerson looked inexplicably sad. "In that regard, Margaret surpassed me. I had gone to Europe to renew my near-empty font of inspiration. I feel I'm treading water here, with only another grim round of lecturing ahead. My words seem increasingly quaint and out of step with the modern, rushing world. To Margaret, I'm a mummified, desiccated husk of a human being, a living fossil." He hung his head. "Even my lectures are old and tired."

Cary threw a handful of acorns at a squirrel flicking its bushy tail.

Emerson kept talking, almost to himself. "I tried to defend myself. I told her, 'We must each do our own work, exercise our freedom as individuals.' She looked at me as if I came from a prehistoric era and said my speeches are irrelevant 'oxygenation of the lungs.' She said I have no new thoughts, projects, or positive goals." He swiped his cane at the tall grass beside the bench, bending the stalks down before they popped up again.

"Margaret is on a different page of history than you," Cary told him. "She wants to liberate Italy, while you seek to liberate the individual spirit."

"Cultivating one's inner being is the true path to universal reform."

"Margaret always says, 'Life is a march and a battle.' I thought that meant hope for progress in a man's world," Cary mused. "Now she's become heroic herself. I admire her courage. She doesn't just lecture about freedom; she fights for it. For herself and for Italy."

"Am I a ghost whispering ideas to the living but not living myself?" Emerson bashed the tall grass with an angry swing of his cane. A gust of wind blew leaves down on his shoulders, and he brushed them off. "When will I act as I write?" He bowed his head. "For Margaret, it's a new day, a new harvest with new fields of thought, new duties, new friends and powers. Her last words to me were: 'I have to let my music play, my flowers open, my starlight shine.'"

His eyes were beseeching. "Am I all brain and no blood?" Emerson—that most phlegmatic of men—wiped tears from his eyes.

He looked at his orchard. "At least my pears will develop into juicy, rounded fruit."

"You and I—are we still developing . . . or stunted?" Cary asked him—and herself.

CHAPTER TWENTY-ONE

Portrait of a Revolution

MAY 1848, ROME, ITALY

In the late 1840s, the continent of Europe seethed with revolutionary upheaval. It seemed to many that the ideal might become real. In Paris, Berlin, Prague, Krakow, Budapest, Vienna—major cities everywhere except in Russia—protestors demonstrated, staged loud rallies, manned barricades, and demanded the goals of the French Revolution: *liberté, egalité, fraternité*. Under pressure from irate mobs, King Louis Philippe abdicated in France. Prince Metternich, the mastermind of the Austrian empire, fled Vienna. "*Viva la Republica*!" was a universal cry.

Italy was hardly immune. In Milan, Naples, Venice, Palermo, Bologna and more, rebels rose up in mass protests against autocratic rulers. They threw bottles, sticks, and stones as they marched and bellowed revolutionary songs in the streets. In Rome, hot-blooded young men joined the Civic Guard in droves and rushed to other city-states to repel the hated Austrian troops. Military drills took place every day. Banners flew. Soldiers strutted. The *rub-adub-dub* of drumbeats swirled through the air.

Margaret exulted, *How fortunate to be here at this moment! A glorious flame burns high in the heart of Europe! I shall return possessed of a great history!* The only American correspondent as eyewitness to the cataclysmic events, she peppered her *Tribune* dispatches with updates on the ferment bubbling up, about to overflow. She wrote observations in her journal every day, intending to convert her reflections into a book on that extraordinary time—a book that would give her immortality and have a happy ending for the Italy she'd come to love.

As her hopes ballooned, something else was swelling. By the end of January, Margaret—at age thirty-eight—realized she was pregnant. When she came to her friend Tom Hicks's studio in May so he could finish her portrait, he was astounded.

"Margaret!" he couldn't resist saying, "how you've grown!" He immediately began altering the contours of her figure on the canvas. With loose brushstrokes, he disguised the girth of her belly, adding highlights to her long blue gown at the hem and bodice to distract the eye. He altered her lips to make her look pensive and—unable to stifle his attention to naturalistic detail—painted lines and weary pouches under her eyes.

Margaret tried to lighten the mood. "I hope you'll flatter me, Tom."

"Flatter?" He sketched in a background of a Venetian lagoon and gondola. "After you abruptly dropped our friendship? This portrait has sat, canvas turned to the wall, for months while you disappeared from my life. And only now I find out the reason!" He mixed dark blobs of oil on his palette, stirring the pigments with uncharacteristic force.

Margaret placed a hand on her abdomen. "Forgive me for ignoring you." She raised her head and stared directly at him. "I don't, however, ask forgiveness of society. I've acted according to the dictates of my character. I implore you, don't paint a hint of shame on my features . . . only perhaps fatigue."

Hicks softened. "As your friend, I must advise you to no longer appear in public. You cannot disguise your condition." "I've kept my condition a secret, and I beg you to do the same." Her eyes implored him. "I've only told my friend Cary in a letter. She'll keep my confidence."

"If people see you, the hounds of propriety will be baying. They'll accuse you of scandal. I've already heard rumors. That young Italian soldier courting you, they say, is after your money."

Margaret laughed with more anger than mirth. "Money? I have none. How absurd." She looked sad. "And how demeaning."

Hicks laid aside his paintbrush and held her hand. "I won't ask who the father is. Or whether you're married. Nor do I wish to know."

"I act as I ought, as I must." She spoke more to herself than to him. "Is it too ridiculous to think that my 'sin' in the Old World may instruct women how to live freely in a new world?"

He looked skeptical but thoughtful, staring towards the street. "The cries for a new world penetrate even the walls of my studio." He cocked his head towards a window. "Perhaps I shouldn't paint what is, but what will be." He snatched a sketchbook from a trestle table and showed Margaret pencil drawings of street scenes. "Look—here's the mob burning wooden confessionals in the piazza to protest rule by clerics."

"I saw it—what a bonfire!" she said. "The crowd was chanting slogans like 'After Rome of the Emperors and Rome of the Pope comes Rome of the people'!"

"They played guitars, banged on tambourines, danced, and destroyed the Cardinals' fine carriages." He laughed, infected by the time's giddy spirit.

"Did you see the cheering crowds in the Piazza del Popolo?" she asked. "They tore down the Hapsburg double eagle over an *osteria* door! They burned the Austrian flag. Rome is simmering, about to boil over. People sing "La Marseillaise," shout *Viva Italia*, and weep with joy. I describe it all for my American readers."

"Americans here are leaving. It's dangerous. You must leave too."

"I'm going to the Abruzzi countryside soon. I don't know if I'll live to see the birth of my child, but I'll spend my time before confinement writing about the birth of the Italian republic." Her eyes brimmed with tears. "Such a coincidence—my own deliverance as an independent woman comes at the same time as Italy's deliverance."

"Not to mention a quite literal delivery awaits you." Hicks laughed.

"Only you, Margaret, can so confound the personal and political." He painted a daub of ivory as a gloss on her pulled-back hair in the portrait. His brush hovered over her fingers. He added a stroke of carmine, conjuring a blood-red ring on her right hand. He painted in a discarded bouquet of flowers on the empty floor in front of her.

CHAPTER TWENTY-TWO

New-Born Hopes

SEPTEMBER 1848, RIETI, ITALY

"*Povera Signora Marguerite, sola* . . . alone, always alone," the *contadini* of Rieti said when passing Margaret riding on a donkey through the countryside. In her mind, she was not alone but filled with stories of revolutionary heroes, which she confided to the pages of her burgeoning book. She filled page after page with fervid stories as her abdomen grew and grew.

Every weekend Ossoli joined her from Rome. In his sergeant's uniform, he strode beside her, picking grapes from vineyards to offer her. The donkey she rode stepped daintily over ruined foundations of ancient Roman temples. It picked its way through crumbling stones marking what used to be a city forum. Broken parts of marble statues—here a beckoning arm, there a sandal-clad foot—and jigsaw fragments of urns and mosaics littered the ground, poking up through mud after a rain. "So much history underfoot," she said. "And we're making new history."

They paused in the piazza outside San Rufo church. Margaret patted her distended belly, looking towards the hills. "This very spot is called the *umbilicus Italiae*," she said, "the umbilical center of all Italy."

"A perfect place for our baby to be born." He squeezed her hand.

The bell tower looming over the Baroque cathedral boomed. "Those bells ring ninety-nine times a day," she complained. "There's no way I can sleep through the night with that incessant bonging—even if

I weren't so uncomfortable." She heaved a loud sigh. "I long for the day when I'm the only person inside my skin again."

"*Cara amore*," he said, "courage! It will happen soon. And if I'm not here, you have the doctor and midwife to help."

She doubled over from a cramping pain and groaned.

Ossoli tightened his grip on her arm. "What can I do, *amore*?"

She let out a deep breath. "Fight for Italy. And come to me as soon as you hear the news of my delivery." She descended from the donkey to lean against him. "How fitting—new life for our babe and new life for this country."

He crossed himself. "May both thrive."

On September 5, 1848, Angelo Eugene Philip Ossoli, a baby boy with turquoise eyes, was born. Margaret and Ossoli were jubilant, even when Margaret's milk proved insufficient and they had to engage a local woman as a wet nurse. Ossoli came as often as he could get away from soldiering.

They strolled together holding hands by the drooping willows lining the Velino River. Among the olive and almond groves, they dodged grazing sheep and exchanged greetings with shepherds who returned their smiles. Ossoli plucked figs and peaches from trees they passed on their rambles, popping them in Margaret's mouth.

The baby, whom they called Nino, grew fat and delighted them with smiles, grabbing their fingers and babbling nonsense. Margaret had never known such a feeling of satisfaction as when she held him tight to her chest and rested her forehead against his. Their hearts beat in unison.

Peasants delighted in having this distinguished American in their midst—*tanta simpatica*—and brought her eggs, mushrooms, and live chickens. She happily ate bread, cheese, and oranges as the autumn light turned from golden to silvery. Indeed, as she paced on the pine-planked loggia outside her bedroom in the moonlight, holding

Nino, Margaret almost felt she was in a new Eden. A baby! At last, she was truly a woman in full!

But even there, the drumbeats of war were accelerating. She would have to return to Rome to see the dreamed-of republic born.

CHAPTER TWENTY-THREE

A Father's Advice for Cary

APRIL 1849, LENOX, MASSACHUSETTS

Cary was surprised to see her father stroll up to the porch of Highwood, swinging his gold-headed cane. "Father! I didn't expect you! Have you come to inspect your new granddaughter? She's perambulating with the nursemaid, but they'll be back soon."

"Of course, I want to see her, but my immediate concern is you. Can we talk?" he said in a grave tone, with no preamble of social niceties.

Cary instructed a maid to bring lemonade and led him to a secluded bench under a pergola in the garden. "Most unexpected, but I am all ears."

Captain Sturgis shifted uncomfortably then plunged ahead. "You know me as not the comforting sort; therefore, I'll not pretend to exude tender sentiments beyond my capacity. Yet I'm not wholly devoid of paternal solicitude." He paused, then mumbled, "You know I perpetually mourn the loss of your brother and my namesake. Now I have another cause to mourn."

Cary raised her head and scrutinized his weather-beaten features. "I don't understand."

"A year ago, I appealed to your mentor Miss Fuller in Italy. I'd hoped to secure her blessing for your marriage to Tappan. She refused in no uncertain terms and cast negative aspersions on his personhood." He paused. A flicker of amusement crossed his face. "I was pleased when you cast your lot with him, even without her endorsement." He reached for his daughter's hand. "Would I had heeded her! She knew you and Tappan better than I. I've heard how unhappy you are since marriage."

Cary waved her arm to take in the orchards and sun-dappled meadow of the grand estate. "I have all this . . . and I have my child. But I also have a cipher for a husband. How deluded I was!" She leaned her head against her father's broad chest. He encircled her with strong arms.

"My goal in coming here is to make you smile, not cry. Let me tell you of my further acquaintance—call it a warm friendship—with your Miss Fuller. I see how her eloquence cast a spell over you, for she enchants me too. When I visited Margaret in Rome recently, we discussed your current situation. She knows your married life is unendurably tedious. Since your sister Elly died, my fears for you have mounted. I can't stop thinking of the streak of madness in our family."

Cary extricated herself from his embrace, stiffening her spine. "There's nothing you can do. It was my choice, not your urging, that landed me in this quagmire. I'll endure it."

"My brave girl!" he said. "Let me continue. I asked Margaret for help. Could she persuade you, dear Diamond, to make peace with your husband?" He sipped his lemonade with a faraway look. "It's astonishing how her thoughts on marriage have changed!"

Cary's face registered surprise. What did he know of Margaret's secret? The baby was not in Rome with her but in the country with a wet nurse. Ossoli was still living with his sister.

Sturgis went on, unaware of his daughter's concerns. "Italy's in turmoil; Margaret risks her life every day, working with wounded soldiers at the hospital. Yet she remains cheerful." He smiled, a conspirator's grin. "Several young men are in love with her, which no doubt contributes to her high spirits. A young Italian soldier shadows her every step, I hear, and a painter named Tom Hicks is an intimate friend." He switched tacks, serious again. "I told Margaret how you seem tortured despite the birth of your daughter. I begged her to write you."

Cary nodded. “I received her letter. I can recite what she wrote from memory: ‘I know Mr. Tappan is shy to the point of torpidity. Permanent love for the same object may not seem possible, but you have cast your lot with him. A union with one for whom you feel fondness is better than being alone. My hope for your happiness in the future, dear Cary, will never abate one jot.’” Cary’s eyes watered.

Sturgis patted her hand. “It’s not a full-throated endorsement, but it’s sincere—and honest. My dear Caroline, you must show the same mettle as your friend.”

Cary drained her lemonade and set the empty glass on the table with a thud.

CHAPTER TWENTY-FOUR

Friends Await Margaret's Return

APRIL 1850, LENOX, MASSACHUSETTS

"How are you doing in the Red House?" Cary asked Sophia Hawthorne as they sat in the farmhouse parlor on a warm summer day.

"It suits us very well. Thank you for inviting us. What a relief after damp old Salem! After the success of Nat's book, he adores everything red."

"We should call it the Scarlet House," Cary said, looking around with proprietary pride. "The fresh paint and wallpaper have livened up the room."

Sophia held up an embroidery hoop. "I'm making Nat a scarlet cravat for Christmas and embroidering an 'H' on it with gold thread."

"An 'H' for 'harlot'?" Cary joked.

Sophia dropped the hoop. "Caroline! The children might hear! I swear, you'll say anything."

"The word is in the Bible, as is 'adultery,'" Cary pointed out with *sang-froid*. "Another theme prominent in Nat's famous book."

"Please don't echo what Puritan critics said of it—that the book deserves 'a scorching rebuke' for investing un-Christian crimes with 'the charms of a highly polished style.'" Sophia tied off a red thread with a hidden knot.

"So much for our literary brethren being able to appreciate daring fiction!" Cary said. "That bishop who reviewed *The Scarlet Letter* wrote that Hester Prynne's 'mind was more debauched than her body'! Hah! Hester is free, brave—like our dear Margaret, in fact."

"I wouldn't go so far as to compare them . . ." Sophia began, interrupted by the Hawthorne children Una and Julian dashing inside. They held out handfuls of blue columbines to their mother. She plumped them in a vase, and the children raced out the door. "The children are brown as berries already. They play outdoors all day."

"We're happy to have you in the Berkshires. Nat's presence has increased the town's literary cachet far beyond Concord's." Cary picked up a copy of Hawthorne's novel, with its red leather cover and brightly tooled gold letter 'A' in the center. "Is the book still selling well?"

Sophia nodded. A grin of fierce pride lit up her face. "Every time it sells out an edition, they reprint another thousand copies. James Fields is so pleased with his company's best-selling author that he sends us cases of claret, boxes of cigars, and lots of books. We just received that lurid novel *Typee* by Mr. Melville. Mr. Fields even sent us tickets to Jenny Lind's recital in Boston. Not that we'll go. I can't tear Nat away from his study."

"He must be pleased at his book's success."

"Yes, for the first time, his writing has earned not only accolades but solid cash. Without a doubt, the subject was a great risk: a shameless woman's adultery and love for a Puritan minister—then bearing his child! Nat was afraid it would be seen as too gloomy or too scandalous. When he read the final pages to me, I sobbed without stop. My heart was broken. I went to bed with a sick headache. Nat glowed—he felt quite triumphant."

"Most reviews were all he could hope for. They called it the 'finest fiction to appear in this country, possessing tragic power and depth,'" Cary recalled.

"When he wrote it, Nat was afraid. He told me, 'It's either very good or very bad. I don't know which.'"

Cary picked up a sheaf of clippings that Sophia had been gluing in an album. She leafed through, murmuring printed words: "Disgusting,' 'filth,' 'nauseous amour of a Puritan pastor.' Hmmm. Not exactly adulatory."

Sophia turned to early pages in the album, reading "'wizard power over language,' 'style above reproach,' 'glorious genius.' Fields is begging for more stories. He promises to publish right away, à-la-Steam Engine." She clamped shut the lid on the glue pot. "Let's go outside. I want to keep an eye on the children."

They joined her son and daughter, who were picking the first ripe raspberries. Their teeth were smeared with red. "More scarlet!" Sophia laughed, then asked Cary, "How is your baby?"

"Well enough." Cary popped a raspberry in her mouth. She seemed preoccupied as she stared at the shining waters of the Stockbridge Bowl. A blinding reflection slanted into her eyes and she shaded them with her hand. "I wish I could say the same for Will."

"Surely the father is pleased with his baby?" Sophia examined her friend's expression with curiosity.

"'Pleased' is not an emotion I attribute to Mr. William Tappan. Impassive, stagnant, soporific perhaps, but nothing so dynamic as 'pleased.'" Cary stripped a pine branch of needles and cones, heaving the pine cones as far as she could. "Ever since we married, I've discovered I stand as much chance of enlivening my husband's alleged 'personality' as moving a star."

"I suppose calmness is preferable to outright neglect of one's babies," Sophia said, thinking of their friend Ellery's disdain for his progeny.

Cary understood the allusion to Ellen's mate. "We can't compare Ellery and Will. You might as well compare a tornado to a turnip."

Sophia changed the subject. "What do you hear from Margaret? Ever since the French army overcame Rome—on the fourth of July last year of all days—her columns haven't appeared in the *Tribune*. What an inglorious end to a republic, only twenty months old."

Una tugged her mother's apron. She gestured to her pail of raspberries. "Look how many I picked! Can we make jam?" She flitted away, back to the tall bushes.

"Margaret was courageous during the siege of Rome," Sophia mused. "With grapeshot, bullets, and cannonballs exploding all around, she tended the dying in a hospital. I did hear they staffed the hospitals with prostitutes released from prison. Imagine—Margaret in charge of those floozies!"

"Of course, the patients were in no position to take advantage of the nurses' profession. Poor young men—university students, tradesmen, farmers—carried on stretchers to the hospital where doctors lopped off their mangled limbs." Cary shuddered. "And, by the way, those maligned harlots are patriots. They carried pans of wet clay to throw on fires raging throughout the city."

"I fear for Margaret's life. No matter how plucky she is, occupied territory is no place for a woman," Sophia said. "Where is she now?"

"Shopping for a freighter, soon to sail home." Cary kicked a heap of leaves with her toe. She put a finger to her lips. "Shush . . . nothing about the secret I told you. She's bringing what will seem to many like a big surprise."

Sophia nodded and said with a twinkle in her eye, "It must be her history of the revolution. It will cause quite a stir; her columns were so popular. Still, with the republic defeated, there's no sublime resolution to brag about."

"I don't suspect she'll be doing any bragging," Cary said.

Sophia tightened her mouth. "Happy endings are in short supply."

CHAPTER TWENTY-FIVE

Plans for the Future

MAY 1850, FLORENCE, ITALY

How to get home was Margaret Fuller's main concern throughout the spring. She tried not to think of what awaited her. Various schemes revolved in her head. She followed the *Shipping News* with greedy interest: comings, goings, the occasional sinking! She shook her head as she read of the alarming number of ships—even new-fangled steamers and luxurious packets—that foundered at sea, beset by storms or pirates. A sea voyage across the North Atlantic was a fearful thing, not to mention costly. Yet she had to go!

Perhaps I should travel by train with Nino and Ossoli to a French port, then board a fast steamship for a swift two-week passage. That would mean less time to suffer sea-sickness, she thought, *but where would I secure the funds?* For half the price, she could take a merchant vessel, powered only by sail, from Livorno to New York. It would take two months to cross, but would it be safe for her precious Nino?

Margaret wrote wealthy friends hinting at her need for a loan to book a well-appointed, fast vessel. No luck. No matter how anxious to see her they professed to be, her New England friends seemed to prefer she remain in Italy. Some, like Waldo Emerson, said so bluntly. What about her good friend Sophia Peabody Hawthorne? After the commercial success of her husband Nathaniel's novel *The Scarlet Letter*, surely they could spare a few hundred dollars? Apparently not, judging from the epistolary vacuum.

It was a conundrum. In Florence she had no prospect of employment, only debt and the terrifying threat of Ossoli's arrest. He had spent an hour interrogated by Austrian officials just the previous week and was only released through the American consul's intervention at Margaret's urging.

Fortuitously, a three-masted merchant brig, the *Elizabeth*, was docked nearby at Livorno. It would soon embark with cargo for New York. Perhaps human cargo as well? She and Ossoli set out to inspect the ship and meet its captain, an experienced helmsman named Seth Hasty. The evident seaworthiness of the ship heartened them, and Captain Hasty seemed most cordial, indeed quite capable and refined.

Margaret invited Hasty and his young wife, Catherine—also very agreeable—to visit her in Florence, where she aimed to extract more information about potential perils of the voyage. Her mind was a maelstrom of indecision. *Go? Stay? How? Where? They don't call it "filthy lucre" for nothing,* she thought, *but the absence of said filth is just as onerous as its presence in the wrong hands.*

She showed Florentine wonders to the couple. Margaret concluded that Catherine, an attractive twenty-six-year-old newlywed, was an amiable, excellent wife and Captain Hasty truly a high-minded gentleman. Hasty played chess with Ossoli, a pastime that required pantomime more than shared language. Catherine advised Margaret on requirements for the long voyage, and they shopped together for oranges, lemons, hardtack, and a medical kit. Margaret accumulated reams of cloth for Nino's diapers and even ventured to a local farm with Catherine to buy a nanny goat for milk.

"Does one wish a goat with floppy or upright ears?" Margaret asked, no detail too miniscule to be debated for the health of her son. Goats milled around them, lactating does with drooping udders and males with beards and horns. The goats bumped their heads against the women's skirts, munching hay and angling to be stroked. Margaret and

Catherine held shawls over their noses to stifle the farmyard's pungent, ammoniac odor.

"These creatures are so agile, I do believe they could climb the rigging," Catherine mumbled as the goats leapt about, clambered up stacks of boards, and jumped over water buckets. Nino squeaked as he lurched towards a brown nanny goat, seizing her neck in his arms. The animal sniffed the child's mouth, tickling his lips with its whiskers. Nino chortled and the goat bleated with no hint of dismay. Margaret pronounced, "That's the one! We'll call her 'Ba.'"

"Ba?" asked Catherine. "Isn't that a bit too common? What about Bottom or Puck from *Mid-Summer Night's Dream*?"

"Ba is my friend Elizabeth Barrett Browning's nickname," Margaret said. "Since the ship is named the *Elizabeth,* it's surely a good omen."

Catherine tapped the goat's shoulder with a long stalk of mullein. "I hereby christen you Mistress Ba of Italia," she said. She pointed to the bare, scuffed-up dirt denuded of any vestige of greenery. Nary a speck of clover brightened the dusty ground, picked clean by the hungry goats. "One more thing we must buy: goat food, although cook and steward can feed her scraps."

"*Andiamo,*" Margaret said, giving Ba's ears a farewell scratch.

Once back in the city, she led her guest on a Grand Tour of Florence, roaming the streets and trotting over the arched bridges of the Arno.

At the dim splendor inside Santissima Annunziata with its colored marble arches and piers, Catherine's voice hushed in awe. Hundreds of silver lamps unspooled threads of light in the shadowy church. When she looked up at the ornate, carved gold ceiling over the nave, her pupils narrowed at its radiance. "What brilliance! It's like looking at heaven!" She spun around and gasped, "So much marble everywhere! We're hauling hundreds of tons of Carrara marble in the hold of the *Elizabeth,*" she told Margaret. "Not just blocks of marble but finished statues, too. There's a full-length sculpture of Senator John Calhoun destined for South Carolina."

Margaret's mouth tightened. "I know that statue. I saw it in Hiram Powers's studio. I begged Hiram to make it ugly, just like slavery, which that scoundrel Calhoun is always defending. Hiram wouldn't do it, of course. He insisted on portraying Calhoun in a toga, as if that disgusting villain were a noble Roman!"

She dragged Catherine outside, where, after the pseudo-twilight of the church, bright daylight made them squint. "Speaking of someone who merits eternal damnation," Margaret perked up, "let's go to the Duomo."

They soon stood surrounded by the multi-colored grandeur of Santa Maria del Fiore church. Margaret waved a hand towards a painting of Dante in a crimson robe holding a folio of his *Divine Comedy*. Below him belched eternal flames of hell. "That's where Calhoun belongs with all slaveholders," Margaret said, scrunching her mouth with distaste.

She pointed to a long winding road in the painting that depicted purgatory. It curled around and around, ever upwards towards a summit. "Purgatory is where I'll be on my voyage back to America, but—" Margaret funneled her hands into a trumpet shape on her lips, "Ta ta! When we get to my native shores, Gabriel will welcome me to the American Garden of Eden." In the painting, Adam and Eve consort atop the mountain in their verdant paradise.

"Heaven and hell and a curving road in between—that painting shows it all," Catherine mused. "But why is our voyage your purgatory?"

Margaret looked grave. "Some people think I betrayed my principles by marrying. I'll be in limbo during the passage. Does heaven or hell await me at home? Will I be vilified or rewarded?"

Catherine caught her mood. "Why does Dante call life's journey a divine comedy? What did he write on the gates of hell? 'Abandon all hope, ye who enter here.' Hardly a droll message. I would never abandon hope, would you?"

Margaret evaded answering. "Perhaps Dante's title should be *Human Tragedy*." She chewed on the implications in her mind. "I suppose it depends on where you are on the path. I'm almost forty. Perhaps I've passed the peak without a glimpse of paradise ahead."

She looked at Catherine with a sense of foreboding. "Tons of marble in the *Elizabeth*'s hold, you say? Won't that make our ship too heavy to float?" She shivered, chilled by the church's cool, marble-clad walls, striped in green and bone-white.

Catherine patted Margaret's arm. "We'll ride the waves with impunity, I assure you. Captain Hasty is a marvel!" Catherine looked again at the Inferno's curls of orange fire and frowned. "Those painted flames look like ocean waves. It makes me shudder." She tightened her shawl across her shoulders.

"My husband has a fear of the sea," Margaret whispered, "ever since a prophecy predicted he'd die by drowning."

CHAPTER TWENTY-SIX

An Ocean Voyage

MAY 17, 1850, EMBARKING FROM LIVORNO, ITALY

When the dreary spring rains finally abated, Margaret bid farewell to Eizabeth and Robert Browning and *arrivederci* to Italy. In the harbor of Livorno she, Ossoli, and little Nino clambered on board a dinghy to row out to the *Elizabeth*. The three-masted sailing vessel sat low in the Mediterranean, weighed down by its cargo of marble.

As the open water between shore and rowboat widened, Ossoli was seized by a need to stand. While the boat rocked unsteadily, he stood straight and saluted his homeland, a soldier without his uniform. Margaret gestured for him to sit down, but he shrugged her off. He bellowed the *Risorgimento* song: "O my country, so beautiful and lost." With tears in her eyes Margaret joined in: "May the lord strengthen me to bear these sufferings."

"Angelo, my dear, we should rejoice we were there when Italy needed us. We're possessed of a great history." She tossed him a handkerchief, and he wiped his eyes. Notes of the revolutionary hymn *O bella libertà* drifted to them from shore. "We'll tell the world—we bring a warning and a prophecy for the future."

Ossoli threw a kiss to his receding land with both hands. "Farewell, until . . ." he said in Italian, then crumpled onto the stern seat.

From the bow, with Nino in her lap, Margaret scooped a handful of water and splashed her husband. "I baptize thee an American. Thou art hereby launched on a grand adventure."

His face brightened, and he straightened. The day was bright and crisp. A briny salt air freshened as the tide began to turn, wavelets racing outward. Flags flew from the *Elizabeth*'s rigging, flapping in the mild breeze, as they clambered aboard the boat. Margaret soon settled her husband and child, along with their trunks, in their cabin. The nanny goat brought to supply milk for Nino brayed at seeing them. Nino ran to it, shouting "Ba!" and hopped on its back, arms encircling the goat's neck. The goat bucked and ran over the deck, scattering sailors who were uncoiling tarry ropes to hoist the sails.

The seamen hauled up the anchor, green seaweed twisted around the line. The sails slithered up the masts with a hiss, then filled with a "whump!" of wind. The ship bolted forward like a horse unleashed. "Mind the boom!" Captain Hasty shouted, although the wooden beams, broad as pine trees, stretched horizontally far above every head.

There was no sign of any storm on the horizon. Captain Hasty and his bride Catherine expected nothing but sunny skies to bless their recent union. Margaret was teary waving good-bye to the shore.

"Why so sad?" Catherine asked.

"I found myself in my element in Italy," she said. "All the encumbrances that used to weary me in Boston vanished. Perchance I didn't become a bird in the air, but I did feel like a fish in water." Margaret watched the land recede. "I found love, had a baby, and I fought for a noble cause. Those were the best years of my life."

With Nino and his goat capering about, Margaret soon became merry. The ship cut a sharp slice through the water, its bowsprit pointed west. After years abroad, Margaret seemed gleeful at the prospect of returning to her native land. Her face lit up when she told Nino of what she called the "rush, bang, buzz" of America. Her descriptions of whizzing trains, giant steamships, and jostling crowds sounded thrilling after years of war.

"I have so much to tell the New World," she told Catherine. "They mustn't repeat the Old World's mistakes." Sometimes she grew pensive and seemed to dread their return. She feared what she told Catherine was the "social inquisition" of her fellow Americans. "Almost no one knows I am married. I only told my mother recently."

Catherine, who knew Margaret was a famous author who wrote for *The New-York Tribune*, expressed surprise that she'd booked passage on their slow cargo ship, powered by sail.

"I lack funds for a fast steamboat," Margaret explained. "Yet, in fact, a slow passage suits my purpose. It affords more time to finish my project." She displayed her fingers, smudged with ink, and hugged a lap desk to her chest. "My history!"

Catherine, Captain Hasty, the ship's cook, and the steward did everything possible to make their guests comfortable. The family was a favorite with the entire crew. The three Ossolis had liberty not only of their cabin and a spacious parlor but freedom to explore the whole ship—the deck, galley, and even the cargo hold below. Nino could be seen swinging on the ropes and sliding across the mopped deck each day. He followed the steward, his particular friend, around to deliver hard tack and oranges to the crew.

Ossoli was a favorite. Every morning he had English lessons with Catherine. At her instruction, he practiced saying, "It is a pleasure to meet you" and bowed and kissed her hand. His face became ruddy from sun and stiff wind. His hair grew so prodigiously, his ringlets were as long as a finger.

On many a night, Ossoli sang Italian ditties to sailors on night watch, and Margaret pointed out constellations in the starry skies. When phosphorescent algae lit up the sea like a milky trough of stars, Margaret woke up Nino to see it. "Look! Stars above us and below!" She cradled the groggy child. "You'll never see this on land!" He had forgotten by morning. "No matter," she told Angelo. "It's the sweetest dream for him."

Margaret spent much time writing her history of the short-lived Roman Republic. Her fingers always smeared with ink, she carried a lap desk everywhere, clutching it tight to her chest. She considered the manuscript so precious that when wind ruffled the pages, she retreated below deck to work by lamplight, fearful she might lose her words.

Not one week after they embarked, tragedy struck. Off Gibraltar, Captain Hasty came down with smallpox. For seven days the boat lay at anchor while Hasty, covered in red sores, thrashed and raved with burning fever. Tangled in his sheets and crossing his arms above his head, he yelled, "Spiders!" and dodged imaginary foes.

Catherine and Margaret nursed him around the clock, taking turns as the ship's bells sounded. They swabbed his brow with cool cloths that soon became hot and put ointment on his blisters. Ossoli wandered in and out of the cabin, setting up Hasty's chess set in hopes he'd soon recover enough to play. He sang Italian hymns, his voice soaring to the topsail on *Ave Maria*.

Catherine wrung her hands with worry, so distraught she wished to fling herself overboard. Margaret rubbed her back and spooned broth into her mouth when Catherine neglected to eat. "Courage, my dear!" Margaret exhorted. "We must keep our strength to help Captain Hasty."

Their ministrations were of no avail. When the captain sucked a last raspy breath, then ceased to exhale, Ossoli knocked over the king piece on the chess board.

"You think he'll be sick forever," Catherine whispered to Margaret. "Then he's gone, and it really is forever."

The last service to the dead was to wrap Hasty's pock-marked body in a canvas shroud. First Mate Henry Bangs, who took over as commander and navigator, presided at the funeral. "May our dear Captain," he said in a scratchy voice, "move gently with the ebb and flow of the tide and come to anchor on the shores of paradise."

The crew doffed their hats and formed a line, heads bowed and silent. One played a harmonica, its drifting notes settling hard like a funeral bell. Two sailors heaved the body onto a wooden plank, which they tipped off the side of the ship. The sailcloth-wrapped bundle, looking more like stained laundry than a much-respected man, slid down. A splash, ripples, then the waters closed.

"Good-bye, my love!" Catherine cried, hanging over the railing. "May flights of angels sing thee to thy rest!" She covered her eyes with a handkerchief. The other vessels in the harbor—instructed by health officials to keep their distance—flew banners in tribute. A solemn drumbeat boomed over the water. Margaret hugged Catherine; they sobbed together.

"A noble man!" Margaret faced the row of mourners and asked Catherine, "If I may?"

Margaret began to improvise a eulogy, half remembering an old Scottish ballad about a sea king and half extemporizing.

> "His battered boat pulls out from shore and swiftly o'er the water glides.
> The swelling sail heeds not the gale but safely through the tempest rides.
> Now sunk below, he rises high . . ."

Catherine tottered, so overcome she could barely stand. Ossoli held her up. Margaret's voice grew stronger as the wind intensified, almost whipping away her words.

> "Like a feather on a mighty wave, now torments cease, he's hushed in peace.
> He rises in triumph from his liquid bed. He died as he lived . . . on the sea."

Catherine wobbled, nearly tumbling to the deck, her eyes swimming in tears. Margaret held out a pebble-sized piece of sea glass, shining like an emerald. "Take this," she said. "Smoothed and polished by the waves, it proves something broken can be made beautiful. One day, your memories of Captain Hasty will also shine."

• • •

With Captain Hasty gone, command passed to First Mate Henry Bangs who did his best. Squinting through the sextant and juggling compass, spyglass, and other implements at the wheel, he could not be sure of their latitude. He scrawled calculations on a chart but came to no useful conclusions. He aimed the ship's trajectory south of the setting sun.

Margaret hardly suspected that her little boy Nino would also catch smallpox, for she'd been sure to get him vaccinated before they left Italy. Yet, while the ship was in quarantine and was swept with sulfur, Nino broke out in pustules and a scorching fever. The darling boy—almost two years old—was such a favorite, galloping over the deck astride his goat. The sailors all said rosaries for him. One carved him a scrimshaw whistle. Catherine was tortured with guilt, remembering how Nino had bounced on her husband's lap and begged for stories before the Captain showed symptoms. Hasty had bellowed sea chanteys as Nino clapped. "Give me some time, to blow the man down!" his deep, bass voice had echoed.

Margaret and her husband were in hysterics. Ossoli, who never talked much because he spoke little English, sat by Nino's side night and day, trying to amuse him with rope tricks. He showed him how to tie a bowline: "The rabbit goes around the tree and into the hole . . . ," but Nino couldn't open his swollen eyes. Margaret chattered and told stories to arouse Nino's spirits. Her husband listened, prayed silently, and fretted.

Their love for Nino and each other was clear, but his illness instigated a quarrel. They disagreed over how to treat the baby's illness, with Ossoli arguing for prayer and Margaret forcing soup on the boy. When Nino vomited, his father cleaned up the greenish bile. "Leave him to God!" he urged, saying the Hail Mary over and over. A quick volley of Italian followed, each firing harsh words before they remembered to lower their voices. "Are we being punished?" Ossoli asked. Margaret threw up her hands.

In the end, all they could do was wipe cool, wet cloths all over the boy's little body. Margaret and Ossoli sang to him as he lay limp in his hammock. Catherine played her zither, accompanying the English tunes. During one serenade, as Margaret sang the Quaker hymn "'Tis the gift to be simple, 'tis the gift to be free," Nino started waving his hands in time to the music. "Thanks be to the Lord!" Catherine said. "He's feeling better!"

Margaret and Ossoli rejoiced. He grabbed her hands and danced her in a circle around the cabin. They laughed, kissed, and hugged until they cried. "Deliverance!" Margaret exulted, wiping her cheeks. Her husband sank to his knees in prayer, making the sign of the cross in forceful stabs at his chest. Margaret hugged Nino and smoothed his sweaty hair after his fever broke.

She was relieved when the pock marks faded, leaving his skin once more smooth and pink. She wanted Nino to look his best when her family saw him for the first time. She wanted him to look like an angel.

Arriving home with a husband and son would be a shock to her friends. Most still didn't know she was married with a child. Given her very vocal opposition to marriage, no one expected her to get married or pregnant. Then there was the fact that she had just turned forty, a confirmed spinster in the eyes of many. She'd celebrated her fortieth birthday on the voyage, not an unalloyed pleasure to her mind. While Catherine, Ossoli, and Nino showered her with hugs and good wishes, breaking out cake and grog for a party, Margaret felt unaccountably incomplete.

"My life is half over," she told Catherine. "What do I have to show for it?" She held her lap desk close to her heart. "Here is my most important contribution. This manuscript, my history of the republic, will vindicate my existence."

Sea gulls squalled overhead. *Are they hailing my pronouncement,* she wondered, *or laughing?*

The ship sailed on, approaching North America with a steadily following breeze that filled the sails and lifted their hearts.

PART TWO

CHAPTER TWENTY-SEVEN

Bad News

JULY 22, 1850, CONCORD, MASSACHUSETTS

Ellery Channing burst into Waldo Emerson's study with the news. His face red, long hair flying, fingers smeared with newsprint, he waved the New York paper above him like a flag flapping wildly in the wind. Emerson wrinkled his brow, startled by the unseemly interruption. It could be no ordinary cause that propelled anyone into the master's most sacrosanct retreat. But then Ellery was erratic, prone to hysterics. His extreme excitability was a quirk that either attracted or repelled acquaintances, depending on one's tolerance for volatility.

So startled was Emerson by such an abrupt appearance, he broke the nib of his quill, which spilled a puddle of black ink over his notes. Only later did he perceive the irony—he was revising his famous essay on Friendship. The terrible news Ellery brought made Emerson rethink the meaning of friendship.

"O blackest day! Margaret is dead!" Ellery yelled as he pressed the rumpled newspaper under his mentor's nose.

Emerson scanned the lead story. His eyes widened when he saw her picture, read her name: Madam Margaret Fuller Ossoli. Drowned, along with husband and son. What? Margaret? No!—his mind raced—but she's on a boat! We're planning a party with pound cake and lemonade to welcome her! "Impossible! Unimaginable! Inconceivable!" Could a mountain melt? No! His mind screamed.

Ellery thought it the better part of discretion not to mention Emerson's frequent admonishment to him: Never use three words when one will do.

Emerson adjusted his glasses, and soon the inky marks congealed into readability. He drooped as he gleaned the tragic particulars. His friend Margaret Fuller had drowned within sight of her natal shores. Instead of welcoming her to Concord as planned, now he must mourn her perpetual absence from his hearth.

He clapped a hand to his chest, feeling a peculiar emptiness. "No, no," he said aloud. "It can't be true! Margaret is unstoppable, unsinkable. She must have escaped the wreck!"

"I'm sorry to be the bearer of such news—my dear sister-in-law is no more!" Ellery said. "You can imagine how Ellen and the children are wailing at home! To lose a sister and a beloved auntie, when we expected to welcome her this week . . . I must write a poem to commemorate her." He flicked an invisible tear from his cheek, evincing histrionic more than sincere grief. He looked keenly at Emerson. "What would you have me do, O best Waldo?" He placed a comforting hand on the older man's shoulder.

Emerson felt an urge to write. He began to compose a eulogy aloud: "My dear friend Margaret will never be absent from my heart." His mouth tightened as he added to himself, *Obstinate, contrary, overbearing, supercilious, I can no more forgive than forget her!*

"We must arrange a memorial service!" Emerson sat up straight. The thought of a formal tribute electrified him like a lightning bolt. After all, he and she had worked together for years on *The Dial*. Her legacy, though considerably more abbreviated, was linked to his own. Commensurate? Hardly, but celebrating Margaret was almost like celebrating himself—at least insofar as they agreed.

"Margaret, dear Margaret," he said, regaining Ellery's attention. "The red room across the hall where we worked together on *The Dial*, now forever bare, will evermore be empty of your resounding laugh.

For those two years, we were like mountain climbers yoked together. We scaled the heights of Philosophy in America—Prometheus bringing the gift of fire to the frozen masses. Now you have fallen from on high." An inconvenient thought intruded: Given her disdain for propriety and her laxity when it came to convention in recent days, would her plunge drag the Sage of Concord down as well?

Why, oh why, he asked himself, *didn't she heed my counsel to remain in Europe? With her defiance of decency, she faced only oblivion on these shores. In Europe, she was a voice for liberty. Here, she would have been a token of licentiousness.*

"I must go to the site of the shipwreck," he announced. "If she's indeed gone, we must find her body—and her little son's—to bury them with honor."

Ellery hesitated. He offered, "The strain of the trip and an arduous search would be injurious to you, my Waldo. You're crushed in spirit. Let me go with Henry in your stead."

Waldo pondered the proposal. It had merit. Ellery and Henry were young and hearty, most experienced in outdoor activities. *While I*—he sighed—*am more fit for sitting at my desk or delivering a lecture.* Rambling over the seashore, sifting through mounds of seaweed, interrogating witnesses—it was hardly congruent with his area of expertise.

Letters! Now that was where he excelled. He'd write Margaret's nearest and dearest to inform them of her passing and invite a select few to Concord for a memorial tribute. Lidian would not appreciate such a gathering. She constantly complained that his hospitality to guests reduced her to an exhausted innkeeper. Plus, she never liked Margaret, except in the early days before *The Dial* when Lidian attended the sessions Margaret called Conversations. Lidian had never conversed much at those gatherings, he'd heard. A wife knows her place.

Aware that Ellery awaited his word, Emerson consented. "Go at once. I'll pay all expenses. Take as long as it takes."

Emerson started upright with a sudden urgent recollection, swatting his forehead with a hand. He leapt from his chair in such a surge, his knees quaked and he came near to crumpling. Ellery caught him and nodded as Emerson charged: "The work she was bringing us, her history of Italy's quest for independence! You must—you shall—find the manuscript. It's imperative we rescue her last, most important work!"

Ellery saluted and vowed to go immediately to Fire Island. He and Henry Thoreau would scour the beach, the shallows, the wreckage for any vestige—corporal or literary—of Margaret. He left in haste.

Emerson had naught to fill his heavy heart save the news accounts.

CHAPTER TWENTY-EIGHT

Reports of a Loss

JULY 20, 1850
OBITUARY *NEW-YORK TRIBUNE*
BY WALTER WHITMAN

S. Margaret Fuller, 40,
Most Famous Woman in the World, Drowned

S. Margaret Fuller Ossoli, 40, *Tribune* literary critic and foreign correspondent, perished in a shipwreck on July 19, along with her husband Giovanni Angelo Ossoli, 29, and their son Angelo Ossoli, aged nearly two. The boy's body was found, but there was no trace of the parents' remains. An investigation is ongoing.

S. Margaret Fuller Ossoli was born on May 23, 1810, in Cambridgeport, Massachusetts. Her father, attorney Timothy Fuller, imposed a rigorous course of study on his eldest child, teaching her to read at age four and translate from Latin by age six. Margaret went on to master German, French, Italian, and Greek. From 1837 to 1844 she taught classes and led a subscriber series called "Conversations" in locales around Boston. From 1840 to '42 she was the first editor of the Transcendentalist journal *The Dial*. *Tribune* editor Horace Greeley praised her eyewitness dispatches to *The Tribune* on European culture and politics for their "passages of rare beauty, vigor of thought, and habitual fearlessness."

Mrs. Fuller Ossoli was returning to the United States after three years in Europe when the merchant brig *Elizabeth* struck a sandbar off the southern coast of Long Island. A fierce gale broke up the ship, sinking it within sight of land. Eight of the twenty-three aboard the ship are believed lost.

Fuller's controversial 1845 book, *Woman in the Nineteenth Century*, called for women's independence and equality. Although the critic Edgar Allan Poe denounced its "unmitigated radicalism," the book was commercially successful. It has been called "doubtless the most brilliant, complete, and scholarly statement ever made on the subject" by Caroline Dall, a leading proponent of women's rights. Mr. Poe termed it "a book which few women in the country could have written and no woman in the country would have published, with the exception of Miss Fuller."

Although Margaret Fuller was accused of egotism, arrogance, and having "a man's ambition in a woman's body," she won converts by force of personality. She charmed by her power of persuasion. Her company was valued by the wisest, most cultivated minds of our era, such as the lecturer Ralph Waldo Emerson and fabulist Nathaniel Hawthorne. She was considered the most entertaining, stimulating conversationalist of our time. She called for an equally original homegrown literature, "an American bard with poems to match our mountains."

Mrs. Fuller Ossoli's blazing light was more like fireworks than a single candle. An inveterate enemy of convention and prejudice, her motto was "the only object in life is to grow." She urged women to think for themselves and act to spur social reform, to resist much and obey little.

The fate of her work in progress on the recent Italian revolution, an uprising that futilely sought to unite the peninsula in a democratic republic, is unknown. Mrs. Fuller Ossoli threw her whole soul into this work. She had manifold opportunities for observation and was herself a gallant participant in the unsuccessful struggle against foreign tyranny. One cannot forgo the hope that this work will be recovered.

Yesterday, this *Tribune* correspondent searched for miles along the Long Island strand, finding only wrack and ruin of the ship. But in penning this obituary, one sight seems germane. A tiny spider was seeking to spin a web by connecting two fragments of oaken spars projecting from the sand. Perched on a splinter, the spider launched silky filament after filament into the void. Tirelessly it projected threads until one caught on another timber, an anchor for its web. Margaret Fuller Ossoli may have melted into the sea, but the gossamer threads of her thoughts continue to unreel, linking soul to soul.

NEW-YORK TRIBUNE CORRESPONDENT, MARGARET FULLER OSSOLI, LOST AT SEA

JULY 21, 1850

EDITORIAL BY HORACE GREELEY, EDITOR AND PUBLISHER

A great soul has passed from this earth by the death of MARGARET FULLER, by marriage Marchesa Ossoli (1810–1850), who with her husband and child drowned in the wreck of the brig *Elizabeth* on Friday afternoon last. From 1844 Margaret headed our Department of Reviews and Criticism, writing with grace and acuity. From 1846, living in Rome, Margaret filed stories of Italy's attempt to form a unified republic and throw off the yoke of foreign sovereigns. After the patriots surrendered to the French army's assassins of liberty,

Margaret and her husband G.A. Ossoli (both of whom actively supported the Republican movement) deemed it expedient to sail for Fuller's native land. She brought with her a manuscript containing a history of the movement, the fate of which is yet to be determined.

We mourn the loss of our gifted friend and possibly of her last work. We lament that the message of one so lofty in intellect, so devoted to human liberty, so ready to dare and endure for the upraising of her sex and all races, may have perished. America has produced no woman who has surpassed Margaret Fuller in mental endowments and acquirements. That she is gone sorely grieves us. What an additional misfortune if her works are not promptly collected, that we may gauge her enormous contribution to humanity!

CHAPTER TWENTY-NINE

Searching for Remains

JULY 25, 1850, LONG ISLAND, NEW YORK STATE

Henry Thoreau approached a bedraggled young woman who was spreading out limp papers on an oak table before a roaring chimney fire. She turned over the damp pages, careful not to tear them. "Mrs. Hasty, I presume?" he asked. When she nodded, unable to speak as her chest heaved, he continued in a solemn voice. "I am Henry D. Thoreau of Concord, Massachusetts. Margaret Fuller is," he cleared his throat, "I mean Margaret Fuller Ossoli *was* my friend."

She buried her face in a handkerchief, hiccupping with grief. Her shoulders shook.

Thoreau was taken aback but persevered. During his train ride he'd rehearsed interrogatory remarks. Timid to the point of tongue-tied when encountering a strange woman, he didn't trust himself to speak *ex tempore*. "I've learned of the recent tragic events you witnessed aboard the frigate *Elizabeth*. I take the liberty of soliciting your testimony. I've been tasked with uncovering intelligence about the fate of the passengers, in particular my friend, Margaret Fuller Ossoli, accompanied by Giovanni Angelo Ossoli and her son Angelino Ossoli."

Catherine's eyes widened at what appeared a formal inquisition. "How may I help you, Mr. Thoreau?"

Thoreau continued his studied recital. "Ralph Waldo Emerson, of whom you've no doubt heard, has charged me with gathering knowledge on the Ossoli family and any of their possessions extant. We wish to locate any papers belonging to Madam Fuller Ossoli, especially the manuscript of her history of last year's Roman Revolution."

"It's not here." She indicated the pages laid out to dry. "These are letters. You should look for her lap desk. She kept the manuscript inside." She shook drops from a damp page already curling, its ink marks smeared. "Margaret thought the book would be her *magnum opus*. She called it 'a drama of blood and tears.' You must find it."

"My friend Ellery Channing and I have searched the site of the wreck. Channing found a few soggy letters, but only detritus on the beach: mangled timbers, ragged bolts of silk, sacks of juniper berries, and casks of bitter almonds."

She spoke softly: "Yes, remnants of our cargo. Bitter relics of an illustrious life, to be sure."

"I realize asking you to describe the heartbreaking event is painful, but I entreat you to give a full account. Madam Fuller Ossoli's friends—indeed all her countrymen and women—will be forever in your debt. We're preparing a memorial to celebrate her life. Her friends will soon meet in Concord to remember the shining light that was Margaret Fuller's presence." He swallowed, having delivered his prepared remarks. Spontaneity was now called for. He gulped. Perhaps this young woman could enlighten him with no further prompting.

Catherine rose to the occasion, telling her story as if burned into her memory. "May my reminiscences offset the dark hole of her absence," she said. She sat on a stool by the fire, its flames coloring her face, and narrated the first part of the voyage almost robotically. When she arrived at her husband's death, she broke down in tears. "If my dearest Captain Hasty had lived, none of this would've happened."

"Everything about that voyage was upside-down," she went on. A stray thought intruded. "Take Margaret and her husband—an unlikely pair to be sure, but so devoted to Nino and each other. Most days, she talked; he listened. Such a handsome young man in his uniform. He spoke little English, never said much, but sang and prayed in Italian all the time."

Her shoulders slumped with fatigue. Thoreau handed her a mug of cider from his flask, and she drank half without stopping. "I'll skip to the day of the shipwreck. We'd packed our trunks for landing in New York harbor the next day. Margaret showed me the sailor hat she'd picked out for Nino to wear. He was sitting on her lap clapping his hands, and she asked him, 'What was your favorite part of our whole, long sea voyage?' That little poppet, quick as you please, said, 'Right now!' For him, what was past was gone. It was the present moment he loved." She sighed. "I wish I could say the same."

"That night the wind picked up with gale force. It wailed so loud, it was like all the hounds of Hell baying at once. We were rocking up and down with the swells. When the boat pitched over, I almost rolled out of bed. I could hear waves crashing over the gunwales with a *whomp*! The wind was whistling, the rigging clanking, the lines whining and sails flapping. Someone yelled, 'Cut away!' and two masts crashed to the deck. *Boom*! Everything hanging on hooks was jerking back and forth. You should have seen the oil lamps rocking. How I wished Captain Hasty were at the helm. I know what he would say: 'If we must die, let us die calmly.'"

Her eyes seemed to be seeing not the chimney fire but the tempest. "Just then a wave picked up the whole boat—if you can believe it—and slammed it down on a sandbar. You never heard such a *thump*—like thunder, and then the keel scraping, dragging, stuck in the sand."

Caught up in the story, Thoreau forgot his shyness. "I heard your cargo in the hold was tons of Italian marble."

"There was even a statue of Senator Calhoun. I know because Margaret complained she didn't want to share her homecoming with someone who favored slavery. She knew the sculptor, Mr. Hiram Powers, from Rome and tried to get him to make the sculpture ugly, 'like slavery,' she said."

"Margaret was always true to the cause of liberty," Thoreau interjected.

"Now that I think of it, the one bad omen when we left Italy was how low the *Elizabeth* sat in the water, with all that heavy marble," Catherine said. "Sure enough, the blocks rammed through the hull, and we started filling up with water. The whole stern was sinking. You couldn't hear anybody unless they shouted right in your ear, but the steward and Mr. Bangs dragged us to the forecastle. It was completely dark, hours before dawn, and rain was pounding down like a waterfall. The ship was breaking into slivers. I almost got dashed overboard by a wave, but the steward grabbed me by the hair and saved me." She stopped to drink the last of the cider.

She looked shipwrecked herself. "I'll go no more a-sailing," she said in a quavering voice. "Salt water doesn't like me."

"Are you able to go on with the tale?" Thoreau asked.

She nodded and pulled herself up straight. "Margaret was holding Nino tight and singing to him. I don't know how she stayed so calm. She braced her legs against the hull while her husband and the baby nurse prayed in Italian. When dawn came, we could see the shore, but we were still stuck fast. Some people on shore finally fired a mortar with a lifeline, but the rope couldn't reach us against the wind. We saw a big life-saving skiff on the beach, which we kept expecting would come save us. The sea was too wild; they never launched it. People on shore could see us. We waved and shouted to them, but not one came to help. They were too busy scooping up salvage that washed ashore. What scurvy thieves, if you'll pardon my language! I heard later they said if they knew someone important was on board, they would've saved her. More likely, they would've stripped the rings from her fingers."

She hung her head. "Nino's nanny goat leapt overboard. I didn't know a goat could squeal like that. Nino saw it go and stopped whimpering, held out his hands as if to catch it. He was soaked inside a blanket Margaret wrapped around him. "Make it stop, Mama!" he cried.

She continued, gripped by memory. "Margaret tried to distract him with a story. 'You know about King Canute who sat on his throne by the sea and ordered the waves of the incoming tide to stop?'"

"'What happened then?' Nino asked. Margaret held up a hand and shouted above the roar, 'I command you! Stop!' The waves still pounded. 'We can stop tyrants but not the tide,' she said. I heard her tell Nino, 'Death is different than you think. It's luckier. The sea is not the end of life.'" Catherine's eyes leaked tears. "Lucky? Not the end? My heart was breaking."

"Many of the crew decided to swim. They jumped off holding broken spars like a raft to float on and tumbled over and over as the breakers crashed on them. Mr. Bangs said we all had to go. The bow was starting to smash up. Margaret said she couldn't swim. She gave her life jacket to a sailor. The steward took Nino, who was clinging to Margaret. He put Nino in a canvas bag tied around his neck and jumped overboard. I went in after them, holding on to a rope tied around a plank. My Lord, how I was lifted up by the waves and slammed down as the current sucked me back out! Only Providence got me to shore, bruised all over. I felt like I swallowed the whole ocean—and half the sand from the beach."

"Is that it?" Thoreau asked.

She shook her head. "I saw a wave big as a cliff sweep over the deck. The cook, who was the last to leave Margaret, said she had her head bent to her knees as if she wanted to die. Her last words, he said, were 'I see nothing but death before me. I shall never reach the shore.' Then a huge wave crashed over her."

"Always a *crescendo*, never *diminuendo* for Margaret," Thoreau murmured to himself.

"For all the howling wind, the air felt so *empty* once she was gone." Her voice choked. "Nino didn't survive. We found his little body on the sand. It was still warm, believe it or not. I carried him to the nearest house and we put him in a sailor's sea chest for a coffin. The next day I looked everywhere for Margaret's book. Scavengers were stealing everything that washed ashore, but why would they steal her book? I doubt they can read. Such a loss—Margaret said the History would make her mark; she'd leave her 'footprints on the sands of time.'"

"Thank you, Mrs. Hasty. History will record your words." Thoreau rose, but she recounted one last memory.

"What I like to remember about the whole voyage is one sunny day on deck, with Margaret's hair blowing in the wind. She recited Shakespeare to Nino. 'These are pearls that were my eyes,' she said. 'Of my bones is coral made. Nothing of me but that suffers a sea change, into something rich and strange.' How Nino laughed!"

She expelled a big breath. "Please tell Mr. Emerson that Margaret spoke of him fondly and looked forward to their reunion. I wish you success in telling the story of her life. Too short by several score but—oh my Lord—it was rich and strange! I'll just add what I said when we consigned Captain Hasty's body to the sea: 'May flights of angels sing thee to thy rest.'"

CHAPTER THIRTY

Lost but Not Found

JULY 30, 1850, CONCORD, MASSACHUSETTS

Thoreau and Emerson walked by the shore of Walden Pond soon after the young man's return from Fire Island. The wind sounded a melancholy groan through the pines. Goldenrod stalks whipped back and forth like a sea of tattered yellow ribbons. "Our friends are coming for Margaret's memorial. Please tell me everything you saw," Emerson said. "Spare me nothing. Seeing the scene will help me accept the loss."

Thoreau sank to a flat rock and put his hand over his eyes, as if an intolerable glare blinded him. "Ellery and I spent three gruesome days searching for intelligence on Margaret's last hours. We looked for any trace of her possessions. We interviewed the crew, the captain's wife, and as many wreck-pickers as we could find before they vanished with the spoils."

"Is it true the ship was stuck fast, so close, just sixty rods offshore, for twelve hours, and *no one* came to their aid?" Emerson sounded incredulous at the divergence from his view of man's innate goodness.

"Yes, a very grim slice of humanity, those scavengers—thirty or forty at first, but then hundreds from all over Long Island. The beach was crawling with them, pilfering whatever washed ashore. The crew on the ship screamed for help and waved bandanas, desperate, but those vultures were too busy scooping up hats, rolls of fabric, and casks of almonds." His voice dripped with disgust. "They never launched the life boat—cowards! Someone eventually fired a lifeline, but it fell short. The excuse: violent wind, surf, and lashing rain."

"Did you find anything of Margaret's?"

"I found Ossoli's Civic Guard uniform jacket washed ashore. I cut a brass button off the coat that I'll send Margaret's mother. Ellery found a trunk with some letters. He and the captain's wife, Mrs. Hasty, laid the papers out to dry on a table in a nearby house."

"Was the ship flimsy? Is that why it was bashed apart? A stout brig should be able to weather a pounding. I know it's possible to get off a sandbar. You fling the anchor fore and aft and haul away with all your might."

"It was a 340-ton brig, only five years old, very solid. But 150 tons of marble in the hold came loose when the ship slammed onto that sand bar—not a gentle jolt but a timber-cracking crash, Mrs. Hasty said. The crew was tossed from their bunks. The marble blocks tore a hole in the hull. The damaged ship could never have floated off at high tide."

"That cursed statue of Calhoun!" Emerson whacked his thigh with a fist. "The slaveholder did her in."

"Insurance agents were already there with mules at low tide to haul up the statue and send it to South Carolina," Thoreau said. "At least Calhoun is saved for posterity."

"Calhoun was resurrected," Emerson said bitterly, "but not Margaret."

"I followed the thieves' trail to a village on the South Shore where they live," Thoreau continued. "I hired some drunken Dutchmen to take me. Now that was dispiriting!"

"What happened?"

"Inside a shack were young thugs playing dominoes, guzzling rum as if they hadn't just witnessed a tragedy. The worst sight, comical really—those ruffians were wearing fancy hats they stole from the wreck. Someone had already sewn on buttons, braid, and fringe. My intuition tells me the frippery came from Margaret's wardrobe. You know she loved haberdashery." He looked inexpressibly sad, although his voice was tinged with anger.

Emerson came near exploding, like a dormant but rumbling volcano. "Sacrilege! Margaret was so elegant—meticulous in her dress. To think of her ornaments on thieving rogues!"

"It was all I could do not to throttle them," Henry said, "and I do not approve of fisticuffs."

"Where was Ellery?"

"He was busy drying letters to Margaret he found on the beach, although who knows if they're legible? He was just as determined as I to find any shred of what might define her legacy."

Emerson looked thoughtful. With a stick he drew spirals in the sand, then stuck it upright in the center. "Ellery . . . he and Margaret had their differences, especially over the distress his—let's call it *insouciance*—has caused her sister Ellen and the children. Yet the dear boy has proposed to write Margaret's lost history."

"A noble or ignoble gesture?" Thoreau shrugged, unsure. "How can one transmute something that springs from another's life?" He sighed. "In his favor, I'll say Ellery was avid to rescue anything of Margaret's."

Emerson swatted his forehead, an un-Sage-like sign of anger. "Why oh why did that moronic captain sail through the night, even with sails reefed, with a southeast gale behind him?"

"He took a sounding and found the depth twenty-one fathoms, the ship's cook told me," Thoreau explained. "Pure ineptitude—he didn't realize they were headed straight for Long Island—with a freshening wind. You wouldn't believe the damage that gale wrought on land: chimneys reduced to piles of bricks, boats torn off the moorings and blown sideways onto shore, trees toppled like straws, root balls heaved up."

The two men clambered to their feet and turned from pond to forest. White-skinned birches creaked as dark clouds scudded overhead.

Thoreau spied a heap of purple flowers and dropped to his knees. Emerson watched without comment, attuned to his young friend's botanical passion.

With his pocketknife Thoreau unearthed a spear of comfrey root buried beneath leaves. "Knitbone!" he exclaimed, pleased with his treasure. "It cures sprains, bruises, and burns." He stuffed the slimy white root in his hat.

"If only it could knit up our ragged pains," Emerson whispered. "That fool First Mate, running with the wind in a hurricane instead of heaving to in a harbor!"

Just like Margaret, he thought. *No safe port for her. Always full speed ahead! And what now?*

CHAPTER THIRTY-ONE

Remembering

AUGUST 15, 1850, LENOX, MASSACHUSETTS

The red clapboard farmhouse was humble, nearly a shanty, with a bountiful apple orchard in back its only compensating luxury. Twisted branches laden with green apples stooped to the ground. In the dooryard, spent lilacs with heart-shaped leaves still retained steeples of skeletal brown relics of spring bloom. The creaky wooden gate hung off its hinges on one side.

Sophia Peabody Hawthorne, a slight, comely woman with fair hair and glowing face, was surprised by a stranger knocking on her parlor door. A gentleman who identified himself as a correspondent for *The Tribune*, a Mr. Walter Whitman, tipped his hat and said, "Call me Walter."

I shall do no such thing, Sophia thought. She had spied the peculiar-looking man outside as he ambled down the path. She thought how she'd describe his gait to Nat: not strolling but *sauntering* lazily in their dooryard. His garb looked like a working man's, one whom she'd heard described as a "rough." On his head a black slouch hat perched at a conspicuously oblique angle. He had glacial-blue eyes and no coat over his unbuttoned coarse-knit shirt, open at the collar to show a somewhat scrawny chest. She would've taken him for a gypsy, were it not for his respectful address.

"Madam Hawthorne, I presume." He performed a bow that was almost a curtsy. He added without taking a breath, "I am enchanted to meet such an esteemed painter as yourself and the lovely wife, to boot, of America's premier novelist, Nathaniel Hawthorne. I'm writing a newspaper story on Margaret Fuller Ossoli's significance for American letters." He pulled out a notebook and pencil. "Will you be so kind as to grant me an interview with yourself and Mr. Hawthorne on the subject of Mrs. Fuller Ossoli?"

Flattered to be asked her opinion, Sophia was forming a suitable quotation when her husband appeared. Unlike Sophia in her simple house dress and apron, Hawthorne was dressed impeccably as always (despite the warm weather) in a flowing cape, figured waistcoat, and silk cravat. "Who is it, my Dove?" he asked.

Mr. Whitman's eyes widened at the sight of the author's elegant apparel and appearance. Hawthorne, ladies said, was as handsome as Lord Byron. Strangers gaped at him on the street, which annoyed the shy man, given to retreating to his solitary study. One day Hawthorne—habitually loathe to converse with strangers—had actually fled when accosted by a gypsy in the woods. The exotic woman, gold bangles clanking on her wrist, had stopped short and gasped, asking, "Are you a man or an angel?"

Embarrassing, to be sure. Hawthorne much preferred to be venerated for literary prowess than for his looks. Still, the engraved photograph of him that accompanied reviews of his novel didn't hurt. His post office box overflowed with letters from gushing admirers.

Hawthorne was reticent, at first content to observe while his wife spoke with the journalist. On receiving Whitman's congratulations on the success of *The Scarlet Letter*, he blushed, rendering his handsome face even more attractive. *A fairer man I have yet to see,* Whitman thought. Tall, broad-shouldered, with dark, wavy hair and arresting blue-gray eyes, Hawthorne looked like an athlete. Or to Whitman, who was an aficionado of male beauty, a Greek god.

It was surprising that a man like Hawthorne, known for his silences, would chat so amiably with a reporter. Perhaps the number of fans who made pilgrimages to his door after publication of *The Scarlet Letter* had softened him. One appreciative reader had just sent a case of champagne. Whitman was quite free with compliments, and Hawthorne radiated approval. Finally he was rightly recognized by the press as a source of belles lettres and wisdom!

Another possible explanation: after all the news reports of Margaret Fuller's demise, characterizing her as God's gift to women's emancipation, Hawthorne was eager to express dissent. "Margaret's erudition was, in fact, excessive," he told Whitman, who scribbled fast as Hawthorne warmed to his subject. "Her mastery of arcane subjects was unbecoming, in my opinion, and unnecessary." He spoke slowly and precisely for the benefit of the note taker. "Women's knowledge should be limited to domestic affairs. That is the truest arena for their talents." He straightened his cravat and pulled his coat sleeves over his cuffs, pleased with his summary.

Sophia was astounded at how voluble her normally terse husband was. They both had much to say on Margaret's merits and demerits, which Whitman recorded as he sat at their table.

Whitman exercised a reporter's prerogative to inquire whether *The Scarlet Letter*'s heroine Hester Prynne owed some traits to Margaret Fuller. Hawthorne looked shaken at the thought and Sophia thunderstruck. "Well, in Margaret's unconventionality, her violation of rules of conduct perhaps," Sophia allowed. "There has always been gossip clouding her, always eyebrows raised."

Whitman's next question surpassed the border of propriety, but he had to ask: "Did Fuller have a child out of wedlock?" The couple exchanged glances.

"Margaret would never . . ." Hawthorne stammered.

Sophia, shocked, considered the much-gossiped-about possibility: "There is the fact that she concealed the wedding, if a Catholic ceremony may be deemed valid. And she was returning home with two unexpected accessories: one possible husband and one obvious child."

She hesitated, then burst out, "Margaret and I disagreed on many things, I'll readily admit. She denigrated the sanctity of marriage, even advising her protégés to maintain their chastity, never succumb to 'domestic slavery,' as she called it."

"Yet she herself married," Whitman pointed out.

"A striking inconsistency," Hawthorne admitted. "Another one I might note is: Although claiming that women are Amazonian in intellectual power, she wished to retain all courtesies men pay women as the *weaker* sex. When she visited us here—after publication of her notorious book—Margaret would habitually wait for me to open a door for her." He barked a laugh at the incongruity. "As I held the door wide, I teased her by quoting her infamous admonition to aspiring ladies: 'Let them be sea captains if they will!'"

"Did she laugh?" the journalist asked.

"Of course. Margaret had a boundless well of drollery, enjoyed light satire at her own expense—just as vigorously as she ladled it on others' hypocrisy. Yet, I tell you, Mr. Whitman, her 'sea captain' ambition is ludicrous. I doubt she could even pilot a dinghy."

Sophia pointed to a bronze vase. "Margaret gave us that as a wedding gift. She brought it to us herself, filled with fronds of fern."

"She *was* thoughtful." Hawthorne was pensive. "When I toiled like a peasant at Brook Farm—what a debacle that interlude was!—and I was ill with an ague, Margaret brought me a bowl of warm gruel and spoon-fed it to me in bed."

At this bit of new intelligence, Sophia raised her eyebrows, picturing the indelicate scene. "Margaret—a nursemaid? You never mentioned it in your letters!"

Unperturbed, he continued, "Even more salutary was her vivacious wit. She entertained me with her silver eloquence. Her force and fluency of speech always threw her writing into the shade, you know."

"She could've been a fiery stump orator," Sophia agreed. Her voice trembled, near breaking down. "Once her child was gone, it was really better she died! There could be no peace or rest for her in this country." Her eyes filled with tears. "Was there ever anything so tragical? The newspaper accounts—she was so close to home, such a dreary image of her on that wreck! So agonizing!"

Hawthorne, assuming an air of moral rectitude, explained: "And if she had lived to disembark with a husband so lacking in force and intellect? Imagine the censure, the scandal in Boston! That so-called Marchese, nothing but a pretty boy who seduced a woman of that age!" He brushed nonexistent lint off his trousers. "Appalling liaison!"

Sophia plucked dry, brown curls of fern from the vase, fluffing up the remaining green stalks. "Margaret was never happy in life. May she be happy in death."

The interview was interrupted by the arrival of a tall, dark-haired visitor who, with his abundant reddish beard, radiated vigor. Husband and wife greeted their neighbor, Herman Melville, warmly. With his advent, the atmosphere in the house changed markedly. It was as if a dovecote with two cooing birds welcomed a sharp-beaked hawk.

"The man who lived with cannibals!" Whitman blurted out, having read the newcomer's best-seller *Typee* about jumping ship in the South Seas. Melville looked pained at the accolade, which Whitman was soon made to understand was an insensitive gaffe.

"Don't let the ruddy countenance deceive you. Mr. Melville is a writer of consequence," Hawthorne was quick to affirm. "The book he's writing will be a leviathan of world literature, as substantial as the whale that is its subject."

"Bravo!" Whitman congratulated him. "We need literature to reflect American strength, instead of whey-faced imitations of European models."

"Margaret would've agreed with you there, Mr. Whitman," Sophia interjected. "She called for a truly national literature. American writers, she said, must extract 'the tapeworm of Europe from their brains.'"

The two novelists prepared to retreat for brandy and cigars.

Discussion of Fuller came to a halt, but not before Sophia asked, "Why not summon Margaret's spirit and put our questions directly to her? We're all—her closest friends—to meet soon in Concord to remember her. Perhaps we could engage a mesmerist to contact her recently departed essence."

"I'd very much like to see such an ectoplasmic apparition," Melville smiled, all game for a supernatural visitation.

Hawthorne was much opposed, expressing himself in uncharacteristically blunt fragments: "Nonsense, my Dove! Impossible! Your interest in mesmerism, what claptrap, bunkum, unalloyed rot!"

Sophia, undeterred, said with dignity: "I will broach the subject with Waldo and Lidian." She turned to Whitman. "If we can arrange a session, I invite you to witness it, Mr. Whitman. I also invite you to accompany us to Concord for Margaret's memorial service. You'll learn much about your subject from her friends who convene there. In the meantime, in response to your inquiries, I'll consult my old journals for evidence of how remarkable Margaret was when we met a decade ago."

Melville, whose speech showed a tendency to specialize in enigma, addressed Hawthorne: "There are more things in heaven and earth, dear Horatio, than are dreamt of in your philosophy."

Hawthorne was speedy with his response: "O brave new world, that has such people in it."

"'Tis new to thee . . . ," Melville responded, taking up the *Tempest* allusion.

Shakespeare's words singing in his ears, Whitman snapped shut his notebook and bid them farewell. *Who was Margaret Fuller?* he asked himself. *Is it a brave new world or a still-shackled old one?*

Sophia accompanied him outside for a last word. "I can provide anecdotes for your tribute, Mr. Whitman, to shed light on Margaret's character. I knew her quite well, and—despite my husband's horror of her radical ideas—Margaret and I were friends."

Whitman promised to come again for more information to round out the profile. As he headed back to his oxcart, Sophia wondered how an acquaintance with a picturesque person like him might proceed. She thought him a harmless—and engaging—eccentric, although she deplored seeing a red flannel undershirt in evidence beneath his open collar. Since Hawthorne needed quirky characters to fuel his imagination, it was plausible the reporter would appear in some future tale.

Besides, publicity never hurt. The newspapers and literary magazines still brimmed with laments over "Our Lost Genius, Margaret Fuller." Shouldn't they pay more attention to a genius living among them?

CHAPTER THIRTY-TWO

The Quick and the Dead

AUGUST 16, 1850, LENOX, MASSACHUSETTS

"What do you make of yesterday's visitor, that Mr. Whitman?" Hawthorne asked his wife. "A strangely charming bird—a bit of a fancy Dan, I suspect, despite his rustic dress."

Sophia floated three waterlilies Hawthorne had brought her in a shallow bowl. "At least his literary sensibility seems quite refined." She wiped her hands. "He certainly grasps the excellence of your tales."

Hawthorne looked pleased and nudged the bobbing lilies into a more symmetrical alignment. "Yes, very gratifying to have one's merit acknowledged. Yet I'm mystified why you invited him to go to Concord with us for the memorial. Surely that was rash."

Sophia turned and busied herself in the kitchen. She scrubbed rust off an iron skillet, scouring it with sand. The question hung in the air between them.

"And, my dearest Dove," he persisted, "your suggestion of engaging a mesmerist to contact Margaret's spirit—sheerest lunacy!" He grabbed her hands, releasing the iron pan into the sink with a clatter. He kissed her fingers. "You shouldn't attempt work like this. Let the char do it."

"Oh Nat," she said, tearful. "I dread going back to Concord. We were so happy in the Old Manse, just after we married. Our children were born there. What joyful memories! And now it will be a place of mourning for Margaret."

"I admit I accepted Waldo's invitation with tears and fears," he said. "To see Concord again will be a pleasure. Yet the occasion fills me with grief."

"I as well," she said, her voice trembling. She paused. "I promised to tell Mr. Whitman more of our impressions of Margaret. What would you have me say?"

Hawthorne retrieved from a vest pocket a page inscribed with a quote-worthy statement. He cleared his throat and read aloud, enunciating each word with precision: "For such an exceptional life as Margaret's, it seems only fitting that her end should be as spectacular. Margaret was a revolution in herself. Perhaps after the revolution in Italy failed, it had to happen that she too would perish, as did her hopes for democracy in that benighted land."

Sophia looked taken aback, and he confessed, slightly abashed, "I've been preparing some written sentiments to deliver as a eulogy." He looked at her with admonishment. "Sophia, I must differ with you on one thing. I know that you, like other impressionable ladies, put faith in that pseudo-science, mesmerism. With so many questions swirling around Margaret's status as a wife and mother, you have the mistaken view that a mesmerist can evoke our late friend's soul. Pure poppycock!"

"I can vouch for the efficacy of mesmerism!" Sophia was adamant. "It helped my headaches. People in Boston, New York—even Margaret herself—they swear by it! Why not try?"

"Imagine the travesty it would be! The foolishness of such an endeavor, especially attended by Margaret's closest friends: Waldo and Lidian, Henry Thoreau, her sister Ellen and Ellery. And now a reporter—that Whitman fellow."

Sophia flung off her apron. "Scoff however much you like, my love." She crossed her arms, assuming an immovable stance. "I intend to discover the truth about Margaret's last days."

Hawthorne, on meeting unforeseen resistance, changed the subject. "I would like to invite our new neighbor, Mr. Melville, to attend the memorial service. Do you approve?"

"Isn't that rather precipitous? We hardly know him, although I concede his nautical yarns are most entertaining."

"He's an up-and-coming young author, one I'd like to encourage. So far, he's celebrated for novels of his South Seas adventures. I think him capable of much more than potboilers. He aspires to write of depths that compel a man to swim for his life."

Sophia was thoughtful. "He's already endured tides and typhoons, but is he a suitable sea dog for turbulent Concord waters?"

"Judging from his tales of living with naked savages while a castaway, his moral code may not accord with ours," Hawthorne said. "Yet, I do think he's worth knowing."

"He has a warm—if not to say passionate—heart, with life to his fingertips," Sophia agreed. "You've spent hours smoking cigars with him, but why bring him to Concord?"

"Margaret once termed me in print 'a man of ice,'" Hawthorne recalled. "I think you'll find Mr. Melville is a raging bonfire. Let's see how he heats up the frigid atmosphere there."

CHAPTER THIRTY-THREE

Back to Concord

SEPTEMBER 1, 1850, EN ROUTE:
STOCKBRIDGE TO CONCORD, MASSACHUSETTS

Hawthorne, his wife, Sophia, and the younger writer Herman Melville jostled along on a stagecoach from Stockbridge to Concord, accompanied by *Tribune* reporter Walter Whitman. Their goal was to join a gathering at the home of philosopher Ralph Waldo Emerson to share memories of S. Margaret Fuller Ossoli.

As they rattled along the bumpy road, the group was thrown against each other's shoulders, murmuring a polite "excuse me" and "I beg your pardon" until they gave up and accepted their cramped proximity. Sophia handed around cider, which they sipped from a communal jug, and golden blueberry muffins, their tops cleft and filled with sweet butter.

It made for a cozy ride, overcoming any pretense at formality. The travelers were talkative, even the usually dour Nathaniel, who chuckled when he recounted a favorite story about Margaret. He told how she insisted the panorama from a mountaintop was much superior to the view from a tangled forest. "That was Margaret," he concluded, "all peaks and no valleys."

A jolt shook up the party as the coach wheels juddered out of a hole.

Melville leaned forward to add his tuppence: "A view from the crow's nest rewards one's fear of climbing the rigging. Yet, always, one has to descend."

Hawthorne consulted his gold pocket watch, tucking it tidily in his vest pocket and ensuring that the gold chain hung in a smooth loop. "Indeed, Margaret achieved a peak of notoriety with her seditious book. I wonder—had she lived, would she have faced a grievous comedown?"

"What," Melville asked, "for example?"

"The alienation of her friends' affections, galled by her unsuitable matrimonial match!" Hawthorne declared with a ferocity born of assured rectitude.

Surprised by the prim set of the author's lips, Whitman responded, "You write of adultery and passion in your *Scarlet Letter*. I'd think you'd understand the lure of love."

"Margaret scolded me for giving up my life as an artist for love." Sophia looked at her husband with no hint of a smile. She shifted uneasily on the horsehair seat. "I became a wife and mother instead of a painter." Did I betray, she wondered, Margaret's teachings, betray my own ambition? Her husband patted her hand to console her. Best to blame society, she decided. "The howling storm Margaret encountered was like the sea of prejudice she would've met on shore." There! She and husband were restored to the same wavelength again, despite momentary doubt.

Burying misgivings on marital felicitude, the Hawthornes volunteered to provide a rundown of the figures the others were soon to meet. As a thumbnail sketch of their host, the venerable essayist Ralph Waldo Emerson, Hawthorne was brief: "You'll find Waldo habitually absorbed in celestial cogitations," he warned.

At Whitman's raised eyebrows, Sophia explained, "Waldo tends to hold Nat hostage, in close, dead-set attack on his ear. Most of Waldo's acquaintances are reverential. They merely echo what Waldo says. Nat has no fear of expressing diametrically opposed views. For Waldo, it's always morning, while Nat's imagination yearns for twilight—the dark, mysterious past."

"What of Mr. Emerson's disciple," Whitman asked, "Mr. Thoreau?"

"A most unmalleable fellow, tedious, tiresome, the most notional chap alive," Hawthorne said with a yawn. "Still, one can have no better companion for a walk in the woods or a row on the pond."

"Henry and Waldo's wife, Lidian, are very close," Sophia said with raised eyebrows. "We'll leave you to judge the young buck for yourself," she added, wiping crumbs from her skirt.

Melville felt it imperative to put his oar in. "After reading Mr. Emerson's essays and attending his lectures, I'm curious to meet him in the flesh. He seems a brilliant fellow. Whether his ideas are begged, borrowed, stolen, or of his own manufacture, he must be an uncommon man." He addressed Hawthorne: "If you think Emerson a cosmic humbug, he's no common humbug!"

The coach lumbered to a halt; clopping hooves ceased abruptly. *Rat-a-tat-tat!* A scarlet-headed woodpecker drilled a rotten tree. A gray squirrel on a branch barked and flicked its curling tale.

"We're here!" Sophia sang out. She unfolded herself and stepped from the coach, stretching her limbs. An orange tabby tiptoed over and sniffed her portmanteau. "We are hard by the site of 'the rude bridge that arched the flood,' as Mr. Emerson's poem puts it," she recited, adding, "'Their flag to April's breeze unfurled, here once the embattled farmers stood and fired the shot heard round the world.'"

She hopped over a puddle, raising her skirts. "This time, I wonder, will we fire a shot for revolution or will there be discord in Concord?"

The cat yowled.

CHAPTER THIRTY-FOUR

Old Friends and New

SEPTEMBER 1, 1850, CONCORD, MASSACHUSETTS

The riders disembarked from the coach. Much hugging, shaking of hands, and manly pats on the shoulder ensued. Emerson's wife Lidian (a tall, stern-looking matron in her mid-forties, thin as a straw) embraced Sophia. A pretty young lady, Margaret Fuller's sister Ellen Fuller Channing, threw her arms around Sophia.

They clung to each other. "I can't believe she's gone!" Sophia gasped, shoulders heaving with sobs.

Lidian felt it her role as hostess to comfort them, although her bromides failed to staunch any tears. "The Good Lord took dear Margaret with her husband and child—a blessing. They will forever be together in the Hereafter, escaping the decay of age, without a pang of separation." She remained dry-eyed as she delivered her homily.

Emerson, more than six feet tall, lofty as his ideals, with a handsome, craggy face and mellifluous baritone that so captivated Lyceum audiences, welcomed the travelers. "Thank you all for making the journey to honor the memory of our dear Margaret." The Sage of Concord fixed his eyes on the firmament and spoke as if declaiming a Sermon on the Mount: "Although there can be no funeral for one swallowed up by the deep, we must determine how best to memorialize her."

"Perhaps a poem?" asked an attractive young fellow with unlined face. As Ellery Channing bounded up, it was immediately evident he considered himself the cynosure of all eyes. He warmed up his vocal apparatus and cast about in his mind for a rhyme with "Margaret," assuming ardent poses. Like a novice actor, he strutted and flung his arms out to the heavens, clearing his throat to declaim.

The others ignored his histrionics, but a smirk and a question crossed Whitman's mind. Who is this outrageous bloke? Mayhap, he's too handsome for common life? He remembered there was a black sheep among the Transcendentalist coterie, none other than Margaret Fuller's brother-in-law Ellery, married to her delicate sister Ellen.

"Allow me to present Mr. Ellery Channing," Emerson said, addressing Whitman and Melville. "Or, as I call him, 'Professor in the Art of Walking.'" He looked stern as he spoke to his young disciple. "Ellery, dear boy, you know I admire your poetry. Yet I envision a more substantial publication for Margaret's memorial. Perchance a biography, memoirs of Margaret by her nearest and dearest, augmented by selections from her journals and letters. We might call it *Margaret and Her Friends*."

"What about *Fuller in Full*?" Ellery offered, "or *Fuller: Full of Herself*?" He plucked a dandelion puff from the ground and blew the gossamer seeds skyward, hanging his head melodramatically. "Scattered like her bones!"

Whitman stifled a nervous giggle.

"Ellery!" His wife shook her golden ringlets. "Please!"

"As a preface for your memorial book, Waldo, I offer a few lines of my own composition." Ellery puffed out his chest in the grip of inspiration and intoned with affected solemnity: "Weep no more, kind friends. Our beloved Margaret is now, like Keats when Shelley eulogized him, free from reviewers' malicious attacks. She is not dead. It is the living who are dead. She is One with Nature."

"Really, Ellery," Hawthorne said, shaking his head. "That's going a bit far, even for a pantheist like you."

"Well then, a poem perchance. You desire a substantial tribute? A poem by me can be substantial, even epic." Ellery threw his hands skyward as if to grasp the sun, and recited,

"Out of the day and night, A joy has taken flight;
Spring, summer, winter hoar—
Move my heart with delight no more."

He lowered his head in mock grief.

A raucous loon's call pierced the air from nearby Walden Pond, an unworldly yodel.

Sophia frowned. "Those are Shelley's words. You can't use them as your own!"

Ellery drew himself up. "If I improve them, they're mine. Besides, who will know? Shelley is long dead. Life is so short, it's a wonder everyone doesn't steal." He evinced no trace of shame, only pride.

An awkward silence fell, which Whitman felt compelled to alleviate. "Thank you, Mrs. Emerson, Mr. Emerson," he offered, removing his hat, cocked at its usual jaunty slant, and bowing, "for allowing me to observe the memorial service and report to my *Tribune* readers. I am a great admirer of your Transcendental philosophy, sir."

"Then you must call me Waldo, not a cloven-hoofed Lord of Darkness, as some detractors are inclined."

Hawthorne broke in on the two men's mutual exchange of smiles—Whitman's combusting with bliss and Waldo's somewhat banked. "Allow me to present my neighbor, another brother of the printed word, Mr. Herman Melville."

Bows and handshakes among the men followed all around. Lidian Emerson, in sharp contrast, drew up her skirts as if in jeopardy of contagion. "The author of those . . . er, Polynesian adventures, *Omoo* and *Typee*?"

"Yes," Melville admitted, "but do not believe me infected with savagery. I spent years before the mast. My novels draw on that experience, but they are fiction."

"Thanks be to heaven!" Lidian stood even more erect than before and clutched a Bible that materialized miraculously from a pocket. "I do hope you did not witness such pagan excesses as I've heard your book describes."

Just then a short, youngish man, so thin he seemed almost a specter, appeared. Emerson made the introduction to Melville and Whitman: "My colleague, Henry Thoreau." Hawthorne clasped the long-nosed rustic to his chest.

Lidian's priggish expression evaporated. She smiled at the young man, whose chin threatened to disappear in his sparse beard as he ducked his head and presented her a pail of huckleberries. "The last of the season," he said to her, followed by "How d'ye do?" to Melville and Whitman, doffing his hat.

Sophia hugged him. "Oh, Henry, how difficult for you and Ellery to scour the beach for Margaret's bones!" Her voice quavered. "And to find nary a trace!"

Hawthorne grasped her hand. "Dearest! We must be strong."

Evening shadows grew long and leggy as the sun sank. Whip-poor-wills called their lonely tune. Pines sighed, and swallows zigzagged to mud nests beneath the eaves.

Lidian indicated the path to the front door of their large white house. "Come. We can talk over supper."

CHAPTER THIRTY-FIVE

Around the Table

SEPTEMBER 1, 1850, CONCORD:
THE LARGE DINING TABLE IN THE EMERSON HOUSE.
DRAMATIS PERSONAE:
MR. AND MRS. EMERSON, MR. AND MRS. HAWTHORNE,
MR. AND MRS. CHANNING, HERMAN MELVILLE,
WALTER WHITMAN, HENRY THOREAU

Seated at one end of a long, walnut table, polished to a high sheen, Lidian Emerson cleared her throat, shot meaningful looks at her guests, and clasped her hands before her in prayer. As conversation sputtered to a halt, she bowed her head and began, ignoring the others' restless murmurs. "O God, our heavenly father, for all thy mercies and for this food that nourishes our bodies and restores our flagging spirits, for the grace that sustains our souls, we thank thee and bless and *praise* thy holy name, through Jesus Christ our Lord and Savior . . ."

She paused in her recital, as Ellery couldn't restrain himself from dragging over the platter of crookneck squash. Soon all guests were passing bowls of string beans, sliced cucumbers, and fat sections of tomatoes—without so much as an Amen. Lidian indicated a leg of mutton with a curt nod as if it were a pile of dung: "For those not inclined to a vegetable diet like myself," she told her guests, "help yourself to some animal flesh."

Ellery lunged for a slice of mutton and announced, "And for those, unlike yourself, who eschew a diet of poppy syrup."

"Shush!" said Ellen, as if scolding an unruly son.

"I am prone to the curse of headaches," Lidian Emerson explained. "My cross to bear."

"And prone to lying prone abed all day in a darkened room," Ellery quipped. Ellen tapped his arm, her signal to desist.

Emerson searched for a less awkward vein of conversation. "You see how admirably Henry has managed my garden, which is still producing bountifully. Tillage! To know the pan and mixture of soil—what a blessing!" he rhapsodized. "Our cucumbers are big as trouts, although I must say insects have so devoured their leaves, they're like lace. And my Bartlett pears . . ."

Sophia would not be lulled into horticultural chitchat. "Have you tried mesmerism for your headache, Lidian? One session cured me in Salem. My father used it in his dental clinic—he put patients in a sleeping state for painless extractions."

"Sweetest!" Hawthorne enunciated carefully: "You know I am unalterably opposed to such humbug. The idea of some charlatan putting you in a trance so he could enter your mind, the holiest of holies! It's obscene." He frowned, his eyebrows in an angry V.

"I agree," Emerson was quick to add. "Such vulgar performances as I've seen in Boston! A crude mountebank in a dark, smoky room supposedly cures an invalid or communicates with a spirit beyond the grave—it's a black art."

"Don't you wonder if a human body might be a conduit to a departed soul?" Sophia asked as she impaled a cucumber coin on her fork.

"Margaret found great relief from back pain through a mesmerist," Ellen nodded assent. "You remember how curved her spine was? After mesmerist treatments, she stood straight and measured three or four inches taller."

"So naïve, my dear—don't be a fool," Ellery patted her hand and spoke to Emerson: "Women are so credulous. They believe any quack who puts on a good show." He shrugged his shoulders—Women!

Ellen looked annoyed more than credulous. She snatched her hand from his grip.

"Women are not expected to know science," Emerson nodded in accord. He assumed his preacher mode to add: "Nor to write or fight or build or compose musical scores. *Woman* does all by inspiring *Man* to do all."

Ellery purred to Ellen, "A wife should be pretty, silent, passive, frail, and dependent on her husband."

Sophia spoke up. "Margaret regarded mesmerism as a source of liberation for women. I remember she told us in one of her Conversations we should give up corsets, as she did. 'Let the female form be free of constraints!'—that's exactly what she told us."

Lidian looked faint and fanned herself with a handkerchief. Discussion at table of female undergarments and possible black magic? "It sounds rather like sorcery, all these claims of peeping into one's mind or soul."

Thoreau spoke for the first time: "The whole world is a wonder. Why just look in one corner? Why seek to find the spirit by putting someone into a waking sleep? We should seek the divine in each of us by waking up to the truth of nature."

"Well said, my boy!" Emerson tapped a fork on his wine glass and made it ring. "I recognize my own sentiments vibrating in all you say, clothed in your own originality, of course."

Thoreau appeared less than pleased at his patron's half compliment.

"Mesmerism is absurd, repugnant," Hawthorne adamantly declared, "a corruption akin to witchcraft."

"I beg to differ, Dearest." Sophia sat up as tall as her small form allowed. "Numberless witnesses in New England and New York who have seen their performances attest to their veracity."

"What about that young woman in a trance who told the mesmerist where to find a missing woman?" Ellen said. "When they went to the place she named, they found the woman's body! Her spirit had communicated the location."

"What an ass!" Ellery burst out. Although he left in doubt to whom he referred, Ellen colored, an angry angel.

"I propose we invite Dr. Théodore Léger, the mesmerist who cured Margaret in New York, to come here for a séance." Sophia was unyielding.

Ellen seconded the proposal: "He can hypnotize me to make contact with Margaret's spirit."

A general cacophony of loud, male voices erupted around the table: "Nonsense! Folderol! What delusions! Sounds like an opium dream!" Fists pounded, hands slapped the table, cutlery clattered.

Their host attempted to restore peace. "Ladies and gentlemen, may I propose a toast?" Emerson raised his wine glass in the direction of the red library where he indicated Magaret was wont to stay on her visits. "May the baneful weed of disagreeable strife be banished from our field of friendship. Harmony! Concord in Concord!"

"Peace and calm are all very well for you," Hawthorne told him, draining his glass rather than hoisting it. "Margaret sought tumult. She would have gloried in a debate." He looked pensive.

"And so it begins." Emerson assumed the mantle of Master of Ceremonies. He cleared his throat and said in his most oracular style, "I am bereaved of part of myself. We meet for memory and mourning. This time for our dear, departed Margaret, my friend, my foe, my equal, who never failed to set my brain on fire, to make me laugh more than I wished and argue with me until the owls hooted us to sleep."

"Hear, hear," the others raised their glasses. "To Margaret!"

Lidian looked green. "Please excuse me; my head is pounding! I must retire."

"What about dessert?" Ellery guzzled his drink and scraped a fork over his empty plate. "I believe I saw rice pudding with currants in the larder."

"How can you even think of sweets?" Ellen's own plate, strewn with a smear of red juice and broken spears of string beans, looked like a battlefield after corpses have been dragged off.

"Margaret may be dead," he said, "but I'm not."

Whitman's fingers itched to record his impressions. The room was a hive of buzzing conflict.

CHAPTER THIRTY-SIX

Ellen and Ellery

SEPTEMBER 2, 1850, CONCORD

Whitman had accepted the offer of a bed for the night in the Channings' small house. The rooms were tiny and low-ceilinged. One held mismatched desks and served as a schoolroom for local children, whom Ellen taught. Ellery boasted that he had no fixed occupation other than impecunious poet. "I am averse to being in the harness" of a regular job, he told Whitman.

As if to prove his poetic *bona fides*, he shoved out his chest and quoted Wordsworth:

"The world is too much with us, late and soon.
Getting and spending, we lay waste our powers.
Little we see in Nature that is ours.
We have given our hearts away, a sordid boon."

Ellen's expression showed such recitals had lost all appeal for her. She had by necessity assumed the role of breadwinner of the family and treated her husband like a delinquent child (along with their three actual tots). Despite her faded calico frock, her Madonna-like beauty, fair complexion, sunflower-yellow curls, and eyes of deep purple-blue were striking. Under that lovely exterior a tempestuous soul smoldered.

She felt beauty was no compensation for her deficiencies as a scholar. Ellen always felt inferior to her illustrious sister, even though her mastery of French and Italian (taught by her tutor Margaret) at age eleven proved her own precocity. Ellery's demeaning comments did not augment her self-esteem.

While she was washing up from breakfast, he popped into the kitchen looking like an unshaven Pan. "Ellery," she reminded him, "you must go to Bush and chop two cords of wood. Waldo already paid me a dollar."

Singularly unmoved by her plea, he radiated good cheer and chirped, "All in good time, my dear. I'm hunting chestnuts and barberries with Henry this morning." He chomped an apple, unbothered as a clam at high tide.

"Ellery can be ostentatious in his disregard for family responsibilities," Ellen explained to Whitman. "I must be patient as with my children, whose character it is my sacred duty to develop." One had the impression her excuse had become an oath for her.

From a back room came the loud clatter of children playing. Ellery clenched his teeth and confided, "I do not find children unpleasing when they are silent, Walter." He added with cheeky pride, "I am chiefly engaged in doing nothing. I have a large penchant for rambling about the countryside. Indeed, it's from nature that I derive my poetic inspirations. You might say, my life is my greatest poem." He bowed as if receiving acclaim.

Ellen's shoulders stiffened, her eyes buried in the floorboards. "The children are a strain on my husband's nerves. He can't be still for a moment. He wouldn't be happy in heaven unless he could see a way out. I must admit, he's a different person when outside. With the sky for a ceiling, he's happy."

Ever the reporter, Whitman asked, "Did your sister approve of your husband's vagabond ways?"

"Of course she finds . . ." Ellen began, "I mean *found* him clever."

"'Genius' is the precise term she used," Ellery said as he began juggling apples, keeping them whirling until one splatted on the floor.

Ellen bent to wipe up the mess. “Margaret called him ‘hopelessly untamed at the core.’ When Ellery and I married after only two months’ acquaintance, my family was shocked.”

“Untamed is my badge of honor,” Ellery winked. He seized a wild fox grape from a basket of tangled vines and chewed it. His mouth twisted. “Sour,” he accused Ellen. “Why don’t you make preserves?”

“If I could afford loaf sugar . . .” she began.

He ignored her remonstrance and skipped out the door, all ebullience: “Farewell for the nonce, my apple blossom. A golden morn of adventure beckons!”

Ellen served her guest a bowl of porridge, saying, “And for me a grind of chores.”

“Pray tell,” Whitman asked, “what are those papers, which I heard Ellery found on the shore after the shipwreck?”

“I asked him to show me, but he only displays reams of poems he composes each night. After traipsing in the woods all day, mind you. I tell you, Mr. Whitman, you are fortunate your calling is journalism, not poetry.”

An inexplicable expression flickered over the reporter’s face. Why, he wondered, do I feel such an affinity for a wastrel like Ellery? He’s unabashed in celebrating himself, singing of himself, glorifying himself—loafing and lounging to observe a spear of grass.

CHAPTER THIRTY-SEVEN

A Lesson

SEPTEMBER 2, 1850, LATER MORNING,
CONCORD

The Channings' children—Greta (six years old, named Margaret Fuller Channing) and Caroline, four—filed into the schoolroom, followed by toddling one-year-old baby Walter. Soon the Emerson children appeared and settled at desks: Ellen, called Nellie (eleven), Edith (nine), and Eddy (six) as well as ten-year-old neighbor Louisa May Alcott. With such a miscellany ranging in age from barely one to eleven, instructing them all seemed nigh impossible.

Before becoming a journalist, Whitman had taught—rather badly—in schools all over Long Island. He wondered if New England pedagogy was more enlightened than his home-grown methods. "I confess to you, Mrs. Channing, that I'm a failed school teacher. I'm utterly incapable of engaging young minds. My students used to pantomime drowning when reading Virgil and tease me by clutching the air, as if sinking in the depths of Latin."

"Surely you exaggerate, Mr. Whitman. And you must call me Ellen. I seek to be a friend, not a lecturer, to my students, and I would be your friend as well."

"I assure you, there's no hyperbole in describing my abysmal defeat as a teacher," he said. "Other favorite tricks by the students were loudly cracking walnuts and uttering squeaking sounds as if a battalion of mice were on the march. Some boys threw themselves to the floor and rolled about in chalk dust, claiming they were 'whited sepulchres'—I'm still not sure what that had to do with their lessons."

Ellen's students, in contrast, were attentive with the exception of the not yet literate or articulate Walter, who chased a kitten on all fours. Ellen said she followed the Socratic approach: asking questions of her pupils, listening to their answers, and pushing them always further to explore a subject.

"What do you think of rote learning as a requirement?" Whitman asked, remembering how his students had mumbled their multiplication tables like weary automatons.

"It makes a straight-cut ditch," she said, "out of a free, meandering brook. My pupils vie to speak. They're almost foaming over with ideas."

"Do you ever have to mete out blows with the ferule to get their attention?" Whitman inquired.

She looked askance at the thought. "No need. Other innovations," she pointed out, "are that boys and girls sit together. They don't stand to recite, and they don't have to parrot dry facts."

Amid all this ferment, Ellen's charges were learning (and mastering) Greek, Latin, French, Italian, German, composition, arithmetic, history, and geography—all at different levels, the elder helping the younger.

"My students were just learning to make quill pens at this age," Whitman told her, "while yours surpass some men at Harvard."

"I pour ideas into their heads," she said, "but unfortunately, much runs out."

In another departure from common practice, play was an important part of the routine. She released her charges for a brief recess, and while they romped in the dooryard, she displayed school books, most inscribed with her sister's name. The sound of joyful voices singing "London bridge is falling down" wafted into the room.

When Ellery poked his head in, the mood shifted from amiable to frosty—even though a fire was blazing. "I was on my way to meet

Henry when I saw the children outside with no supervision," he said. "Isn't your primary job to keep them from falling down the well? Why are the girls attending school anyway? The brass needs polishing, feather beds must be aired; there's sewing to do. You're stuffing their heads with useless learning. Why waste their time with Latin?"

He plucked some books from the shelf. "Margaret's books! I won't have you turning my daughters into pedants like her!" He tore out pages and stuffed them in the woodstove. "That's all they're good for!"

On seeing Whitman's shocked expression, Ellery changed his demeanor from rebuke to charm. "Watch how I'd conduct their lessons, Walter." He called the children back inside, strutting as he delivered his instructions: "All of you—boys and girls—*know* your proper bone."

They looked confused, glancing down to see if any actual bones were called for. Little Walter reached up to be lifted by his papa, but Ellery nudged him aside with his boot and continued to orate: "Gnaw at it, bury it, unearth it again. Be not simply good, but good *for* something, whether that be as a wife, a mother, a father, or a free spirit."

Inordinately pleased with this directive, he addressed them more like an impresario than a schoolmaster: "Now, students, if physical activity is on the curriculum, I'll teach you a dance from medieval Italy."

He gathered them in a circle with himself in the center. "Watch and learn!" Ellery danced, humming a double-time tune, and they attempted to repeat his leaps and hops. "The saltarello!" he shouted, drawing Ellen by her hands into the jig. "Walter, can you play the pianoforte for us?"

Whitman twirled round on the stool and pounded on the keys, thumping out the tune to "Camptown Races." Children and adults all sang together at topmost volume, as Ellery shouted, "Faster, faster!" Whitman's fingers flew over the keyboard.

De Camptown ladies sing dis song (one leap, two leaps),
doo-dah, doo-dah!
De Camptown racetrack five miles long, oh, doo-dah day!"
(leap, leap, hop!)
Den fly along like a rail-road car, Doo-dah! doo-dah!
Runnin' a race wid a shootin' star, Oh, doo-dah-day!

The children spun and twirled, faster and faster, laughing hysterically. Ellery led the chorus, bellowing in fine voice: "Gwine to run all night, gwine to run all day!" Tension vanished, replaced by high spirits and rollicking ruckus. Wide pine planks shook under pounding feet in percussive concord. Ellery scooped up baby Walter from the floor—lest he be trampled—settled him on his shoulders, and continued dancing and singing.

"Now the tarantella!" Ellery cried, leading them in a wild gambol around the room, arms and legs flailing, feet kicking high. A frenzy of raucous laughter before Ellery cut it off with an orchestra conductor's swipe of his hand: "Now that, my dear wife, is how to reach young minds and hearts! Not instruction in dismal numbers but dancing our way to celestial life."

The children panted, giggled, and flopped on the floor like rag-dolls—pushing and pulling each other in a heap of skinny arms and legs. Greta planted a wet kiss on baby Walter's dirt-smeared cheek.

With a radiant smile, Ellery waved farewell and sailed from the room. "Don't expect me back for a while, my dear. I go to the woods to unearth my font of creativity."

He waltzed out, leaving Ellen to restore order and resume teaching. "I have a foolish wish to do something great, to help children *be* great," she sighed. "It may be that the world is not ready for utopia. I will probably spend my life in the kitchen . . . *if* we don't end up in the poorhouse."

Whitman pounded an ominous chord on the piano. *Ellery! What a man of multitudinous gifts. . . . And frailties?*

CHAPTER THIRTY-EIGHT

Henry and Ellery

SEPTEMBER 2, 1850, LATER THAT MORNING
BY THE SHORE OF WALDEN POND, CONCORD

Rambling through the woods, Whitman scuffled and kicked piles of crackling chestnut leaves. He turned at the sound of unbridled laughter, a virtual jubilee of joy sifting through the trees. He saw Thoreau and Ellery shaking branches of a chestnut tree, and spiney conkers raining down on their heads. They hopped about to catch them in their straw hats.

Ellery beckoned Whitman over. "So glad you're able to join our expedition, Walter!" His handsome face was full of fun, with apple-red cheeks, a smile lighting it up like sunshine.

"I hope I don't interrupt your enterprise," the reporter said to Thoreau, who appeared shy. *Or perhaps,* it occurred to Whitman, *he's not thrilled at my joining their duo?*

"No such thing, Mr. Whitman." Thoreau handed the newcomer a hiking stick he'd fashioned from a slim column of striped maple. "You're welcome to join our brotherhood. Ellery and I are frequent trekking companions. We've meandered all over Cape Cod, the Catskills, even Mt. Katahdin in Maine."

"We just as often go rowing on the river, skating on the pond in winter, swimming, and, of course, berry-picking, nutting, and mushroom hunting." Ellery kicked a pile of chestnut leaves, which drifted in the direction of a pond. He pointed to it and said, "Look, Walter—let's be first-name friends—there lies what remains of a small shanty Henry lived in for two years, all alone."

Thoreau looked towards a pile of foundation stones, residue of a cabin he'd built, and said, "The idyll was thanks to your urging, Ellery. And your help in cutting down hemlocks for posts and raising the walls."

"What's that lake called?" Whitman asked.

Thoreau answered with a proprietary air. "Walden—a kettle-hole pond, very deep."

"Henry has just finished a manuscript account of his time at Walden Pond," Ellery added. "Do you think Greeley would like to serialize it in *The Tribune*?"

"Right now, Greeley is fixed on memorializing Margaret Fuller, which brings me to seek your reminiscences."

"It just so happens I've composed a poem for the occasion, which you are welcome to use in the newspaper, *gratis*." Ellery assumed an orator's pose, hooking thumbs behind his suspenders.

"We weep the radiance that is flown
O night of agony and awful morn!
Thou art not lost though sleeping in the deep
A heart too strong, a will unchecked,
The dream is sunk beneath the surge."

"Not my finest effusion," Ellery said with faux modesty, "but 'twill do, 'twill do. Should I rhyme 'surge' and 'dirge'?"

"Perchance, my friend," Thoreau said, "it's still a bit more slipshod than sublime. As I've often told you, a little judicious editing does no harm."

"And, my friend, as I've often told *you*," Ellery shot back, "spontaneity is closest to inner divinity. My verse dethrones the bugbears of prudence, reason, and logic to crown the worship of irrefutable impulse. "

Whitman—who had a job to do—interrupted the poetic theorizing. "May I ask your thoughts on Margaret's writing on the wave of revolutions in Europe in '48? When I read her dispatches in *The Tribune*, I thought to myself, "God, 'twas delicious, that brief, tight, glorious grip upon the throats of kings."

"Blood-red socialistic views! The howling wolves of enmity to her radical ideas were already baying!" Ellery responded with fervor, his face rhubarb-red. Controlling himself, he added, "Why is everyone so fixed on *her* version of events? Margaret has no monopoly on profundity. I've been to Italy too; I know how foreigners think. Across the continent in 1848—not just in Italy—uprisings broke out—France, Austria, Spain, Germany—everywhere! What did all those rebellions achieve? Nothing! Monarchs rule again, just as before all the bloodshed. What's imperative is not political revolution but radical, personal reform."

Thoreau came to his aid. "I agree with Ellery. Waldo's philosophy, which the public calls Transcendentalism, bids us cast off all earthly chains. We must each heed divine inspiration within. By connecting with nature, we wake from the stupor of conformity." He cast his eyes down, unaccustomed to preaching.

"Precisely," Ellery nodded. "The common tribe sees Henry and me as misfits because we do not march to the beat of their drummer. We have broken our chains. We live in daily rapture."

"Simplify, simplify, simplify!" Thoreau murmured, so low Whitman had to lean forward to hear.

"If only rapture were a cure for moral slumber," Whitman stated, defending his view. "The rebels in Europe may have only temporarily toppled the autocrats before they were routed . . ."

"Before they were slaughtered," Ellery butted in.

"But," Whitman persisted, "they planted seeds of victory in their graves. Revolt is dormant, not dead. The people will rise up again."

"*The people* are no concern of mine. I believe in the Sovereignty of the Individual." Ellery tossed back his mane of long hair. "I can hardly find rest for the soles of my feet. The open road calls me. Waldo says, 'Hitch your wagon to a star.'"

"And Margaret?" Whitman asked. "Will her star sink to oblivion?"

Thoreau shrugged. "Death is not a failure, and continued life not necessarily a success. It depends on whether you truly *live*."

"I shall quote my most famed line of poetry," Ellery announced: "If my bark sinks, 'tis to another sea."

The two friends' heads jerked upwards when they heard a squawk. They burst into laughter and pointed at the unlikely apparition of a porcupine wedged in the cleft of an oak tree. Ellery's exuberance overflowed. "Look, Walter, a porkypine! Speaking of sinking—do you know that creature's quills are filled with air?"

"Porcupines are good swimmers," Thoreau added, "because their quills keep them afloat in the water."

It occurred to Whitman to describe the two young men in his article as buoyant and prickly themselves, just like a porcupine. Unpredictable, given to sudden outbursts of merriment as well.

Thoreau plopped down on a stump, pulled out his flute, and tootled the tune of "Skip to My Lou." Ellery kicked up his heels, jumping and dancing. "Faster, Henry, play it in the key of joy!"

Whitman shook his head in disbelief. Margaret Fuller dead, but not a care in the world for those two. I'll leave them to their high spirits, he thought.

Margaret Fuller had prophesied the dawn of an egalitarian Golden Age, when all men and women of whatever race could rise to their fullest potential. *May it be so!* Whitman said to himself. Thus abstracted, he stumbled over an oak root. Beside him a partridge flapped into the air with whirring wings. Overhead a black rope of geese undulated in the sky, their honking carried on the wind.

Ellen's voice sounded faint in the distance: "Ellery, where are you? Come home!"

CHAPTER THIRTY-NINE

Boating

SEPTEMBER 2, 1850, LATE MORNING,
ON THE CONCORD RIVER

On his way back to town, Whitman saw Emerson and Hawthorne shoving a double-masted rowboat into a particularly lazy bend of the Concord River. Nearby Melville paddled a canoe with sleek J-strokes.

"Ahoy, ye land lubber!" Melville hallooed. "Hop aboard!" Nosing the canoe towards a flat boulder, he steadied it while Whitman flopped in, hardly a vision of grace.

From the rowboat, Emerson surveyed the woods lining the riverbank. The first reds and yellows of maples and birches blazed. "A redundance of splendor," he said, beaming as if he had personally invented autumnal glory.

Hawthorne waxed nostalgic. "Just like old times," he said, "on board Henry's *Pond-Lily*, exploring the river."

"Ah, but usually we glided by moonlight with Margaret in the bow." Emerson stared into the depths.

"Yes," Hawthorne replied. "Do you remember how she chided me? 'Your work is too placid, too dainty and picturesque. You should paint with blood-warm colors.'"

"I received the same critique," Emerson admitted. "I am too 'aloof from life,' she called me, paralyzed on my empyrean peak, removed from the perturbations and conflicts of the world. I should give up self-reliance, forget efforts to improve myself. Social reform—nay, transformation, she was after. She called me a 'poor hermit,' said we need the animating influence of discord here to shake us up."

"You have to admit utopian schemes have been refulgent in our times," Whitman reminded the Sage. "Brook Farm, Fruitlands and Shaker villages right here, scores of communes across the country—Red Hook, Oneida, Hopedale, New Harmony, and more."

"We live," Emerson agreed, "truly in an era of aspiration. Or, at least so I remind my audiences."

"It's an era of inhumanity as well," Melville muttered. He back-paddled with an abrupt flourish to prevent the other boat's ramming Whitman's seat in the canoe. "Nat, watch where you're going!"

"A bit difficult, when I'm facing backward," Hawthorne said. "Waldo, please point in the desired direction. You were saying, Herman?"

"I merely wanted to note the abomination of our so-called civilized government annexing Texas," Melville finished.

"Which was," Whitman was impelled to tell them, "a pretext for the Mexican War, which was part of a plot to grab 850,000 square miles of Mexican land in the West."

"All of which was a plan to admit more slave states, as Henry constantly reminds me," Emerson said. "Henry and Margaret—not to mention Lidian—accuse me of shunning the abolitionist cause." He trailed his hand in the cool water.

"And what is your reply?" Whitman very much wished to know.

Emerson sighed, "How idealistic we were when Margaret lived with us. How young and innocent! 'I have other slaves to free,' I always told her. 'I must first liberate my imprisoned spirit, locked in the far recesses of my brain.'" He continued, almost speaking to himself, "'Snap your chains,' she told me. 'Release your emotions.'" Emerson looked at Hawthorne and whispered, "She may have been the best of us."

"Margaret called you 'The Intellect' and herself 'Life.'" Hawthorne recalled. "I sympathize with you, Waldo, for I too am an observer. We both require peace and serenity for our work. For Margaret, it was the heat of action, not cold thought, that signifies."

"I loved her like a sister, but I confess: I was born cold. I always froze when she came near. Corpse-cold, she called me. She hated my fatal incapacity to express regard. She once said I lack the kind affection of a pigeon!" Emerson looked to the heavens for exoneration.

Hawthorne seconded Margaret's judgment: "You're not exactly demonstrative, Waldo."

Stung, he answered in a self-congratulatory tone. "Calm, introspection—even passivity—I daresay, are obligatory for pondering the truths of human existence." He assumed an orator's mantle: "You know what I say: A foolish consistency . . ."

"Is the hobgoblin of little minds," Hawthorne finished, a bit too fast. "Margaret was nothing if not consistent in her self-regard."

Whitman was suddenly struck by a new idea and sat up straight to announce: "Contradiction is the enemy of consistency. If you contradict yourself, you can be large; you can contain multitudes!"

"A mountain of maximum Me-ness—that was Margaret," Emerson said, "a consistent tornado of unalloyed Much-ness. The most irritating conversationalist in the Americas."

"I wish I had known her." Melville spoke wistfully. "She sounds like a phantom one pursues but can never catch. No smooth sailing for her; always a squall." He scanned the sluggish current as if hoping for rapids.

"Speaking of catching something, shall we wet a line, gentlemen?" Hawthorne pulled out a bamboo fishing pole.

They baited their hooks and cast their lines. Sunlight vied with shadow through overhanging leaves. Bubbles on the surface burst. A swan glided past, all quiet serenity on the surface while its webbed feet churned furiously below.

“Is it true,” Whitman asked, “that swans unlock their silent throats and sing beautifully right before they die?”

“I have heard it so—a swan song,” Melville murmured. He started in surprise as a foot-long trout leapt in a silver arc near the canoe. A shower of cool drops splattered his hands. “Would that I had a harpoon!” Melville shouted.

CHAPTER FORTY

Lunch with Lidian

SEPTEMBER 2, 1850, MIDDAY, CONCORD

The Meeting House bell boomed twelve metallic bongs as Whitman approached Bush after his excursion on the river. The door to the big two-story house swung open. Lidian leaned out as if hoping for company.

A stately, pale-faced matron—angular, lithe and very graceful like a dancer—she exhibited all too clearly an air of bitter discontent. After Emerson's first bride—his beloved Ellen—had died, the Sage characterized his second marriage—a more practical arrangement—as "a very sober joy." Even the unmarried Walter knew such terminology was not endearing.

"Mr. Whitman, won't you come in and have midday dinner with me? The children are at school, and the house is deathly quiet. Not even Mr. Emerson scribbling away in his study with his door closed, as usual. There's no 'usurping conversation'—as he terms my attempts to chat—to bother him today."

"Gladly," he accepted, "if it's no trouble to you, Mrs. Emerson."

She bustled about and loaded a tray with food. "I hope you won't object to baked beans with molasses, cornbread, cheese, and apple cider. Gustatory options are limited here, unlike the choices in a city."

"What excellent cornbread!" he said as he took a generous bite, mouth stuffed to prevent an injudicious reply.

Lidian spied a disturbing object on the table—a vase located adjacent to the edge. She rushed to move it and arranged it precisely in the absolute dead-center of the table. At Whitman's questioning glance, she informed him, "I have a passion for symmetry, Mr. Whitman. If the vase were not centered, it would cease to be an ornament and become litter." A mild air of revulsion at the disarray, a slight shudder of her shoulders, overtook her.

She spied a pile of books on a side table and showed signs of alarm at the incipient clutter. Earnest, she placed the smaller books just so, atop the larger, creating a pyramidal, as opposed to cantilevered, stack. She emitted an audible sigh of relief—disorder averted!

"Mrs. Emerson—or, if I may—Lidian, it is my hope you will enlighten me about the miscellaneous players assembled for Miss Fuller's memorial." He swallowed a spoonful of beans before forging ahead. "Will you be forthright with me? I confess, ever since I heard Mr. Emerson deliver his lecture on 'The Poet' in New York, I've been consumed with hero worship. Not the best frame of mind for a journalist."

"I cannot promise objectivity." She wiped crumbs from her lips with a linen napkin. "But I am evermore bluntly honest. What do you wish to know?"

"I'm most curious about Mr. Ellery Channing. What do you think of him? I was predisposed to think him a poet of exceeding ineptitude. In person, he seems a true bon vivant, exuberant and uninhibited, like a coiled spring poised to pop."

She chunked a tray of dishes in the tin sink and worked the pump handle up and down, with a force unseemly for one so decorous. "Even now," she answered with a frown, "whenever Ellen is about to give birth, that young man decamps for a prolonged excursion in the wilds. The children are nothing but an irritation to him; he finds a newborn's squalls intolerable."

"He hardly seems the paternal type," Whitman acknowledged. "But I just saw Ellen and Ellery dancing together this morning. He didn't appear distant but exuberant. A thoroughbred, not a mule."

"If you only knew the half of their impetuous courtship . . ." she began. "Marry in haste, repent at leisure. The stories I could tell."

"I'm eager to hear them." He picked up a dishrag and began to rub pewter plates in a circular motion.

"There's one young woman—a perpetual thorn in the garden of their marriage—Cary Sturgis. She's now Cary Tappan, Ellery's first love." She rinsed a plate and dried it, placing it on a shelf. She shook her head as if the subject was distasteful. "Ellen has the patience of a saint, but when Ellery throws his tantrums . . . . Between you, me, and the fencepost, she ought to amputate herself from her matrimonial half."

She pumped another gush of water from the spigot, then stopped the flow with a final *thunk*. Notes from a flute drifted in the air, and Lidian lifted her head, a smile playing on her lips. One foot tapped in time to the music. She was almost dancing!

A clump of bittersweet vines wrapped in paper sailed through the open window. Lidian smiled broadly as she unwrapped the bundle of red berries, which were popping open to reveal golden cores. She waved at the launcher of the bouquet, none other than Henry Thoreau, standing outside wearing a sheepish grin.

"Do you often receive vegetal tributes pitched through the window?" Whitman asked.

"Henry cheers me up with poems and posies." She unrolled the paper, scrawled with ink. "You must excuse me, Mr. Whitman. Another time, I can add more color to your picture of Mr. Emerson and acolytes."

She handed him his hat and ushered him out.

CHAPTER FORTY-ONE

Mourning

SEPTEMBER 3, 1850, CONCORD

Sophia Hawthorne was quite happily sketching a speckle-breasted chicken hawk, penciling in its sharply hooked beak and smudging stipples of graphite to depict mottled feathers. The bird suddenly spoiled her study by swooping off a branch with a stiff flap of its wings. It glided in a soaring circle and uttered an ominous *kek-kek-kek* cry. She had intended the drawing to be a symbol of Avian Dignity. Instead, it became an Angel of Death as it dropped like a stone to seize a chipmunk. The hawk ascended, squeezing its writhing trophy in its talons. Unwary chickadees were hopping about the lawn, and Sophia hastily shooed them off, lest they be next on the menu.

Why, she wondered, do I think of death when we return to Concord? It was the scene of so many happy days after she and Nat married! Living near the Emersons in the home where their children were born was idyllic, so why, on this return visit, did she feel a cold shiver down her spine? It must be that she could still see little Wallie Jr. capering about with his hoop or riding on "Uncle" Henry's shoulders.

Emerson eternally grieved his son's death—his first-born! Part of the reason Lidian retreated to her bed every day, Sophia was sure, was her sorrow over her darling son's death. No matter how many years ago—losing one's child, barely five years old—the anguish would never recede.

She knew Henry felt the loss as well. He was almost more of a father to Wallie than was Waldo himself. All the days and weeks when Waldo was away lecturing, Henry was there, not just caring for the garden and restocking the woodpile but taking care of Wallie and Lidian too. They went on picnics together. Henry showed Wallie secret spots for berry-picking. He whittled boats, whistles, pop guns, all sorts of toys for little Wallie.

Feeling a pang, Sophia suddenly remembered when Wallie's pet bunny died. How the little boy had loved that creature! When the child peeked into the hutch one winter day, the rabbit was still and stiff, its fur matted and hard. Henry had wrapped it tenderly and buried it in the garden—hacking away at the frozen ground—and Wallie said, "In springtime, Bunny will sprout into a whole tree of baby bunnies hanging from the branches by their ears." Sophia could never think of that without a catch in her throat.

She remembered how Lidian had described the trio popping corn one gloomy day. Henry had shelled the kernels into a warming pan. Lidian shook them over the fire, while Henry wound up a music box and played "Home Sweet Home," accompanying it on his flute. Wallie tooted his whistle and clapped his hands. When the chorus of snapping corn reached its apogee, Lidian lifted the napkin off the pan, and white puffy blossoms showered them, lighting all over Wallie and the rug. Henry said it looked like a snowstorm, so, of course, they pounded each other with fistfuls of popcorn.

The house was so colorful inside, a contrast to the liver-colored skies outside. Lidian had placed sheaves of red and yellow maple leaves and clusters of blue asters on every table. Happy days of yore.

How Lidian doted on that child! Once she found Wallie had constructed a tower, stacking up cards, spools of thread, and an awl-case with a flower box on top, all balanced precariously. "Wallie!" she said. "What a stairway to heaven you've built!" She was so overcome with admiration, she lay on the floor and kissed the pyramid. It tumbled down. *An omen, perchance?* Sophia wondered.

Enough of Wallie thoughts! Now they had to manage another loss. Draping the Emerson house in mourning would multiply Sophia's melancholy, but it had to be done before the ceremony. Lidian had already hung a black wreath on the front door. Together with Ellen, who was standing on a barrel, Sophia helped drape strips of black crepe on the top and sides of the door. Women's work—preparing a house for mourning.

She wondered where Lidian could have found so much black bombazine so soon after hearing the news about Margaret. *Perhaps Wallie's death gave her a funerary cast of mind,* Sophia thought, *and she stores black crepe the way others hoard ribbons or buttons.* Lidian's own wardrobe contained no jaunty colors, only fabric of dismal gray or charcoal hues. "Ashes to ashes" was her sartorial strategy. At least it eliminated the need to choose a color each day, allowing more space for her mind to dwell on grievances.

"Every Fourth of July," Ellen told Sophia as they worked, "Lidian swathes the door and front gate in mourning, an emblem of the death of liberty for enslaved people in the South."

Everyone knew that Lidian's fervor for the Abolitionist cause was all-consuming. "I cannot celebrate our country's birth as long as our colored brethren are denied freedom. Every time I picture their suffering on slave ships," she said with a quaver, "not to mention the poor souls whipped by overseers, it makes my gorge rise and almost undoes me."

Inside the house, there was no jolly scene of popping corn now. Long gone were those halcyon days, although Sophia could almost see Wallie hiding behind a door to pounce out and surprise Uncle Henry.

She and Ellen followed Lidian's instructions. They placed silvery daguerreotypes facedown and turned paintings to the wall. They hung mourning ribbons on looking-glass frames, then covered the mirror faces with cheesecloth. To prepare the parlor, they fluffed cushions and straightened doilies.

"Nat and Waldo may consider mesmerism a farce," Sophia said with uncommon resolution, "but I'm determined to attempt it. I have so many questions for Margaret."

"Her marriage to that young Italian seems so out of character," Lidian said, "yet I'm frankly terrified." She paced hither and yon, all aflutter. The grandfather clock ticked steadily in its mahogany case, an unfailing reminder of mortality. "I don't know if I should stop the pendulum now or just before the ceremony."

Sophia could no longer delay delivering what she feared would be unwelcome news. She slowly took a letter from her reticule and addressed Lidian and Ellen. "Did you know that Cary Sturgis Tappan and her husband are our landlords in Lenox? They allow Nat and me to rent the Red House at greatly reduced rent. Very kind."

Only a bare shrug of acknowledgment from Lidian and Ellen.

"Hmmph—you call that generosity?" Lidian could not desist from carping, equanimity not her strong suit. "As well she might, since Lady Bountiful's husband is wealthy as Croesus. Not that Cary herself ever wanted for a shekel. Her father—the Merchant Prince of Boston—is many times over a millionaire."

"People say Cary married Will Tappan for money," Ellen sniffed, "but how can that be, when her family has a fortune?"

Her lack of charity was understandable, Sophia thought, given Ellery's flirtatious history with Cary. Sophia felt obliged to assert what they knew to be true: "Family fortune does not insulate a woman from needing to marry well. Men control the purse."

"Why are we talking of Caroline?" Lidian eyed the letter in Sophia's lap.

"Cary is coming here today—with her father. She wants to witness the mesmerism." Sophia said. "Cary says she was Margaret's confidante, so her presence will induce Margaret's spirit to speak."

Lidian looked alarmed. "How dare she?" Her voice squeaked into an upper register. "I sent her no invitation, although that heathen has a marked tendency to barge in unexpectedly."

Sophia supplied the obvious answer: "Waldo must've invited her. Surely they've communicated about Margaret's death."

"That man's hospitality is insatiable," Lidian huffed. "It's like living in a hotel."

"Cary was my sister's favorite pupil," Ellen had to admit, "her most intimate friend. When the rest of us were still ignorant, Margaret told Cary about her baby."

Lidian minced no words, revealing a vindictive layer beneath her ostentatious piety. "Be that as it may, I remind you that Cary Sturgis Tappan is an incorrigible flirt." She looked both sad and angry. "She is also an 'intimate' friend of Mr. Emerson, and, as Ellen knows all too well, Ellery's boon 'companion' to boot."

"You hardly have to remind me, Lidian." Ellen busied herself flicking an invisible speck of dust from a sideboard. "Ellery insisted we name our second daughter Caroline Sturgis Channing, in tribute to their *special* bond."

"Why did you agree?" Sophia couldn't forbear asking.

With as much dignity as she could muster, Ellen said, "Since I named our first daughter Margaret Fuller Channing after my sister, Ellery said it was his turn. And, Lidian, you are hardly immune to beloved namesakes. You named your first daughter Ellen Tucker Emerson, after Waldo's first wife."

"Yes, but I call her Nellie," Lidian admitted. She looked at the floor. "I had the foolish thought that our daughter might replace Mr. Emerson's memories of his first love."

A knock at the door interrupted their colloquy. Whitman sallied in, cocking his head and putting a hand on a hip in his jocular fashion. "Greetings, fair maids! Why the long faces?" Taking in the funerary décor with a circumferential glance, he quickly amended his mien from cheerful to woeful. “I beg pardon, ladies. Of course, ’tis a most solemn day.”

“Not just solemn,” Sophia corrected, “but momentous. Today we’ll hear Margaret speak.”

CHAPTER FORTY-TWO

Fear and Trembling

SEPTEMBER 3, 1850, CONCORD

After he absorbed the mortuary ambiance of the altered surroundings, Whitman offered to help. "May I be of service, ladies?"

"We've finished preparations." Lidian looked around, satisfied at the atmosphere of gloom. "Unless you see anything that suggests cheer."

"No, an excellent job you've done. All that's missing is a coffin . . . and a corpse, but no matter!" he said. "Most lugubrious."

"Mr. Whitman, you'll recall I was speaking yesterday of Cary Sturgis," Lidian began. "You can soon judge her for yourself. I've only just learned that Cary Sturgis Tappan is to attend our mesmerist session this evening." Her posture was stiff, her mouth a thin line of disgust.

"I remember reading her poems in *The Dial*," he said. "At the time I thought them anonymous, signed only with the letter 'Z.'"

"Mr. Emerson was always begging her to send drawings for the magazine and her blasphemous poems." Lidian's mouth turned down as if tasting something sour. "When that brat stayed here for lengthy visits, I was relegated to domestic drudge. Queen Caroline was Mr. Emerson's exalted Muse."

She assaulted the floor with a broom, dust whorls her enemy. "Do you know what that imp wrote me, when I had just given birth?" She stirred up a cloud of dust and coughed. "'I shall not send my love to the baby, for I never like anything that can only express itself by doleful cries.'"

"She exults in flouting convention," Ellen said. "I suppose that's why she and Ellery are compatible. Both are the epitome of Transcendental self-reliance, true to their inner urgings, and to the devil with manners!"

"According to my lights, self-reliance is a fancy term for ego." Lidian was firm in judgment. "Imagine the conceit of believing God is inside—ego-theism, I call it."

Whitman couldn't resist saying, "I look forward to meeting such a paragon of individualism!" The ladies were noticeably silent, failing to applaud his anticipation.

"You'll find her a free spirit," Sophia said, her words circumspect. "She can be quite charming, if one is attracted to bold, vivacious redheads. I believe even the artist Mr. Eastman Johnson was smitten when he sketched her. Only charcoal, not an oil portrait, but nonetheless . . ."

"She is willful, heedless of pleasing others. Cary will say anything. She delights in offending one's sensibilities." Lidian wielded a feather duster with vicious swats. "If one's father is a rich nabob, one can defy manners and still be the brightest bubble of high-society foam."

"Five years ago, Cary boarded with Nat and me at the Old Manse," Sophia said. "Nat was not impressed with her prominence in the young 'Newness' circle, using slang and aping the lingo of that coddled generation. When I attended Margaret's Conversations, Cary delighted in acting like an impudent child, misbehaving just to incite outrage. When Margaret asked the serious question 'What is Life?' Cary was flippant: 'It is laughing or crying, depending on one's constitution.'"

Ellen chimed in. "She never blots a line in her verse. Spontaneity is her mantra."

"Mr. Whitman," Lidian said, brimming with disapproval, "you've seen Ellen and Ellery at their sweet little cottage. Do you know what

Cary had the temerity to say after visiting them? 'I never saw a prettier external life, but pearls are hollow.'"

"Hollow!" Ellen pounded a bolster into shape on the divan. "Well, we all know she was in love with Ellery when he met me." She turned the wedding ring on her finger and smiled with more than a speck of triumph.

"I remember Cary told Margaret she did not think you were Ellery's equal, Ellen, not 'noble' enough for him," Lidian divulged with unseemly zest. "She said it was more like he adopted, rather than married, you."

"I suppose that's why Ellery disappeared right after our honeymoon to see her—to assure her of the rightness of his choice." Ellen smoothed her gingham skirt.

Whitman's inclination to meet a person eliciting such various opinions grew. He felt giddy at the prospect and sang out, "Batten down the hatches, ladies! Hurricane Caroline is a-comin'."

"Ellen, please draw the curtains." Lidian unlocked the glass door of the grandfather clock. "I believe I'll halt the pendulum now." She arrested its swing and tied it off.

The wind picked up outside, began to wail. A flock of crows took flight, their raucous caws trailing behind.

CHAPTER FORTY-THREE

Guests Arrive

SEPTEMBER 3, 1850, EVENING SUPPER, CONCORD

The usual cohort (Emersons, Hawthornes, Thoreau, Melville, Channings, Whitman) gathered around the supper table as the Meeting House bell tolled six. The fare consisted of boiled beef and horseradish, potatoes freshly dug up, brown bread and butter, bottles of capers, pots of pickles, and applesauce. Except for a grief-stricken Ellen, everyone ate with gusto. Anticipation of the soon-to-come mesmerism session ran high.

Without so much as a knock at the door or a how-d'ye-do, an elderly man and an attractive young lady burst into the Emersons' dining room. The men leapt up to surround them, bubbling jovial greetings. Lidian and Ellen sat silent through the introductions.

"Cary! How delightful to see you!" Emerson embraced the fashionably clad newcomer. In a scarlet silk dress, she appeared a bright flower in an enveloping sea of black. "Let me bring you a chair!"

"You can bring me a glass of wine, too," she said with a saucy toss of curls. "Let me present my father, Captain Bill Sturgis. He's eager to see if we can truly summon spirits."

All eyes swerved to her companion, a burly, muscular man of nearly seventy years. Looking more like a monument than a mortal, the distinguished gentleman sported a gold-headed cane and cape of the finest fur. His bushy hair was slicked into obedience with fragrant pomade.

Lidian rose to take his top hat and cape. "Welcome, sir! In my hometown of Plymouth, we've heard of your naval exploits." She caressed the velvety cape with her long fingers. "I've never felt anything so soft."

"Next to a beautiful woman and a lovely infant," Captain Sturgis (the acme of well-rehearsed suavity) said, "a prime sea otter is the finest natural object in the world."

The others could summon no similar examples of excellence; they seemed nonplussed. Waldo seized the reins of conversation to put his guest at ease. "We've heard how your company dominates the Northwest fur trade with China, Captain."

Sturgis, seated, raised a glass of Madeira to Waldo. "And I've heard how your presence is the pride and boast of Concord, Mr. Emerson."

Lest anyone forget his claim to naval expertise, Melville interjected, "I'm a seafaring man myself. I look forward to hearing your tales of oceanic adventures."

Ellery could no longer cede the spotlight. "As one who has a roving nature *and* is Cary's close friend"—he shot her an insinuating glance, unwelcome to Ellen, who stiffened at his wink—"I would welcome the opportunity to discuss trade with you. I've always felt there is a difference between *making* a living and *living*." He sat up straight, convinced he had delivered a telling bon mot straight out of the Transcendentalist playbook.

"I say, Lidian," Emerson asked, attempting to tamp down controversy, "do we have any Durham mustard to go with this excellent beef?"

"One thing our whalers learned from your merchant brigs," Melville said, filling the breach, "is to paint the bottoms of our ships with copper. Otherwise, barnacles snag so much seaweed and bushels of kelp, it slows down the hunt."

"Speed is indeed imperative," Sturgis agreed, "especially when attacked by pirates."

"Father, not again!" Cary put a restraining hand on his arm.

"Oh yes! Do tell!" the table clamored. The diners leaned forward to hear.

"Off the coast of Macau, a fleet of Chinese pirates came abreast us, broadside to my sloop," Sturgis began. "In addition to 2,500 otter pelts from Oregon and Alaska, I had 300,000 silver dollars in the hold. Fortunately, I had also loaded on board four small swivel cannons. A fortunate precaution! We repelled the pirates with cannon fire while running at full sail to safe harbor."

"How dreadful!" "How frightful!" Dramatic expressions of dismay sounded around the board. The ladies were aquiver, the gentlemen steely-eyed to show manly resolve.

His story having made its impression, Sturgis addressed Ellery directly. "Mr. Channing, I assure you that uppermost in my mind at that moment was *living*—or mayhap dying—not *making* a living. I was prepared to detonate the ship and scuttle our cargo, perishing with all hands rather than fall into the pirates' clutches." He confided in an aside, "Pirates are known for treating captured sailors with exquisite torture."

Ellery, determined to have the last word, muttered, "Better than living with a chronic disease, that is, an enlarged bank account."

Sophia ignored him and turned to Sturgis. "It's no wonder you're called a hero."

"Father is a man of action," Cary said, "which reminds me of our dear Margaret. Waldo, remember how you once called her *Mr.* Margaret Fuller? You thought her life of action made her more of a man than you with your life of thought."

"Margaret was so active—even as a child—that her schoolmates used to say she could eat an apple, rock a cradle, knit a stocking, and read a book all at the same time," Ellen interjected with pride.

Fidgeting, Emerson stared at his plate, perhaps suspecting his life of thought was less than valiant. Laboring to muster his usual serenity, he swept the room with his gaze, hoping to alight on a change of subject.

"What is it Mr. Edgar Allan Poe said of Margaret?" Cary asked with seeming guilelessness. She began to quote: "'Humanity is divided into men, women, and Margaret Fuller.' Poe intended a compliment."

At the mention of the critic Poe, those at the table exchanged nervous—if not a bit eager—glances. *Whoa,* Whitman thought. *Hunting dogs are about to be unleashed.*

Ellery's face turned ominously red. Ellen seemed full of dread. "We don't need to mention Mr. Poe," she was quick to say. "We all know his reviews are balderdash."

"Nonsense!" Cary countered. "You refer, I gather, to Poe's estimate of Ellery's poems, a supreme example of the reviewer's skill as a wordsmith."

"Spiteful garbage!" Ellery leapt up, hammering a fist on the table, making the pickle pots jump.

Unwilling to drop the subject, Cary kept on. "Spiteful or no, that review is a tour de force of literary dissection. As I recall, Poe said Ellery's book 'contains about sixty-three things, which he calls poems, which he seriously supposes so to be. They are full of all kinds of mistakes, the most important of which is that they were printed at all.'" She giggled like a schoolgirl.

"Cary loves to set the cat among the pigeons," Sophia whispered to Whitman, who noticed Ellery looking more a murderous hawk than harmless pigeon.

"You have to admit, Ellery," Hawthorne said, failing to suppress a touch of glee, "Poe had your number when it comes to certain affectations. He said your verse is quite enamored of the word 'sumptuous,' as in 'sumptuous trees' and 'sumptuous girls,' employing the epithet at all hazards and upon all occasions." Hawthorne checked his napkin for stains and, finding none, continued, "What else? Oh, yes—You seem unaware that the word means expensive or costly; and, as Mr. Poe said, 'we are not quite sure either trees or girls are the one or the other.'" Hawthorne laughed aloud, a departure from his usual gravity.

"Why are you all deliberately torturing me?" Ellery's face was an angry mask, his fists clenched.

"I've seen my share of nasty reviews," Melville broke in as Ellery's scowl intensified, "but, my God, Poe can turn a phrase like a stiletto. He said you set yourself up as 'a poet of sublimity and profundity, a poet of unusual depth and very remarkable powers of mind.' That man can land a harpoon."

The whole room—with the exception of a nervous Ellen and infuriated Ellery—hooted with laughter.

"Sometimes blubber is just blubber," Melville added enigmatically.

"A pity that Poe died last year," Whitman ventured in an effort to restore peace, "found in an alley in Baltimore, I believe."

"Good riddance to that drunken scribbler!" Ellery shifted from foot to foot, like a bull about to charge. His hands clasped and unclasped, fist and fingers beyond his control. "Poe's mind was sunk in a pile of manure. Every word he penned adds to the ordure!"

The saintly Lidian wiped her eyes and chuckled. "Remember how Poe said Boston critics have a notion that poets are porpoises, for they always talk about running in schools? He classed Ellery in the school of pompous Transcendental poets." She paused, adding, "Perhaps he meant to include Cary and Mr. Emerson as well?" Her assumed expression of innocence fooled no one.

"Now, Queenie—that's enough. We can't credit that jingle-man with anything but cruel wit." Emerson tried to divert the conversation: "Don't we have a fruit cobbler coming, baked with our own plums?"

Thoreau resolved to defend his friend. He overcame his meekness in the presence of their august visitor to tell the Captain, "You must understand, sir. Ellery is quite sensitive about his poetry."

Sturgis nodded. With a barely concealed twinkle, he remarked, "Thank you, Mrs. Emerson, for a most *sumptuous* repast."

Ellery threw down his napkin and shouted, "If I am to survive this supper, I will finish my meal in the kitchen!" He stomped off.

Ellen started to rise, but Lidian put a hand on her arm and whispered, "I hope he won't vent his anger on you tonight. I know you can ignore his rages, but I'm worried. Of late, he seems so on edge."

"He's changeable as a drop of mercury. I'm habituated to Ellery's ups and downs. Nothing lasts long." Ellen folded her linen napkin and smoothed out its wrinkles.

Lidian patted her hand. "You'd better stay with us tonight or barricade your chamber door."

CHAPTER FORTY-FOUR

The Spirit Speaks

SEPTEMBER 3, 1850, LATER, SÉANCE,
EMERSON HOUSE, CONCORD

In the parlor, sitters gathered around a walnut table: Sophia and Nathaniel Hawthorne, Herman Melville, Lidian and Waldo Emerson, Henry Thoreau, Ellen and Ellery Channing, Cary Sturgis Tappan, William F. Sturgis, and Walter Whitman. The room was dim, illuminated by flickering candles and oil lamps. The ladies, most dressed in black, hugged themselves as if cold. The men wore black armbands and tapped their feet nervously.

The French physician Dr. Théodore Léger was a commanding presence. With his tidy beard and charcoal-colored frock coat, he appeared nothing like a showman or a quack. He stood to greet them: "*Bonsoir, mes amis*! We are gathered to commune with the spirit of Margaret Fuller, a patient of mine, whom I healed through mesmeric treatment. I will be your operator this evening." He looked around the room and made eye contact with each attendee, deadly serious. "Who will be the medium?"

"I will!" Ellen and Cary both volunteered. They glared at each other.

"I share Margaret's blood," Ellen affirmed, secure in her claim. "Surely, I am the one she is most eager to contact."

"I heard you need some token of the departed for the session to succeed. I have the last letter Margaret wrote before boarding the ship." Cary waved a much-folded and unfolded letter like a banner.

Ellen declared: "I have letters as well. Should not a family tie dominate?"

Emerson settled the argument. "Cary was Margaret's closest friend," he told Dr. Léger, "her most esteemed assistant during all her Conversations. Since this is to be a conversation, she should be the means to contact Margaret."

Ellen sighed, a huff of indignation more than resignation.

Lidian was incensed. "Did Cary not blaspheme by saying that Christ was the first hypnotist? How can we allow such sacrilege in this procedure?" She quivered like a jelly mold. Under her breath, she intoned a prayer: "Our Father, who art in heaven . . ."

"Let us begin." Dr. Léger darted a sympathetic glance at Ellen but deferred to Emerson. Cary handed him the letter. He held it above her head. "Ladies and gentlemen, please sit in a circle, holding hands. Your feet must also touch to produce an unbroken chain. No one should speak while I induce the medium to enter a mesmeric trance. Later, you may pose your questions to the spirit, who will speak through Mrs. Tappan."

Cary sat in an easy chair, knee to knee with Dr. Léger. He placed his thumb on her forehead and asked her to fix her eyes on a candle he held in his other hand. He waved the candle back and forth in slow motions, its flame elongating and shrinking. He spoke in a low voice: "I am linking the energy of your body to the energy of the spirit world. Relax, allow your limbs and eyelids to grow heavy, heavier, heavier."

As he continued to speak in a monotone, Cary gradually slumped until she appeared to be in a trance. Around the table everyone held their breath.

A curtain fluttered in a sudden draft. A tall candle flamed up, then winked out. The circle of viewers started, jerking upright. Goosebumps sprouted on arms, teeth chattered. A doleful *whooooo* swept the room.

"It's that blasted owl in the black walnut tree," Emerson reassured them. "Did it wake her?"

Léger, unperturbed, clapped his hands next to Cary's ear. No reaction—she was still as a stone, unhearing.

"I summon our spirit-sister Margaret," he said. "Speak to us!" Everyone leaned forward, bent like a jackknife. To their astonishment, Cary opened her eyes, staring without appearing to see.

"Margaret, have you completed your journey?" Léger asked.

Cary squinted as if near-sighted, blinking her eyes and elongating her neck in a fashion most unnatural for her. She articulated each word with precision. "I am still wandering."

"Uncanny!" Thoreau gasped.

Sophia trembled. "Just like Margaret!"

"Margaret," Léger said, "please lend Cary your vital energy to speak to us. We implore your help in understanding your wishes." He turned to Ellen and indicated she could address the medium.

Ellen's voice quavered. "Where are you, dear Margaret?"

"I am with you, but far away, in a place with no name," Cary said in a voice strikingly like Margaret's. "It is a place with no today, no yesterday, no tomorrow—only forever. I float in the sea. I drift. The sky is deep purple. I am awash in murky water; breakers bash apart wooden planks, tearing open crates."

"What do you see?"

"I see a ship underwater. I grasp a rope of sand, but it dissolves, and the waves tumble me. I am cold, I am wet. I see a man of marble, taller than life. He wears the toga of a Roman Senator, but he is no republican. He is a subjugator."

"A miracle! The Saints be praised!" Lidian gasped. Her abolitionist sympathy was fully aroused. "It's the statue of John Calhoun, the one that tore apart the ship. Tell us more!"

"The marble man holds a scroll carved with the words 'Truth,

Justice, Constitution,'" Cary continued speaking. "His left arm is broken off. The words 'Truth' and 'Justice' have disappeared."

"There is no justice for slaves." Lidian's eyes widened in awe.

"Tell us what you saw in Rome," Léger directed.

"I saw beautiful young men mowed down in their prime. I saw mothers wailing over their martyred sons' bleeding bodies, their limbs gashed or lopped off, perishing in a hopeless contest but holding fast to the idea of liberty."

Léger held an almanac above Cary's head. He pointed to a date ten years in the future. "Tell us what will happen next. In our own country."

"Turn the page," she ordered. Her voice became haggard. "In 1861, I see muskets, sweat, dust, panic; dirty, hungry, beaten men. I hear bugles and booming cannons. I see torn flags and blood-soaked bodies on the ground, piles of chopped-off limbs in tents, clouds of smoke covering battlefields. I see ghosts—hundreds of thousands—of young men who will never return to their wives, mothers, and sisters."

Whitman squeezed his eyes shut imagining the horror—a generation of young men, who were once so handsome and joyous, maimed or dead, their bodies strewn across fields, woods, valleys, and battlefields, a bloody promenade. Behind a mist that clouded his eyes, he seemed to see a vision of brown-faced men, their rifles flashing in the sun. Then he saw charred plantation homes covered in weeds, the soul of the South blackened in shame. He shook off the premonition—*not a fight for liberty in my own country too!*

"Margaret," Emerson said, "we must know. Where is your History of the Roman Revolution? Tell us what happened to your manuscript."

Ellery blanched and grew pale, as if shot with an arrow.

"*Viva la Republica! Viva Italia!*" Cary shot an arm into the air, her open eyes still frozen. Her brow wrinkled. "The history is lost to me, but it is not lost to all."

Everyone exchanged confused glances. Ellery abruptly shattered the spell. "This is rank superstition!" he shouted. "You are dupes to believe this folderol!" He jumped up and shoved away Ellen's hand, breaking the circle.

Hawthorne supported his wife, who fell in a swoon against his shoulder. Consumed with disgust, he felt his reservations were amply justified. "Light the lanterns!" he ordered.

Melville wiped Sophia's damp forehead with a kerchief and addressed Hawthorne. "My God! I felt a hand tap my shoulder—was it you?"

Pandemonium reigned. The women felt terrified or faint, limp as a torn kite. The men milled about the table scoffing and exchanging outbursts like "My word!" "Never have I seen such an outrageous sham!" "What a humbug!"

As the clamor swirled about her, Cary blinked, her trance spent, and said in a small voice, distinctly her own, "What happened?" She shook her head and cleared her throat.

Her father knelt before her and bowed his head to her lap. "It worked!" he whispered. "You found her spirit."

Drained, she clutched his lapels and spoke only to him. "I found so much more."

CHAPTER FORTY-FIVE

Lidian and Henry in the Garden

SEPTEMBER 4, 1850, CONCORD

The next day, Whitman followed Thoreau and Lidian to the vegetable garden, intent on learning more for his story. These Concord folks were not turning out to be the happy utopians he'd imagined.

Thoreau plunged a spading fork into a hill of potato vines and pressed the tines down with a boot-shod foot. He unearthed a handful of oval spuds, brown as the soil, and stooped to shake off a cloud of dirt. He placed the spuds in a basket, which Lidian, standing close beside him, carried.

Lidian was fretful, anxious, tearing to tiny pieces a sprig of primrose she'd pulled up. "If only my dread from that scene yesterday could be shaken off like dirt from those potatoes. I swear, Henry, didn't it sound just like Margaret's voice? I always suspected she had devilry in her."

"Horrific as it was," Whitman said, trying to calm her, "it seemed to have a ring of truth."

"What nightmares that prophecy gave me!" Thoreau grunted as he heaved up a mound of potatoes. "Yet with Daniel Webster's betrayal, the wicked Fugitive Slave Law pushed by that devil Calhoun, and now more slave states in the Union, how can the future be other than a nightmare?"

"More tragedy than nightmare," Lidian said. "I beseech Mr. Emerson to speak up for Abolition, but he never heeds my counsel." She stomped her foot. "I cannot believe he let Cary take precedence over

Ellen as medium! That man is still infatuated, just like when she was a slip of nineteen and he a married man of thirty-five!"

"Waldo gets a vicarious thrill from her rebellious spirit," Thoreau explained to Whitman. "Cary is like a child of whim, impulsive and irreverent."

"If only the arctic chill he shows you and me applied to her!" Lidian complained. "He forever tells me he has an 'incapacity to demonstrate affection,' but with Cary it's different. I remember how they used to walk together every single day, while you and I, Henry, were hard at work. And their moonlight paddles on the river!"

"He values your housekeeping, while Cary's talents veer more towards the decorative," Thoreau said, continuing his attempts to calm her. "You have practical skills; Cary frolics in the ether."

"I wouldn't object to his acknowledging my contributions from time to time."

"You know, Lidian, his compliments cut both ways." Thoreau wiped sweat from his brow with a bandana, leaving a brown smear on his forehead. "Waldo praises what he calls my 'simplicity in this double-dealing, quacking world,' yet he thinks me provincial. He told Nat I have no appetite for food and drink—as if that were a fault! He said, 'What can you have in common with a man who sees no difference between ice cream and cabbage, who has no experience of wine or ale?'"

"Being abstemious is no fault," Lidian nodded in approval. "The temperance movement gains every day! Remember Ephesians: 'Do not get drunk on wine, which leads to debauchery. Instead be filled with the Spirit.'"

Thoreau kept digging, filled with agrarian zeal, and Lidian stood close by him, ready to receive the fruits of his labor. The two seemed to forget Whitman's presence, immersed in their domestic ménage. Whitman was feeling a bit peckish—not to mention left out. "I like a gulp of hard cider now and then," he said.

From a branch overhanging the garden came a chorus of musical chirps that sounded like "po-ta-to, po-ta-to."

Lidian's eyes lit up and she challenged Henry, evidently in a game they played. "Well, my classifying friend, what bird call is that?"

He pointed to a small, yellow bird hopping on a pine branch: "A male goldfinch, of course. Bluish-gray eggs, in a cup-shaped nest of plant fiber." Proud of his ornithological expertise, his mouth formed a smirk.

"Henry knows more facts about birds than there are stars in the sky," Lidian informed Whitman. "All animals are his friends. You may have noticed how he always wears green and brown homespun clothes."

Whitman surveyed Thoreau's baggy attire. "A bit of cerulean wouldn't be amiss," he ventured to jest.

"No," Thoreau assured the journalist. "The better to harmonize with Nature. Sometimes animals don't see me creeping up to observe them." He held his hands an arm's length apart. "I once got this close to a mink scurrying by the river."

He wiped his hands on his trousers and plucked a rose twining around the split-rail fence. He inclined his body in a half-bow and presented the flower to Lidian. "The last of the roses, I'm afraid."

Petals of the full-blown blossom dropped to the ground before she could tuck it behind her ear.

They resumed their dissection of Emerson's foibles, a favorite topic. "Waldo always apologizes for showing me 'his most unfriendly friendliness,'" Thoreau said, "but that is his nature—reserved."

"Call it what it is—cold and hard," Lidian said. "With everyone except Cary. And Margaret before her."

Her jealousy twirled in the air like a barely visible dust mote. Curious, Whitman asked, "Tell me about his friendship with Margaret. Was he warm?"

"Ah, Margaret . . ." reflected Lidian. "She was the hot wave—intense, passionate—that washed over his frigid stone."

"He was never washed away by her," Thoreau said.

"Mr. Emerson is too adamantine in his rectitude for that. His pale light could never understand her fire." Lidian bent to wrench a handful of weeds from the garden, turning her head, but not before tears wetted her eyes. "Margaret is—I mean was—like a prism, refracting light into rainbow arcs. Waldo's light emits only a single bone-white ray. It sears without warming."

"He appreciated Margaret's company, welcomed her vision and society," Thoreau put in, "but he withdrew from her intensity."

"Her extreme nature," Lidian theorized, "paralyzed his art." She went on. "Margaret once said Mr. Emerson had raised himself too high, too 'perpendicular'; that he should be more horizontal to learn truth from real life, not from high heaven." She kicked up a clod of dirt as if it might reveal buried facts.

Outside the garden fence, hens cackled, pecking away at the dirt in search of a tasty bug. A flock of geese flapped in chevron flight, honking in a decrescendo as they flew south.

Thoreau looked towards the orchard, where branches bowed down, laden with apples and pears. "Waldo's peaches and plums didn't do well last year at the Middlesex Harvest Fair. No prizes. Judges said the orchard soil is too thin, too rocky for robust fruit. Of course, everyone knows you're the best gardener in Concord, Lidian, but Waldo's orchard fruit is another matter—rather skimpy in flavor."

"That man dotes more on his pears than on his children," Lidian huffed.

CHAPTER FORTY-SIX

Herman and Nat's Target Practice

SEPTEMBER 4, 1850, A BUGGY RIDE, CONCORD

Melville was the only one at the gathering besides Whitman who was not intimately acquainted with Margaret Fuller. After the séance, he was eager to flee the gloom and put his thoughts in order. He wasn't even sure why he'd come, except out of respect for his new friend Hawthorne. He had a nagging feeling that there was something about Fuller—her intensity, her quest for freedom perhaps—that might inspire the book he was writing.

He begged Hawthorne to join him and escape the monotony of mourning. Even though the older author was known for his lack of sociability, he consented to take a buggy ride. To be friends with such a literary eminence was a dream for Melville. The more they talked about literature, the more Melville thirsted for respect. So far, no one considered him a serious writer like Hawthorne. With this next book, he'd prove he was no featherweight.

What a dandy he is, Melville thought of his companion, impeccably arrayed even for a pastoral jog. The very clods of earth seemed to respect his brilliance. Although dollops of mud spattered Melville's boots and the hem of his frock coat, Hawthorne's elegant attire remained pristine. The gold silk of his waistcoat glowed like autumnal maple leaves; his black velvet collar was as smooth as his skin. A handsome man, a pleasure to behold—with a fine mind and a beautiful wife to boot! Melville couldn't even speak of *The Scarlet Letter*, lest he turn scarlet with envy.

"What do you think of last night's occult encounter?" Melville asked as the horses lumbered over the rutted road.

"Complete lunacy!" Hawthorne ranted, not equivocating a jot. "I've inveighed against such vulgar performances with Sophia repeatedly, but she still believes in that fiddle-faddle."

"What about Margaret Fuller? I've heard of her Conversations—they aroused so much attention, and I've read her reviews in the *Tribune*. I know she had a formidable intellect. What do you make of her?"

"Margaret . . . now there's a conundrum for you," Hawthorne said. "Altogether too argumentative for a member of the gentler sex. Talking with her was like a gladiatorial skirmish. A contest she was sure to win, especially with me, since I'm generally as taciturn as the moon. Talk about contentious! Her mode wasn't *joie de vivre* but *joie de guerre*! By God, she could make me laugh, though!"

He reached up with both arms and stretched to rake his fingers through the low canopy of overhanging leaves. "I disapproved of nearly every aspect of her philosophy and person. But I must admit, while any dead fish can be swept along with the mainstream, only a *live* one can swim against the current."

Melville translated Hawthorne's opinion into nautical terms. "You're saying she lacked ballast and rudder, never reefed her sails, never feared a jibe?"

"Safety last! for her." Hawthorne seemed torn between scoffing and admiring. He decided on disapproval. "Do you know, Queen Margaret called marriage 'mutual degradation'—implying it was akin to slavery for women? Even though she considered my own marriage to Sophia an ideal of perfection!"

The idea of ethereal Sophia as "degraded" seemed an oxymoron to Melville. In their brief acquaintance, she always spoke her mind, while revering her husband's wisdom. Theirs was a mutually worshipful union.

"Does Sophia share Fuller's views on women's emancipation?" Melville asked.

"That you will have to ask her," he said. "I know Sophia shares my opinion that Margaret's ideas were more destructive than constructive. She wanted to tear down time-honored traditions without offering anything to replace them." He went on, "Margaret was disappointed when Sophia abandoned painting to care for our children. Yet aren't children a mother's supreme work of art?"

"If marriage was anathema to Fuller, why'd she wed someone so beneath her in education and culture?" Melville asked, voicing the question that haunted all her friends. "Was she a desperate old maid?"

Hawthorne had no ready answer. "Aye, there's the rub." He considered his reply before elaborating, each word appearing as if dragged out of him by a team of oxen. "Margaret wrote Sophia a description of her so-called husband Ossoli, saying he was like a wild violet growing in the deep woods, 'ignorant of great ideas, ignorant of books, but enlightened as to his duties.'"

They exchanged conspiratorial smirks. "Did that mean marital duties?"

"He was—by all accounts—stunningly handsome," Hawthorne responded, offering no further description. He fell into one of his trademark silences as they trundled along. Melville tugged on the reins, and they stopped in a forest glade. Hawthorne alighted from the buggy with a graceful hop and bent down to scoop up a handful of acorns. "Here, Herman, try your aim. Pretend that oak is your prey."

Like competing schoolboys, they threw acorns at a knot in the tree, each naming a foe he wished to vanquish. "Bleeding-heart Abolitionists!" was Hawthorne's target as he hurled a handful, spraying the trunk. "Slavery is not our problem; it's an evil that will one day vanish like a bad dream. Let the South crucify itself!"

Saying "readers who wish only to be entertained!" Melville let fly a fusillade of acorns. "Today's market craves sensation, and the penny papers give them plenty: murder, mayhem, madness!" His acorns overshot the target, so riled up was he at the thought of fluff-headed readers.

"My *bête noire*—editors who seek transparency." Hawthorne hurled a spray of acorns that hit the tree with a satisfying hiss. "What an inhospitable country for fiction! I need shadows, antiquity, mystery—picturesque, gloomy scenes—but this country is all sweetness and sunlight!"

"Whither unfathomable blackness?" Melville asked. "We will never grow up as a culture until we can imagine the demonic."

They pretend-sparred a few blows at a philistine public, waving canes like swords. Then they climbed back in the buggy with Hawthorne manning the reins for the return trip.

"Can a book succeed by aiming at a higher truth?" Melville peppered his friend with questions. "Captain Sturgis fascinates me. Might he be of use for my new novel?"

Hawthorne seemed absorbed in thought, not answering.

"Do you think I can corner him and ask him questions? He and Fuller have the same passion and intensity. Is that a blessing or a curse? Damnation! This gathering stirs me into a tempest. So many conflicting currents—will the tribute to Fuller be celebratory or damning?"

"Margaret . . ." Hawthorne began, still chewing on the same bone. "Sophia and I felt she should not return from Italy, not with that man who may or may not have been her husband. Who was, in any case, totally unsuitable. Margaret was always running amuck in the world. I grieve for her loss of reputation as much as I lament her loss."

Melville dared to ask, "Was her child a bastard?"

At first it seemed the older man wouldn't answer, but after a moment he said in a low voice, "Her death was a calamity, but her return would have been an even graver catastrophe. There's no place for her here and who she had become. Taking a lover! The end—when she refused to make a leap for shore and said, 'I see nothing but death before me'—that sums it up."

"But surely," Melville ventured, "her reputation as a genius would have kept her alive for the public. Geniuses are permitted eccentricities —at least, male geniuses. Certainly her History of the Revolution would have been successful."

Hawthorne let out an audible "Huh!" and shook his head. "Ellery thinks the History is a myth, only Margaret's attempt at self-aggrandizement. He claims to be writing his own history of the three R's—rebellion, resistance, reform." He added a defense of Ellery, of a sort, calling him a "contemplative loafer, always musing and writing, refusing to be sucked into a mindless job."

"Henry certainly thinks highly of him," Melville admitted. "He told me Ellery is the best man in the world for a ramble and that he rejects a life of mediocrity, which would 'wear away his life by inches.'"

"Henry is hardly one to talk," Hawthorne said. "If Waldo didn't hire him as handyman, he'd have no trade. One cannot live on foraged blueberries."

"Still, I can't imagine Ellery Channing writing something that doesn't burst full-bodied from his own inspiration," Melville said. "Channing giving birth to a book that requires focus and structure? Not to mention sustained work?" He shook his head. "Unlikely."

"These Emersonians are all the same," Hawthorne allowed. "They see the world through rose-water imbecilities. Ellery is as unfit for actual work as his sparkling shallowness can make him. He probably feels a weighty book by him would be earthshaking, a riposte to Poe's mockery. It would prove he's not a shallow tinkerer."

"In some way I understand that motivation," Melville replied. "My first books were popular, to the point where I was hailed on the street for my autograph and invited to fancy dinner parties. Yet I am *not* just the Man who Lived with Cannibals," he insisted. "Write that way again, I cannot."

CHAPTER FORTY-SEVEN

Cary and Sophia Wander and Wonder

SEPTEMBER 4, 1850, CONCORD WOODS

Sophia and Cary strolled through the woods near the Concord River.

"What memories being here at Bush arouses! Makes me feel like the nineteen-year-old virgin I was when I first came," Cary said.

"I know what you mean. I'm also flooded with memories," Sophia agreed. "Eight years ago—what a fine time of life it was—just starting out in my marriage."

"Waldo is as handsome as ever. I swear that man hasn't changed a whit. Still has that thrilling voice, still dreamy with his head in the clouds." Cary walked to the riverbank and threw pebbles to mar the placid surface, watching the concentric ripples as they widened.

"Last night, when we were all aghast at the mesmerism, how did he keep as buttoned up as his dress shirt?" Sophia wondered. "I was all a-flutter!"

"That high collar so throttles him, it's a wonder he can breathe—it's tight as a strangler's grip," Cary said. "I suppose he has to live up to his reputation as the serene Sage of Concord." She laughed. "Margaret and I used to try to provoke him, make him show his feelings. We said we'd convert him into the Rage of Discord. It never worked. You might as well ask a block of ice to dance."

"He's like a walnut," Sophia agreed, "a hard nut to crack open."

"In my case, I think I cracked him open a smidge," Cary said as she fluffed her hair, streaming down her shoulders without a bonnet. "He liked me. Still does, I can tell. To him, my boldness makes me the perfect example of the Self-Reliant Individual he's forever preaching about. I am Transcendentalism Come To Life. So is Ellery."

"I've found relying on a partner is far more agreeable than self-reliance." Sophia, thinking of Nat, smiled smugly.

"You're lucky," Cary told her. "I have no one to rely on but myself. Don't even mention Will, my torpid husband. And my father? He was always too busy, gone halfway 'round the globe. And Mother? Crazy as a loon since my brother died."

"For so many years, since you were her pupil, Margaret was your partner in crime." Sophia sank down on soft moss. She picked up a stick and began to peel it.

"Margaret was like a mother to me, or a big sister," Cary said, swelling with pride. "She was big in every way—in ideas, ambition, charisma. When she spoke through me in the séance, it was the greatest thrill of my life! I can't tell Ellen, but I feel Margaret is reincarnated in me." She looked to see if Sophia thought her foolish.

"Someone has to preserve her legacy. You? I know what those men will do. Waldo says they want to publish memoirs to immortalize her, but they really want to sanitize her and file off her rough edges," Sophia said. She shifted uncomfortably and brushed a spiderweb from her shawl.

"I'd bet a thousand silver dollars their 'memorial tribute' won't mention her marriage to Ossoli or the birth of Nino, who was to be my godson. Or how she was friends with the 'scandalous' adulterers George Sand and Chopin; how she approved of free love. Everything about her—who she was, what she believed, all her ideas that threaten them—they'll bury. That stuffy old pedant Thomas Carlyle called Margaret an old maid, but she was a goddess. She compared herself to Minerva, but really she was Aphrodite!" Cary was breathless after her impassioned speech.

Sophia began piling rocks, one on top of another, to make a cairn. "Well, I certainly didn't agree with many of Margaret's ideas—especially after she wrote that outlandish book on women's rights." The pyramid of stones toppled over, and she rearranged them in a circle.

"Those prudes! Margaret was too immense for their tiny minds," Cary said. "She was to be the keynote speaker next month in Worcester at the first-ever Women's Rights Convention. 'Let them Think! Let them Act!' That was her call to arms. I'd wager her so-called biography will really be Waldo's autobiography, more a recital of his dogma than her doubt."

Cary flicked pine needles from her skirt, took a breath, and continued. "In Italy she outgrew Waldo. She gave up Transcendentalism. In this country, even in Manhattan, she was called a bluestocking. Only in Rome could she free her spirit and become a woman of the Now era. 'I love my country,' Margaret wrote me. 'Will it love me back?'"

"Why did you come here, Cary? To make trouble?" Sophia vacillated between admiring Margaret and maintaining loyalty to her tight-laced husband. "At one time, I wanted to be a New Woman too. Then I became a wife and mother. You're married now. What about you?"

"*Forza e corragio*! I want to present the uncensored Margaret Fuller, with all her radical ideas intact. Even if it makes Waldo faint. I plan to record everything at this memorial. I'll reveal every betrayal by her timorous 'friends.'"

"It's a fool's errand, Cary. You'd best return to your husband and baby. No one here will support you, not even Ellen."

Cary folded her arms, defiant. "I know Lidian hates me. Mrs. Saintly Martyr is still jealous." She tried to make light of her resolve. "I give her credit for creating the proper atmosphere for this wake. The house reeks of Doom and Death. I may even don my own black crepe mourning dress for supper tonight."

"I can't wish you luck in your mission." Sophia looked Cary in the eye. "Not that you ever give a fig for what others think."

"Only for what Margaret thinks." Cary paused, then whispered to the wind, "And what posterity will think of her."

They rose and began walking back to town. Rather than linking arms, Cary walked faster, a few paces in advance of Sophia, who stopped now and then to gather black-eyed Susans.

Hell's bells, Cary thought, *I may even write a History of the Roman Revolution for Margaret. If I could just see those papers Ellery found on the beach. Why does he hide them? If they were Margaret's, why squirrel them away? He says Ellen is Margaret's heir, and as her husband, that means a wife's property is his. Hell's bells!! He's up to something.*

CHAPTER FORTY-EIGHT

Cary and Waldo Debate

SEPTEMBER 4, 1850, LATER UNDER THE ARBOR, CONCORD

Ahead of her rendezvous with Emerson in the grape arbor, Cary thought what she might title her intended tome—perhaps *My Friend and Inspiration, The Real Margaret Fuller: A True Tribute by Caroline Sturgis Tappan.*

At his request, she was meeting the Oracle of Transcendentalism, who believed he had created an intellectual haven in Concord. He cultivated colleagues and fruit—both tart as his ideas.

Emerson and Cary sat in the arbor behind his house, encircled by vines laden with purple, musket-ball-sized grapes, of which he was preeningly proud. The Sage hoped his philosophy—the fruit of his intellect—would be as nourishing to the masses.

"Is there a serpent in Paradise?" Cary wrinkled her nose. The carpet of squashed grapes underfoot emitted a sickly-sweet smell of decay. "Are we closer to Hades than Heaven?"

Emerson regarded the streams of inky juice crisscrossing his paving stones with distaste. "I must get Henry to sweep up the overripe fruit. I do hope it won't stain." He examined the sole of his boot, dislodging grape skins with a stick.

"If it stains, think of it as walking on crushed violets," Cary suggested. "We'll 'walk in beauty, like the night.'"

"That sounds like something our noble Margaret would say." His voice was so low it was a bare whisper, unlike his vigorous speech from the podium.

"The highest compliment," she said.

"One half the world died to me when we lost Margaret." His eyes were clouded by moisture that looked suspiciously like tears. "Nothing looks the same as when I saw the world through her eyes." It almost seemed he was descending from his Olympian peak of Higher Thought to the terra incognita of true sentiment. *What will this new, Margaret-devoid world be like? Would it melt his icy froideur?* Cary wondered.

In the distance the faint scratching of a fiddle—the town music master conducting a lesson—floated through the air. Cary sang along with the tune: "Go and tell Aunt Rhody, the ole grey goose is dead . . . the one that she's been saving to make a feather bed."

"She was conceited and histrionic," Emerson said, reverting to judgmental mode, "but sparring with Margaret made me feel alive! She said I need a foe as much as a friend to hone my ideas."

"We all warmed ourselves by her blazing intellect."

"A blaze, indeed. Alas," he added, "I always tried to trim her wick."

"It only takes one spark to start a fire. You always try to tamp out ideas you don't agree with. Tell me, Waldo . . . do you grieve for the friend we've lost or for our lost time together, when we all were happier, younger, perhaps more deserving of love and honor?"

Emerson plucked a bunch of grapes from the trellis and stuffed them in his mouth, as if an abundance of fruit proved his worth as a steward of seedlings. He spat out the pits and flung the bare stems to the ground.

The fiddler switched to "Oh! Susanna, don't you cry for me." Cary didn't sing along. She just let the notes flit over the two of them—and sink into her heart.

Emerson, with an imperious gesture, waved off a fuzzy bee that was inspecting too closely the interior of his ear. "Some of her dictates were dangerous. They deserve to be suppressed."

"Such as?"

"Her distortion of a wife's role! A wife should be like a clinging vine, supported by the firm post of her husband." He gestured to the overloaded grapevines strangling the arbor poles. "Without such support, the vines would fall—nay, they would creep along the ground, where the fruit would rot." He looked smug, always the omniscient mentor. "Nature ever Teaches us Lessons for Life." He vocally capitalized his topmost points, a long-established habit of oratory.

I too can derive homilies from Nature, Cary thought, and replied, "Margaret said a submissive woman is like a blueberry bush hidden in the forest, laden with fruit no one harvests. Its fruit is wasted, just as a woman cannot use her talents when strangled by custom."

He looked uneasy. The pupil challenging her master? Cary didn't back down, asking him, "What about your call to independence in your 'American Scholar' speech? You said, 'We will walk on our own feet; we will work with our own hands; we will speak our own minds.' Surely, 'we' includes women?"

"I gave that address to the *men* of Harvard College," he answered stiffly, looking as if he had a ramrod up his back. "Dr. Oliver Wendell Holmes called my discourse 'our intellectual Declaration of Independence,' challenging us to cut the cable from Europe, risk the dangers and reap the glories of our own deep blue waters."

Emerson looked proud, then embarrassed as he surveyed the garden for potential eavesdroppers. Only a bushy-tailed gray squirrel paid him any mind, pausing in its task of scrabbling at the ground to bury a nut. "At the end of the séance, you said you found out so much more. What did you mean? Before Ellery interrupted, I wanted to ask if Margaret really married that Italian fellow Ossoli. Do you know?"

Cary hesitated—a stance wholly foreign to her nature—and finally answered, "I believe they married in Florence, shortly before embarking on the ship."

He seemed stunned. "By then, the boy was almost two years old?!"

He plucked a bursting grape and popped it in his mouth, conveniently turning away so she could no longer observe his expression. "Did her spirit say anything on the subject to you?"

"Only," Cary said, breaking off a trailing vine and flinging it to the squirrel, "that Margaret sends you her dearest love and wishes to remind you of the time you met in Marseille—the outset of '48, I believe." She arched her eyebrows at him, eager to see his reaction. "Take that as you will."

Emerson bounded up to his full six-foot height, bumping against an arbor post and incurring a grape-juice stain on his spotless cravat. "Mourning is messy," he sputtered. "That séance—I never saw such an impudent imposture in all my life! A load of rubbish!"

"Maybe not," Cary murmured.

CHAPTER FORTY-NINE

Ellery's Surprise

SEPTEMBER 4, 1850, EMERSON HOUSE
NOON DINNER, CONCORD

Present at the table were Mr. and Mrs. Emerson (Lidian silently seething, her husband maintaining an air of abstracted remove), Mr. and Mrs. Hawthorne (basking in their usual glow of nuptial bliss), Henry Thoreau (with tousled hair and baggy gray trousers, exuding a spicy-turpentine aroma of pines), Herman Melville (regarding all with his mariner's sharp eye), Cary Sturgis Tappan and her father Captain Bill Sturgis, Walter Whitman, and Mrs. Ellen Fuller Channing, who rubbed her forearm and tugged down a sleeve to conceal . . . what?

"Where's Ellery?" Cary asked Ellen. "Isn't he hungry?"

"Lord only knows," Lidian answered. "The way that rascal gets around, he could be at the North Pole or in Timbuktu. How many pairs of boots has he worn out this week, Ellen?"

Ellen reddened and mumbled, "He's locked in the attic I suppose. I heard him riffling through papers and scribbling away. He must be in the throes of creative ecstasy, writing new poems." She didn't intend sarcasm, but around the table a sly smile or two broke out.

"Our loss," Emerson pronounced, ever the *pater familias*, "but, please, I urge you all to eat heartily. We have much to discuss, much to decide concerning our raison d'etre—that is, how to commemorate our dear Margaret."

He served himself two stewed plums with a side rasher of bacon.

"I commend Henry for his skill in grafting. You'll find these plums delicious, with just a soupçon of tang." He chewed like a contented bovine ascended to stone-fruit heaven.

"*À propos* of Margaret, it behooves me to say aloud what we're all thinking," Hawthorne interposed. "Since many of her ship's crew made it to shore alive, and land was actually within sight of the wreck, we must consider the possibility that Margaret didn't wish to survive. The crew begged her repeatedly to leave the disintegrating vessel, yet she remained. Did she choose to die?"

Around the table were heard gasps of outrage and confused yelps.

"Sir, are you implying that a memorial praising her would, therefore, be inappropriate?" Sturgis asked. Others divided into two camps, either aghast at the idea or complicit in disapproval of Margaret's inaction.

Cary bent her head in sorrow. "Margaret was so fearless. She'd plunge into any storm of controversy. Why o why didn't she plunge into the stormy sea?"

Ellen started, her head popping up as a new thought struck her. "Do you think she might be alive but in hiding?"

Sophia shook her head to signal it wasn't possible, then felt obliged to second her husband's reservations. "We must face facts. Her end was agonizing, infinitely sad, but she would've had no peace here." Defiant, she said, "She was better off dead."

Everyone except her husband registered shock at her bluntness.

Sophia refused to backtrack. "There! I've said it! The storm that killed her was nothing compared to the storm of scandal she would've encountered if she'd lived. No wonder she stayed aboard 'til the end!"

"It took a hurricane to extinguish her flame," Melville said under his breath.

Cary was quick to defend. "No one is without flaw. She always had grit in her oyster. We come not to consecrate Margaret. She consecrates us—with her work, her ideas, her example for future generations."

"Margaret's writings, her Conversations," Ellen agreed, "they all vindicate women's right to think and speak for ourselves. Will you stifle my sister's voice?"

"Her gift was like the sun shining on buds. We all burst open under her warmth, blossoming like flowers," Cary said. She went on with a challenge to the men: "Think of her two main questions for women: 'What were we born to do? How shall we do it?' Apply that now to yourselves!"

"I must admit," Sophia ventured, "Margaret spoke brilliantly—verbal virtuosity was hers. But," she looked at her husband for approval, "she often wrote obscurely. She said, 'Man is vain and wishes to be more important to woman than by right he should be.' That is *not* the reality of marriage—at least, not the reality of *my* marriage." She linked hands with Nat.

"Aye, my Dove," Hawthorne patted her arm. "Margaret was a sizzling conversationalist. Her writing is vastly inferior to her talk. She dressed beautifully too—and what an entrancing laugh—like a little gamine." His dark eyes shone in memory.

Sophia, encouraged, went further: "Her death was merciful. She was too much a reform woman."

"Her reform proposals show the mooniness of dreamers," Melville said, "yet who the devil ain't a dreamer?"

Emerson weighed in with his habitual air of authority: "Whatever Margaret's faults, they arose from exuberance. She was always in a hurry; hence, her ardor for reform—too much of the man and not enough of the woman in her haste."

"You speak of exuberance as if you possess any, Mr. Emerson," Lidian spoke with false mildness. "Working alone in your study all day, silent as the tomb at family supper. Solitude on your summit of imperturbability—it is not just a misfortune but right-down selfishness."

Cary spoke in rare unanimity with Lidian: "Margaret was not loath to express her emotions, unlike certain members of our current party. That doesn't negate our obligation to her memory."

Thoreau, who'd been silent, no longer refrained. "I'll say this for Margaret. She urged her reforms not with a sword but a word. And she cared not for wealth or material possessions. He who does not possess can never be possessed. She was free." He bowed towards the millionaire in their midst. "No offense, Cap'n Sturgis."

An amiable plutocrat, Sturgis dipped his head. "None taken, my boy."

Wagon wheels clattered outside on the Cambridge Turnpike. The clip-clop of horses' hooves stopped as a stagecoach halted with a screech. At full speed Ellery then burst into the room. Not even removing his straw hat, he brushed cascades of dust off his jacket. Ellen averted her gaze and focused on her plate.

"Cheerio, fellow seekers!" Ellery sang out. "I come bearing tidings of great joy—I've secured a contract to deliver *the* authoritative book on the history of the Roman revolution!" He removed his hat and bowed elaborately, one hand at his waist, the other behind. "You may congratulate me." His smile resembled that of a fox penetrating a henhouse.

Before anyone recovered wit to speak, the unmistakable sound of a rooster crowing leaked through the window. Thoreau was confused. "It's not sunrise! What . . . ?"

"He's marking his territory," Sturgis said. "There must be an interloper."

Ellery flicked his copious mop of hair back from his forehead and looked expectantly at the diners. Murmurs at the table ranged from disbelief to astonishment. From all corners, a clamor of questions erupted.

Ellen's voice was loudest, her face blotchy with color, as if a Harlequin's coat had rubbed off on her. "Pardon me for alluding to the subject of funds, but tell me—what payment did you receive?"

Whitman was overcome with professional curiosity. "Who will print and distribute the book?"

Ellery laughed, delighted at the attention, and acknowledged the latter question. "Fowler and Wells will publish. Lorenzo Fowler himself read the bumps on my skull. He discovered my most pronounced cranial contour is for *Literary Flair*."

Melville questioned with an undercurrent of disdain: "I believe their list consists of books on phrenology?"

"Exactly," Ellery assented, proud, "and my book will be as accurate and scientific as phrenology."

Ellen persisted, cutting through the blather. "What are the terms? How much will the royalties be? Is there an advance?"

Ellery preened like a peacock. "Royalties? I want no royalties! I'll pay all expenses to produce the book—you are all welcome to contribute—five hundred dollars for an edition of one thousand. Fowler and Wells will distribute deluxe copies with leather covers and a gilded title at a price of one dollar per book."

Ellen stared at the filigreed carpet, mumbling, "Five hundred dollars we do not possess."

"When profits accrue from sales," Ellery informed her, "I told Lorenzo to apply them to reduce the price of future editions."

Lidian smacked her lips audibly, as if the virtues of vegetarianism placed her on a summit of superiority.

"I must ask, in all sincerity," Cary said, overcoming temporary muteness, "what qualifies you to write such a book?"

"Why, isn't it obvious?" he sniffed. "My poetic sensibility."

Semi-stifled guffaws sounded from nether portions of the room.

Ellery glared at the snickers. "I have been laboring—don't laugh! Yes, actual, unstinting labor, every single night, perusing a trove of letters from Italian revolutionary leaders to Margaret. They form the basis of my book, filtered through our Transcendental philosophy, of course." He looked at Emerson for sanction.

Commotion and questions from all sides flew at him: "What? How can it be? Why are you entitled to compile the letters into a book?"

"Why? Because I am headstrong, ungovernable, ardent, without limits! Only untamable energy like mine can crush the dragons of conformity! In short, I am the perfect vessel to deliver a tale of how to perfect society through individual reform."

"That is *not* Margaret's message!" Ellen threw up her hands. "She believed in community action, not individualism!"

"Well," he said, "it is *my* message. It belongs to me, as do you!" He regarded the faces ringed 'round him—open-mouthed in degrees of disbelief—and tried to recover his dignity. "A single man is stronger than a whole city of men if his mission is divinely inspired." Thoreau nodded his approval as Ellery continued, palms up *(to accept nails to the cross of Transcendentalism?)*, "My solitude and self-reliance are more worthy than a whole crowd acting in concert. I offer my toil as sacrifice for the benefit of humanity." He bowed his head in a semblance of humility. *Saint Ellery, the divine?*

Sturgis drew his daughter aside to whisper, "This is an attempt to revive his reputation after Mr. Poe so ruinously lampooned his 'poetic sensibility.'"

"I admit he was the target of ridicule—possibly malignant—but that," she answered, "doesn't give him the right to steal Margaret's project! He'll mangle her ideas!"

"By Jove, remember what she told you in the séance," her father replied, his eyes widening in wonder. "The History is lost to her, but not to all. The prophecy comes true!"

Cary was thunderstruck, while her father looked lightning-struck. "We have to get that mesmerist back! I would give all I possess to know . . ."

In the ensuing hysteria, his voice was drowned out.

CHAPTER FIFTY

Questions Persist

SEPTEMBER 4, 1850, HOME OF ELLEN AND ELLERY CHANNING, CONCORD

Whitman retired to his room at the Channings' for a brief lie-down after all the hubbub. He planned to peruse his notes of the séance. Was his story changing from a profile of Fuller and friends?

He didn't mean to invade his hosts' privacy, but the walls in the Channing house were porous as a fishing net. From downstairs he could hear both Ellen and Ellery's raised voices—more than raised: shouting, screaming, crying, yelling. Ellery was in a rage.

O, dreadful day, Walter thought, *and me a pacifist!* He heard loud stomping and fists hammering on wood, glassware shattering.

Ellen sobbed, "How could you? A history of the Roman revolution? It's Margaret's story to tell!"

"You're so full of being a Fuller!" he screamed. "You're a Channing now!"

"Where can we get five hundred dollars? Our only income is from my teaching," she cried, "one dollar a month per pupil."

"You know the law—what's yours is mine, and what's mine is mine," Ellery retorted. "Don't rage against limitations of your sex. As for how to pay for my efforts—optimism, my dear! I smile at poverty. Never will I desert the muse!"

"My sister worked on her book until the end. And now you . . ."

"I assure you, dear one," he interrupted, "it is better for me to write it. I'm stronger than a woman in facing opposition. I care not if my writings bring no bread. Poverty is the proud lot of a poet."

Whitman clapped his hands over his ears but he couldn't blot out the quarreling. An idea came to him: *I'll sing loudly, at the top of my lungs; they'll know I'm here and stop!* He began to bellow "Turkey in the straw, turkey in the hay! Well, the bullfrog danced with his mother-in-law, and the tune that they whistled was Turkey in the Straw!"

Although not a particularly melodious performance, it had an effect. The Channings lowered the volume of their arguing. Still Ellery couldn't stop himself from shouting, "You always thought she's better than me! Smarter, a better writer, more famous! She's not the only one who knows about revolution! Did I not undergo a personal revolution when I married you?"

Anxious thoughts assailed Whitman. *Lidian was right to caution Ellen about Ellery's temper. Can I help her? How? It's their business—not mine to interfere, but what if he harms her? She kept tugging down her sleeves at dinner. Her arms—are they bruised?*

Before he could rally his resolve to intervene, a door slammed. Blessed silence.

After his heartbeat slowed, Whitman went down, tiptoeing on the stairs as if to avoid broken glass. Ellery was in the kitchen by himself. He kicked aside shards of crockery.

"Walter, my boy, what a boon you're here to record my big announcement." His expression was smooth as a kitten lapping cream, with no acknowledgment of any altercation. Apparently thinking a trick was in order, Ellery grabbed a broad-brimmed hat off a hook, tossed it circling high in the air, and caught it on his head. He laughed merrily, his mood ebullient.

"Ellen," he explained, "is slightly cross at my refusal of remuneration for my History." *Slightly?* Whitman looked incredulous. No shadow of shame crossed Ellery's milk-smooth brow. He repeated the hat trick over and over, flipping and flopping it like a P.T. Barnum sideshow.

"Don't know if you've seen the tannery in town, Walter," he said. "There's a dray horse, and all he does, day after day, is trudge around in circles, turning a millstone to grind oak bark into tannin for leather. I vowed never to be that work horse. I have no remorse for not having a plodding profession, a routine dogtrot around a ring." He added what he considered his topmost lesson: "I do not postpone life. I *live*. My word is not tomorrow or yesterday but *today*. Rather than hear a lecture on the stars, I *see* them."

Proud of his rejoinder, Ellery continued to throw and catch his hat on his head until Whitman felt dizzy. Ellery, man of manifold tricks, transitioned to tossing grapes in the air and trapping them in his mouth.

The man is a virtual automaton, Whitman thought as he left the room. *More than a scamp, a scalawag!* Once alone again, he could still hear every sound from the kitchen. Ellery hummed "Turkey in the Straw" slightly off key. The sound of a box or trunk bumping upstairs, dragged from the root cellar, was next, then the crunch of twigs being broken and fed to a crackling fire. A tea kettle screeched.

A door opened. Thoreau hailed Ellery, pounding his shoulder and offering congratulations. "When did you have time to write a history of the Roman revolution? I didn't suspect you knew much about it."

"I've been working at night, ever since we got back from Fire Island," Ellery said. "Look—here's my book. I made a fair copy and sewed the pages together myself."

Thoreau was curious. "How came you to write a history? Is it a philosophical treatise? On revolution in general? I never took you for a historian."

"It's exceedingly factual," Ellery assured him. "I include heaps of anecdotes, local color, and telling details. I've been writing like a scrivener—wore out four pen nibs already. The goose hates me for plucking her feathers."

Thoreau seemed skeptical. "It's not like you to hole up inside working."

"The wise man needs no perch to observe petty mortals. Freedom of mind is all that's needed." Ellery puffed up with dramatic certitude. "My history relies on divine revelation. The tale came to me in a flash."

Thoreau scratched his head. Would this new identity supplant the happy-go-lucky Ellery who was his sidekick? "I'm surprised. History is a story of the past. But you and I live in the Now."

The new Ellery aimed to enlighten humanity, insisting, "More than a historian, I'm a prophet! My book illuminates Resistance and Rebellion, two of the three R's. At the end, I unveil the third, the ultimate goal. I instruct the world with our ideas."

Thoreau drew back, startled. "*Our* ideas?"

"Yes! *Reform!* Personal reform of the individual, self-reliance, civil disobedience, not collective social action. I urge the Emersonian concept of nature as our teacher. Guided by intuition, we find divine inspiration within."

"Heeding intuition rarely works in war. If it's every man for himself, anarchy replaces strategy." Thoreau's doubts were evident. "Are you sure your book is about the revolt in Italy?"

"Henry, have faith! In your lecture, you said it yourself: 'That government is best which governs least.' Forget solidarity! Individual improvement is key. My book substitutes Transcendental truth for Margaret's gibberish. The basis for revolution is self-reliance, not female pedantry. My book is American to the core."

Whitman, eavesdropping in his room above, could no longer restrain himself. He descended the stairs. In the few days he'd been in Concord, he'd spoken to bakers, seamstresses, millers, blacksmiths, farmers, and more. He'd learned that townspeople regarded Henry and Ellery as twin oddities. Both were considered idlers and dreamers who did nothing but shun work.

Whitman greeted Thoreau in the kitchen. Thoreau scuffed his feet on the floor, relieved at the distraction.

"Perchance you'd like to review my book in the *Tribune*?" Ellery asked the journalist. "My prior book of poetry sank without a glimmer of public awareness, more's the pity."

"Waldo is disappointed that Ellery and I have not achieved a 'circumstantial' position in American letters," Thoreau muttered as he stared fixedly at his boots. "He thinks our continued insignificance inexcusable."

"That's about to change!" Ellery crowed. "Soon the world can judge me aright!"

"Ellery has long felt overlooked," his friend explained.

"Readers see Margaret as opening a new world!" Ellery's tone was aggrieved. "In my opinion, her Conversations, teaching genteel ladies how to think, are wildly overrated. My book will be both *New* and *True*—Confrontations, not Conversations."

"You plan," Whitman put it succinctly, "to kick over the pail."

"Exactly!" Ellery puffed up. "No more talking to the wind. Inform and reform! Tell your *Tribune* readers! May I provide paper and pen?"

When Whitman failed to record his words, Ellery seemed disappointed. He continued his critique. "Margaret's writing was artificial, if you ask me. She presented each sentence like a rehearsed, treasured thought. Her stream of ideas always seemed pumped, rather than flowing naturally."

In a kinetic fit, he flipped what looked like a coin over and over, catching it in his palm with a smack after multiple revolutions in the air.

"What is that?" Thoreau asked as it flipped.

"It's nothing," Ellery said. Thoreau caught the object in the air and examined it.

"Where did you get this? It looks like a button from Ossoli's Civic

Guard jacket, identical to the one I found on the beach." His brow furrowed.

"I also found one in the sand." Ellery snatched it away and stuffed the button in his pocket. He began to whistle "Turkey in the Straw" at full volume and asked, "Say, gents, would you like a cup of elderberry tea?"

A mildewed trunk spilling over with scrawled, smeared papers sat on the floor. "Is that where you keep your source material?" Whitman asked. "May I see the contents?" He stepped towards the trunk.

Ellery snapped the lid shut and shoved it bumping down the cellar steps. "No need. I have my handwritten copy." He held it out with a beatific smile. "Now, my good Henry, shall we undertake our afternoon ramble? I've discovered a boggy spot where we can find whortleberries."

He and Thoreau skedaddled. At the gate, not waiting for his companion to open it, Ellery vaulted over, his long legs spread wide like scissors.

CHAPTER FIFTY-ONE

Lidian and Ellen—A Snake in the Henhouse?

SEPTEMBER 4, 1850, CONCORD

Lidian and Ellen walked in the fenced-in chicken run near the wooden coop. The hens were scratching the dirt and clucking, avoiding a self-important rooster who strutted nearby. Lidian scattered a pailful of grain for the chickens to peck. A comely Rhode Island Red gave herself a dust bath, flapping her wings, rolling in a cloud of dust.

"Tell me, Ellen. What will become of your family now that Ellery fancies himself a famous author?" Lidian asked as she hurled feed.

Ellen shook her head. "Who knows?" She flung a handful of grain, and hens flocked around her feet pecking. "I don't want to complain of my situation." She raised her chin. "Yet hearing the voice of my sister gives me courage to confront my troubles."

Lidian patted her arm. "I've seen how tortured you are. Even teaching the children doesn't relieve your misery. We must think of how Our Lord would deal with Ellery's conduct."

"Lord knows, I've been patient with him," Ellen said. "I've tried to inculcate the virtues he so desperately needs." A hen appeared with a gauzy tube dangling from its beak. "Look! A cast off snake skin! There's a serpent in the chicken pen!" Ellen held up the skin for Lidian to see. "It will eat all the eggs!"

Lidian's initial alarm turned to calm. "Nonsense! Just a harmless grass snake." She tossed the snake skin to the chicks, who descended on it, tearing it to bits.

"What he requires foremost is discipline and the will to provide for his family," Lidian said firmly.

"Discipline? Hah!" Ellen huffed bitterly. "Do you recall, when Margaret sent a volume of Shakespeare sonnets as a gift, he told her, 'I do not read. I am chiefly engaged in doing nothing. I own I have a large penchant for this species of occupation.'" She imitated his air of superiority, then wilted. "How could I have ever thought that shunning ambition was a sign of superior character?"

"You do have a tendency to be impetuous," Lidian said, not unkindly.

"I was only twenty-one when we met. He was so handsome. What a beau he seemed! I was flattered that Ellery preferred me to beautiful, rich Cary Sturgis. I know Margaret fretted, but Ellery called me his 'savior,' said I rescued him from an ill-spent youth."

They ducked under the low door of the coop and held kerchiefs to their noses to block the strong ammoniac smell. The broody hens fluffed their feathers and cooed as they sat in nest boxes.

"For years, I hoped his character would alter, but we live at swords' points," Ellen explained. "He says my desire to amend his faults blocks his 'starry path.' He claims I'm 'injurious' to his genius!"

Lidian slipped a hand under a hen and withdrew a brown egg, still warm. She placed it in her basket, nestled in straw. "The most ridiculous thing is how he's convinced himself he's a devoted husband and father, which would be laughable were it not so absurd."

"His temper is frightful! His moods terrify me. Today he grabbed Greta's doll from her arms, tossed it to the floor, and stomped on it! I collect the children in bed with me at night. I bar the door. I cannot bear another pregnancy, another lying-in while he rambles."

"Right you are!" Lidian approved.

"I wish I had Margaret's gift to say to him what ought to be said, then do what ought to be done. The thought of losing my children has kept me fast in his orbit. It's not just the ills of my condition but, as Margaret has written, of all women."

"You know my motto," Lidian said, 'Husband knows best!' However, it doesn't seem to apply in your case." She continued to gather eggs, petting the hens' feathers and speaking softly to them.

"What shall I do?" Ellen sounded desperate. "I thought of fleeing with the children to my mother. For the last few years, I've been saving for an emergency. But I must tell you the worst." She grabbed Lidan's sleeve, her voice breaking. "I fear Ellery has stolen my savings. I've looked everywhere. The jar I was stashing coins and notes in—it's gone! Will he pay for his book with my savings?"

"You must not allow him to steal from you or Margaret!" Lidian swerved towards her and nearly upended the basket on her arm. "From her dispatches, I know Margaret wanted to warn our own country to return to our founding principles, which we abandoned with slavery and the Mexican War."

"I suspect this memorial the men are devising—like Ellery's book—will twist her message. Working together—not self-reliance—was Margaret's way, the true way."

Lidian considered it: was her husband's credo of self-trust a euphemism for egotism? She straightened her backbone and decided, "We women must band together." She covered the eggs with a red-and-white-checked gingham cloth and marched from the henhouse, purposeful.

Ellen's courage faltered. Outright defiance? "Lidian, no. I must hope for the best. I chose this man. Inside him lurks a good man. It's my duty to bring it out, to hold on and endure."

Lidian jerked around. Spineless child! An egg tumbled from her basket and splatted in the dust. Streaks of sunshine-yellow yolk turned a soupy gray.

CHAPTER FIFTY-TWO

Cary's Concerns

SEPTEMBER 4, 1850, THE OLD MANSE, CONCORD

"Why do I bother patching his stocking?" Sophia asked Cary, as her needle darted in and out of a woolen sock. "Now that we have coin in our coffers at last, Nat will surely buy new ones. Probably silk."

"Old habits die hard," Cary answered. "Take me, for instance. I know Ellery's a cipher. Why did I ever think he was my true love? God knows, his poetry is foggy, twistified, pompous. You could galvanize a pumpkin, and it would be as lively a poet as Ellery. But when he chooses to be charming. . . . My heart still beats fast when I recall those love sonnets he wrote me!"

"I suppose you found his tortured history romantic," Sophia said. "The scion of such distinguished forebears throwing over his pedigree to forge his own path, even living in a log cabin on the prairie! To me, he's like a little boy desperate for love."

"Yes, a *handsome* boy, full of hijinks! Why are women attracted to Bad Boys?" Cary wondered. "I could never guess what Ellery would do next: a kiss or a miss?"

"With Will Tappan you don't have that problem," Sophia said. "No surprises there."

"He's predictable as the sunrise." Cary yawned and stretched her arms. "I should've known marrying Will would be no fun. Never anything unexpected."

"If I may be so bold as to ask," Sophia ventured, putting her sewing basket on the floor and leaning forward, "why *did* you marry him?"

"Waldo encouraged the match, as did my father. And, with his dark curls, Will looked like a Spanish privateer. A big mistake. His eyes are dead. He's not so much retiring as retired from living. I can anticipate to the moment when he'll take a nap."

"Quite different from Ellery," Sophia acknowledged. "I understand why Waldo promoted Will's suit. Waldo abhors disruption."

"It's like looking into an opaque cave with Ellery. Anything could pop out. He does have an unfortunate weakness for puns, however—a grave liability for a poet." Cary shook her head and closed the door on her past romance. "Well, enough about him."

"What do you think of Mr. Melville?" Sophia's cheeks reddened and she busied herself sifting through her sewing basket, eyes cast down.

"That virile seadog! Our new Neptune invited me for a row on the river. What do you think? His books are labeled indecent, but why should I be demure? The idea of a jaunt is intriguing. We are both married, so no chaperon required. Why not?"

Sophia looked momentarily envious, then picked up her daughter's pinafore to mend and settled back into matronly habit. "Nat Hawthorne and Mr. Sailor Man—what an odd friendship!"

Yes," Cary agreed. "Mr. Melancholy and Mr. Mystery."

"One so cautious, steady-as-she-goes, the other full-speed-ahead," Sophia added. "Herman, you'll find, is an irresistible raconteur."

Cary was eager to hear more. "I read *Typee* about his life in Polynesia—titillating, nearly obscene. Nautical tales are usually as enthralling as bilge-water, yet that one! I flew through it in two hours!"

"The same for me," Sophia said. "His description of native islanders, especially the girl Fayaway—now that is something rare! I heard that Mr. Putnam, who published it, said he found the manuscript so consuming, he forgot to go to church."

"My sister couldn't put it down and so was late making supper," Cary said. "She vowed to never again read anything with the taint of a story. The old Puritan hostility to fiction if it doesn't have an uplifting moral."

"Even Nat says Herman describes native girls with . . ." Sophia said, pausing to emphasize her husband's words, "'voluptuous clarity.'"

"Voluptuous or scandalous?" Cary asked. "In the book his women frisk about naked, with streaming coils of ebony hair and—at most—a slender belt of bark. So much for modesty! They delight in anointing the hero (*Herman?*) with oil, massaging his body all over with their smooth hands. *All over?*"

Sophia blushed and admitted, "Chastity seems an unknown concept to them—as is shame over its absence. We must remember—as Herman assures us—it's fiction."

"Fiction or fact? I intend to find out. I accepted his invitation for a row on the river."

• • •

"Call me Herman," was the first thing Melville said once Cary was settled in the rowboat.

"And I should be Cary to you," she responded with an arch smile. *A bit premature for first names,* Cary thought, *but we're all friends here.* Nevertheless, she intended to keep him at arm's length and quiz him about his book. "Surely," she said, "you exaggerate the natives' proclivity for cannibalism?"

Herman rowed with great energy and dodged answering, snagging some peppery watercress from the bank and taking a bite. His mouth puckered.

She pressed him to answer.

"I assure you, I indeed jumped ship in the Marquesas and evaded recapture."

"And did naked savages take you to their jungle village and shower you with kind attentions?"

"Just so," he admitted. "I was their guest and their captive."

"How unsettling," she murmured. More unsettling was his animated recital of the adventure. When he told of his escape once he suspected he was being fattened for a stew, his eyes shone with a piratical gleam.

"Running at full-tilt across the strand, pursued by a savage with a knife clamped in his teeth, I fled back to the bosom of civilization," Herman concluded. "Paradise Lost."

Paradise? Cary thought, deeming his tales more gas than glory. Yet her pulse had throbbed at his vivid reenactment. He had raced like a lightning bolt from his pursuer, bare feet slapping the sand, he said. With his fast talking and wild gestures, the drama seemed heart-stopping. So convincing was he that, while listening, she actually looked around for the cannibal's knife.

"That's not why I wanted a private audience with you," he said. He steered the boat into a lazy current, shipped the oars, and she waited for what might come next. "Would you be so kind," he asked, "as to afford me a conversation with your father?"

Not what I was expecting! Cary thought. *We're both only thirty, in our prime. True—I just had a baby, but I've got my figure back.* She opened her parasol to protect her complexion. Her reply was somewhat chilly: "I see no impediment, but why do you wish to speak to him?" She feared he wanted money. Once people knew about her father's fortune, pleas for aid were common. Herman might be a rugged Salt, but he could have mercenary aims.

His explanation floored her. He made Ellery as a Master of Surprise look like a timid mouse!

"I'm writing another seafaring tale, but this time, it's not intended to amuse readers with exotic adventures." Embarrassed to admit his ambition, he explained, "No razzle-dazzle. I would fain create an epic allegory, even if it courts unpopularity." His eyes shot sparks of intense resolve. "I mean to dig deep into human aspirations—the divine and the satanic. I wonder if the Captain's experience might fertilize my own ideas—still inchoate."

Blow me down! So he's not just a handsome sailor! Cary was astonished. "Do you know much of my father's life story?"

He knew the basics: How Sturgis came to command a ship (the *Caroline*, Cary's namesake) at age nineteen when the captain proved inept. How he cornered the Northwest Territory–China fur trade in sea-otter pelts, fought pirates, made a fortune. How his sails whitened every sea. How, with her mother Elizabeth, he had five daughters and one son.

Cary stopped him. "One thing you must know. My brother Willy Junior is dead. My father never allows his name to be uttered. His room has been untouched for sixteen years, awaiting his return."

She hurried through the story, telling him that when Willy was sixteen, the summer of his sophomore year at Harvard, her father put him on a packet boat off Provincetown to learn navigation from a retired captain. "Poor Willy didn't learn fast enough," she said. "A gust of wind swung a jibing boom around and smashed his head. He fell, bloodied, into the sea, where a host of fish enveloped him."

"Please go on." Melville seemed avid for details.

"If only I had been there!" Cary wailed, her voice breaking. "I would have seen the tell-tale yarn shift with the wind and yelled 'Jibe-ho!' Willy would have ducked beneath the boom. He was my playmate, my best friend. It didn't have to happen." She was near crying.

She couldn't stop jabbering. "My father still grieves. Stronger than despair is his anger and, I suppose, guilt. He's gripped by the question: how can a good God perpetrate such evil on an innocent boy? It drove Mother mad and my father . . . well, you can judge for yourself, Herman."

"He's a man with many demons."

"Ever since Willy died," Cary said, "Father prefers a howling gale and the monotony of the sea to safety on a lee shore. It's been stormy for all of us. For me and my sisters, Paradise Lost—the end of childhood, the end of happiness." Her eyes gleamed with tears.

"I'm sorry," Melville said.

"After the accident, Mother was no mother to us, in and out of hospitals, pacing and pacing all day, her mind gone into the beyond with Willy, her eyes blind to the world. People see my family's mansions, our fine clothes and servants. They think we live in clover. No one sees the pain."

Melville, a big, robust man, seemed to shrink into a little boy. "When I was twelve I lost my father. He went bankrupt, went mad, and died within two weeks. I can't forget—I worshipped him. He was raving, ranting Bible verses, maniacal really. It was the end of childhood for me. After that, even though Mother lives in the same house with my sisters and me, she's never really present for us."

"We're both like orphans," Cary said. "Perchance you can understand why Father keeps sailing, searching the sea—for what? Willy? He still dreams of Willy, agonizes over him. He's gone. Let him go, I say." She closed her parasol and tucked it under her arm like a lance.

"Does it show strength to avenge a grievance or to let it go?" he asked.

Cary had no answer. "Father wanted Willy, his namesake, his heir, to take over the business. He never considered that *I* can do it. Only a girl—what do I know? He calls me 'Diamond' for my red hair and fiery spirit, but he fails to see the real me. Margaret said of women, 'Let them be sea captains!' My whole life, I'm ready."

A trout jumped in a looping arc by the boat, then disappeared into the depths.

CHAPTER FIFTY-THREE

Dying Light

SEPTEMBER 4, 1850, CONCORD RIVER

Melville rowed. Captain Sturgis sat in the bow facing him. Although the younger man needed no instruction, Sturgis prompted him to avoid obstacles and use proper technique. Sunset was above and below them, its blood-stained reflection painting the river. Stars began to wink overhead, and golden glints of moonlight—or more likely the last glimmers of a sinking sun—streaked the water's surface.

"Given your expertise with otters, sir," Melville said, "I thought you might find river otters of interest."

At that moment, the sleek head of a bewhiskered otter popped up, swimming in front of their boat. An inverted V of ripples trailed behind the animal, widening until it lapped the river bank. The men froze, as still as logs, rewarded by the sight of three baby otters, half-hidden among the pickerel weeds. The babes tumbled over each other like a romping ball of soggy fur, until their mother approached with a crayfish. Of a sudden, their capers turned serious, as they snapped for the crustacean.

How should I broach my subject? Melville wondered. *I can't mention his long-gone son.* The display of the otter's maternal solicitude prompted an opening. "If only my own mother were as nurturing of her offspring," he sighed, a bit histrionically.

"Oh? Is that so?" Sturgis's ears perked up. *Perchance my wife isn't the only neglectful mother?*

Melville told the tale of his father's insanity and death when he was a young lad and of his mother's cold withdrawal. He was careful not to allude to the Captain's loss but circled around it.

"The otter is a slippery creature," Sturgis said, steering the conversation into safer waters. "The Chinook name for sea otter is 'Elake.' Sea otter pelts from Oregon Country are so lush—and costly in China—that they call them 'soft gold.'" He seemed determined to keep the conversation out of the depths. "Watch out for that log off your starboard!"

"Aye, aye, Cap'n!" the oarsman said.

"I'll give you the advice my captain gave me on my first voyage," Sturgis said. "I was sixteen, barely out of short pants: 'Always go straight forward, and if you meet the devil, cut him in two and steer between the pieces.'"

Melville thanked him for the advice, but the captain wasn't finished. "If anyone imposes on you, tell him to whistle against a nor'easter and to bottle up moonbeams." He looked pleased at his adage, composed of both piety and defiance.

"What do you advise if Fate deals you an irrecoverable blow?" Melville asked. "Something so painful, like the loss of a beloved father, that nothing can assuage the heart-sickness?"

From a man on top of the world, Sturgis seemed to wither, looking like the last dry leaf on a stem. "Cary would spout Transcendentalist blather to buck up," he answered. After a long pause, he went on. "She'd say the sun still rises each day, that new dandelions bloom from last summer's brown stock."

"Dandelions are dormant," Melville broke in, "not dead. Should one face the abyss and keep breathing, knowing that spring follows winter?"

Sturgis dragged a line in the water, saying, "To me, landscape never re-blooms. It's empty as a desert. That's why I go to sea. Only the ocean looks right. The endless waves . . ."

"Is it whistling against a nor'easter," Melville asked, "if a man injured by fate through no fault of his own refuses to accept the wound? If your dinghy springs a leak, do you abandon ship or pump it out and keep going?"

Sturgis wrapped a rope tightly around his fist. The question touched his inmost core. His eyes looked like boarded-up windows. "Let's turn back," he growled.

"Forgive my impertinence." Melville held one oar upright in the water to turn the boat. "I'm struggling with a new book, one I fear will be wicked. One character is a sea captain like yourself. I hoped you might have some insights."

"I surmised you didn't invite me solely to show me otters. Tell me bluntly—what do you seek?"

"Only the answer to the meaning of life. *Is* there any meaning? In the face of tragedy, should one rage against it or retreat? If tragedy—or the devil—is at the heart of life," Melville asked, "should one go to meet it—sail right through it, as you said—or head to port?"

The river was darkening now, not so much moonlit as hell-lit. "You ask if one must fight human limits just as one braves physical danger?" Sturgis mused, twisting and untwisting the bow line around his arm. "The eternal Why?" He seemed sunk in thought.

"Is resistance godly or ungodly?"

"If you lose a dog," the Captain mused, "you know how to hunt for it. But if you lose your heart, how do you seek it?"

"A ship plunges deeper as it rises," Melville said. "That's the question! How do you regain what fate steals?"

Just then they came broadside the otter family. The mother was teaching her young to hunt their own crayfish.

"Have you ever thought of retiring, Sir, of letting your daughter take over your burdens?" Melville, the master of non sequiturs, asked.

Sturgis pretended to shoot the mother otter, taking aim with an outstretched arm and finger. "Hah! Haven't you heard what happened to King Lear when his daughters took the crown?"

Melville landed the boat, and his passenger scrambled out without a backward look. As Melville pulled the rowboat to shore and tied it up, an owl serenaded with mournful hoots.

CHAPTER FIFTY-FOUR

A Raw Wound

SEPTEMBER 5, 1850, CONCORD

Cary had to know. For Margaret. To save her reputation, which gossips and rumor-mongers in Boston were already shredding. She felt she must record all the details. She asked Thoreau to accompany her to Goose Pond.

"I must know everything you learned about the shipwreck. You've never particularly liked me, but I know you share my interest in the truth."

He flushed, as he habitually did in the presence of ladies—except Lidian. "I would say I'm indifferent to you," was his mild reply. He reached down and picked a handful of leaves. He brandished them like a trophy and announced, "*Arnica mollis*, known for its healing properties. When I once fell and skinned my shin, at that very spot I saw some *arnica* and smeared it on my wound. If you get a cut, this is your balm. Unparalleled."

Not to be deterred, she asked, "What is it you *do* like, Henry?"

He didn't pause to consider but answered: "A south wind, books, old trees, a boat, a friend."

"Are you, peradventure, jealous of my friendship with Waldo?"

"I will not dissect friendship, even as I would never eviscerate a rose." He kept his eyes averted and scoured the ground, searching for more vegetal remedies. "We'll find excellent chokecherries at Goose Pond. I can smell the sweet scent of waterlilies now."

They kept walking through the underbrush. Henry arrested his stride every time a song bird warbled. "Hear that?" He held up a hand. "It's a stake-driver, or bittern—sounds like someone hammering, right?" He imitated the bird's glottal banging: "*Gulp-Thunk!*"

In the distance they saw a fallow field, which prompted another botanical lesson. "See how pigweed and chickweed have taken over those furrows? Despite the farmer assaulting weeds all spring and summer with a hoe, they always win. With their pluck and vigor, they cover every garden, meadow, and pasture. On every melon hill, I plant one hundred seeds rather than eight or ten. Wild and cultivated nature can co-exist."

Cary dragged him back to the subject. "Please tell me what you found, what you saw and heard on Fire Island. I can't get the image of Margaret holding her baby in the storm out of my head. Holding him tight as the last mast crashed down." Cary covered her eyes with a hand.

Thoreau told her of his search, ending with, "The cook said Margaret was singing to little Nino until the end—to calm him."

"What was she singing?"

"*Amazing Grace* . . . 'I once was lost, but now am found' . . . ," he quavered.

"Now she's lost," Cary mourned. "Why, oh, why did that imbecile captain not go to a safe harbor when the gale blew up?"

Thoreau shook his head. "I can't help you there."

"Is there nothing to cure this pain?" she asked, in tears.

"It's a wound," he admitted, "no *arnica* can heal."

"That fool First Mate," Cary lamented, "running with the wind in a hurricane instead of heaving to in a harbor—unbelievable! If only *I* had been captain of that ship! Margaret would be alive."

CHAPTER FIFTY-FIVE

About Henry

SEPTEMBER 5, 1850, THE EMERSON KITCHEN, CONCORD

The Emersons' cook was roasting a haunch of venison for the guests' supper. *Seems as if all I do is feed them,* Lidian groused to herself. *If it weren't flogging a dead horse, I'd tell Mr. Emerson that if we lived in a decently sized city, he wouldn't have to constantly import guests for culture. Nor would he have to travel as far for his lectures. But what do I know?*

The back door banged shut. Sophia entered bringing sprigs of lacy juniper. "Here, Lidian, this is for the sauce to go with the venison." She stuck the stems in a pail of water. "I'll host supper at the Old Manse soon. I hate for you to bear the burden of feeding everyone."

Lidian sighed, long-suffering. "My role is hostess. I have gold to give. Mr. Emerson sees only tin." She brightened to add, "Henry and I are collecting mint for sauce for a leg of lamb. If our guests weren't so avid to decimate my barnyard by eating the flesh of my chickens, pigs, and lambs, supper time would be simpler."

"Herman has promised to shoot a brace of pheasants for us, bless him," Sophia said, using Melville's given name with—to Lidian—shocking informality.

"Although I deplore their slaughter," Lidian replied, "at least it means I won't hear them anymore. One pheasant lives in that walnut tree outside our front door. I see its tail feathers drooping down every time it screeches. What an unearthly sound. The scream sounds like strangled babes." She shuddered.

"How are you holding up today?" Sophia inquired.

"Holding on is more like it." Lidian dabbed at her forehead with a cologne-soaked handkerchief. She took a deep breath, indicating her resolve to cling to life, even though her ailments were taken so cavalierly by others.

"Thank goodness you have Henry to help with the chores," Sophia said, hoping to soothe her.

"Dear Henry! I'm eternally grateful for his care," Lidian looked fully restored to health as she chattered about her young boarder. "Henry is not so hostile to affection as Mr. Emerson. He understands how vital my garden is to me. The clever boy devised and fitted cowhide claw covers on my chickens' skinny legs, so they wouldn't scratch up my roses! Who else could imagine such an invention?"

Sophia looked amazed at both the concept of claw covers and of Lidian's sudden transformation to cheer and volubility. "Brilliant!"

Lidian smiled so wide it almost split her face. "He built a wooden drawer with my Sunday gloves inside to slide out from beneath my favorite chair. The dear man! So thoughtful."

"I remember how, on the children's birthdays, he always carved squash into pipes and made whistles out of rhubarb stalks," Sophia recalled.

"What jolly times!" Lidian's headaches seemed to have dissipated along with her hangdog look.

Sophia began to strip juniper berries from the green stalks. Lidian crushed them with a mortar in a porcelain bowl. "Do you know these are not actually berries?" she asked. "They're more like tiny pine cones. Henry taught me that. He knows everything about botany."

Sophia sniffed her fingers. "They do have a piney smell—a bit of rosemary too." She added, "It must have been hard on you when Henry moved out to live by Walden pond."

Lidian perked up even more. “I just finished reading a draft of the book he’s calling *Walden: Life in the Woods*. Last night in my chamber, I couldn’t stop ’til the end.”

“What do you think of it?” *Another* local author, Sophia thought. *Concord is crawling with scribes!*

Lidian raised her voice. “I wanted to shout ‘Bravo!’ At last Henry has found his métier. Not poems but inspired prose—clear as a mountain rill! The dear young man. I knew he could do it! He nails words to his observations of Nature. The narrative almost doesn’t matter. It’s just a slender thread of two years’ experiences, with dazzling beads and ingots of thought strung on it.”

“How lovely,” Sophia said. “I must admit, when we heard he planned to build a cabin by the pond and live alone, we thought he was daft.”

“I had my doubts. When he asked Mr. Emerson if he could build a hut, I thought, why?” Lidian crushed the juniper berries with extra force, mashing them into a paste. “I wanted Henry to live with us in his room upstairs, but why should my wishes be considered?” She waited while Sophia added another handful of berries to the bowl, then continued, “Naturally, Mr. Emerson consented to the move.”

“Waldo told Nat that having Henry underfoot was an ‘inconveniency,’” Sophia remembered.

“As if my having a friend to talk to is of no consequence!” Lidian bore down on the berries with vigorous chops of the mortar to split them.

“I don’t suppose Henry would have done it if Ellery hadn’t tried the experiment first years ago, on the Illinois prairie,” Sophia said.

“Not that Ellery’s sojourn in a log hut was a success!” Lidian said with undisguised disgust. “The poems he wrote there are deadly dull. And Ellery’s shack! It had a dirt floor. His 160-acre ‘farm’ had no fence, no oxen, no barn, no plough. Not that he’d know what to do with a plough. All he did was eat salt pork and potatoes and sleep until noon.”

"That man knows how to be idle better than anyone," Sophia noted. "He certainly can lie in the sun."

"I have to give Ellery credit. He urged Henry to go live by himself. Ellery used to say he dreamed of building his own 'hermitage' by the pond, where he'd write poems all day long."

Sophia asked, "Did Ellery help Henry build his cabin?"

"Yes, they raised the frame and plastered the walls," Lidian recalled. "Those two are so unlike and yet so similar, I'll never understand how they're best friends."

"Two years' housekeeping alone in the woods—no one knew what Henry was doing or why," Sophia said.

"I used to bring him cherry pies, and, of course, he often stopped by for a chat. He had supper with us every Sabbath. He wasn't a hermit. His book explains it. He said: 'I went to the woods because I wished to live deliberately, to front only the essential facts of life, and see if I could not learn what it had to teach, and not, when I came to die, discover that I had not lived.' A bit wordy, but thrilling!"

Sophia looked up, impressed. "He proves you don't need possessions for a full life. A single room will do, if one has an open heart and a spacious soul."

"Mr. Emerson will be pleased," Lidian agreed. "His faith in Henry's genius will finally be vindicated. I remember when Henry first began to cultivate Mr. Emerson's friendship. We were in our thirties, Henry a young man of nineteen, fresh out of Harvard College."

"We were living here then, too," Sophia said. "When Henry first fell under Waldo's spell, people said he was like a pocket Waldo. His speech, pauses, enunciation, even his mannerisms seemed to mimic Waldo. People said Henry brushed his hair—when he remembered to brush it, that is—like Waldo." She laughed.

"He's sick of being compared to Mr. Emerson. He doesn't want Mr. Emerson to be his patron; he wants to be his equal!" Lidian was forceful on Henry's behalf. "This *Walden*! At last, Henry's found *his* voice. He doesn't imitate anyone or anything! He's nobody's shadow now."

"I wonder," Sophia mused, "if the book will vault Henry to the forefront. Waldo's talent is for aphorisms. 'Whoso would be a man must be a non-conformist' and so on. It sounds like this book goes beyond pithy sayings."

"Henry's book has Art and Heart, which is more than I can say for Mr. Emerson, no matter how sagacious a Sage he may be," Lidian said.

"There!" Sophia finished picking berries from the juniper fronds. "I'll see you later, Lidian."

Lidian hadn't finished her confidences. "Wait! I don't know why I think of it now, but I remember one time when Henry showed who he truly is. Our cat Milcah was acting strangely. She flattened her body, crept forward, leapt and crashed against the wall, then began clawing, trying to climb up to a framed picture. We turned the painting around and saw, clinging to its back and hanging upside down, a bat! I shrieked."

"Goodness!" Sophia interjected. "What happened?"

"Mr. Emerson said, 'In the name of God, don't touch it!' Useless man. Taking the Lord's name in vain. Henry not only touched it, he cradled the bat and confined it under a glass bowl while he identified it as a hoary bat. He called it Batty and gently transferred it to his arms before releasing it out the window. What I thought was tiny like a mouse was in truth big as an eagle. It spread its wings wide with a *whump!* and flapped off into the heavens."

Sophia nodded and said, "That sums up the difference between Waldo and Henry."

"I thank God for Henry. If he hadn't been here, that animal might still be hidden, its back to the wall. I would never have seen its magnificent wingspan." She paused, then whispered, "At the end of *Walden*, Henry wrote: 'Only that day dawns to which we are awake. There is more day to dawn. The sun is but a morning star.'"

CHAPTER FIFTY-SIX

Appreciating Ellery

SEPTEMBER 5, 1850, CONCORD

Whitman, out for a jaunt in the apple orchard, ran into Emerson and Ellery similarly escaping the cloistered halls of mourning. He readily attached himself to their twosome, not only to bask in the glory of his idol Emerson but to glean any tidbits useful for his article.

"I require some deacon of trees and grass and cranberries," Emerson lamented, "to tend this disheveled property. I would fain ponder philosophy instead of pruning these scraggly branches." He held up a leaf punctured by insect bites, as full of holes as a lace doily. "Exhibit A for the prosecution."

"Isn't that why you employ Henry?" Ellery asked. "And look what a magnificent job he does." He gestured to the red globes of apples that littered the grass, tumbled from trees by yesterday's windfall.

"But who will gather them before they rot?" Emerson sighed, helpless and hopeless.

"Allow me." With a flourish, Whitman began to pitch apples into a nearby barrel. They landed with a *boom-boom-boom* like a flurry of drumming.

"Careful!" Emerson warned. "You'll bruise them. Each should be lain on top with care."

"Bruised ones," Whitman assured, "are fine for cider."

Ellery picked up three apples and juggled them in a circular blur. Emerson burst out laughing, chuckling more loudly when Ellery added circus tricks like standing on one leg or whirling apples behind his back. With the velocity of his foolery, he resembled a Hindu god with eight arms.

"I can always count on Ellery to cheer me up," Emerson said, wiping his eyes and subsiding into his usual gravity. "I treasure his antics. It's like being on holiday, a perpetual picnic!"

"À propos of such positive influence," Whitman addressed the Sage, "may I say that your lecture 'The Poet' is a mighty source of inspiration to me?"

"Which sentiments, may I ask, did you take to heart?"

"Your call for poetry that's commensurate with the grandeur of our American continent—its teeming races of people, its cataracts and canyons, shining lakes and roaring rivers."

"Alas, when will such a bard appear?" Emerson asked.

A rhetorical question, which Ellery welcomed, ripe to promote himself as the longed-for Messiah of Letters. He opened his mouth to declaim.

Whitman hastily opined, "We need a poet who will sing and celebrate ourselves. A revolution in poetry—no rhyme or meter, just pure energy and vigor! No tame, orderly stanzas like Longfellow's but stirring and strapping, like the salty speech of a riverboat man or trapper, a blacksmith or a chambermaid."

Ellery was not to be stifled. "You describe the character of an ideal man—free, unconstrained by rules or custom, unconfined, exuberant." He puffed out his chest and threw wide his arms, clearly considering himself that paragon.

"Exactly!" Emerson nodded. "'Tis a great delight to saunter with Ellery," he said in approbation. Ellery glowed.

The older man and his disciple trod into the woods. Whitman trailed behind.

"What a balsam for the soul to abandon home and hearth for

immersion in Pure Nature," Emerson went on. "Ellery is an incomparable companion for walks. He's as good as an Indian guide, an inhabitant, not a guest, of Nature—knows every inch of land better than the Algonquins."

"Do you care to see where pennyroyal grows or the wild cherry or wild plum?" Ellery asked, basking in his mentor's praise. "I've discovered a secret garden brimming with lady slippers."

Ellery's attention shifted. His eyes scanned the ground with sudden focus. He stooped and picked up a maple leaf with small, brown objects on it. He shoved the hand-shaped leaf beneath Waldo's eyes. "Regard, my dear sir! Proof from the animal kingdom of the irrefutable differences between male and female."

Emerson scrutinized what looked like two curls of worm-shaped dung. Both he and Whitman were flummoxed.

An obvious triumph for Ellery, who touched the droppings and informed them: "Excrement from the male turkey [pointing] is J-shaped, while the female turkey excretes spiral-shaped dung! The larger the droppings, the older the turkey." On the path ahead, a half-dozen wild turkeys strutted, tail feathers spread like fans. They bobbed their heads and gobbled, beard feathers wobbling, unperturbed by the proximity of carnivores.

"In our walks, I always see what was never shown before," Emerson affirmed. "After Ellery points out the wonders, I afterwards never cease to see them."

They heard a chirping "cheep, cheep, chevet." With professorial aplomb, Ellery pointed towards a Norway pine branch. "A redstart," he proclaimed, as if he had conjured the rarely seen bird with a feat of prestidigitation.

"Sorry to distract from your discoveries," Whitman said, truncating the zoology lesson, "but I have a job to do. I must ask: What are your plans for Mrs. Fuller's memorial?"

Emerson's face fell from delight into lines of grief. "How to honor our Queen of Discourse?" He paused, then offered a proposal. "A book, I think, a collection of her writings, letters, journals, and eulogies by her friends."

Ellery stopped midstride and said firmly, "Not a hagiography—no halo or crown for her. The biography should display her strengths and flaws. After all, she was human." His mouth wrinkled, as if humanity's taste was sour. "Ellen weeps half the day, says she can't imagine living without Margaret. Such a racket! We don't want to be crybabies." He tossed a pinecone into a boggy puddle, saying, "This way, oh best Waldo." He took his mentor's arm and steered Emerson, as if he were blind, around the muck.

"You see, Mr. Whitman?" Emerson's voice was sententious, lectern-ready. "Ellery is like a flower in the wind, with an immense dispersing power. The seeds that fly off him germinate and grow in my brain into full-fledged thoughts."

Ellery, that man-boy and consummate disperser, pretended to go crusading. With a sword that looked suspiciously like a barkless stick, he hacked off the purple tops of thistles and sliced stalks of mullein. "En garde, infidel!" he cried, hopping from one foot to the other.

They stepped over the decapitated thistle blossoms.

CHAPTER FIFTY-SEVEN

Herman and Nat

SEPTEMBER 5, 1850, CONCORD

Hawthorne and Melville sat in a blue fog of cigar smoke. Both were restless, rocking their chairs back and forth like a bull about to charge.

"When, o when will we be liberated from this tiresome bonhomie?" Hawthorne burst out. "I long to rescue my Dove from the cackling hens and hie ourselves away. Oh, to be back in our Red House in Lenox, secluded in my study, no matter how drafty! I'd gladly stuff rags in the crevices and count myself lucky to be there."

"I have to agree," Melville said. "My new book is growing in my mind, about to crack my skull."

Hawthorne looked thoughtful, taking a deep drag of the cigar. Its tip glowed red. "Waldo has always amused himself with collecting 'originals,' whom he considers geniuses. When he recruited Sophia and me to the Old Manse eight years ago, I doubt he considered me one of his bizarre crew. I'm too laconic by far to enliven his brain, although at that time—immediately after our marriage—Sophia was a convert to his and Margaret's so-called Transcendentalism."

"I gather you are not so inclined?" Melville asked.

"Poppycock-ism, I call it! As if Man is infused with the divine! I had enough of that idiocy during my sojourn at Brook Farm. What gems of thought can one find in a midden-heap? If ever there was proof that Waldo's notion about self-trust is claptrap, it's the tragic alliance of Ellen and Ellery."

"Has Ellery no redeeming features?" Melville asked, tapping a cylinder of ash from his cigar.

"I enjoy rambling with him, ice-skating, or rowing and fishing on the pond, but to live with such an irresponsible clown?" Hawthorne spread his fingers in disbelief. "Impossible!"

"Waldo has called an all-hands-on-deck meeting," Melville said. "You're to discuss his project of immortalizing Madam Margaret's memory. What will you say?"

"My opinion?" Hawthorne narrowed his eyes. "Her shocking conduct with her lover and their probable bastard should not be celebrated but covered up. I shudder to think of the dangerous influence on impressionable female minds if such loose behavior is condoned. If my own sensible Sophia could be enthralled by Madam Fuller in her youth, imagine the harm to a less strenuous mind! Will the flower of Boston maidens take themselves off to Italy and acquire lovers?"

Melville thought of his own experience with native maidens, for whom the Western niceties of dress and morality were dispensable. "Don't we owe it to her memory to understand her reasoning?"

"There's nothing rational about it! Pure hedonism!" Hawthorne scoffed. "The demand from the ladies that we hold another mesmerism session is deplorable. I regret the impulse that led me to invite you to come. What a waste of your time! A mockery!"

"Please don't apologize, Nat. It's been most stimulating. It may even provide me with characters for my whale story."

Hawthorne looked relieved. "If truth be told, I too have found fuel for my imagination. My thoughts kindle at the idea of incorporating a Margaret-like character into what may become a story of my Brook Farm experience. What happens when intensity meets extremism or idealism runs smack into reality? My Margaret character might commit suicide by drowning, unable to live without her unsuitable love. I could name her Cleopatra . . . no, perhaps Zenobia, after the prideful queen of Palmyra. We'll see."

"And my project to investigate Captain Sturgis?" Melville said. "I've just scratched his surface. He's like an iceberg, with four-fifths of the mass hidden below."

"I need to know more as well. I'll not create another Hester Prynne in the old Puritan days. My new story will be contemporary, exposing the madness of these reformist times. Margaret's life was a revolution. It's the fate of all revolutions to die."

He stubbed out his cigar and drank off a last gulp of claret.

"And her memory?" Melville pondered. "Will that die as well?"

CHAPTER FIFTY-EIGHT

Vanished Arcadia

SEPTEMBER 5, 1850, CONCORD

Cary entered Emerson's study and plopped down on a chair opposite his desk. He looked up from scribbling in his journal. "Sorry to interrupt," she said, casting her eyes around at piles of books on the desk, floor, and bulging from bookshelves. "I've never been in here before, the Holy of Holies. So this is where you spin straw into gold."

He blotted a page, then stood his pen in the inkwell. "Every day of my life for the past sixteen years—since we came to Concord—I've recorded thoughts in my journal. After pie and coffee every morning, I retire to read, think, and write. All morning I'm cloistered, only emerging for dinner before resuming work."

"You don't have to explain your habits to me," she said. She leafed through a book on a table at her elbow.

"I wish Lidian were as forgiving as you. This is not recreation but creation. For my profession, seclusion is mandatory."

"I've heard her chide you for withdrawing from life. Margaret understood; she appreciated the fruit of your labor," Cary said, hoping to draw him out.

Emerson sighed. "How happy we were when Margaret visited—both working at our inkhorns in rooms opposite each other. After writing all day, we walked for an hour before supper and then rambled for more moonlit hours after. We debated, sparred, questioned, disagreed, and criticized. Above all, we laughed. We were opposites—I aloof and she ardent—but we met in the middle. *Et ego in Arcadia sum.*"

"Now she's gone," Cary said, clapping the book shut. "I long to hear that inimitable voice again—even if it's only through a medium."

Emerson crossed and uncrossed his legs, troubled. "I shrink from what her voice might say. I know what I'd say to her—in fact, what I *did* say in my last letter—'Do Not Come Back!' I told her I would arrange for publication of her History. I would ensure its distribution and favorable reception." His words poured out like a confession. "I told her, 'My dear Margaret, do not risk condemnation by returning home!'"

"I wanted her to come back," Cary said. "Whatever reception awaited her, she was strong enough to face it."

"Understand me," he begged. "It's not my reputation as her associate but her own that concerned me. The opprobrium would be too much even for a consummate battler like her."

"She had nothing to be ashamed of," Cary declared, stomping her foot. "Her role was to show America what a New Woman, a Complete Woman, looks like."

"No, no," Emerson retorted. "Her reform ideas were too radical. Universal suffrage! No hierarchy of the elite! The howling wolves of public opinion would have mutilated her! Imagine—no man to be lord over another, whether woman or slave! We're not in Arcadia, alas!"

"No, we're in Concord," Cary whispered.

Emerson confessed, relieved to lay his guilt at someone's feet. "When Margaret wrote asking to borrow funds so that she, Ossoli, and Nino could book passage on a fast steamship instead of a slow freighter, I failed to answer. I must live with that shame."

"If only I had sent funds . . ." Cary's voice broke.

Emerson continued as if she had not spoken. "In my defense, when Margaret and I met in Marseille in '48, I offered to bring her back with me, at my expense, to settle her in a house nearby in Concord. There was no Nino then, just her brilliant self. I realized how much I'd missed her since she'd been abroad. When I told Lidian I wanted to invite Margaret to live in Concord, she was obstinate in naysaying. And this from a woman whose motto is 'Husband knows best'!" He shook his head.

"We can still talk to Margaret!" Cary said. "Let's bring the mesmerist back!"

Emerson was distraught. "Might it reveal too much? Truth, truth, all the truth is the quarry Margaret and I pursued. Must every personal truth be revealed to the chattering mob?"

"The truth is what she wants!" Cary stood, books sliding off her lap, and shook a finger at him.

She softened when she saw his expression of profound sadness. "I would fain have met her child Nino," he said. "The little sprite sounded like my own long-lost Wallie Jr. We were going to have a pound cake and ice cream party for them. With lemonade. All these years I've saved Wallie's hoop. I wanted to present it to Nino. Imagine an almost-two-year-old babbling in Italian and English. He must've had Margaret's fluency, her gift of gab."

Cary murmured to the air, *Arrivederci, piccolo ragazzo . . . goodbye, little boy.*

CHAPTER FIFTY-NINE

Interview

SEPTEMBER 5, 1850, THE OLD MANSE, CONCORD

Whitman sat at tea with Nathaniel and Sophia Hawthorne in the house they had occupied when first married. Hawthorne circled the table with his swinging gait before settling in a chair and assuming the pose of a sedate Greek god. Whitman was awed—*how can anyone be so handsome, imperious, and glacially removed from the messiness of ordinary life?* Sophia served tea accompanied by a firm cracker and pungent cheese. Never had the reporter witnessed a husband and wife so in harmony, so fused in unbreakable couplehood.

"Pray tell me," he asked, "your suggestions for how I should frame my story on Madam Fuller Ossoli. To put it bluntly, was she a saint or a sinner?"

Hawthorne made a sucking noise with his teeth, surprising in one so dandified. "We enjoyed Margaret's shenanigans before she became so radical on issues like women's rights and emancipation. Since then, I've been thoroughly disgusted by her pursuit of dissolution."

Whitman looked startled, prompting Hawthorne to elaborate. "Her attraction to Ossoli—it must've been purely sensual." He shielded his eyes with a hand as if to blot out human frailty.

Sophia rushed to expand on her husband's reply. "Margaret was anxious to try all things, to fill her cup of experience to the brim."

Hawthorne held a walnut in his hand, studying it. "She would rip off the shell to taste the kernel. The ways of Catholic Rome are not the ways of Boston."

Sophia added, "Margaret's view of the sacred institution of marriage was abominable, immoral, and irreligious. It pains me to say that her pronouncements were devoid of all delicate sentiment."

How far from her early idolatry of Margaret! Back then, Sophia had called her "Priestess." Marital compliance, Whitman observed, extracted a price, one Sophia was loath to acknowledge.

Her husband nodded assent. "Even for such a moonstruck age in which every tobacco-chewing philosopher races to join a utopian community, the reforms she proposed are farcical. As if human character can ever be improved!" he huffed.

Sophia set her teacup down with an unladylike clatter. "These advocates of the vote for women, for temperance, for all the rabble-rousing revolutions of '48—it's unnecessary, bizarre—a grand conspiracy to overthrow the Christian social order."

"However," Hawthorne was quick to clarify, "Waldo's view that individualism is the proper antidote for communitarian folly is equally absurd."

Whitman's optimism was not so easily dampened. "Yet shouldn't man be always striving to improve himself and society?" he asked. "Of what use is a rainbow or a firefly? Transient, ephemeral, but without them—without dreams—life is barren."

"Are you proposing sexual anarchy?" Hawthorne asked, biting off a cracker. He added with a visible shudder, "Do you intend to join that perverted Oneida Community, where Free Love is the guiding ethos?"

Sophia reddened. "My dear, such things are not to be spoken of. Perhaps some toast and molasses, Mr. Whitman? We also have hard cider, if tea is too tame for you."

"'Tis against the best conduct of humanity to crush butterflies," Whitman rejoined, with more vehemence than coherence. "Why can't we live like grasshoppers? Why renounce floating soap bubbles for the heft of convention? Let us tune our lyres for the greatest symphonies!"

Hawthorne stood and brushed crumbs, like the fancied bubbles Whitman cited, from his lap. "I fear, Mr. Whitman, your own lyre is missing a few strings. Good day, sir."

Whitman, his dignity dented though free spirit intact, slunk away. *Hawthorne's novel may feature a gloriously embroidered Scarlet Letter*, he thought, *but its author sees only irredeemable blackness. I'll seek sympathy for my views elsewhere.*

CHAPTER SIXTY

A Mesmerizing Experience

SEPTEMBER 5, 1850, THE OLD MANSE, CONCORD

The Concord cohort, including Cary's father, convened at the Old Manse to attempt to contact Margaret again. Only Ellery refused to participate, deriding the mesmerism, in his orotund lingo, as a "ridiculous travesty" and "pusillanimous flummadiddle."

Flummadiddle or not, the ritual commenced as before. Dr. Léger announced with due solemnity, "Mrs. Tappan will again assume the role of medium to voice Margaret Fuller Ossoli's spirit."

"Or so we are led to believe!" Lidian whispered in Thoreau's ear. "Just as likely, it's Beelzebub's voice."

Dr. Léger intoned, "Margaret, lend Mrs. Tappan your force to speak to us. We implore you to help us understand your wishes." As before, Cary sank into a deep trance.

Everyone held hands around the table. Emerson's damp hand seemed to shake with palsy, while Thoreau's grip on Lidian's other side was dry and firm. Candles flickered, the only illumination in the room. The blackened walls of the Old Manse were streaked with what looked like centuries of hell-fire soot, fitting décor for the ceremony.

Again, Cary's eyes were open without seeing. Her voice and posture seemed a bully imitation of Margaret's. Anyone who closed their eyes would've thought Margaret was speaking.

Sophia appeared to regard the performance as God's truth. Her voice quaked when she asked, "Margaret, dear, do you regret anything?" She seemed genuinely afraid of the answer.

Margaret's voice replied, "Only that my friends are relieved I can no longer plague them with aspirations for their destiny."

"Aspirations!" Hawthorne erupted. Although he was never known to raise his voice—even if pigs trampled the corn—the reticent author actually shouted, "What you call aspirations are nothing but temptations to immoral behavior!" Then he sputtered, addressing Sophia more than Margaret: "Independence is dangerous for women! Only dependence on a husband's guidance saves them from ruin."

"You will have more to say on uppity women and their sad demise in your next novel," Cary, as Margaret, said to him. "At Brook Farm, you resisted my arguments for the rights of women. Then you converted Sophia into your Dove, when she was born to soar like an eagle."

"She's telling a thumper there," Hawthorne muttered. "Providence was kind in putting her and that clownish Ossoli on that doomed ship."

"Comments like that," Mr. Whitman whispered, "will wake the snakes."

Sophia stared steadily at her lap, then asked in a barely audible voice, "Did your marriage change your opinion of matrimony, Margaret? Are not the bonds between husband and wife different from bondage?"

"My marriage to Angelo changed nothing. Only the birth of my son taught me how happiness accrues from a union between man and woman."

"Your son, little Nino," Hawthorne began, speaking like a barrister determined to batter down a defendant's superior airs. "Was he conceived *after* the sanctity of marriage or as a result of your exercising your independence from Christian virtue?" Under his breath he muttered, "That will fix her flint!"

"As to Nino's conception . . ." Margaret's voice began, speaking through Cary, who swiveled like an automaton to face Emerson.

At this juncture, Emerson turned white as a corpse, raising his voice to protest, "Stop at once! This nonsense has gone on too long. It's approaching the witching hour!"

Ellen hushed him. "Let's hear my sister!"

"Waldo," Margaret's voice continued, "remember when you urged me to be a celibate woman warrior? But when we met in Marseille before your return to Concord . . ."

When Cary turned towards Emerson, Lidian felt a frisson of fear, as if a ghost were tapping on her coffin. Emerson's arms twitched wildly, and he knocked over the candles, extinguishing them. A clamor of frightened voices overpowered Margaret's. Everyone looked pointedly at Emerson, whose eyes were shut tightly as Cary delivered Margaret's message, her voice blurred and garbled.

"Are you saying Waldo is Nino's father?" Whitman was confused at what he thought he heard.

"And the devil loves Holy Water!" Lidian cried. "Holy Lord, our Father, cleanse this room of evil spirits!"

Before anyone could attempt to untangle the indecipherable remarks, Sturgis roared, "Wait! I must know—Margaret, did you see your boy drown, covered by the waves? How could you resign yourself to death? Why didn't you fight?"

Melville, fired up to a pitch of passion, yelled, "Wasn't it the better part of valor to battle cruel fate with all your strength? Why did you submit? Why not rage against death and live to wreak vengeance on that fool First Mate Banks? His idiocy caused the catastrophe!"

Everyone babbled all at once. All except Emerson, still as a steeple, his eyes drilling through his lap. The connection was broken, as all the participants' hands were in motion, gesticulating, hammering the table. Only Emerson's were tightly folded in his groin.

Lidian clutched her chest, her heart pounding. "Lord, Lord, it feels like the valves of my heart have snapped shut! My head is ringing like a brass gong." She leaned against Thoreau in a near faint.

The spell shattered, the men (except Emerson, frozen in his seat) jumped up, pushing their chairs back so fast, they fell over with a bang. Sturgis stormed off like a bolt of lightning, giving Melville a piercing look before he left. The women slumped, unable to move. Cary rubbed her eyes, emerging from her trance. Dr. Léger flapped a handkerchief near her face to rouse her.

Sophia looked ashen. "Was it really Margaret talking?" she asked Lidian. "Perhaps Ellery is right: mesmerism is nothing but hogwash."

CHAPTER SIXTY-ONE

The Aftermath

SEPTEMBER 5, 1850, LATER, CONCORD

Sophia sat beside Lidian's bed, trying to soothe her nerves. "Here, Lidian, drink this laudanum. It'll help you sleep."

Lidian was spent. "A black art—that's mesmerism, pure-dee quackery," she raved in a voice clouded by fatigue. "I reckon it was Satan speaking. The Prince of Darkness wants me to question my marital vows. Begone, Lucifer!"

"Forget it, dear. Just sleep," Sophia said.

Lidian couldn't unwind her mind. "Nothing about that séance makes sense. Mr. Emerson will not even meet my eyes. What am I to believe?" She drifted off to sleep.

"I'm not sure what we heard." Sophia tucked a quilt under Lidian's chin and talked to herself. *How could he? My own Apollo, the most high-minded of men, how could he accuse Margaret of conceiving a child out of wedlock? And then to hear what is surely a falsehood that Waldo and Margaret . . . I can't even say it!* She heard quick steps pattering up the stairs. Ellen, near tears, burst into the room, shaken. "What did Margaret say? What did she mean? Was it truly her spirit speaking? Was Cary playing a prank?"

Sophia shook her head. "None of us knows."

"Margaret supported the whole family after Father died—teaching, writing, never thinking of herself. She was always the soul of integrity. How much did living in Europe change her?" She looked at the bed.

"Poor Lidian, exhausted by hysterics. Thank goodness she's asleep now. And Waldo? He looked cleaved in two by a lightning bolt."

Sophia wrinkled her brow, trying to make sense of what they'd witnessed. "Of course, we all saw how Margaret used to make sheep eyes at Waldo, how she hung on his every word and colored whenever he showed her the least approval. It's no secret Lidian wasn't pleased when Margaret stayed here. Margaret and Waldo would go strolling every evening and tangle to high heaven on every subject under the sun."

"True," Ellen admitted. "Waldo thrived on their arguments. To see his eyes light up at Margaret's barbs irked Lidian. Especially since he kept to his peak of seclusion with her."

"Still, I would never suspect Waldo of a romantic indiscretion. Such an honorable man, the epitome of propriety," Sophia mused. "If anything—the idea, years ago, did cross my mind—I would've thought he'd succumb to Cary."

"We all know she's a barefaced flirt—I'll never understand how she came to be my sister's best friend. Cary was just one of the young disciples Margaret attracted. Waldo's a Pied Piper, too. You'd think he's Lord Byron, the way he enchants listeners. I've seen virtuous young ladies all but swoon over him lecturing on the platform. Few of them understand him, but no matter! They call him the Buddha of the West."

Sophia seemed deep in thought. "What Margaret said about her friends relieved that she's gone, so she can't challenge us to 'be all that we can be'. . . . That hurts."

"Because it contains a kernel of truth?" Ellen asked.

"It's true she encouraged me to paint. She was thrilled when my work was shown in Boston and when I won commissions for portraits. She believed in me almost more than I believed in myself. Then I gave it up."

"She loved you," Ellen reassured her friend. "She would've understood."

"Even when I didn't touch a paintbrush after the children were born? Then later, when I had to paint teacups, lampshades, and screens for money—was that a betrayal? I painted flowers, bees, and butterflies on totty ornaments!" Sophia looked at the floor.

"For all her bluster," Ellen comforted her, "Margaret hoped to find love. And she saw you found the perfect partner in Nat. Your children are your dearest treasures."

Sophia sat up straight. "It was my choice. Nat didn't force me." She tucked escaped tendrils of hair behind her ears. "I am content to be his Dove. I have no desire to be a screaming eagle with sharp talons. Can she forgive me?"

"Do you forgive yourself?"

CHAPTER SIXTY-TWO

More Questions

SEPTEMBER 6, 1850, CONCORD

After the mesmerism session, Whitman knew he had to confront Emerson. He spent all morning pacing in a circle, asking himself, *Is everything I believe about my idol a sham? Is Emerson, the most idealistic man in America, hiding a sin of adultery?*

Not that Whitman believed sexual freedom was a sin. In his lexicon, carnal love was spermatic in the best sense, a force for creativity. *We should all be audacious, bawdy, rowdy*, he thought.

Perhaps I'm on the verge of a scoop for Tribune readers! Who is the Real Ralph Waldo Emerson? His reporter's antennae were quivering. The prevailing image of the Sage of Concord was oracular, a Goody-Two-Shoes even.

The parrot Holly sat in its habitual place on the boot scraper by Emerson's front door. Despite everyone's efforts to teach it to say "gingerbread," the scruffy featherbrain continued to emit only raucous, unintelligible squawks. When Whitman reached to open the door, the green demon flew at him, a maelstrom of feathers and claws, fastening its beak on Whitman's cowhide boots. Then the bird flapped up his leg, snapping in intimate proximity at tender parts. Lover of Nature that Whitman claimed to be, he nonetheless backhanded the beast, shoving it towards a less sanguinary perch. Holly let out a barrage of outraged screeches—none of which sounded remotely like "gingerbread."

Discombobulated by the attack, Whitman entered the house without righting his garments, in a state of semi-dishabille. Emerson and Hawthorne were deep in a low-voiced parley, surrounded by a fog of cigar smoke. They seemed kindred spirits, even though one believed in man's innate depravity and the other, innate divinity.

"Walter," Emerson said, "this is the first time I've seen you without your hat hugging your head obliquely." He chuckled, believing his comment revealed the reporter's inmost character.

Whitman tipped his slouch hat in its customary jaunty slant. "I cock my hat as I please, indoors or out. No thanks to your diabolical parrot, a fowl most foul."

"May I offer a recommendation that goes beyond millinery?" Without waiting for a by-your-leave, Hawthorne flung his silk scarf over his shoulder with confident insouciance. "To be taken seriously as a man of letters, you'd do well to trade your coarse overalls for proper wool trousers. You might consider a cravat in place of an open-collared shirt. No rolled-up sleeves, I beg you. A gold pocket watch would do no harm."

Emerson seconded Nat's critique, oblivious to Whitman's mounting dismay. "Walter, if you wish to be read not only in a tavern but in genteel parlors, you must button up. A touch of orderliness would elevate your standing."

Whitman bristled: "I drink beer in a tin cup, not claret in crystal. I am no stander above man and woman or apart from them. I am content to be myself, brawny, direct, and—above all—forthright. If I am a brute, very well then, I am a brute. I am not a bit tamed. I sound my barbaric yawp over the roofs of the world!"

Barbaric yawp? They were taken aback at the peroration, mouths agape. The Sage tried to smooth the waters, "I assure you, Mr. Whitman, we're quite charmed by your deviation from sartorial norms."

"Which brings us near a topic Waldo and I were just discussing,"

Hawthorne began. "Should literature hew to a higher plane of thought and reflection—refinement, in short—or debase itself to the common parlance of the mob?"

It was clear, from his attitude of distaste, that he favored refined diction.

"Some young writers, I've heard, reproduce the slang of the unlettered masses," Emerson noted, proof he was au courant with the latest literary trend.

"Let me speak," Whitman interrupted, "in defense of what you call 'the unlettered masses.' You may not be aware that civilization *does* exist outside Boston. The arts are alive on the prairie as in the parlor! Why, on the frontier, all saloons install a piano and musician first thing. Streetwalkers and bar girls robe themselves in the latest fashions. Cowboys and hurdy-gurdy players and stevedores sing, as do Irish gandy dancers laying railroad tracks. I've heard the most flavorful blab from horse car drivers."

Hawthorne chose to ignore the speech, so at odds with his own practice, and swiveled to face Emerson. "I commend you, my dear Waldo, for keeping standards high. You're unabashed in offering lectures alluding to the ancients in the most eloquent phraseology. I do, however, have a bone to pick with your irredeemably optimistic pronouncements. How can you believe, as you write, that 'Evil is just Good in the Making?' Your cheery faith—unfounded in the reality of man's depraved nature—is impermeable to exceptions."

"I have to admit," Whitman ventured, "with the expansion of slavery and looming clouds of secession, preaching sunny ideals from the '40s seems stubbornly blind."

"Slavery will disappear in due course," Emerson assured him with Olympian aplomb. "The interest of men is always driving them to what is right, making all crime and tyranny mean and ugly. I'll never condescend to address my audience in anything less than the most elegant prose, and I adhere to my view of the perfectibility of man." Waldo was firm, although his voice faltered on the word "perfectibility."

"As to the question of human frailty . . ." Whitman's voice trailed off, his attempt to steer the conversation towards his purpose ending when Lidian came gliding in. The three men fell silent as she approached the kitchen window. A gleam of panic flashed across Emerson's eyes.

"What was that clamor from Holly about?" She threw open the window and saw two bluejays cleaving to the windowsill, their glittering eyes fixed on her. "Are you menfolk still jabbering about heathen pantheism? You ought to be feeding our little friends." She pinched off bits of hasty pudding and offered them to the birds. "Here you go, Peter. Wait your turn, Atrocious." The bluejays devoured the morsels and rowed their wings aloft to the nearest pine tree. "Henry says bluejays carry the sky on their backs," she murmured, as if to herself.

"I was about to introduce the subject of marriage," Whitman said, once more steering the discussion. Emerson stiffened at Lidian's glance.

"Do continue!" She dropped into an armchair and leaned forward.

"Sir Thomas More said getting married is like putting your hand in a sack with ninety-nine snakes and one eel," Emerson said, striving for a digression. "Of course, in my experience, the marital sack is full of rosebuds and apple brown Betty." He gave Lidian a weak smile.

Hawthorne summoned another literary reference: "Byron compares love to marriage like wine to vinegar. Hardly my experience, however."

"Reminds me of my observation on Ellery deserting Ellen whenever their babes are born. He champs at the bit, but eventually he goes the way the bridle leads," Emerson said. "Ellery rambles but returns. Isn't that the measure of a successful marriage?"

"Ellen is a martyr to that stake!" Lidian retorted, shaking her head so vehemently that her lace mobcap threatened to fly off. "Your reasoning butters no parsnips!"

Just then—as Whitman closed in on his goal—Ellery burst into the room. Oblivious to the tense atmosphere, he stamped his feet and hollered, "Damnation! I stepped in a cowflop on my way here, then got stung by a bee. But nothing can quell my joy!"

Emerson, grateful for the interruption, urged him on. "To what do we owe your excess of joy?"

"A poem best describes it." Ellery struck a pose and declaimed: "I tire of shams, I rush to be/ Fizzing and dazzling, as a comet free."

Whitman, underwhelmed at the outpouring, asked, "Why, pray tell, do you feel so free and fizzing?"

"For all that *some* people criticize my nomadic spirit, it's done! I've finished my book! My independence may be ragged and ambulatory, but it's all mine, as is this book!"

Through the open window came a blood-curdling scream. The hairs on Whitman's neck stood on end and he jumped to his feet. The others merely shrugged as the screeches faded in intensity. Waldo leapt up to slam the window shut.

"It's mad Nancy in the Poor-house across the brook," he explained. "Whenever I pride myself on living in the best possible of worlds, her screams shatter my dream."

CHAPTER SIXTY-THREE

Sorting It Out

SEPTEMBER 6, 1850, CONCORD

Cary and Sophia meandered in the Sleepy Hollow woods. Swallowtail butterflies flitted about, sucking nectar from tall cardinal flowers to fatten up for migration. Pine trees tossed their branches overhead in the gentle breeze.

"Well, of course, it's obvious. Waldo is human," Sophia told Cary. "No matter how much he's revered locally—even nationally—he's a man. I myself have fallen under his sway. In my younger days, I worshipped him as a prophet."

"That must've been before you found your true calling as helpmeet to Nat," Cary said with undetected sarcasm. "Tell me what that mesmerist session revealed about Waldo. I remember nothing."

"You don't know that Margaret, speaking through you, all but named Waldo the father of her child?"

"Unthinkable!" Cary was so surprised, she wrenched her shawl from her shoulders and threw it to the ground.

"I agree," Sophia said. "After the session, Waldo stayed to speak to Nat. I was in the kitchen but I could hear every word. It confirmed what I suspected from her writings: Margaret had thoughts that should never be expressed, much less acted upon! Her conduct in Europe was shocking, immoral, un-Christian. Alas, the influence of Italy upon her character was wholly malign. It transformed her not just into a radical, but a fallen angel."

"Whose opinion is that—Nat's, Waldo's, or yours?"

Sophia shrugged. "I confess Nat and I both lamented Margaret's extreme views on woman's role. For me, marriage is my true destiny. Margaret felt that men treat women as slaves, whose sole purpose is to do their bidding and minister to their comfort. Appalling!"

"What does that have to do with Waldo and Margaret?" Cary asked.

"Waldo said when Margaret met him in Marseille at New Year's in '48, she criticized *me* for my 'excessive devotion' and living 'so entirely' for my precious husband. She said my 'obedient goodness' prevented following my own polestar. She called our indissoluble union 'solitude *à deux*'!" Sophia looked affronted.

"Well, you changed." Cary bent to collect goldenrod fronds and black-eyed Susans. "I still don't see your point."

"Waldo denied responsibility for Nino's paternity, which is surely true. The things he told Nat, speaking man-to-man! Waldo believes Margaret was already pregnant when they met, that she'd had what he termed 'earthly union' with probably that young Italian soldier Ossoli and possibly other men, like the artist Thomas Hicks, the Italian Mazzini, or that Polish poet she idolized, Adam Mickiewicz."

"She failed to disclose anything like that in her letters to me."

"Nat had the presence of mind to ask why Waldo suspected Margaret was with child when they met. 'She glowed!' Waldo said! I couldn't help but feel sorry for Waldo. Margaret had begged him to open up his life, but when he took her advice and went to Europe—did that unleash his inhibitions?"

"Hardly," Cary said. "He's stiff as ever. Margaret called his work too much thought and not enough feeling. 'Literature is not the whole of life,' she told him. 'There's too much suffering to indulge in a life of contemplation! You never reach either the center or circumference of life.'"

"Writing and thinking are hardly a retreat from life!" Sophia said. "As if thinking were an indulgence rather than a boon to one's readers!"

"Margaret said Waldo touches only the glass over the picture, not an actual person," Cary recalled.

"I hardly recognize Margaret in what Waldo told Nat." She hesitated, then divulged, "In Marseille, Margaret made *advances* to force Waldo to recognize what she called her 'legitimate needs as a woman.' She told him, 'I've learned things you can't learn from books.'" Sophia's mouth twisted. She could barely continue. "Then she took his hand and pressed it to her bosom!"

Cary dropped the bouquet she'd been assembling. "Margaret a seductress? I can't picture it."

"I never would've believed it, except I remember her attraction to my Nat. The way she followed him around Brook Farm years ago and lounged in the moonlight with him here in Concord—it made me uneasy. When Waldo rejected her advances, she had the gall to accuse him of being 'undeveloped.' She was absolutely brazen."

"Brazen," Cary asked, "or brave?"

Sophia could only say, "For shame! As Nat says, her untimely demise was—sadly—both timely and Providential."

CHAPTER SIXTY-FOUR

Confronting the Enigma

SEPTEMBER 6, 1850, CONCORD

Lidian eyed the bottle of creamy liquid, turning it over and over in her hands. Just a little sip, she thought. Then I can go to bed and forget all this.

"Husband knows best" had been her motto throughout her marriage. When he was off lecturing; when she had to feed and care for the many guests he invited to their house; when he mooned over those juvenile poems written by his first wife or went jaunting with Margaret or Cary, ignoring his own wife, Lidian had accepted it. Part and parcel of her role as better half to the Great Man. But this!

She knew they had to talk about it—the revelation from the mesmerism session. Lidian was a Christian, enjoined to forgive those who trespassed against her. Yet, if he'd violated the sanctity of their marriage vows, how to forgive her husband? It had not occurred to her, when she wrote her Transcendental Rules, to include "Thou shalt not commit adultery."

I know Mr. Emerson complains I'm increasingly invalided and despondent, but I do not believe the trespass is mine, she thought.

When the Emerson children were at their lessons, she made bold to confront him, no longer pretending nothing had happened. "Why do you seem so dyspeptic?" she asked when he emerged from his study for an afternoon cup of tea.

With a sour face, Emerson described his last night's dream: "I bent down to pull a weed lurking behind a cornstalk, only to discover four thousand and one weeds choking the ground. I awoke with a start, sick in my heart, with the conviction that I myself am a weed." He looked woebegone.

"Why do you fear your character is weedy?"

He sank into an armchair, hesitated, then plunged ahead. "I neglected to write you of my visit with Margaret in France," he began. "Our interview was astounding—unsettling, humiliating, and embarrassing, which is why I tried to erase it from my memory."

"How so?" She had to know the particulars.

"I was very glad to see Margaret after several years apart," he began, shifting from side to side, his teacup rattling in his grasp. "You know there's no one to whom I can talk with as much profit as Margaret."

"I certainly *do* know. Margaret was the intellectual partner I hoped to be."

"I first spoke to her in a spirit of friendship, inviting her to live near us in Concord," he said. "I discovered—to my chagrin—she wished a nearer relation than as neighbors." He cleared his throat, unable to continue. He gulped more tea.

"Just say it, Mr. Emerson. Don't be delicate with me. Did she express a desire for physical union with you?"

He looked her in the eye for the first time and added more honey to his teacup. "Margaret told me, 'You inspired me. You set me free, and in Italy I have added action to inspiration.'"

"Did she mean . . ." Her voice nearly faltered but she continued, "Did she mean—sexual freedom? Freedom from proper behavior?" Lidian, repelled, could not refrain from asking.

"I regret to say that is the case," he admitted, straightening his cravat. "I believe she attributes Nino's conception to my philosophy of freedom from convention. Only in that sense—allegorically—is Nino the spawn of my friendship with Margaret."

"Thank the Lord!" Lidian flung her arms around his neck.

He extricated himself from her embrace. "Openness does not come easily to me, as you know. In that regard, Margaret surpassed me. I tried to defend myself, saying, 'We must each do our own work, tend our own gardens instead of rushing to support the latest reform.' She looked at me as if I were a relic from a far-off era. 'The only lasting, meaningful reform,' she said, 'will be in the social sphere, achieved through collaborative action.'" He pushed aside his tea. It had grown cold.

Emerson nodded towards a chunk of masonry on the sideboard. "Margaret brought me that piece of porphyry from the Pantheon as a gift." He fixed his gaze not on the purple tile displayed there but on some distant sight—or insight. "I could accept that present—a cold stone—but not the gift she offered of herself."

CHAPTER SIXTY-FIVE

Kindred Spirits

SEPTEMBER 6, 1850, CONCORD

Cary strolled in the woods to clear her head and almost tripped over the recumbent form of Whitman, loafing on the grass.

She gave his knee a playful kick. "Tell me, Walter, why have you attached yourself to our Concord cohort? Is it because Margaret charmed you when you met in New York?"

"She fascinates me," he said, dropping his head to the turf, "and this group of friends makes my mind go spinning off to the stars. Even more than when I began this assignment, I don't know who she was." He chewed on a stem of grass and looked to the sky for an answer.

"It's clear she wasn't the Vestal Virgin that most people thought," Cary said as she sat down beside him. "But intimate relations with Waldo? Impossible!"

"Your friends seem to have a very uncharitable view of who she became in Italy."

"Let me enlighten you about these fair-weather friends," she offered. "Nat is a prig and detests any woman who dares be true to herself. Sophia is thoroughly indoctrinated. She used to love Margaret; now she fears her ideas. My father lives in the past, Lidian wraps herself in the mantle of saintly martyr, and Waldo is paralyzed by cowardice. Even Henry endures a lonely life."

"What about Ellery and Ellen?" he asked.

"Tragic!"

"And our heroic Margaret? Did she succumb to despair and choose to die?" He locked eyes with her, keen to understand.

"She wrote me that the liberty of Rome was not advancing with seven-league boots, but she still believed its future was dawning." Cary shook her head in disgust and pounded a fist on her leg. "And me? Is it dawn or dusk for me? I'm tied to a ninny of a husband."

"Why'd you marry him? Why not stay the independent woman you were?"

"Waldo liked him; he likes Will's inane poems. Why did I listen to Waldo instead of to my heart?" Cary's voice rose to a cry of anguish. "If only Margaret were alive, I'd ask her to tell me, show me—how do I live fully?"

Whitman challenged her. "You must be born anew. It's true for you, for me, for all of us. Nothing can replace our soul's desires."

Cary met his eye and raised her chin. She jumped up and threw her arms high, towards the slabs of clouds gathering above like a ladder to heaven. "You're right! I spit in the eye of despair! I have dreams more solid than bubbles, all made for me. Everything is there for my taking—if only I can seize it. I can grow and bear fruit, flaunting my wings like a grasshopper on a summer day. The open-sesame of the universe is courage!"

Whitman leaped up so fast his hat flew off. He grabbed Cary's hands and spun around with her in a circle, shouting, "Yes! That's the spirit!"

Cary laughed, giddy. "Margaret once told me, 'Never strike sail to anyone. Man the yardarms and come into port greatly, all flags flying!'"

CHAPTER SIXTY-SIX

Sketching the Unknown

SEPTEMBER 6, 1850, CONCORD

As he left the Old Manse, Melville encountered Sophia in the parlor writing a letter. He half-bowed and addressed her: "I fear I've overstayed. I expected this tranquil town to be as unrippled as the lazy trickles of the Concord River. It was to be a few days' respite before plunging back into my novel, only half written. Instead, my thoughts are stirred up to a cataclysm, roaring and pouring like Niagara Falls."

She looked up, surprised at his outburst. "I'm also eager to return home. This visit is so upsetting." She threw down her quill and wiped ink from her hands.

He raked his fingers through his curly hair. "Everything is rising to a thundering tumult inside me!" He stalked back and forth like a caged tiger. "The submerged whale can never be harpooned. I have to bring it up—acknowledge the titan! Then, go deeper."

She rose and reached for his hands. "Nat will be sorry to lose your company, but if you must go," she advised, "you can take the Fitchburg line from Concord to Stockbridge. Check the train schedule at the post office."

"Thanks!" He bolted out the door with a perfunctory wave. Once outside and en route, Melville felt his jitters ebb. Back to my whale book! He began humming. The prospect so energized him, he loped down the path with long strides. He sang a few bars of a nautical melody:

"The skipper's on the quarter-deck a-squinting at the sails
When up above the lookout sights a mighty school of whales
Blow, ye winds in the morning, and blow, ye winds, high-o!
Clear away your running gear, and blow, winds, blow!"

Time to haul away my running gear and get back to work, he promised himself—*deeper and deeper into the depths. Too much fairy dust hereabouts.*

Walking past the grape arbor in Emerson's back garden, he spotted Cary sketching with a pencil. In a sprigged muslin frock, she looked fresh as a blooming orchard—no deathly black crepe for her. A ray of sunlight poured over her figure. Her red hair shone like polished copper. He halted his song and came alongside.

Cary looked up with a melting glance and flipped over a page in her portfolio. "Herman, can you sit for a quick sketch?"

"Why not? I'm no beauty, just a weathered sea dog, but have at it," he said, sitting opposite her. *Mayhap I can quiz her about her father*, he thought. *A model for my captain?* He leaned back against the arbor struts, pulling a handful of grapes from a vine.

"Bacchus?" she laughed and declined a taste, her head bent over the paper where she scrawled rapid lines.

"Poseidon is more my ideal."

"Didn't he have an affair with Aphrodite?" she asked, her eyes on her subject.

Melville's face took shape on her sheet, first the oval outline of his head, then eyes squinting in the sun. As she sketched his lips, Melville was surprised to see they turned up in a smile. He rolled his shoulders, uneasy. *When*, he wondered, *did a woman last look at me so keenly? Am I really composed of such straight scratches? Surely my hair and beard have circular tendencies.*

He broke the silence to ask, "Waldo speaks of 'the tragedy of limitations.' Does he mean we must accept our imperfections, or fight them?"

"You really have no talent at all for small talk, do you, Herman?" Cary laughed. She grayed in the sketch with the side of the lead nib, her pencil in motion.

"I aim at big game." He was aware of how pompous he sounded. "I have to figure things out. My novel . . . still a rough draft, but I'm getting there—if it doesn't annihilate me first!"

"Accepting limitations . . ." She seemed to be tasting the words in her mouth. "I despise those who speak of 'woman's lot.'" She threw down her pencil, adding, "As if women must be limited by the status quo! *That* I will never accept."

"But if you don't acknowledge reality," Melville said, "if you don't admit you're not all-powerful and accept that circumstance will likely thwart your will, you'll never be happy." Somehow he felt Cary—with her own sad family history—would understand.

She scribbled whorls of his beard on the paper, then answered, "We're not born to be happy. We suffer. Pain teaches the truth of human existence."

He leaned so far forward, he almost fell into her lap. "What truth?"

"If you don't suffer, you don't live. The only worthwhile happiness is to look pain and evil in the face without denial. Only then can limitations not stymie you."

"You triumph over them?" Melville asked, his mind stirred up to a pitch. He couldn't sit still but vibrated on the bench like a telegraph transmitter.

She tossed back her hair and scrutinized her sketch. She shook her head, dissatisfied. With bold strokes of the pencil she drew a thick X over the portrait and sliced the eyes with black graphite lines.

"My view of your head will never do." She placed a fresh, blank sheet atop the rejected one. "I was drawing a jolly tar, a sailor who sings sea chanteys and dances a hornpipe, with a woman in every port. That's not you." Her pencil paused, then scrawled the outline of a man, seen from the back, facing the vast deep of the sea.

"A more tragic portrayal then?"

"If tragedy is at the heart of life, let's meet it head-on. There's no benevolent deity ruling our fate, just the sovereign self muddling through." Her pencil moved fast over the page like a ravenous crow. Lines curled and crashed, here a darkening spot, there a diagonal slash.

"Live while you're alive—is that the message?"

"Even though no one escapes pain—yes," she said, hashing the image with lacerating lines. "It's better to be wounded than to always walk in armor. Margaret taught me that. She said that love brings sorrow, but solitude without love is worse."

Melville looked intently at her sketch. As she limned the outline of a ship, it seemed to disintegrate. "You must miss her."

"No one can understand!" Her words crackled with emotion like a bonfire of thorns. "To think of her voice forever silent, her husband and babe gone . . ." The pencil pressed so hard, it inscribed deep dents in the paper.

Melville remembered a line from his novel. He whispered, "She dropped a tear into the sea; nor did all the Atlantic contain such wealth as that wee drop."

Cary started in surprise and reached to touch his hand, tears welling in her eyes. Their eyes locked for an instant.

Her sketch became clear on the page: rolling waves battering a foundering ship.

A passing cloud darkened the arbor as Emerson arrived at a trot, panting and straightening his cravat. "Cary! I've been looking everywhere for you!" He raised the picture to his eyes and said with characteristic composure, "A bit morbid for a fine day, eh? I suggest you draw my apple orchard—now there's a sight to inspire both hunger and sublimity! 'Ripeness is all,' you know." He chuckled, a paragon of good humor.

Melville tipped his hat and stamped off towards the post office. *Waldo wouldn't know a depth if he fell head-first into it*, he thought. *His benign world is shallow, placid, orderly.*

Or is it?

CHAPTER SIXTY-SEVEN

Seeking Counsel

SEPTEMBER 6, 1850, CONCORD

Lidian sat at the big walnut dinner table, an array of silver cutlery, bowls, platters, and a tea service spread across the surface. She rubbed a cloth in a coarse solution of baking soda, water, and salt and scoured a knife with the paste. As the tarnish transferred from knife to cloth, she smiled at her reflection in the blade.

Ellen tiptoed into the room, her eyes cast down. *Everyone creeps around me, as if I'm a glass pitcher with a cracked lip,* Lidian thought. She rubbed harder on a spoon.

"Ellen, how is Ellery?" *Now there's a safe subject,* Lidian thought. He hadn't witnessed the second mesmerist session. He had no idea what happened. His latest shenanigans were always distracting. Dragged out of her worries, Lidian felt sympathy for her younger neighbor, who looked as if she'd shatter.

"We must be strong, whatever he's up to," Lidian cooed. "The good Lord sends us travails. You must stick to your husband, respect your marriage vows."

"How can I ever steer Ellery to the path of righteousness?" Ellen asked. She picked up a cloth, dipped it in the paste, and polished a silver fork.

"What troubles you, dear?" Lidian asked. "What has he done now?"

Ellen dipped the fork in a pan of hot water. "Ouch! I burned myself!" she cried. "Oh, Lidian, I despair! You know how winning Ellery can be when he tries. When I think of our courtship, how in love we were . . ." She sniffled.

"Mr. Emerson thinks highly of his talent, but the man's temperament—that's what you must deal with," Lidian advised. "I remember well when you married Ellery. He'd been quite the gypsy. He told us he'd found 'a home and a shelter' in you. You must help him."

"Help him ruin my sister's legacy?" She was distraught. "When I say that he shouldn't publish his blasted book, he shouts at me, 'All my hopes of the heart are dashed to the ground, broken, dead, mutilated!' What am I to do? What would Margaret do?"

"Is it possible the book will honor Margaret's memory?"

"More likely, he'll poison it. Since Margaret died, Ellery's mood is so bent I almost think he's mad." Her voice squeaked, near-frantic. "You know his little terrier Frizzy?"

"That little rodent always nipping at his heels?"

"He brings Frizzy to the supper table, seating her on a chair beside him. Then he proceeds 'to teach her manners.' When she puts her paws up, he says, 'No elbows on the table!' When she gobbles from her bowl, he says 'Don't gulp your food, Frizzy.' I wish he cared to teach our children proper manners."

"I imagine it's his idea of a jest, playing the fool to brighten the day. It must make the children laugh."

"There's no laughter in our home. You should hear him rave when my hen darts through the door. He detests Mollie, that Rhode Island Red, my best layer." She leaned forward. "Mollie prefers to be inside the house. Her favorite spot to lay an egg is Ellery's shoe, no matter how muddy. The pine-needle smell must attract her. If the door is open for a bare fraction of a second, Mollie makes a beeline for his shoe and plops down to lay an egg. Then, if Ellery steps on the egg in the morning, you wouldn't believe his curses!"

Lidian tried to arrange her mouth in an attitude of disapproval but couldn't stifle a smile.

"Wait! You haven't heard the worst!" Ellen continued with no sign of mirth. "Mollie wanders all over the house, clucking and fluffing her feathers. When she scratched holes in his papers and stirred them into a nest, Ellery was even more wrathy than ever! He roared against her and threatened to wring her neck. He almost caught her this morning before she flew into the rafters. If we don't have eggs, how will I feed my children? We're too poor to even keep a pig."

"He does sound unstable," Lidian agreed. "I have an idea. You know how Henry can soothe Ellery. Why not ask Henry to calm him down and dissuade him from the book?"

The idea bubbled in Ellen, gaining traction. She rubbed a silver sugar bowl to a high sheen. "Perhaps if the proposal comes from you, Lidian . . . you know how Henry puts such store in everything you say."

"I'll touch on the subject," Lidian promised, "but it'll be a sticky culvert to cross. Henry is so honorable, without a selfish bone in his body—more than I can say for certain celebrated lecturers of my acquaintance," she huffed. "Ellery is Henry's best friend, but Henry will do what's right."

"Will he do what's right for Ellery, or for Margaret?" Ellen gave up on polishing a tarnished ladle, dropping it with a clang to the table.

"So different, those two young men," Lidian mused, picking up the ladle to scour it. "If Mollie laid an egg in Henry's shoe, he'd kiss her beak and thank her."

"The children love his collection of birds' eggs—so beautiful!" Ellen said. "When I take them to the barn, they're astonished. Each egg is cradled in a nest of woven pine needles."

"That eagle's egg is huge—how did Henry get it?" Lidian wondered. "The hummingbird egg is teeny-tiny, while the oriole egg is all marbled and mottled. Oh, the colors! From robin's egg blue to speckled. Henry and I value our feathered friends. Henry throttle that sweet hen Mollie? Never!"

CHAPTER SIXTY-EIGHT

Enlisting Help

SEPTEMBER 6, 1850, CONCORD

Thoreau sat on a bench in the orchard whittling a new flute. Lidian walked towards him, a scowl brewing on her face. He tooted a few notes, fingering the holes, then reamed the interior with his knife. Each time he tested a note and found it off-key, more curls of wood spiraled to the grass.

"Henry, I have a strange request to make of you," Lidian said.

"Ask me anything," he said. "Without hesitation, I'd follow your tracks into the deepest, dankest wood."

She paused, then began. "You've helped me with household tasks and child-rearing these many years." She smoothed out a coiled wood shaving on her knee and blurted, "I must tell you that Ellen—with no evidence, only suspicion—fears Ellery will claim Margaret's work as his own."

He bleeped a discordant note on the flute. "What are you saying?"

"Ellen suspects he has stolen her sister's history, claiming it as his own. She wishes you to find out if the book is his. Could you search the house for it?"

"Whoa." He wiped the knife blade on his trousers and set it down. "This commission is a weed-strewn row to hoe. I foresee briars and brambles ahead."

"You said you'd brave the deepest wood. What about the briar patch?"

Thoreau fidgeted. He looked at his boots as if they held an answer. "It makes no sense. How could Ellery have seen Margaret's manuscript to copy it? We searched the wreckage together July last. All he found were some soggy letters. Her lap desk was empty."

"Could Ellery have found the text after you left, hidden it, and copied her book to present as his?" Lidian asked. "Ellen wants you to look for any original pages of Margaret's he might have. Sound him out on the subject."

Henry began sanding rough spots off the flute, his hand working while his mind raced. "I admit, something's amiss. Ellery's look, tones, gestures, and his—let's call it—aversion to labor make me doubt he could complete such a mammoth project. He always begs me to comment on his new poems, but he hasn't allowed a glance at this new book."

"Very unlike his usual hunger for praise!" Lidian noted.

"When I told him it's bold to become an expert on the rebellion, he only said, 'Don't you want a wild man, not a tame ditch-digger, for an expert?'"

"You'll be no less his friend for being truthful with him, Henry. If you perceive a wrong, you must condemn it."

Lidian saw Ellery approaching and turned to walk back to the house. She hissed to Thoreau, "Have at it!"

Ellery doffed his hat theatrically and pulled a green apple off a branch of a nearby tree. He took a bite and tossed the apple for his little dog to pursue. "Fetch, Frizzy!" he said.

My chance! thought Thoreau. He greeted Ellery and said, with as much presumed innocence as he could muster, "Tell me how you finished your book so fast." His half-finished flute rolled off his lap to the ground.

"My muse has dancing feet but not for trotting on a treadmill. When I apprehend a subject, it comes like a flash of divine revelation!"

Ellery claimed. He tossed another apple to Frizzy, who bounded in the air like a furry spring.

"What did divine revelation conclude about the revolution? Do you draw on Margaret's dispatches from Italy, or are the ideas wholly your own?" Thoreau asked, affecting a pose of mild interest.

"Look," Ellery said, "we all know what our Delphic deity Margaret Fuller would say. To free Italy of despots, she'd require *collective* action."

"True," Thoreau nodded.

"Her idea is a sham! What's indispensable to make a better world is self-improvement. Individual, not social, action!"

"Indeed, that's what Waldo teaches," Thoreau admitted. "It's what I've always believed."

"Inner reform—that's what my history preaches!" Ellery grabbed a thin cylinder of wood Frizzy was gnawing and held it out of reach to tease her. The dog yipped, jumping and tumbling. Ellery waved his hand in a circle, coaching the dog to somersault. "Good dog!" he said.

"Oh, look!" he laughed. "This stick Frizzy picked up to gnaw—it's a half-formed flute! Henry, you shouldn't be so careless with your instruments." He put the mouthpiece to his lips and blew a screeching note. "Hmm. Needs work."

• • •

Thoreau didn't care to know what pretext Ellen had manufactured to lure Ellery away—and didn't know how long he'd be gone. *How much time does this give me?* he wondered in a misery of trepidation. The children had disappeared with Ellen for a nature walk. Their cottage was quiet, empty. Let it also be empty of deceit, Thoreau prayed.

With not a few misgivings about the wisdom of his undertaking, he skulked into the house. He searched for any trace of either Ellery's book or Margaret's manuscript, turning over cushions, looking under rag carpets. *Damme! I'm no detective*, he thought, putting back the upended cushions in their original position.

He climbed creaking stairs to the top floor—the children's rooms and Ellen's bed chamber. He didn't want to know if it was a conjugal chamber or not. The armoires held faded and tattered clothes; even the chamber pots were chipped. The remnants of a fire in the chimney had long gone cold. Many of the children's toys were broken, but he recognized wooden boats he'd whittled for them in the toy chest and handmade puppets with cornsilk hair. He leafed through every book on the shelves: Latin, French, Italian, English, a few with pictures.

He carried a gunny sack in case he found anything suspicious. At first, the bag was flat, limp, but gradually it fattened as he stuffed in stray ribbons, scraps of fabric, bits of birch bark, spiderwebs, and puffs of cotton wool escaped from quilts. This would probably be a fruitless search, but at least he would acquire some dribs and drabs to use for birds' nests in his egg collection.

Downstairs, he sifted the ashes in the wood stove—no fragments of burned pages, only silvery dust. He emptied and refilled the ice box in the kitchen—not much to eat there—and overturned every jar of preserved string beans or pears in the larder. Nothing!

Frizzy barked somewhere outside, her high-pitched squeals getting louder. Thoreau's heart thumped as he swiveled his head from side to side. He hurried, turning over piles of mending, bumping his head on a hat rack. Where else? He looked behind pictures on the walls, shuffled logs in the woodbox, and stirred the kindling pile in haste.

Thoreau pulled the handle on the door to the root cellar. It was locked. Done! Nothing! He breathed a sigh of relief and shouldered his sack. One last glance around as he stepped towards the back door.

But—just before leaving—he saw a curious mass near Ellery's slippers on the parlor floor. *Is it a mouse's nest, right there on the planks?* It wasn't like Ellen to allow something so untidy. He heard a flutter of wings, and down from the rafters flapped Ellen's prize hen Mollie.

She carried a scrap of paper in her beak and, clucking, added it to a helix of torn paper on the floor. Mingled with downy feathers, the jumbled papers resembled a nest. Mollie fluffed her feathers and plopped down on top, waggling her tail to get settled. Gently Thoreau lifted the hen from her perch, scooped up the twisted papers, and added them to his bag.

Frizzy's barks were louder; her paws scrabbled on the threshold. She whined. Ellery whistled. Thoreau darted out the back door and headed to the barn to unload the nest-building materials he'd gathered.

CHAPTER SIXTY-NINE

A Curious Nest

SEPTEMBER 6, 1850, CONCORD

Whitman was itching to get back to New York. Quiet Concord—with its industrious citizens and philosophizing gentlemen—was too sedate. He took a last ramble with Ellen and the children, hoping to absorb her teaching methods by osmosis.

As they walked by Walden Pond, she asked the children questions. Whitman noted how she waited for their answers rather than lecturing. A nest of sticks and reeds floated near the shore, anchored to a stand of pickerel weed. "Why do you think this loon's nest is in the water rather than on shore?"

"Because loons are crazy?" Emerson's eleven-year-old daughter Nellie ventured.

"Good guess, but try again," their teacher laughed.

Ellen's four-year-old Caroline piped up, "So the baby loons can eat fish straight out of the pond?"

"I know! I know!" Emerson's daughter Edith waved her hand in triumph. "Because mama loons can't walk! They have to swim to their nests to take care of their babies."

"Right you are!" Ellen patted her arm. She pointed to a bowl-shaped nest of grass and twigs, lined with soft down. "Who lays eggs in a nest on the ground?"

Emerson's six-year-old son Eddy looked towards the pond and saw a female wood duck paddling by, her ducklings trailing in a line. "A duck!" he shouted.

The children all began to flap their folded elbows and quack like a flock of hysterical waterfowl. Everyone laughed. Whitman noted that fun was an essential part of education in Ellen's practice.

"The expert in birds' eggs and nests is really Henry," Ellen said. "Let's go see his collection."

"Mama," six-year-old Greta asked, pointing to the top of a pine tree, "what bird builds a giant-sized nest like that one?"

"That's a bald eagle's nest," Ellen explained. "They re-use the same nest year after year, adding mud and more branches to it. Sometimes it gets so big and heavy, it collapses. That means it falls apart," she added for the benefit of her youngest, little Walter, still in nappies.

Greta spotted something on the ground—a translucent tube that broke apart in her hand as she lifted it. "Mama, what is this strange thing?"

"That's a snake's outgrown skin. When baby snakes get bigger, they shed their old too-tight skin and wear brand-new, larger skin. Now who knows which other animals do that?"

"I know, I know!" Nellie jumped up and down. "Lobsters and crabs!"

"Right you are!"

Greta looked thoughtful. "Can people shed skin when they grow bigger? Can Daddy change his skin for something bigger?"

Ellen looked deep into the pond, searching for an answer. Whitman perked up his ears. "No," is all she said. She kicked a pile of leaves that swirled into the air, caught by a breeze.

The children caught her mood and became restless. "Can we go see Uncle Henry's eggs?" Edith asked. "He promised to show us the new ones."

"Come along, my little ducklings," Ellen said. Her pupils trailed behind her quacking and waddling.

The Emerson barn was neat and orderly, smelling like sweet hay. Glints of sunlight spilled through cracks in the weathered walls. Thoreau nodded to the children without pausing in his task. He removed material from a bulging sack and arranged the odds and ends on a bench. "To what do I owe the pleasure of your company?" he asked. "You're not migrating so soon, are you?"

They giggled, and Louisa Alcott, at ten full of dignity, informed him with a touch of pride, "It's our *onitholopy*, no, I mean *ornithology* lesson. Will you show us your eggs? Oooh, look at that one!" She pointed to a tiny, pea-sized egg in a nest no bigger than a thimble.

"That's a ruby-throated hummingbird's nest," Thoreau said. "It's made to look like a knot on a tree, covered in lichen held together by spider silk. Gnatcatchers, too," he said, showing them another nest cradling an egg, "use spiderwebs as glue for their nests."

"We all need glue to keep our homes together," Ellen told them. "For people, that glue is love."

Edith pointed towards a bank of dirt-colored cylinders high up in the hay loft. "What are those mud holes up there?"

"They're barn swallows' nests. The mama swallows fill their beaks with mud and use their own saliva to paste it together," Thoreau answered.

"Is it always the mother bird who builds the nests?"

Whitman remembered how his mother created the family home over and over when his father made them move every year.

"Almost always the mother," Thoreau said.

"A fact I know all too well," Ellen mumbled.

They spent half an hour surveying the eggs, marveling over the finely woven nests, as ethereal motes floated like gold dust in the barn's raking light.

Ellen drew Thoreau aside and whispered something. She gave him a searching look, but he shook his head in negation. She looked down, disappointed.

Greta, who'd been investigating the miscellanea unloaded from Henry's sack, picked up a twisted scrap of paper from the bench. She examined it closely, then called out, "Mama! This paper has words written on it! It looks like the handwriting on Auntie Margaret's letters!"

Ellen snatched up the scraps, flattened the papers, perused one side of each page, and turned them over. She furrowed her brow as she tried to decipher the blurry writing. She waved one in the air and spoke in a voice that mingled surprise and wonder: "This one has a page number—page 208—and it is certainly Margaret's handwriting! She writes about Italy!" She asked Thoreau, her voice trembling, "Where did this come from? Where did you find it?"

Whitman raked his hands through his hair, feeling as if a phantom had just materialized.

Thoreau squeaked, "Your hen Mollie was making a nest out of scraps like these in your parlor. I scooped them up. I didn't think it was anything special, just one more poem fragment by Ellery."

Whitman's face lit up. *A hen discovers a purloined text! Oh my! It's like finding buried treasure. My story gets more intriguing by the minute! Too rich—Mr. Edgar Allan Poe couldn't have composed it any better!*

He decided it was premature to I can't leave. What would happen next?

CHAPTER SEVENTY

Help Needed

SEPTEMBER 6, 1850, CONCORD

Lidian contained her curiosity with difficulty. To occupy her mind, she undertook her usual Sisyphean task of polishing household silver. She was arranging shiny silver candlesticks—just so—at opposite ends of the dining table when Ellen came into the room. Her face was flushed, her hair escaping from her bonnet, disarrayed by her hasty run to Lidian. She collapsed into a chair, catching her breath.

Lidian clasped Ellen's hands. "Tell me! What happened? Did Henry find anything?"

Ellen looked around, fearful of being overheard. Lidian pulled a chair near her and leaned close, their foreheads in contact. She touched the Bible in her apron pocket, in case an instructive verse was required.

"We have proof Ellery stole it! I just saw a fragment of Margaret's book—a torn page, which he must have copied. He stole not only her ideas but her actual manuscript! He must've found it when he and Henry searched the site of the shipwreck."

"So that's the root of his sudden desire to publish a book on the revolution," Lidian said. "He failed as a poet. He'll be reborn as a historian!"

Ellen slumped. Her words were a wail. "Oh Ellery! Not a thief!"

"So much for self-reliance!" Lidian was electrified. She thumped her Bible like Gideon blowing his horn to bring down the walls of Jericho.

Ellen's head drooped low. "Now I know why he let no one read his text. He knows I'd recognize Margaret's style and vocabulary."

"Her prolixity is so different from Ellery's haphazard prose," Lidian agreed. "What now? He brings the book to the publisher this week."

"The subject was so dear to Margaret's heart and hopes. Ellery's version will ruin her message—I'm sure of it. What should we do?"

"Who else knows?" Lidian barked the question as if she were a general plotting a battle.

"Henry and Mr. Whitman were with me when we saw the scrap of paper with Margaret's handwriting. They offered to take the children to Sleepy Hollow while I went to speak to Ellery. The hardest thing I ever did."

"Mr. Emerson is planning a bonfire tonight to commemorate Margaret. It's well you confronted Ellery first. What did he say? How did he explain? One page doesn't prove anything." Lidian was turning over facts in her mind. "What did he say, child?"

"He was in the parlor petting Frizzy when I came home. I was so hoping he'd have an explanation. When I said I had proof that Margaret's manuscript exists . . ." Ellen broke down in tears and wiped her eyes with a sleeve. "His face turned white, then dark red. I asked him bluntly if he's pretending her history is his."

"And?" Lidian could hardly restrain herself. Ellen struggled to continue.

She took a deep breath. "You know his temper. He sputtered and stood up so fast Frizzy fell off his lap. Then he berated me—hurtful words I won't repeat. Mainly he said it's a wife's duty to obey her husband and never question his judgment."

"Husband knows best!" Lidian spat out with heavy sarcasm.

"Ellery gave no hint how page 208 of Margaret's history came to be on our floor. Before he stomped out, he shouted that his book will make the world recognize his talent. He said he'll be a person of consequence like Waldo. His poems will finally be seen as first-rate."

Lidian paced up and down in the parlor, straightening drapes and positioning gewgaws precisely in the center of side tables. She circled the room, muttering, "What to do? We cannot countenance theft!"

Ellen clapped a hand over her mouth, trying to restrain a cry of despair. "Ellery threatened that if I accuse him publicly, he'll take the children—as is his legal right—and force me to leave the house!"

A thought struck Lidian, acutely aware of men's weakness for a pretty face. "We must ask Cary's help. That imp has more wiles than Delilah! Perchance she can inveigle Ellery to admit he copied Margaret's manuscript. You know how susceptible he is to flattery!"

"I couldn't ask her!" Ellen's voice rose near hysterics.

"Margaret would say, 'Do it! Seek the truth!'"

"It might work," Ellen admitted. "We'll see what she discovers. But if she can't get Ellery to confess—for Margaret's sake—I'll risk the worst. I'll reveal my suspicions at the bonfire." *Is it too much to hope that Margaret's friends will force Ellery to reconsider?*

CHAPTER SEVENTY-ONE

Packing the Basket

SEPTEMBER 6, 1850, CONCORD

Lidian was stocking the wicker hamper with victuals for the Sleepy Hollow service for Margaret. *I do nothing but feed them*, she hmmphed to herself, feeling put-upon as she set jars of preserved peaches in the basket with a thump. Through the window she heard plaintive notes from Thoreau's flute. "Come over and practice by me!" she called to him. Even though the tune he played, "Nearer My God to Thee," was mournful, she was lonely.

He entered the kitchen without the usual spring in his step. In fact, he seemed to be dragging, his head bent down.

"Why so droopy? Here, you can help me." Lidian put him to work packing the hamper. "Champagne and lemon-sugar punch on the bottom, please, then the pickled gherkins."

He brightened a bit, becoming almost frisky, as they packed cress sandwiches, ham and mustard, pears, gingerbread, and hard-boiled eggs. At the sight of the eggs, a shadow fell over his face.

"What ails you, Henry?"

"Will you promise to keep a secret?"

"Honor bright." She placed a hand over her heart.

"You know how a cowbird always lays its eggs in another bird's nest, and leaves that bird to raise its young?"

Always the birds with Henry! She nodded, aware of cowbirds' negligent maternal style.

“I suspect Ellery is guilty,” he frowned, “of a similar flaw.”

She had an inkling where he was going, but she affected to be mystified, hoping to learn more than Ellen had told her. “Tarnation, Henry! Just say what you mean straight out!”

He folded a checkered picnic blanket over the hamper, then drew her to a chair, where he unburdened himself. He confided that he, along with Ellen and Whitman, had discovered a scrap of writing in Margaret’s hand that looked like an extract from her History.

“I know,” she admitted, wishing to preserve her primacy in unraveling the mystery. “Ellen suspects Ellery’s book is really Margaret’s book.”

“A book we all thought was lost!”

Lidian ran with the avian analogy. “Is Ellery a catbird usurping Margaret’s nest? I know he’s a neglectful parent. He loves Frizzy more than his own children. He locks them in their bed chamber rather than listen to their prattle . . . but *this*?”

“Hard to believe.” Thoreau looked inexpressibly sad, as if he’d discovered his best friend had leprosy.

“Zounds!” Lidian couldn’t stop herself from an intemperate outburst. “That would explain how the lazy rogue managed to produce in short order such a weighty tome.”

“One scrap proves nothing, of course,” Thoreau said, his voice shaking.

“Have you inquired of him?”

“Yes,” he said. Henry’s demeanor was troubled, his mind all astir and buzzing like hornets in the attic. “I saw him lounging in the apple orchard, throwing apples for Frizzy to fetch, as if he hasn’t a care in the world. I told him, ‘I fear, my friend, you’re concealing something from me.’ ”

“What did he say?”

“He was insulted; said, ‘Balderdash! You know me better than anyone. My true persona is always front and center to you, as to everyone.’

I told him, 'True friendship doesn't countenance dissimulation, so I'll say it bluntly: You disappoint my expectations.'"

"Exactly!" Lidian beamed.

"Ellery held Frizzy up to his face and pretended to speak to the dog: 'Do you hear that, my most accomplished pup? My beloved friend doubts me!' He even pretended to wipe away tears."

"The scamp! Always play-acting!"

"I said, 'Friendship can't rob me of my eyes. If you do something that darkens my own character by association, I'll have none of it!'"

"Bravo, Henry!"

"He didn't seem to grasp—indeed, I myself have trouble grasping it—what I suspected," Thoreau said. 'Tell me what you mean!' Ellery demanded. 'Your speech is all pumpkin and no pie!'"

"Willful ignorance!" Lidian was adamant, stomping her foot. "I hope you told him we need to know if the history he intends to publish is really the result of his labor. We all know he never slogs away until he finishes anything."

"'Tell me true,' I pressed him, 'did you copy Margaret's history?'"

"And?" Lidian had to know.

"Ellery couldn't meet my eyes, so he talked to Frizzy: 'Can you believe my best friend is accusing me of theft? It must be Ellen spreading lies.' Then he spoke to me: 'How can the book be Margaret's, Henry, when I told you the final chapter stems from *our* ideas—yours, mine, and Waldo's? Individual effort—*independence*, not *interdependence* as our benighted Margaret advocated—is the triumphant conclusion to my book!'"

"Do you believe him?"

"He believes himself. He shows no sign of guilt. He really thinks his book will uplift humanity."

"If Ellery is resolved to be a scoundrel, he should at least have the decency not to invoke you and Mr. Emerson as co-conspirators!" Outraged, Lidian patted Thoreau's hand, not knowing how to comfort him.

"Have a piece of spongecake," she said, cutting him a triangular piece, then pivoting with a sudden thought: "Perhaps Ellery is adhering too closely to the commandments of my Transcendental Bible."

Thoreau looked perplexed until she explained, "Don't you remember the rule: 'Never confess a fault. You should not have committed it, and who cares if you're sorry'?"

"The absence of confessing a fault is certainly here," Henry said, adding, "if, indeed, Ellery did appropriate Margaret's work, which is not proven. We don't know where that scrap came from."

"Also evident," Lidian retorted, "is the absence of sorrow for misdeeds—real or hypothetical." She rapped a hard-cooked egg on the edge of the tin sink, peeled it, and gave him the egg. "Let's see what he says at Margaret's memorial service tonight."

Her children ran in, all dusty with dry leaves crackling in their hair. Eddy clung to Uncle Henry's knees while Thoreau hoisted Edith on his shoulders. They jaunted around the kitchen, Eddy dragging behind as he encircled Thoreau's ankles. Nellie grabbed what remained of his spongecake slice and stuffed it in her mouth.

"Oooh, your flute!" she said, spotting it on a chair. "Play us a tune, please!"

CHAPTER SEVENTY-TWO

The Bonfire

LATE AFTERNOON, SEPTEMBER 6, 1850, CONCORD

In attendance at the Sleepy Hollow memorial were both Hawthornes (enacting their customary tableau of marital unity), Melville (somewhat abstracted as the odd man out who didn't know the honoree, Mrs. Fuller Ossoli), Lidian and Waldo Emerson (sitting apart on the grass, she dispensing items from a wicker basket, he pointing out autumnal tints of trees with proprietary approval), Thoreau (playing a soulful rendition of "Amazing Grace" on his flute), Ellen and Ellery Channing (sitting at a conspicuous remove from each other, Ellery perched on a bulging knapsack), Cary Sturgis Tappan, Walter Whitman, and sundry Emerson and Channing children drinking lemon punch, throwing acorns, and scuffling through fallen leaves.

It looked more celebratory than funereal. Here and there, leaves of maples blazed scarlet and waved like fluttering flags. Yellowish-brown fans of elm leaves, pale as sheaves of wheat, tossed overhead, and purple asters dotted the green grass like stars. The pungent aroma of wild thyme, crushed underfoot by gamboling children, wafted through the air. The sun sank low, irradiating the blue sky with streams of yellow and pink.

As the last notes of the flute faded away, young Eddy plopped down on Uncle Henry's lap, asking, "Is there licorice? I smell it." He pawed through Thoreau's gunnysack.

"No, that's the smell of goldenrod when you trample it," Henry—ever the naturalist—explained.

The group fell silent. Wind whispered through the pines. Emerson seized the moment. "Friends, we are gathered here, at our noble Margaret's favorite spot, to remember her and eulogize her departed spirit. When darkness falls, we will light the bonfire symbolizing the light she shed on all of us. With her loss," he hung his head, "I'm impelled to ask: is the best behind us or ahead?"

Hawthorne sat up straight, tumbling Sophia's head abruptly off his shoulder, where she had nestled it. "Allow me to express my reservations," he said. "Early in our marriage Sophia and I were Margaret's boon companions. Sophia delighted to sit at Margaret's feet in awe of her honeyed tongue. That was before Margaret's book on the role of women in society. From that moment, alas—Margaret as a prophet was dead to me."

"Not to mention," he huffed, "her hypocrisy in disdaining marriage for others and then 'marrying' a dolt who couldn't tell the difference between his thumb and his big toe!" He sat back, straightening his cuffs, as everyone stared open-mouthed.

The crowd shifted uneasily. The adults gulped down their champagne and returned gherkins to their plates with nary a chomp. *What? Haven't we come here to praise her? Why does Nat speak ill of the dead?*

He ignored the clenched jaws of those around him and went on. "She was too radical in her gender views." *There!* he congratulated himself. *It's settled.*

The ever-loyal Sophia showed her indissoluble respect for her husband. "Margaret wanted to set the world on fire, to burn down everything. But she burned too brightly and too fast for most of us."

Thus emboldened, Hawthorne elaborated his much-rehearsed opinion. "The storm in which she perished presaged the storm of disapproval she would face in her native land."

Ellery, constitutionally incapable of yielding the spotlight, piped up: "Margaret always took everything to its utmost. Her earnestness was too extreme."

Cary, her contempt evident, asked, "What, pray tell, is too earnest about Margaret saying 'Throw open the doors of colleges, courthouses, and Congress! Let our sisters in'?"

Melville exchanged a look of solidarity. "She sounds to me like a thought-diver. Any fish can swim near the surface, but it takes a great whale to go down five miles, then come up with lungs bursting and bloodshot eyes."

Well said! Whitman thought, mentally noting the finny analogy for his story—*Margaret the Deep Diver!*

"Margaret escaped our bigoted, Puritan New England." Cary glared at Hawthorne. "She found a more expansive fellowship, first in New York, then in Italy. No more in thrall to stuffy school masters"—she darted a glance at Emerson—"she freed her spirit, giving herself over to love. We should all navigate by her star."

Emerson was uncomfortably aware of brewing discord. He offered soothing words: "She certainly climbed high and burrowed deeply into every subject. Her curiosity was without limit." He surveyed the others. "Margaret and I once shared dreams of building an ideal community here in Concord. Let us lift up a glass to toast her: To Margaret, whose most illustrious halo is neither her intellectual nor her aesthetic achievements, but urging us to fulfill the promise of our American Revolution, begun right here in Concord!"

"Hear, hear!" Most of the group seconded his sentiment.

"May I add a note of reality?" Ellery interrupted. "Margaret always wanted to grow forward and outward. I hold that growth should be inward."

Ellen, unable to remain silent, exploded. "She wanted everyone to go forward—men and women—to full equality. Her voice is silenced, but her ideas will never die!"

Lidian sat at full attention, thinking, *now will she bring up the missing book*? Her heart thumped.

"Indeed," Emerson intoned, voicing more platitudes to divert disagreement, "it's a tragedy that she perished before her task was finished. Rest assured, dear Ellen, that wherever there is knowledge, beauty, and striving for freedom, justice, and equality, Margaret is there."

Thoreau shuffled amid the crackling leaves, settling himself. "Let us recall that Nature shows no sorrow when leaves decay and fall each year. Instead, they nourish future growth. Violets will still sprout in the spring. The note of the lark will sound each morning. How beautifully the leaves—that once soared so high—go to their graves. They teach us how to die."

"Poppycock!" Cary shouted. "Margaret taught us how to *live,* not how to *die*!"

Lidian, with a mien faux-innocent of any intent to arouse dissent, said, "If death, followed by rebirth, is the law of life, what seeds did Margaret plant that will bloom in the future?"

Ellen jumped on the wagon: "Her History! That will be my sister's lasting legacy!" She stared hard at Ellery, who bolted upright from his lounging posture. Thoreau, Lidian, and Ellen were tense.

Ellery tapped his fingers on a knee, feigning unconcern. He hissed at Ellen, "As your husband, I command you not to speak!" To the group, he said, "Her legacy? As the old lady, when she saw her late husband's gravestone, said: 'Very nice'!"

"I don't understand," Cary spoke up. "Her legacy is what she lived for. It's in me, in all women, in the fight against tyranny! Why speak of her lost book? It's gone."

"Be that as it may," Ellery said with studied nonchalance, "I remind my wife that her dear sister's dream of women's emancipation is just that—a pipe dream. As your husband, *I* control all property, even to the hens in the coop."

Everyone shivered as a cool breeze nipped their arms. The sun's dying rays created an eerie glow, silhouetting the pines like tall candles. Emerson resumed his Master of Ceremony mantle. "Time to light the bonfire!" He threw a torch on the pyramid of logs. The fire crackled. Twigs and dry leaves kindled into licking flames. A gust stirred it higher. Sparks leapt and swirled like dancing fireflies. The sharp scent of crushed leaves and singed bark floated over all.

Whitman recalled bonfires on the beach he'd experienced as a child, how he and his brothers waved the flaming ends of sticks to draw circles of light in the darkness. He couldn't resist saying aloud, "I know I shall not pass like a child's curlicue cut with a burnt stick in the night."

Emerson brought up his own memory: "In her book *Summer on the Lake,* Margaret wrote how distressing it was to see a magnificent eagle at Niagara Falls chained up like a plaything." He tipped his head back, raising his orator's voice above the throbbing flames: "Margaret, you're released from earthly chains to soar in the heavens! Once a citizen of the world, you are now a citizen of the universe!" He spread his hands in benediction.

Greta led the children in a shout of hurrah. "I wish I had a kite to send soaring up to Auntie Margaret!"

"May I remind you," Cary said, her voice cutting into the cheers, "when Margaret first saw the roaring magnificence of Niagara, a gentleman walked up near the edge, regarded the falls without emotion, and *spat* into the cataract." The shouts died.

"Thus reality," Hawthorne murmured, tossing down his champagne, "conquers the ideal."

The irredeemable showman Ellery stalked to the pyre. He removed great wads of papers from his knapsack and tossed them by the armload into the roaring flames. The fire, like a voracious dragon, consumed the pages, curling them into black cinders that whooshed and spiraled into the air. "Margaret, I consign these foreign letters, found on the beach and of no use to posterity, to the Great Beyond." He upended the knapsack and shook out reams of scribbled pages. "My book will tell their tale."

"Wait!" Ellen cried out. "Put out the fire! Don't let him burn . . ." Ellery shot her a withering look.

Thoreau and Cary jumped to their feet, rushing towards the conflagration like a fire brigade. Cary shouted, "No, no, no!" and poured the dregs of her champagne on the fire, igniting a loud sizzle and plume of smoke. Thoreau kicked ashes on the embers, causing silvery dust to erupt in a powdery flash. He reached into the flames to grab fragments of burning paper. Futile! They jumped high on a jet of hot air.

Ellen sobbed in great gulps, her hands covering her eyes. All others stared, as if witnessing an occult ritual of fire worship.

"What the blazes is that all about?" Emerson whispered. He squeezed his eyes shut as a belch of smoke stung him to tears.

CHAPTER SEVENTY-THREE

Flirting with the Truth

SEPTEMBER 7, 1850, CONCORD

Ellen found Cary packing her clothes in a carpetbag. "I really must get away, back to Lenox. Should I take the train? Not alone—I can't bear it. Perhaps I can order a brougham and ask Herman to drive? He lives near me in Pittsfield. Where is Father?" Cary's mind was in such a muddle, she couldn't stop babbling.

Ellen put a hand on Cary's arm and dragged her to a chair. She looked into her eyes with great seriousness. "You must do me a favor," Ellen said, "for Margaret."

"The best thing we can do for Margaret is go," Cary answered. "I thought we would honor her memory, but last night, from Nat and Ellery, I heard dishonor!"

"Please, Cary, let's set aside our disagreements. You're the only one who can get Ellery to admit the truth." She explained the mission.

Cary was disbelieving. "You ask me to do what? To worm my way into his confidence, only to betray him? How can you ask me to expose Ellery's treachery, if that's what it is?"

"We must find out if those pages he burned were Margaret's! Ellery claims they were letters to her, not her manuscript, but we have reason to think he copied her book." Ellen shuddered. "Such an unearthly sight last night! The sparks whirled up like a tornado engulfing Ellery in fire."

"Why do you think *I* can persuade him to admit he copied Margaret's work? How could I get him to admit anything?"

"You have a way with men," Ellen said.

"If I do it, it would be for Margaret—to keep her History from being stolen—and changed into Ellery's freakish version." She smiled at her reflection in the mirror, then took from the carpetbag a low-cut frock and held it up to her chest. "I do think my feminine wiles are intact, and Ellery is always liable to flattery. . . . We used to court. Before he met you, of course."

Ellen's mouth tightened. "He and I were both so young. We fell in love instantly! I thought my life's duty was to tame him."

"As if anyone could!" Cary blurted. "That's precisely what everyone loves about him: how wild he is. Savage even."

Ellen burst into tears. "Our Margaret is gone: my sister, your best friend! And my husband. . . . You must help!"

Cary tried to buck her up. "You don't see me crying. If it doesn't break us, we get stronger. Stiffen your spine, keep going! Look forward, not back!"

"Looking back is my only source of happiness . . . when Margaret was alive and Ellery and I were newlyweds."

"I remember when Ellery came to see me right after he married you. Our flirtation was finished, he said. He spouted poetic blather about his married state: 'Let floods beat, winds rave, let the sun be eclipsed!' he ranted. 'Nothing can harm me. I have found shelter in Ellen's arms, as under a wide-spreading tree.'"

Cary neglected to divulge what Margaret had written her about Ellen's marriage: "Their connexion is so precipitately formed, I feel a shadow of tragedy overhanging the match. I shed tears not to stain the marriage," she wrote, "but hoping it will be a radiant dewdrop in the morning of a golden sky."

"I accept your charge." Cary stiffened her backbone. *I must be clear-eyed,* she thought. *I know Ellery's latitude and longitude. How to trick him? I'll invite him for a stroll at candle-lighting time.*

• • •

The crickets were chirping, geese cackling and waddling, cows lowing as they wended their way back to the stable, tin bells tinkling. The light was fading, pearly-pink and golden. Striding beside Ellery, Cary made sure her face was rouged by the setting sun, her cheeks blazing. She wore a fetching purple bonnet, trimmed with ribbon and a flower in front.

Her wide linen skirt grazed his limbs as they meandered over the meadow. Their swinging hands nearly touched. He's still a devilishly handsome man, Cary thought, rather enjoying herself. When they came to a flat rock overlooking the river bend, she sank down, spreading her crinolines and pulling Ellery down beside her. She dimpled prettily, smiling at her prey. He regarded her with more approval than surprise, pleased to receive his due of admiration. Cary tossed curls out of her eyes and slid her paisley shawl down her back. She could smell bay rum tonic drifting from his silky hair.

"Ellery," Cary crooned, "it's been an age since we had a good chat." All seductive innocence, eyes wide, eyelashes fluttering, soothing, entreating. "Do tell an old friend. How goes it with you and Ellen? At the bonfire last night, she seemed in distress. Is it possible she doesn't appreciate you?"

Ellery's mouth tightened. He whined, "Our house is a rotten trap, a prison to curtail my roaming. Ellen's sole purpose is to confine me! My rambles—so necessary for my poetry and my very being—are anathema to her. Ellen is teaching the children to hate me. They are anvils dragging me down, the rowdy brats, their heads stuffed with useless Latin. The girls can barely sew a hem."

"Oh dear," Cary soothed, batting her eyes. "I'm so sorry to hear she doesn't understand you. And here I thought yours is a marriage made in heaven." She patted his hand, casting consoling looks.

His voice brimmed with ill-used self-pity. "She accuses me of falsity! As if I could be other than I am! I have not a crooked bone in my body!" He was working himself up to spite. "When she accosted me last night, away flew all my hopes of the heart! They fell to the earth, heavy, broken, dead." He cast his head down melodramatically. "Oh Cary, I will never be young and light-hearted again." He edged closer. She could feel his breath on her face.

"And you so diligent in producing a book of great worth to the nation! With your gift for poetic expression! Please tell me how you did it!" Cary affected to beg.

Ellery became suddenly sly, with both pride and subterfuge flitting across his face. "It wasn't easy! I've worked like a slavey, writing, thinking, brooding, pacing the floorboards all night long and bent double over a desk to make a fair copy. The candle guttered in its socket. My poor eyes were stinging, my hand is near crippled, my back twisted like a pretzel."

"Making a fair copy?" she asked, the epitome of guileless sympathy.

"Waldo says Margaret was like an overloaded wheelbarrow, with original ideas heaped up and tumbling out willy-nilly. Well, *I* have original ideas too!" He sat up straight, glaring at the yellow sea of swaying goldenrod, as if it accused him of mediocrity. "Waldo says surprise is the woof Margaret weaves in the web of her every thought. Well, *I* can be even more surprising." Petulant, he squared his shoulders.

"Tell me more." She aimed melting glances at him under lowered eyelashes and leaned against his shoulder. "Your 'original ideas'—where do they come from: your intellect or imagination or . . . ?"

"I'll tell you . . ." he began, "and only you."

A yellow sassafras leaf spun down, flopping onto his knee. Ellery's face brightened, suffused with delight. "Here—chew on the stem," he said, shoving the mitten-shaped leaf in her mouth. "Doesn't that taste like root beer?" He watched, anxious to see her reaction.

Cary licked her lips, distressed at the delay but determined to maintain the play. "Hmmmm, spicy-sweet."

"If you crush the leaves and rub the oil on your skin, it heals bug bites," he said, full of botanical lore, then sighed. "If only there were a salve for Ellen's complaints!"

We must get back to The Book—time to play the coquette, Cary thought. "Shall I rub your aching back with this leaf, Ellery?" He bent forward, and she lifted the hem of his shirt and slid her hands beneath it. She massaged his shoulders, spinning the crumpled leaf all over his back. She couldn't help noticing how strong he was, muscles bulging like iron oarlocks from all his rowing.

He revolved his neck, sighing, "Why did I ever think marriage to a Fuller would bring happiness?" His sideways glance at Cary carried considerable heat.

"You were saying, Ellery? The source of inspiration for your book?"

He opened his mouth, bringing his lips near her ear. "The source—you may not believe this . . ." She could feel his warm breath tickling her neck.

Just then, a ringing "Hallooo!" sounded from the meadow. Melville tramped towards them in his peacoat, his long legs marching at top speed.

Ellery's mouth clamped shut, the valves of his speech closed tight. He stood, brushing grass from his shirt sleeves, ready to bolt. "Excuse me. I must collect sassafras leaves to make root tea. I feel in need of a pick-me-up." He nodded, tossing a farewell over his shoulder: "I bid you good evening."

Cary clenched her fists, seething in frustration, almost groaning. *Mission thwarted! So close!*

"You're looking peaked." Melville was oblivious to the debacle his interruption caused. "Is something wrong?"

"Dang blame it!" she erupted. "Everything is wrong! I was on the verge of taking the measure of the man, getting the truth out of him." She growled, all pretense of gentility flown out the window.

"I'll tell you the truth," he said. "That man is a feather. Light stuff floats, and the smallest barrels are soonest filled."

"Never will I fathom your gnomic utterances!" Cary told him, angry.

Melville pulled her to her feet and together they headed back to Bush. Unladylike though it was, she drew back her boot and kicked a stone clear across the grass as they strode. Melville joined her in attacking the stones, but she whacked them with more ferocity than he, as if each one were an implacable enemy.

"My book summons me with increasing urgency," Melville said. "When will your father be back? I must sound his depths."

"All you care about is talking with Father! How do I know when—or even if—he'll come?" Cary groused.

"This Concord gathering has stirred me up to high heaven," Melville said. "Henry and Walter too—we're all in a state of molting. Only Nat and Waldo seem content to sip their brandy and stagnate."

"What does your book have to do with Margaret?" she asked.

No reply.

In the distance, Cary saw Ellen awaiting her return and waved her hand in a wide arc like a white flag of surrender.

Margaret taught me well, Cary thought. Failure is not an option. Now what?

CHAPTER SEVENTY-FOUR

Walter Wonders

SEPTEMBER 8, 1850, CHANNING COTTAGE, CONCORD

Whitman straightened his stack of notebooks as he thought, *It's time to wrap up my fact-finding tour. Back to Gotham tomorrow, accompanied by Ellery. He'll deliver the book to his publisher. The game is lost. He wins. No proof.*

Ellen saw him packing. "Must you go so soon, Walter? You can't have the whole picture of my sister yet."

"We have no trace of her book," he answered. "Its loss is hardly a triumphant conclusion to my story."

"What will you write?"

"Perhaps I will disappoint Mr. Greeley. Margaret's true story can't be told in prose, only poetry."

In contrast to their sagging mood, Ellery entered and frisked about the parlor, dancing, whistling, and humming "Camptown Races." He seemed to have not a care in the world—so soon to be a famous author!

"Walter," he caroled, "you can be first to announce my *History of the Revolution*. Be sure you note that the solution to the world's ills is personal change."

If Margaret had a grave, Whitman thought, *she'd be kicking off the dirt clods to rise up in protest.* He said with false mildness, "If self-improvement is the cure, shouldn't you start by improving yourself?"

Ellery laughed, buoyant. "Improve what is already so near perfection? You jest, Walter!" He clutched fat folios of his manuscript tight to his bosom, as if they sprouted from his heart.

"Waldo and Nat appear eager to censor Margaret in their tribute," Whitman said, as Ellen remained quiet, knitting a sock and eavesdropping.

"Yes, it's important not to over-praise her," Ellery said, blithely untroubled.

"Must my story whitewash her too? In their so-called biography, they won't mention her views on marriage or the role of women. No admission that she birthed a child, either."

"A child of dubious parentage—better let it go." Ellery thumped a finger on his text.

Whitman had to speak. "Isn't it wrong to rub off the raw edges of truth? What today seems like blasphemy may be sacred writ tomorrow. It could be they're threatened by a woman who refuses to be silent."

Ellery, unperturbed, resumed humming. "Best to bury her in silence."

"What if Margaret's dearest wish was to leave footprints for others—generations of women—to follow? It could be they're not burying a corpse but planting a seed."

Whitman saw Ellen nod in approval. She could no longer pretend to be indifferent. She stabbed a ball of yarn with her knitting needles and, like a Valkyrie, rushed towards Ellery to declare, "You and Waldo refuse to admit the concept of Wrong. You insist 'Evil doesn't exist,' that what appears to be evil is just the absence of good, 'a negative entity soon to become positive.' How will erasing Margaret be positive?"

"Will wrong disappear with a wave of a magic wand?" Whitman asked.

"Poof and piffle!" Ellery dismissively replied.

"Tell that to women crushed by husbands!" Ellen exclaimed. "Or tell colored slaves who are denied their humanity!"

"Silence!" Ellery hammered a fist on the sideboard. "Reasoning with you is useless. Pack my bag. I depart for New York tomorrow." He strode out, Frizzy capering at his heels.

Ellen seemed galvanized. She told Whitman, "Odd—Margaret speaks to me now more clearly than at the mesmerism."

"Yes, I too hear her pounding heartbeat. It arouses an echo in me. I want to sing her song, but is it a funeral knell or a hymn of praise?"

He opened a notebook and wrote, "I will look for you under my boot-soles, growing from the grass I love. I must keep encouraged—missing you in one place I must search another. You stop somewhere, waiting for me."

"Tonight," Ellen sighed, "we gather at Bush for a final meal—the last supper. Will Judas be revealed?"

As she bowed her head in grief, he scribbled a poem:

I hate the swift-running eddies that dash her head-foremost
    on the rocks.
What are you doing you ruffianly red-trickled waves?
Will you kill the courageous giant? Will you kill her in the
    prime of her years?
Steady and long she struggles,
She is baffled, bang'd, bruis'd, she holds out while her strength
    holds out,
The slapping eddies are spotted with her blood, they bear her
    away, they roll her, swing her, turn her,
Her body is borne in the circling eddies, it is continually
    bruis'd on rocks,
Swiftly and out of sight is borne the brave corpse.

CHAPTER SEVENTY-FIVE

A Rift Between Friends

SEPTEMBER 7, 1850, BUSH, CONCORD

Ellery, all fired up with glee, pranced about the Emersons' parlor, fit to bust his waistcoat. To Lidian, who observed his high spirits with a jaundiced eye, he seemed so tip-top ebullient, it was like he stood on stilts. Circling the room, he was impatient for Emerson to emerge from his study, so he could brag about his trip.

"Fare thee well, Lidian," he informed his idol's wife before the Great Man appeared. "Tomorrow I leave for a higher calling!"

"Good riddance!" she said under her breath, retreating to a nook and opening her sewing basket. How would Mr. Emerson react, she wondered, to boasts by this man of moderate intellect, glib tongue, and execrable morality? She resolved to listen quietly, trusting that a wife's invisibility would allow them to speak freely.

Thoreau stumped in, jostling a leathern bucket of logs. He dumped the faggots in the scuttle with a clatter. Ellery jumped in surprise and turned towards him with a superior smirk. "Sorry you can't accompany me to the city, Henry, but I know domestic duties are more your calling."

Thoreau frowned.

Ellery has set the snakes to dancing, Lidian thought as she darned a sock. The two friends were at odds. Usually they hiked together for hours every day—sometimes all day. They were like twins, always on the same page—same line, same word even—especially if the word was "saunter." The two men shared a philosophy: instead of working six days and reposing on the Sabbath, they preferred to work one day and ramble six. Now Henry seemed in a snit completely foreign to him. Never would Lidian have expected a rift. She couldn't resist listening as they squabbled.

"I've seized my destiny in my hands!" Ellery proclaimed. "One day, my friend, it may be your turn." His pride was unmistakable, as was his condescending assumption: Thoreau would lag behind as Ellery ascended.

"You leave tomorrow to deliver your History for printing, I believe?" Thoreau's voice was even, nonjudgmental, yet a hectic circle of carmine splotched his cheek. He regarded Ellery keenly, like a barred owl circling above a field mouse. He let out a sharp puff of air. In sorrow more than anger, he was blunt: "More than any man, you disappoint me." His eyes engaged Ellery's without flinching.

Ellery's bravado melted like morning mist on the river. "Your words land like blows, Henry. How do I disappoint?"

"I am your best friend, your fondest companion and admirer," Thoreau persevered, "yet you are strange to me."

"Why . . . what do you mean, Henry?" Ellery asked, his voice quavering.

Thoreau kept his voice level, like Diogenes in search of an honest man: "I can't picture you a bona fide historian of the Roman revolution. It's a most peculiar cloak you're wearing."

Ellery smiled like a crocodile, so cool that butter wouldn't melt in his mouth. "It's indeed a new cast of skin for me. I've turned my energies in an outwardly productive direction. It's not intended to be lucrative—I scoff at Mammon, as you well know. Yet I have every reason to hope my readers will reap ample riches of wisdom, thought, and wit."

Lidian wanted to poke her needle in his chest. *Lord forgive me!* she thought, *but you'd think his braces would pop, his ego's so inflated!*

"Pardon my frankness." Thoreau came to the sticking point: "You're a man of genius but no discipline. If I suspect this work isn't yours, I can't respect you. I beseech you, dear friend: stop. Take a deep breath. Tell me the truth."

Ellery flushed, his voice near strangled with escalating anger: "You and I, Henry, are very alike. The world marks us both failures. People shake their heads; they tsk-tsk at our lack of ambition. To them, we're village oddities, loiterers. Gallivanting is our sole purpose, they say. You've heard the whispers behind our backs: we don't choose to work. We're devoid of go-get-'em gumption. It's a badge of honor for me." Swelling up, he continued, "Now, like a hermit crab, I come out of my shell. I am become a Prophet to the Nation!"

Lidian could almost hear a drumroll and trumpet blast in his declaration. George Washington, Thomas Jefferson, Marquis de Lafayette all rolled into one deluded young man.

"I want that for you," Thoreau nearly pleaded. "I want your story to be not just a bushel of nuts, but glorious, coherent, and true."

"Henry," Ellery replied, his words spoken as to an ignorant child, "you and I have been hibernating—you in your wooden inkstand at Walden Pond and me consigned to Poverty, which the world deems fit for a Poet. I've endured the world's indifference. If, however, there is *anything* beautiful in me, now it will bear fruit." He paced in a tight circle, his voice lifted to the rafters: "I'm trusting my inward vision, heeding my inner voice!"

Thoreau minced no words. "Why then do I suspect you deal in stolen goods?"

"Sir, you insult me!" Ellery's voice, unrepentant, climbed into a near-shrieking register. "I must assume—with infinite regret—your hostility stems from jealousy. *I* am launching my barque on the seas of public acclaim. You, dear friend, are content to drift underwater, an invertebrate jellyfish tossed by the tides."

Thoreau thrust his hands deep in his pockets, shaking his head.

"Trust thyself!" Ellery was determined to have the last word. "Every heart vibrates to that iron string."

Lidian could no longer be silent. Just as Ellery was high-stepping out—the picture of self-regard—she stood. "Those are Mr. Emerson's words!"

"Yes, and they are true for all humanity," Ellery deigned to say over his shoulder.

Thoreau slumped, collapsed in an armchair, his head in his hands, a look of despair on his face. "I thought I knew him all to pieces."

Lidian patted his shoulder. "Pay him no mind! He thinks he's the biggest toad in the puddle."

At that juncture, Emerson—head in the clouds and nose in a book—strolled in, supremely ignorant of the drama. "What," he asked from his peak of abstraction, "did I miss?"

• • •

As he staggered away from Bush, Thoreau heard a flock of geese squawk, flapping through the pale sky in a wavy black ribbon. Monarch butterflies, with their black-rimmed saffron wings, undulated above the milkweed, dipping in and out like thirsty drinkers. They cheer me not, Thoreau thought. All Nature is in retreat. It does not speak to me.

Lidian followed him. "Henry, don't run off. Talk to me!"

He turned to face her, his face tortured by doubt. "Is it true I'm jealous because Ellery's leaving me for wider pastures? Abandoning me to oblivion?"

"You two have been so fused," she said. "He said very hurtful things. No wonder you're upset."

Thoreau looked to the sky, spreading his arms. "We've been like fish hawks, flying high, circling against the storm of opinion. Together we scorn manners, pooh-pooh ideas of proper dress, even reject polite speech. We proudly spurn wealth."

"It's time to spurn *him*."

"Oh Lidian . . ." He picked a purple coneflower and began to rip its petals off. "I imagined he was someone else entirely, someone he isn't. What a fool I am! I know he has a secret. I must condemn what's wrong in him."

"Of course, you must. My question is, Why won't Mr. Emerson condemn him? Is it because he wants a man to get credit for Margaret's work? That he can't bear for her to surpass him—even in death?"

"Don't blame Waldo."

Lidian let out a resounding "hmmph!"

"No, no—together, Waldo, Ellery, and I stand for freedom, self-reliance, inspiration from Nature. Is that wrong?" he asked.

"Not wrong," she said, "but not entirely right either."

"Ellery leaves me for society. What do I do?" He seemed about to cry.

Lidian pulled out her omnipresent Bible and held it like an offering to the gods. "Examine your soul, root out pride, find what will sustain you in this deepest hollow, and claw your way back to light and air."

Thoreau slouched, looking like a windblown scarecrow, all askew, its stuffing leaking out. "I'm a laughingstock in Concord. When I went to live at the pond, everyone jeered at me. One said I'd rather live with woodchucks than in town, which he said is very hard on the woodchucks."

Lidian stifled a tiny smile at the joke but said to him, "You must tell them why you went and what you learned."

He pressed her hand. "I will! I can't be what I have been. I'll part company with the best friend I ever had. I'll pursue my own path."

CHAPTER SEVENTY-SIX

Bringing in the Sheaves

SEPTEMBER 7, 1850, CONCORD

The last gathering of Margaret's friends before they went their separate ways approached. Ellery prepared to leave the next day to deliver his History to the publisher. He stuffed in his valise a silvery daguerreotype of himself. *Not as handsome, perhaps, as the real article*, he thought. *Yet 'twill do for the frontispiece as a Portrait of the Author. For my next book, I'll commission a drawing from Sophia. The publisher can use it for an engraving, send it to magazines and newspapers.*

In his mind he was already celebrated across continents for his scholarly acumen. He brushed his wavy hair and hummed, a picture of jovial charm if not exactly of Sophoclean wisdom. All was right with the world. He clutched his manuscript, unwilling to let it out of his sight.

Cary's mood was at an opposite extreme. Her father had written of his imminent return, letting her know why he'd inserted himself into the gathering. "When I learned a mesmerist would contact the spirit of your friend, I hoped I could speak to your brother beyond the grave as well. It would give me solace if I could beg forgiveness." He felt it his duty to attend the final farewell.

She went to the stable, where the carriage would arrive, to await her father.

It was Indian summer at its best, mild and dry. The air tingled with a nimbus of red-gold brilliance. Boys were cutting corn, hacking the tall spikes down to stubble. Men swung scythes and sickles in a hypnotic rhythm—whoosh, whoosh—mowing the last of the hay. They pitchforked the stalks into tall haystacks, singing "Jimmy Crack Corn, an' I don't care." The whole outside world seemed sunstruck, yet Cary dreaded the first frost—not far off.

She had always had a fondness for corn-husking and haying season, when everyone worked together, laying in the sheaves before winter. They'd tear off the corn's outer, bleached-gold husks—how they crackled!—to reveal the brighter gold kernels inside. Cornhusking time meant a party. Lanterns were hung in the barn. The cows lowed and creaked in their stanchions. Inside the house, a long table was spread with a checkered tablecloth. Candles were stuck in the stub ends of cut carrots as sockets. There were baskets of apples, piles of brown bread, soft gingerbread, fresh cheese, and pumpkin pies.

Cary remembered those halcyon days of youth as she lay back on the sweet-smelling hay. Little Eddy's pony nickered. She pulled her shawl tight.

A bass voice punctured her revery: "Do you hope to find the answer to your questions in here?"

"Would that were true, Herman," she said. "Do you?"

"In fact, yes. I await your father. If I am to glimpse the inner spring of my novel, I must plumb his depths. I feel a shock of recognition with the Captain."

"Father? Why—what has he to do with an imaginary tale? Aren't you writing a yarn of high adventure on the sea, of pirates and cannibals?"

"No, I write in blood, not ink." In the dim light, his features looked tortured. "Only in the most profound grief is there total honesty. When one has nothing left to lose—then we see truth. Your father has dwelled in this maddened state, I think, since your brother's death."

She didn't hide her exasperation. "You really have no trivial chit-chat! How do you ever manage when a Parson comes to call?"

Her gut felt a throb of pain, as happened whenever she thought of her fractured family: a dear brother and sister dead, mother insane, father forever launched on the sea, alone in infinite sorrow. "Does a character in your novel suffer a loss?"

Melville reminded her of a true story about an albino sperm whale that attacked and sank the ship and crew of the whaleship *Essex*. "That's the germ of my book. A sea captain who's been dismasted by the whale, his leg bitten off, and his search for vengeance."

"What does that have to do with me?" Sturgis bellowed, having quietly entered and overheard them.

"Forgive my bluntness!" Melville said. "My captain is driven mad by his loss. He's enraged, obsessed, a godly, ungod-like man."

"And I?" Father asked. "Am I also maimed by my loss?"

"*Our* loss," Cary corrected. Her voice was tearful. "Since the day Willy died, our whole family is lost. I've lost you."

Sturgis flung a bucket of oats against the stable wall and knocked down a row of pitchforks with a loud, metallic clang. He paced, batting the air with his arms as if throttling a ghost. "My son is gone—my heart ripped out of my chest, my right hand cut off! I can't comprehend his fate. Of explanation—I have none, consolation none, only bitterness and oblivion!"

"You can't bring him back by force of will!" Cary shouted. "You live alone, nursing a grievance against the universe! We're still here—your daughters who share your grief."

"Am I being punished for my adventuresome youth? How do I dare love again?" His questions were a yowl to the pit of hell.

"Love *me*!" she implored. "Even in the midst of life, the specter of death is at our shoulder. No one gets out alive. You just keep going until the end!"

Melville spoke softly to them. "You both carry too much sail. Take a reef. No grief is incommunicable. It'll poison you like swallowing arsenic if you don't spit it out."

"We can't conquer the universe, Father." Cary gentled him with a pat on the shoulder as you would a rearing horse. "Please don't refuse my comfort. Come back to port."

Melville uttered one of his trademark non sequiturs: "It's a joint-stock world, sir. You have but one share in a company of friends. Seek solidarity, not solitude. In the trying pots, when we squeeze whale blubber to extract sperm oil, we often hold a neighbor's hand."

Cary had no clue what to make of his analogy, but Sturgis's eyes were moist. With a near-crushing grip, he jerked Melville's hand up and down like a pump handle.

Melville, looking mournful, murmured to himself, *However many a man will brag of his science and skill, to the crack of doom, the sea will insult and murder him.*

Her father kissed Cary's cheek. "When, dear daughter, will we be done growing?" He left for the Old Manse, marching like a soldier armed with resolve rather than a musket.

"Thank you, Herman. I've never been able to speak so honestly to Father. Meeting you here is a gift from Providence." She shook Melville's hand.

"When big hearts strike together," he said, "the concussion is a bit stunning." She looked perplexed, so he went on. "It's a strange sort of book I'm writing. I promised it would be 'enjoyable' but a Polar wind blows through it. I fear it'll be terrifying." He dropped his head, cursing, "Dollars damn me!"

CHAPTER SEVENTY-SEVEN

History or Her Story?

EVENING, SEPTEMBER 7, 1850, THE OLD MANSE, CONCORD

Gathered at one end of the walnut dining table were Waldo Emerson, Nathaniel and Sophia Hawthorne, and Ellery Channing (hugging a wrapped bundle to his chest). Seated a considerable distance away from them were Lidian Emerson, Henry Thoreau, a downcast Ellen Channing, Cary Sturgis Tappan, Captain William Sturgis, Herman Melville, and Walter Whitman. Tension, rather than joviality, prevailed.

"Why do they cluster around Ellery?" Lidian whispered to Thoreau. "Is it to shield him from disapproval?"

"They're like a covey of bobwhite quail," he said, "roosting shoulder to shoulder and facing outward to spot predators."

The hosts tried to instill collegial cheer. "Do help yourselves to provisions!" Sophia urged with exaggerated spirit. "Let's pass around the ham and mustard. There is boiled tongue, bread and cheddar, beets, turnips, and carrots."

"Don't forget the lemon punch and cider." Hawthorne, fastidious as ever, tucked a linen napkin over his spotless cravat.

An awkward silence fell, relieved only by the sound of chewing and clang of cutlery. Most of the diners avoided looking at Ellery, instead inspecting their plates with assiduous attention.

Finally, he could no longer abide the lack of notice and announced, "My friends, I hereby inform you that—as of tomorrow—I give up my poetic vocation for the role of Historian." Ellery took a deep swig of punch and wiped his mouth with a threadbare sleeve. False was his modesty, but his pleasure in surprising them was real.

"Now, Ellery, that's not necessary," Emerson reassured his protégé. "Your talent is such that you can produce both prosody and poetry. Look at Henry and me as exemplars. I flatter myself that both forms are valid. Aye, Henry?" He looked at his disciple for the acquiescence he felt sure to receive.

Thoreau clamped his mouth shut, stiffening his shoulders.

Ellery filled the gap. "No, Waldo, I'm hanging up my fiddle. I wish to enlighten the wider world. My previous utterances, I avow, are not worth a fart in a whirlwind."

Lidian gasped, turning purple. Not just a liar, but a crude vulgarian! "I can no longer remain silent! Sir, you are a brigand and a thief! That History is Margaret's!"

Ellery barked a mirthless laugh. He sat up straight, thrusting his head forward as if displaying an encircling halo. "If I'm a brigand, it's doubtless in the same way as Moses and Jesus. We prophets have no need to steal. Our revelations come from the Divine."

Lidian's mouth dropped open in horror. "Blasphemy! I never . . ." she sputtered. A Bible emerged from her apron pocket, which she brandished like a protective talisman. "Sacrilege!"

Emerson put a finger to his lips: "My dear Queenie, please hush! You accuse our friend with no proof!"

"Let us see your so-called prophetic manuscript, Ellery," Ellen said in a firm voice, hands clenched. "Only then can we judge if the words are yours."

"Be silent, woman!" Ellery clutched the bundle on his lap with a death grip, looking straight at her with burning eyes. "Do not play the fool!" He nodded towards Waldo, as if for his guidance: "Heed the Great Man." The others looked askance, uneasy witnesses, helpless.

Hawthorne, an urbane observer well above the fray, attempted to divert his guests. "This poor little country village seems overrun, does it not, my Dove" (addressing his ever-compliant wife) "with strangely dressed, antic mortals who consider themselves appointed agents of the Divine?"

"Just so, my Love," Sophia agreed. "Present company excluded, of course."

"In truth, Waldo's eccentric devotees who presume to solve the riddles of the universe, while being disdainful of all decorum, are intensely irrelevant to the mundane world." Hawthorne blotted his mouth with a napkin.

Eye-rolling at the table suggested a healthy dose of sarcasm was perceived in his remarks.

"No disrespect intended, Ellery," Hawthorne said. "It's only that we have yet to learn precisely what divine revelation you've received."

Ellery shrugged as if unconcerned—a mere detail soon to be revealed in all its glory! He struggled to remain silent, a paragon of unconcern, and then—unable to resist—replied, "Irrelevant, you say? To my mind, it's Margaret who saw the world through colored glasses. The frogs in our swamp, which are young and alive, make finer music than her tired words. You think her musings on Italy would have been more equal to her talents than anything previously published? Rubbish! Margaret's writing bleats, while mine booms!"

Hawthorne frowned. "Regardless of the provenance of your book or of its booming style, I advise you to curb your peculiarities when you go to Gotham. When you meet your publisher, it behooves you to rectify your lamentable sartorial choices and lapse in cleanliness." He stroked his sable moustaches with two delicate fingers, taming an errant hair projecting towards an otherwise pristine nostril.

"As for the question of Margaret's so-called masterpiece, presumed lost," Hawthorne continued, "we all deplore her poorly timed mortality, certainly premature. Of course, she was always precocious—in life as well as in death."

Even Sophia registered shock at the shallow well of his emotion.

She veered in another direction, looking keenly from Ellen to Ellery. "I wonder, dear Channings, if your disagreement is not, in truth, rooted in a measure of discord in your marital experiment." She lifted her husband's napkin to wipe a smudge of mustard from his cheek. They smoldered visibly with affectionate harmony.

"I say, Lidian, is there any sweetflag-root powder?" Emerson asked, turning a sickly pale. "I fear the onset of a bilious ache." He discreetly burped behind his handkerchief. "Bring on the pears—a most salubrious aid to digestion!"

Melville, suddenly recalling his distrust of Transcendental verities, came to life. "Shall we entertain a philosophic debate?" He outlined the points: "Ellery, true to Waldo's ethics, argues that his judgment alone is to be trusted. He perceives Truth through intuition and records it for posterity. Does not such individualism amount to monomania?"

"Exactly!" Cary exclaimed. "Ellery distrusts joint action, fearing a threat to his singularity!" She seemed to be working out her thoughts as she spoke. "Your alleged History, Ellery, is vaporous as *thoughts*, while Margaret's is concrete as *action*. You speak of 'booming.' It was Margaret, not you, who heard real bombs blast and cannons fire. She dodged musket balls roaring through the streets. She tended the wounded and mopped up their blood!"

"You merely play at being a Historian," Ellen piled on. "Through a flash of intuition—all at once—your 'book' appears. Hers came from years of labor. Her history is real! Yours is false!"

Ellery shushed her. "Curb your tongue, woman. Be silent or begone!"

Captain Sturgis spoke softly, as if to himself: "'The voyage is long, night is coming, the body is tired and cold, with no harbor in sight.' That's what Margaret told me in Florence just before she embarked for home."

Ellen, stunned: "What? You saw her before she left Italy?" Surprised voices sounded around the table.

"I meant to tell you, Ellen," Sturgis said. "Margaret and I became friends during her sojourn in Europe. Before she left, she entrusted some papers to me, which I've brought. 'Should I never return,' she said, 'and sometimes I despair of doing so, please know that I have given my all to write this story.'" He pulled out a fat packet of papers spilling out of a folder.

A hullabaloo erupted. Everyone clamored with astonishment. What? Where? How? When?

Ellery—vermilion-red—ransacked his mind for an appropriate facial expression, settling on Confident Imperturbability. He scrutinized the floor as if searching for his missing halo, his star turn overshadowed, thrust from center stage to the pit.

Ellen crossed her arms and looked hard at him. Everyone gabbled at once: "Is it true? Margaret's History! Is it saved? Let's see it!"

They looked towards Emerson, silent on his peak of Higher Thought. He shifted from side to side on his chair, hands exploring his waistcoat pockets, as if searching for a written essay addressing the problem. *What now?*

Emerson cleared his throat, a gambit to buy time. It always worked on the lectern, building suspense by delay. He surveyed the agitated assemblage, clearly at sixes and sevens, and made a Solomonic proposal: "Since we are bifurcated into two streams on the subject of the Book, I suggest we adjourn to Egg Rock and seek guidance from Nature to determine our course. On the banks of the Concord, we can compare the two texts."

"Egg Rock," he told Melville (unacquainted with local topography) "is where two smaller streams, the Assabet and Sudbury Rivers, merge to form the Concord River. It was one of Margaret's favorite spots. Perchance the harmonious confluence will spur reconciliation."

Reconciliation seemed unlikely. But once the two dueling versions of the History were compared, a dénouement of some sort could at least be effected. Perhaps Ellery's parcel contained his own original contribution, as he claimed.

Following Emerson's suggestion, the diners wiped gravy off their chins and pushed back their chairs with a brisk scrape. Donning chapeaux, shawls, and jackets, they tramped en masse from the Old Manse to a large rock, whose rounded surface bulged upwards in an egg-shaped hump. Twilight was turning the river into a rocking cradle of salmon-pink hues borrowed from the sky. They carried torches, while Whitman—ever resourceful—pulled a wagon loaded with magnums of champagne and a lantern.

As he walked, lagging behind, Ellery muttered to Emerson, "Writing is an art that makes the invisible visible, as you of all authors know, O Best Waldo. That's what I've done: pulled from the ether a stirring account of faraway events."

Emerson, absorbed in thought, either ignored his appeal or didn't heed it, lost in a brown study.

Failing to enlist his mentor's aid, Ellery appeared disturbed. He looked from side to side anxiously. How best to conceal his book? An exit strategy came to him—he had only to misplace evidence that might be construed as damning. Shrubbery could hide his package, to be retrieved at a more propitious time.

As if on a theater's proscenium, this master of coordinated athletic grace tripped with exaggerated panache. He stumbled headlong into a buttonwood bush and fell to his knees. He thrashed about in the underbrush, fending off spiderwebs and branches, then clambered to his feet to extricate himself from the verdure's clutches. He brushed thorny twigs from his sleeves and groused, "Brambles! An ever-present danger!"

He pretended absorption in the local vegetation. He stooped to turn over rocks—playing the innocent naturalist—and pick daisies. He continued his slow walk. "Onward ever," he muttered, "backward never."

Whitman was first to notice Ellery was no longer encumbered with the sacred package containing his text. Frizzy brought this deficiency to everyone's attention by scampering to her master and hurling herself into his empty arms, barking in a jubilee of joy at their reunion.

Not only eagle-eyed but stern, Whitman demanded, "Where's the book? What have you done with it?"

Everyone pivoted to face Ellery. "He hid it!" Ellen shouted. "We must find it!"

A hubbub ensued as all except Ellery began beating the tall grasses, parting the reeds in a frantic search, tromping in puddles, and hunting like frenzied children in pursuit of Easter eggs.

Frizzy, unaware of her master's devious design, leapt from his arms. She propelled herself like a cannon ball towards the buttonwood bush. From its depths, she dragged out a brown-paper parcel, its cover, firmly clamped between her jaws, impregnated with ham gravy from the truncated repast. Frizzy licked the package in a haze of hungry delirium until Ellery wrenched it away. He held it above the leaping Frizzy, saying, "Good pup, you've saved the proof of my innocence. I do hope it's not damaged." He affected a look of relief and trudged on.

As pilgrims heading to a shrine, they continued the trek and arrayed themselves like a tribunal on the curved rock, which extended into the river's sandy shallows. Curiosity, skepticism, and accusation floated through the darkening air. Captain Sturgis took charge, intoning with solemnity, "Although these papers, which Margaret entrusted to me, are doubtless an unfinished draft, I will read her words."

Margaret's words at last! Suspense and dread mingled with expectation. With the notable exception of Ellery, everyone held their breath. Not a few slapped hands over their throbbing hearts.

Thinking no one was watching, Ellery heaved a rock in the water behind his back. *Plink*! Ripples spread in a widening circle. "Hark! I hear a pickerel jumping," he said, all *faux*-enthusiasm. "What say we do some evening fishing, gents?"

"Does our court jester hope to distract us?" Whitman muttered.

Ellery prattled on: "We can catch minnows for bait and cut a sapling for a pole. Grapevine for a line, and I'll carve a hook with my pocketknife. You're in for a fight with pickerel. They run with the line—"

"As do you, Mr. Channing," Sturgis said reprovingly, curtailing his chatter. "If you will cease your babbling and allow me to proceed . . ."

Sturgis began reading from Margaret's text in sonorous tones, as Melville—to illuminate it—held a torch near the manuscript. "'Sad but Glorious Days' is the title of this section of Margaret's account," Sturgis said. He read: "That shore by the Tiber, towards which I had yearned all my life, was a place where it seemed the heart would expand and all of Nature be turned to delight. There I hoped a radical, though peaceful, revolution would be achieved."

Ellen clapped her hands in rapture. "Margaret's voice!"

Ellery tried to stand straight and appear defiant, but his posture increasingly drooped. He clutched his bundle tightly, even as Thoreau tried to yank the package from him. They tussled, pushing and pulling the bundle until finally Henry was victorious. He unwrapped it, rifling through the pages and shaking his head. "Ellery," he said, "you've never worked long enough to produce a work of such length!"

Ellery was tight-lipped and turned his head away.

Henry held the first page near the nebula of torchlight. As Sturgis read, Henry traced the lines in Ellery's manuscript with a finger. As Sturgis intoned words aloud and Henry silently mouthed the same words, the group watched the pantomime and concordant recital: "It is here that my sublime hopes for a future without foreign oppression reside, where a great but still incomplete revolution will be won at a dear cost."

Certainty was dawning, and Henry signaled it was his turn. He cleared his throat and raised his voice, reading from Ellery's pages. This time, it was Sturgis who followed along, mouthing words written on the pages he held. "Enmeshed in a combat grand in its motives, surrounded by barricades, I hear earnest words of faith and love. I see deeds of brotherhood of an extent far beyond what the world has known."

Sputtering bursts of outrage erupted from the listeners. "The exact same words! Identical in both manuscripts!" Hawthorne exclaimed.

A cacophony of voices overlapped. "How could you, Ellery?" Ellen howled, heart-broken.

"Those are Margaret's words," Cary shouted, "not his!"

"My boy! I took you under my wing," Emerson scolded. "I praised your poems. I never would've thought . . ."

Ellery slumped like melted ice cream. Then he drew himself up as a possible explanation flashed through his mind: "Just as Margaret's voice spoke at the mesmerism," he blustered, "so she must've spoken to me, dictating what I should write!"

"Shameless jackanape!" Lidian accused. "Far-fetched is mother's milk to you, you scoundrel!"

Even the ladies who praised mesmerism were unpersuaded. Cary challenged, "What 'barricades,' pray tell, were you surrounded by? Which 'deeds of brotherhood' did you witness?"

Ellery mounted his high horse: "I assault the barricades of conformity! In combat between self-trust and submission!" His eyes pleaded for sympathy, but only coldness greeted him. He made one final appeal: "Henry, my dearest companion, go a-berrying with me! I know where wild cranberries grow nearby. If you love me, do not abandon me to this pack of wolves!"

Thoreau struggled, his friend's entreaty vying with disgust. "I prefer liberty to love," he said. "I have several more lives to live. I cannot spare more time for life with you." He kicked up a patch of moss from the rock.

Ellery shifted his plea to his ever-faithful defender Emerson: "This whole thing is a fool's errand. You at least must excuse me, dear teacher. I've only followed the dictates of Nature!"

Emerson seemed to soften, saying, "My boy, I've always believed in your brilliance—"

That was too much for Thoreau, who fairly spat, "Brilliance! What about integrity?" Decisive at last, Thoreau addressed Waldo, his mentor, his idol: "I must break my dependence on you as well. Living under your patronage, I'm like a withered leaf, hanging shivering on a stem. I've been living a life of quiet desperation, chained with golden fetters." Turning away from his fellows, Thoreau added, "If humanity betrays me, Nature will henceforth fill the gap and be my intimate friend. Hereafter I will communicate with Her and express the truths She imparts to me."

Lidian looked unaccountably sad and lifted her hand in both salute and farewell. She kissed her fingers and held them out to him.

Ellen brought them back to her mission. "No more squabbling! Action is called for!" She seemed giddy as she asked, "Can we publish Margaret's book? Not the one Ellery copied and—I fear—perverted with his ideas, but her original words, the ones Captain Sturgis brought? Cary and I can edit it. Waldo, you'll help, won't you? You can write your publisher to recommend it."

Cary frowned, barely perceptibly. Something troubled her.

Infected with impudence without limit, Ellery proposed his own solution: "What if the title page has co-authors—my name and Margaret's? The last chapter is entirely my own. I'm sure my publisher will agree."

Everyone looked daggers at him. "All right," he conceded, pounding a fist in his other hand. He offered what he considered the ultimate concession: "We don't have to list the authors alphabetically. Her name can go first." He scuffled his feet on the rock, as if he had not a care in the world, just a small matter of authorship to arrange. In a show of nonchalance he kicked a pine cone into the water.

Whitman blurted out what seemed an incontrovertible fact: "Impossible! Her book, like her life and that of her son, is unfinished. You can't publish her words without her approval! Margaret would never release anything less than perfect."

"Well then," Ellery stepped forward to the shore—a destroying angel, vengeful yet trying to assume a mantle of selfless dignity. He began to tear pages from his manuscript, saying, "If you all are so eager to reject my offering . . ." He crumpled the pages and heaved them in the river.

"No!" shouted a chorus led by Ellen. She dashed to Ellery's side and grabbed his arm. "Help me!" she screamed, flailing at his face, threatening to knock him into the river. He steadied himself and elbowed her away, ripping pages from the bound manuscript even more rapidly. He balled them up and flung them far out into the current. One projectile skipped like a rock over the glittering water, as ripples diffracted torchlight into prisms of colors.

"The world is not ready for utopia." Ellery hurled pages faster into the depths where green water turned dark blue.

Everyone stood frozen in place, stupefied. Their cries diminished to a shock of paralysis, even as Ellen—shrieking, fighting alone—couldn't stop the destruction. Cavalier in the extreme, Ellery chunked the remaining pages in the stream, where they floated away, grew heavy, and sank.

More unpredictable was what happened next. Sturgis strode to the edge of the rock and held Margaret's manuscript aloft, at arm's length. A breeze rippled the pages as he waved them in the air. "We must move on!" he shouted. "I say, let it go!"

Ellen, like a desperate Joan of Arc, dashed to the Captain's side. She stood on tiptoe and stretched to grab the out-of-reach pages. "Please, sir—it's all that's left of my sister!"

Sturgis was gentle and told her, "This is what she would've wanted."

"How," Ellen begged, "can you say that?"

"Before we said good-bye the final time," he told her, "Margaret was ready to pass the banner to another. 'My faith sings no more,' she said. 'I am weary.'"

"I don't believe it!" Ellen's chin quivered.

He was firm as the rock on which he stood. "I remember well. Her words were like an elegy or a eulogy." He recited: "'Woman's day has not yet come. My perception of the ills of women's condition and remedies that could be applied is sharp. If I live, I will have much to say on that subject, but I am tired of the battle. I'd like someone younger and stronger to say what ought to be said; still more, to do what ought to be done.'"

Even the waves ceased lapping and were silent.

Cary stood, erect as a pillar, and faced Ellen. "In her last letter, Margaret made it clear she was ready to move on. She wrote: 'Had I but energy to tell what ought to be told! Yet if God does not grant me long life to speak of remedies that might be applied, let some other, more worthy person, I pray, assume the duty.' Ellen, you must believe—what Margaret taught us will never die! It's not her written words but her example. She's gone, but she's inside us and will live on!"

"Yes!" Melville rushed to stand like an unbreakable triumvirate with the Captain and Cary. "Remember, Mankind is One, and beats with one great heart."

No one was sure what the Man of Mystery meant, but the others were silent in apparent consent. Sophia and Hawthorne nodded, saying in unison, "Let it go."

Lidian assented. "Her brief, radiant moment is over."

Ellery, perhaps relieved, hunched his shoulders and emitted a sigh through clenched teeth.

Near the water's edge, Ellen sank to her knees as tears trickled down her face, her arms limp. Cary and Melville, together with the Captain, flung Margaret's pages into the bigger river where two streams became the Concord. The inky papers bobbed on the surface, grew sodden, sank, and were carried away by the current. Margaret's tear-stained words dissolved, like her bones, in the flowing water.

Silence engulfed them as the river rolled on. Near the soggy pods of paper bobbing and melting away, a river otter and her pups floated on their backs, their little paws crossed over their chests. Cary, her father, and Melville laughed at the sight and threw the remaining wadded-up papers near them. As the projectiles plopped like snow-balls all around, the otters flipped their sleek bodies into furry balls to dodge the missiles and plunged.

As the critters disappeared, Sturgis sang "Pop! goes the weasel." He laughed loud and long. The release from tension was welcome to all, who joined in the chorus. They sang with ragged voices, "The monkey thought it was all in fun, 'til Pop! goes the weasel!"

"Reminds me of our refreshments," Whitman announced. He prodded corks out of the champagne bottles with his thumbs. Pop! Foamy bubbles exploded in spurting geysers, and streams of wine flowed down the bottles' necks as he passed them around.

"*Viva la revoluzione*!" Cary cried as she took a swig and handed a bottle to Melville.

He upended it and piped up, "*Viva*! Better to live in revolutionary times than deadly dull days!"

Ellen declined a drink. "Dullness has its attractions," she murmured in a monotone.

Amid the jollity, Ellery was strangely mute.

Thoreau turned from the group to face the forest, saying, "I vote for personal revolution. I must be true to my calling. I can't be what I was before."

Melville raised the bottle to toast him. "Hear, hear, my good man! I feel a new resolve as well. My ship now has weighty ballast to plough through the waves. My hand is firm on the tiller!"

Thoreau picked up the metaphor. "No more to drift but to observe and report, steering through treacherous straits!"

Sturgis put his oar in. "Steer true, lads! Deliver the cargo, my hearties, no matter how high the billows."

Leaning against her father with a tipsy grin on her lips, Cary chimed in: "Let us sail to parts unknown, then drop anchor on a lee shore."

"Precisely!" Thoreau, who never touched liquor, had a suspiciously moist beard. He looked at Ellery sadly. "I'll part company with the best friend I ever had to pursue my proper path." He shook off his despair, eyes flashing. "I don't need the public, but the public needs me. People speak of the divinity of Christ. I'll speak of the divinity of the individual soul!"

"By writing of housekeeping in your cabin at the pond?" Emerson asked, skeptical. "A History of Yourself?"

"It was a bold experiment!" Lidian rushed to his defense. "And wasn't Margaret doing the same thing in Rome—meeting the vital facts of life, not in books, but face to face?"

"She added her own insights, don't forget," Ellen inserted "gleaned from life."

"Margaret's work need not be lost." Thoreau slurred his words slightly, feeling the bubbles lift his mood and dull his tongue. "She built her castles in the air. Now we must put foundations under them." He took a long pull from the champagne bottle and preached, "I do not wish to hug the walls of my cabin but to go on the world's deck. Only there can we see moonlight amid the mountains. *Sic ad astra*!"

You can wash the starch out of a Harvard man, Whitman thought, *but not—it appears—the Latin.*

A breeze rustled dry aspen leaves, sounding like distant applause. More stars than they ever imagined pulsated with energy, raining shining rays on the river.

Inspired by the champagne, Whitman orated, "Farewell and fair travels, all! My job here is done. It's time for new beginnings!"

He stripped off his shirt, then shucked his red flannel undershirt like a dry corn husk. A delicious tingle of cool air licked his skin. "My tongue's use was sleeping 'til today!" he shouted, toeing off his cowhide boots. Ignoring Lidian's expression of dismay, he bellowed to the wind, "Now in a moment I know what I am for! An outsetting bard, I awake. A thousand songs start to life within me, never to die!"

Undeterred by the others' mounting surprise, Whitman peeled off his trousers, then his drawers. He stood naked and proud. "The fire, the sweet hell within me, the unknown want and destiny of me awake from this hour!" He dived off the rock into the river, plunging deep and popping up with a glad cry. "Join me, brothers and sisters!"

Cary was first to follow, shedding her shawl, dress, boots, and crinolines. No corset for her—she'd adopted Margaret's recipe for bodily freedom. Stripped to her chemise and drawers, she dived headfirst into the lapping waves. She hooted with laughter as Melville and Thoreau tore off their clothes and jumped into the stream with two great plops. They ducked each other and splashed, rollicking and frolicking.

"No whales here, Herman!" Thoreau yelled.

"Just a flotilla of loons!" Melville responded.

Cary called to Ellen, Sophia, and Lidian, "In the name of freedom and equality, come in!" She waved her hands like an orchestra conductor to beckon them. With only her head visible above the water, her russet hair streamed down her neck, a ribbon of iridescence in the gloaming.

Sophia, with a look mingling defiance and delight, doffed her outer garments and gestured to her husband, who stood stock-still in irresolution. "My Love," she said, inviting him with outstretched hand, "join me!"

He hesitated but removed his hat in a deliberate motion. "Together we can brave anything!" she encouraged, bracelets jingling on her wrist as she extended her arm to him. She flung the gold-link bangles to the sand atop her clothes. Her eyes glittered with audacity, re-enacting the pre-Nat Sophia when she was an avant-garde artist, not an ornamental piece of marital upholstery.

Hawthorne removed his polished boots and broadcloth cloak, folding it and placing all with care on a dry log. Before he could shed his trousers, Sophia pulled him into the waist-high water, laughing and ducking him, then folded herself in his arms. He grinned like a boy who had shot his first bear.

Lidian averted her eyes from all masculine states of undress and paused, sweeping the rock with her worried gaze. Finally, she unhooked her boots and shucked off her shawl and lace cap. Her hair, usually confined, streamed down her shoulders in chestnut waves. She took the Bible from her apron pocket and placed it on an altar-like tuft of moss. Linking hands and raising their skirts, she and Ellen waded into the river, their toes gripping the sand. Lidian shivered and quoted Genesis: "And they were both naked, Adam and Eve the man and wife, and were not ashamed." Her challenging look to Waldo did not go unnoticed.

He reproved her from his planted stance on the shore. "Lidian, Queenie, I'm astonished at this want of delicacy! Modesty, my dear!"

"Mr. Emerson," she countered, "won't you come try the fine and froggy art of swimming?"

Sturgis, taking advantage of Waldo's distraction, placed his hands on Emerson's back and shoved him in. The Sage of Concord came up spouting water and batting the waves. He laughed like a child and held out his hand to Sturgis to rescue him. The older man grasped Emerson's arm to reel him in, but Emerson emitted a whoop of glee and tugged Sturgis in fully clothed. The two removed their boots and poured out streams of silty water like syrup from a pitcher. They tossed their boots and sodden cloaks to shore.

"Such a healthful form of recreation," Hawthorne said, expelling a vertical spout of water and floating on his back like a placid emperor of the waves. The swimmers rolled about and flapped their arms energetically, hysterical with glee. Hawthorne called out, "Think of the medicinal value of aquatic activity, Waldo. This should cure your aching stomach!"

Emerson posed like the central statue in a fountain, spitting a gush of water from his mouth. "I feel better already," he admitted, his voice tinged with uncharacteristic juvenility.

After a joyous interval of cavorting, they grew quiet and started to shiver. The torches stuck like spears in the sand flickered and guttered. A cloud blew away to reveal a full moon. The water turned silver, its mirrored surface streaked with fire, speckled with stars like confetti on a parade route.

Ellery appeared, carrying a heap of quilts and blankets. He didn't speak but draped the coverlets over his horizontally outstretched arms—an offering. He affected a blank expression, although his posture resembled a miscreant nailed to a cross of deception. His eyes shifted like a thief's encircled by detectives.

One by one, then in groups, they kicked off from the water, dripping wet, and seized a blanket, wrapping themselves in warm wool. In the dark sky above, glittering pinpricks of Orion the Hunter aimed his bow at the endless universe.

"Orion was the son of Poseidon," Thoreau whispered, "god of the sea."

Cary, bundled in a quilt, mused, "I wonder if Margaret prayed to Poseidon when she made her final voyage. Minerva was always her favorite."

From the wagon, Whitman took out a lantern and lit it, then gave lit candles to each person. They stood in a circle, their faces flaring when a sudden draft whipped heavenward a lick of flame. Silent, they looked at the flood of mystical, moist night sky, milky with spilled stars like chandeliers of the universe. The stars pulsed in tune with the blood pumping in their veins and formed asterisks of light sparking in their widened pupils.

The river below, which seemed like a path of darkness, throbbed with centrifugal spokes of starlight. The luminous flecks rose and fell with the waves.

Whitman took it upon himself to ask, addressing the stars, "Margaret—large and lustrous to the last, are you sending a message to us? At the edge of the horizon, are your beams drowned in the depths? Or will your light shine forever?"

A streak of white light, dazzling as crystal, raced across the sky, leaving a long, chalky trail before fizzling into darkness.

"Margaret signed all her *Tribune* articles with a star," Ellen said, her voice infused with awe. "The star was her symbol."

Cary whispered, "She just told us good-bye."

AUTHOR'S NOTE

"IF YOU HAVE KNOWLEDGE, LET OTHERS LIGHT THEIR CANDLES IN IT." —MARGARET FULLER

I often use the actual words of my novel's characters, found in their writings in the public domain. I've taken liberties with the facts, in order to create a plot rather than a history. Fact: Ellery Channing was both charming and self-centered. Fiction: No evidence exists that he found Fuller's lost manuscript on the Italian revolution. It was probably swept away by the waves, just as Fuller's body was.

In addition, no evidence testifies that Fuller met Whitman, although he admired her writing and was influenced by Transcendentalism. Nor do we know if Melville, through his friendship with the Hawthornes, ever discussed Fuller's legacy. To illustrate Fuller's audacity, I've taken a novelist's prerogative to imagine events in her life and the concerns of these other literary giants.

After Ralph Waldo Emerson laid the groundwork for Transcendentalism, he invited free-thinkers to live near him and make Concord a hub of progressive thought. Uniting characters to debate Fuller's ideas was the seed from which the novel grew.

The ground-breaking authors of the 1850s blended innovative content and style with lofty philosophic ambition. Their works reflect a dynamic social milieu, an era of ferment, when radical idealism and a passion for improvement—at least in the North—were widespread. The "Roaring Forties" was an age of exuberant expansionism, fueled by unbridled optimism. The lure of a Manifest Destiny caused homesteaders to roll westward and forty-niners to "light out for the territory" in pursuit of gold nuggets. The gospel of "The Newness" encouraged literary rebels to cast off tradition. They emancipated their work from aristocratic European models and diverged from the sentimental, sensational pulp fiction then popular.

Courtesy of National Portrait Gallery, Smithsonian Institution.

In this Golden Age of American authors including Emerson, Hawthorne, Thoreau, Melville, and Whitman, a glaring omission stands out: **Margaret Fuller** (1810–1850). After her death in 1850, this brave insurgent was relegated to near obscurity, partly due to the bowdlerized "memoirs" that Emerson and friends published.

Often caricatured as a minor Transcendentalist, only in the 1970s did Second Generation feminists and scholars thwart Fuller's undertakers and anoint her a major figure. Randall Fuller's 2025 *Bright Circle: Five Remarkable Women in the Age of Transcendentalism* reiterates how much Concord male savants owed to Boston female pioneers. Since her rediscovery, Fuller has been the subject of many biographies, including Megan Marshall's Pulitzer Prize–winning *Margaret Fuller, A New American Life*. Fuller's works are in print, most recently in the Library of America's *Margaret Fuller: Collected Writings*. She is lauded as author of the first book on women's rights in the United States, the first female critic and journalist on a US newspaper, and first foreign correspondent.

We cannot know if Fuller's last, lost work (a history of the 1848–49 *Risorgimento*, or Italian revolution) would have launched her to the pantheon of literary immortals. Yet, in this telling, she seizes the imagination of these pioneers, who, whether as doubters or disciples, embody her example in their works.

• • •

The following are brief profiles of the main characters, those I've undertaken to give voices and imagine their thoughts and feelings.

Courtesy of Concord Free Public Library.

Ralph Waldo Emerson (1803–1882), the first great American man of letters, was Fuller's close friend and colleague. He collaborated with her on their Transcendentalist magazine, *The Dial.* She was a frequent guest in his Concord home, and many thoughts from her journals and letters found their way into his essays and lectures. His belief in the power of the individual is a permanent feature of the American psyche. Emerson co-authored *Memoirs of Margaret Fuller Ossoli* (1852) after her death. It outsold all his published writings.

Portrait of Nathaniel Hawthorne by Charles Osgood. Courtesy of the Peabody Essex Museum.

Both **Nathaniel Hawthorne** (1804–1864) and his wife, the artist **Sophia Peabody Hawthorne** (1809–1871), were Fuller's friends in the 1840s when she visited Concord. Yet Nathaniel's tales of moral downfall contradict the sunny optimism of Emersonian Transcendentalism. Melville called Hawthorne's tragic sense of life his disposition to say "NO! in thunder." Fuller's iconoclasm made such an impression that she may have inspired Hawthorne's characters, such as Hester Prynne in *The Scarlet Letter*, Zenobia in *The Blithedale Romance*, and Miriam in his final novel, *The Marble Faun*. Although initially fascinated by her, the Hawthornes disavowed Fuller's call for women's equality in her book *Woman in the Nineteenth Century* (1845).

Portrait of Sophia Amelia (Peabody) Hawthorne by Stephen Alonzo Schoff. *Courtesy of the Peabody Essex Museum.*

Courtesy of National Portrait Gallery, Smithsonian Institution.

When she stayed in Concord, Fuller went hiking and boating with **Henry David Thoreau** (1817–1862). As editor of *The Dial*, she refused to publish some of his early work, giving him constructive criticism to improve his writing. *Walden, or Life in the Woods* (1854) is a brilliant memoir, a paragon of Transcendentalist philosophy and naturalist lore, inspiring today's environmental movement. His essay "Civil Disobedience" influenced seminal figures including Mahatma Gandhi and Martin Luther King Jr. to seek social justice through nonviolent protest.

Courtesy of Library of Congress.

Herman Melville (1819–1891) published *Moby Dick* in 1851. Although formerly known as a writer of exotic yarns, Melville transformed his whaling tale, influenced by his intense friendship with the Hawthornes, into a complex allegorical epic. Critics now hail the novel as a breakthrough example of modernism. Melville died in obscurity, his dark fiction not appreciated until the mid-twentieth century. His work is now considered at the apex of nineteenth-century American literature.

Courtesy Rare Book Division, The New York Public Library.

Walter (Walt) Whitman (1819–1892) revolutionized American poetry, discarding rhyme and meter for lengthy bursts of free-flowing verse. He introduced taboo subjects, such as sexuality, into his life's work, *Leaves of Grass* (1855). This compendium of poems embodies his passionate love of nature and his advocacy of individualism, fraternity, and compassionate inclusion. After working as a hack journalist for newspapers in New York City, he devoted himself to poetry and was immediately acclaimed by Emerson as a long-awaited, liberating American bard. Whitman is considered the first modern American poet.

Courtesy J.C. Marriner and Megan Marshall.

William Ellery Channing (1818–1901), known as Ellery, was Margaret Fuller's brother-in-law and a minor poet championed by Emerson. When he married her sister **Ellen**, Fuller wrote that "the connexion has been so precipitately formed that I feel overshadowed by it as by a deep tragedy that I foresee, but, as in a dream, cannot lift my hand to prevent." She found the ne'er-do-well Channing of "hobgoblin nature" and "like a wretched little boy," although—to help the couple—she published some of his slapdash poems in *The Dial*. A great friend of Thoreau, Channing became his first biographer after Thoreau's death at forty-four. Channing died a lonely, isolated man. His wife **Ellen Fuller Channing** (1820–1856) left her irresponsible husband in 1853 and died shortly thereafter. Their five children were reared by relatives.

Courtesy of Concord Free Public Library.

Lidian Jackson Emerson (1802–1892) remained Waldo Emerson's faithful wife, although increasingly estranged, until his death at age seventy-eight. A fiercely intelligent woman and fervent abolitionist, she tended her husband after his memory began to fail in 1871. As his dementia increased, he cheerfully admitted, "I have lost my mental faculties." When he was asked to name his best friend, he required Lidian's prompt, asking her, "What was my best friend's name?" and then repeating after her, "Oh yes, Henry Thoreau."

Charcoal sketch by Eastman Johnson. Courtesy of Sturgis Library, Barnstable, Massachusetts.

Caroline Sturgis Tappan (1818–1888) was Margaret Fuller's best friend and confidante, as well as a friend to Emerson, Thoreau, the Channings, and the Hawthornes. A talented poet and artist, she was wealthy, beautiful, and irrepressible. She married William Tappan in 1847 with the encouragement of Emerson, a marriage that proved disappointing. She spent many years in Europe. Her Berkshire estate became home to Tanglewood Music Center after her heirs donated the house to the Boston Symphony Orchestra.

Courtesy of Sturgis Library, Barnstable, Massachusetts.

Captain William F. Sturgis (1782–1863), the father of Caroline Sturgis, was a successful and wealthy entrepreneur, owner of sailing vessels that plied the lucrative fur trade between the American Northwest coast and China. The sea otter trade made him a millionaire, one known for his humanity towards Native American fur trappers (he compiled a dictionary of their language) and as an enlightened supporter of women's rights.

These thinkers debated the positive and negative aspects of Emersonian optimism, which came crashing down with the Civil War. Fuller argued that overcoming injustices like slavery and oppression of women required a radical change of institutions, not just an individual change of heart. The novel's characters vacillate between the two poles: collective action, or individual reform?

ACKNOWLEDGMENTS

I've benefited from the encouragement of family and friends while writing this book, an act of compensation for omitting Margaret Fuller when I taught American literature. I'm grateful to readers of the book in draft form who supplied constructive feedback, including my daughters Alison Rini and Eliza Strickland and good friends and voracious readers such as Susi Boeke, Kathleen Wells, Donald Dillport, and Laura Corwin. I thank friends like Pam Michaelcheck, Larry Shapiro, Bill Martin, and Ginny Tuman, as well as family members like Lora Rini and Acadia Strickland, for their support.

My book designer, Barbara Aronica, was instrumental not only in creating the design of the book's interior and exterior but in introducing me to my superb team: copyeditor Kate Petrella, photo researcher Melissa Totten, and publisher David Wilk.

I thank Margaret Fuller scholars and biographers including Megan Marshall, whose research has inspired my story. Members of the Margaret Fuller Society and Society for the Study of American Women Writers have done much to bring overlooked female writers to public attention. I beg their forgiveness for any historical inaccuracies that crept in. My intention is to inform but also to entertain readers, while preserving the truth about a remarkable woman.

Researching and creating *Sparks Fly Up: The Lost Story of Margaret Fuller* has been a labor of love, so it's only fitting to conclude by acknowledging my undying love for my husband Sid Strickland, without whom nothing I've done would have been possible.

ABOUT THE AUTHOR

Photo: Kathleen Wells

Carol Strickland earned a Ph.D. in American literature from the University of Michigan. She has taught writing and literature at various universities but never included Margaret Fuller's work in course syllabi. Her novel, *Sparks Fly Up: The Lost Story of Margaret Fuller* is an attempt to compensate for omitting a giant of American intellectual history.

Strickland has contributed features to newspapers including *The New York Times, Washington Post, Wall Street Journal,* and *Christian Science Monitor* and to magazines including *Art in America, Art and Antiques,* and *Momus.*

Her introduction to art history, *The Annotated Mona Lisa: A Crash Course in Art History from Prehistoric to the Present*, has sold more than 400,000 copies in three editions since 1992.

She lives in Amherst, Massachusetts and New York City. Find out more at carolcstrickland.com.